Alix jerked around and saw the man at the edges of the forest; leather-clad in jerkin and leggings, black-haired and dark-skinned. Her eyes widened as she saw the heavy gold bands on his bare arms and the grey wolf at his side.

'Carillon!' she cried, backing away from the stranger. She heard the hissing of Carillon's sword as he drew it from its sheath, but saw only the streaking grey form of the wolf as it hurtled silently across the space between them. The animal's jaws closed on Carillon's wrist.

Alix turned to run but the stranger caught her easily. Hands grasped her shoulders and spun her; she stared wide-eyed into a laughing face with yellow eyes.

Beast-eyes? she cried silently. 'You are *Cheysuli!*'

Jennifer Roberson writes:

'The *Chronicles of the Cheysuli* is a dynastic fantasy, the story of a proud, honorable race brought down by the avarice, evil and sorcery of others — and its own special brand of magic. It's the story of an ancient race blessed by the old gods of their homeland, and cursed by the sorcerers who desire domination over all men. It's a dynasty of good and evil; love and hatred; pride and strength. Most of all it deals with the destiny in every man and his struggle to shape it, follow it, deny it.'

Chronicles of the Cheysuli: Book One

SHAPECHANGERS

Jennifer Roberson

CORGI BOOKS

For all those who believe in fantasy,
and the special few who believed in me.

SHAPECHANGERS
A CORGI BOOK 0 552 13118 0

First publication in Great Britain

PRINTING HISTORY
Corgi edition published 1987

Copyright © 1984 by Jennifer Roberson

This book is set in 10/11 pt. Palatino

Corgi Books are published by Transworld Publishers Ltd.,
61-63 Uxbridge Road, Ealing, London W5 5SA, in Australia
by Transworld Publishers (Australia) Pty. Ltd., 15–23 Helles
Avenue, Moorebank, NSW 2170, and in New Zealand by
Transworld Publishers (N.Z.) Ltd., Cnr. Moselle and Waipareira
Avenues, Henderson, Auckland.

Reproduced, printed and bound in Great Britain by
Hazell Watson & Viney Limited,
Member of the BPCC Group,
Aylesbury, Bucks

BOOK 1
'The Captive'

CHAPTER ONE

She sat by the creek, half-hidden in lush grasses. Carefully she twined purple summer flowers into her single dark brown braid, and dabbled bare feet in the rushing water. Stems and crushed blooms littered the coarse yellow gown she wore and damp earth stained the garment, but she paid it no mind. She was purposefully intent on her work, for if she allowed her thoughts to range freely she would be overtaken by the knowledge — and the hope — that he still might come.

A songbird called from the forest behind and she glanced up, smiling at the delicate melody. Then her attention was caught by an approaching rider, and she let fall the flowered braid from limp fingers.

Sunlight glittered off the gold of his mount's trappings and painted the chestnut warhorse bright red. She heard the jingle of bit and bridle and the heavy snort of the big stallion. His rider, who had yet to see her, rode unconcernedly through the meadowlands.

She drew her knees up and clasped her arms around them, resting her chin on their tops. She felt the familiar leap of excitement, anticipation and wonder within her breast, and quickly tried to dismiss it. If she allowed him to see it she would be no different from anyone else to him, and therefore of no account.

And I want to be of account to him, she thought intently.

His tawny-dark head was bent as he rode, blue eyes on the shedding of his gloves. He wore black hunting leathers, she saw, and had thrown a thin green woolen mantle back from broad shoulders. A flash of green and gold glittering at his left shoulder caught her eye: the emerald cloak-brooch he favoured. At his heavy belt was hung a massive two-handed broadsword.

The warhorse splashed into the creek, splattering her liberally. She grinned in devious anticipation and straightened in the deep grass, wiping water from her sun-browned skin.

'I did not think you would come,' she said, pitching her voice to carry over the noisy horse.

The animal reacted to her unexpected appearance with alacrity. He plunged sideways, halfway out of the creek, then unceremoniously slid down the muddy bank into the water again. His rider, equally startled, reined the animal in with a curse and shot a glare over his shoulder. When he saw her his face cleared.

'Alix! Do you seek to unseat me?'

She grinned at him and shook her head as he tried to settle the horse. The creek bottom offered treacherous footing to any beast, and the warhorse had yet to find a comfortable spot. Finally his rider cursed again in exasperation and spurred through the water onto the bank, where he stared down at her from the chestnut's great height.

'So, you wish to see Homana's prince take an unexpected bath,' he said menacingly, but she saw the amusement in his eyes.

'No, my lord,' she responded promptly, very solemn and proper. Then she grinned again.

He sighed and dismissed the topic with an idle wave of his hand. A ruby signet ring flashed on the forefinger of his right hand, reminding her of his rank and the enormity of his presence before her.

By the gods, she whispered within her mind, *he is prince of this land and comes to see me!*

The prince stared down at her quizzically, one tawny eyebrow raised. 'What have you been doing — harvesting all the flowers? You are fair covered with them.'

Hurriedly she brushed her skirts free of clinging stems and blossoms and began to pick them from her braid. Before she could strip them away entirely he swung down from the horse and caught her hands, kneeling.

'I did not say you presented an unattractive sight, Alix.' He grinned. 'More like a wood nymph, I would say.'

She tried to draw her hands from his large weapon-calloused ones. 'My lord . . .'

'Carillon,' he said firmly. 'There are no titles between us. Before you I am as any other man.'

But you are not . . . she thought dimly, forcing a smile even as she let her hands stay trapped. After a moment he released one and lifted her to her feet. He led her along the creek, purposely matching his steps to hers. She was tall for a woman, but he was taller still than most men and twice as broad, for all his eighteen years. Carillon of Homana, even did he ever put on the garments of a common crofter, was a prince to the bone.

'Why did you think I would not come?' he asked. 'I have ever done it before, when I said I would.'

Alix watched her bare toes as she walked, not wishing to meet his steady blue eyes. But she was honest before all else, and gave him a blunt answer.

'I am only a crofter's daughter, and you heir to Shaine the Mujhar. Why *should* you come?'

'I said I would. I do not lie.'

She shrugged a shoulder. 'Men say many things they do not mean. It does not have to be a lie. I am, after all, not the sort of woman a prince converses with ordinarily.'

'You put me at ease, Alix. There is a way about you I find comforting.'

She slanted him a bright, amused glance. 'Men are

11

not always seeking *comfort,* my lord. At least, not in conversation.'

Carillon laughed at her, clasping her hand more tightly. 'You do not mouth idle words with me, do you? Well, I would not have it another way. That is part of the reason I seek you out.'

Alix stopped, which forced him to. Her chin lifted and she met his eyes squarely. 'And what is the *other* part, my lord prince of Homana?'

She saw the brief conflict in his face, following each emotion as it passed across his boyish features. Carillon, even at eighteen, was an open sort, but she was more perceptive than most.

Yet Carillon did not react as she expected, and inwardly dreaded. Instead of embarrassment or condescension or arrogant male pride, there was only laughter in his face. His hands rested on her shoulders.

'Alix, if I wanted to take you as my light woman and give you chambers within Homana-Mujhar, I would seek a better way of telling you. For all that, first I would *ask* you.' He smiled into her widening eyes. 'Do not think I am indifferent to you; you are woman enough for me. But I come to you because I can speak with you freely, and not worry that I have said the wrong thing to the wrong ears; hearing it later from the wrong mouth. You are different, Alix.'

She swallowed heavily, suddenly hurt. 'Aye,' she agreed hollowly. 'I am an unschooled crofter's daughter with no fine conversation. I am very unlike the sleek court ladies you are accustomed to.'

'The gods have made a place for every man and woman on this earth, Alix. Do not chafe at yours.'

She scowled at him. 'It is easy for a man of your rank to say such a thing, my lord. But what of the poor who live in Mujhara's streets, and the tenant crofters who must live on the questionable bounty of their lords? For all that, what sort of place has Shaine left to the Cheysuli?'

12

His hands tightened on her shoulders. 'Do not speak to me of shapechangers. They are demons. My uncle's purge will rid Homana of their dark sorcery.'

'How do you know they are demons?' she demanded, arguing out of fairness rather than conviction. 'How can you say when you have never met one?'

Carillon's face went hard and cold before her; aloof. Suddenly she longed for the even-tempered young man she had known and loved but a few weeks.

'Carillon—' she began.

'No,' he said flatly, removing his hands to stand stiffly before her. 'I have no need to see demons to know they exist. The breed is accursed, Alix; outlawed in this land.'

'By your uncle's doing!'

'Aye!' he snapped. 'Punishment for a transgression which required harsh measures. By the gods, girl, it was a Cheysuli who stole a king's daughter — my own cousin — and brought civil war to this land!'

'Hale did not *steal* Lindir!' Alix cried. 'She went willingly!'

He recoiled from her, though he did not move. Suddenly before her was an angry young man who was more prince than anything else, and therefore entitled to a short temper.

'You freely admit you are an unschooled crofter's daughter,' he began coldly, 'yet you seek to lesson me in my House's history. What right do you have? Who has said such things to you?'

Her hands curled into fists. 'My father was arms-master to Shaine the Mujhar for thirty years, my lord, before he became a crofter. He lived within the walls of Homana-Mujhar and spoke often with the Mujhar. He was there when Lindir went away with the Cheysuli she loved, and he was there when Shaine called curses on the race and outlawed them. He was there when the Mujhar *started* this war!'

13

Muscles moved beneath the flesh of his jaw. 'He speaks treason.'

'He speaks the truth!' Alix whirled from him and stalked through the grass, stopping only to remove a thorn from her bare foot. Her slippers, she recalled glumly, were back where they had begun this discussion.

'Alix—' he said.

'By the gods, Carillon, it was the Cheysuli who settled this land!' she said crossly. 'Do you think they seek this — purge? It is Shaine's doing, not theirs.'

'With just cause.'

Alix sighed and set down her foot. They stared at one another silently a long moment, both recognizing they jeopardized the tenuous friendship they had built. She waited for his curt dismissal.

Carillon's hand idly smoothed the hilt of the sword at his belt, caressing the glowing cabochon ruby set in gold. He was silent, thoughtful, not the blustering or coldly arrogant prince she anticipated.

Finally he sighed. 'Girl, for all your father had my uncle's ear, he was not privy to all things. He could not know everything about the beginnings of the war. Nor, for that matter, can I. I am but newly made heir, and Shaine treats me as little more than a child. If you will listen, I will tell you what I know of the matter.'

She opened her mouth to reply, but a third voice broke into their conversation.

'No, princeling. Let someone who has experienced Shaine's purge tell her what *he* knows of the matter.'

Alix jerked around and saw the man at the edges of the forest; leather-clad in jerkin and leggings, black-haired and dark-skinned. For a moment she stared speechlessly at him, astonished, then her eyes widened as she saw the heavy gold bands on his bare arms and the grey wolf at his side.

'Carillon!' she cried, backing away from the man. She heard the hissing of Carillon's sword as he drew it from its sheath, but saw only the streaking grey form of the wolf as it hurtled silently across the space between them. The animal's jaws closed on Carillon's wrist.

Alix turned to run but the stranger caught her easily. Hands grasped her shoulders and spun her; she stared wide-eyed into a laughing face with yellow eyes.

Beast-eyes! she cried silently.

'Come now, *mei jha*, do not struggle so,' her captor said, grinning. A gold ornament gleamed in his left ear, flashing against black hair and bronzed skin. Alix was conscious of his soft sleeveless leather jerkin and bare arms as he held her against him. 'You championed my race but a moment ago, *mei jha*. Surely you do not lose your principles so quickly.'

She froze in his hands, staring into his angular, high-planed face. 'You are *Cheysuli!*'

'Aye,' he agreed. 'Finn. When I heard you defending my race to the heir of the man who nearly destroyed us, I could not bear to let the princeling force your beliefs against us. Too many will not hear the truth.' He grinned at her. 'I will tell you what truly happened, *mei jha*, and why Shaine has called us accursed and outlawed.'

'Shapechanger! *Demon!*' Carillon called furiously.

Alix twisted so she could see him, afraid he had been badly injured, but she saw only an angry young man on the ground, hitched up on one elbow as he cradled his wrist against his chest. The wolf, a big silver male, sat at his side. There was no question in Alix's mind the animal stood guard.

The Cheysuli's hands tightened on Alix and she winced. 'I am no demon, princeling. Only a man, like yourself, though admittedly the gods like us better. If you would have us called demon-spawn and consign us to the netherworld, you had best look to the Mujhar first. He cried *qu'mahlin* on us, not the other way.' The contempt in his voice sent a shiver through Alix. 'And you make me think you wish to be his heir, princeling, in all things.'

Colour raced through Carillon's face and he moved as if to rise. The wolf tautened silently, amber eyes slitting, and after a moment the prince remained where he was. Alix saw pain and frustration in his face.

'Let me go to him,' she said.

'To the princeling?' The Cheysuli laughed. 'Are you his *mei jha*, then? Well, and I had thought to make you mine.'

She stiffened. 'I am no man's light woman, if that is what your barbaric word means.'

'It is the Old Tongue, *mei jha*; a gift of the old gods. Once it was the only tongue in this land.' His breath warmed her ear. 'I will teach it to you.'

'Let me go!'

'I have only just got you. I do not intend to let you go so quickly.'

'Release her,' Carillon ordered flatly.

Finn laughed joyously. 'The princeling orders *me*! But now the Cheysuli no longer recognize the Mujhar's laws, my young lord, or his wishes. Shaine effectively severed our hereditary obedience to the Mujhar and his blood when he declared *qu'mahlin* on our race.' The laughter died. 'Perhaps we can return the favour, now we have his heir at hand.'

'You have me, then,' Carillon growled. 'Release Alix.'

The Cheysuli laughed again. 'But it was the woman I came for, princeling. I have only got you in the bargain. And I do not intend to lose either of you.' His hand slid across Alix's breast idly. 'You both will be guests in a Cheysuli raiding camp this night.'

'My father . . .' Alix whispered.

'You father will come looking for you, *mei jha*, and when he does not find you he will assume the beasts of the forest got you.'

'And he will have the right of it!' she snapped. His

16

hand cupped her jaw and lifted it. 'Already you join your princeling in cursing us.'

'Aye!' she agreed. 'When you behave like a beast there is little else I can do!'

The hand tightened until it nearly crushed her jaw. 'Who is to blame for that, *mei jha*?' He turned her head until she was forced to look at Carillon. 'You see before you the heir to the man who drove us from our homeland, making outlaws of warriors, denying us our rights. Is not Shaine the Mujhar a maker of beasts, then, if you would call us that?'

'He is your liege lord!' Carillon hissed through gritted teeth.

'No,' Finn said coldly. 'He is not. Shaine of Homana is my persecutor, not my liege lord.'

'He persecutes with reason!'

'*What* reason?'

Carillon's eyes narrowed. 'A Cheysuli warrior — liege man to my uncle the Mujhar — stole away a king's daughter.' He smiled coldly, as angry as the Cheysuli. 'That practice, it seems, is still alive among your race. Even now you steal another.'

Finn matched Carillon's smile. 'Perhaps, princeling, but she is not a king's daughter. Only her father will miss her, and her mother, and that will pass in time.'

'My mother is dead,' Alix said, then regretted speaking at all. She took a careful breath. 'If I go with you, willingly, will you free Carillon?'

Finn laughed softly. 'No, *mei jha*, I will not. He is the weapon the Cheysuli have needed these twenty-five years of the *qu'mahlin*, for all he was born after it began. We will use him.'

Alix's eyes met Carillon's, and they realized the futility of their arguments. Neither spoke.

'Come,' said Finn. 'I have men and horses waiting in the forest. It is time we left this place.'

Carillon got carefully to his feet, cradling the injured wrist. He stood stiffly, taller than the black-haired

17

warrior, but somehow diminished before the fierce pride of the man.

'Your sword, princeling,' Finn said quietly. 'Take up your sword and return it to its sheath.'

'I would sooner sheathe it in your flesh.'

'Aye,' Finn agreed. 'If you did not, you would not be much of a man.' Alix felt an odd tension in his body. 'Take up the sword, Carillon of Homana. It is yours, for all that.'

Carillon, warily eyeing the wolf, bent and retrieved the blade. The ruby glinted as he slid the sword home awkwardly with his left hand.

Finn stared at the weapon and smiled oddly. 'Hale's blade.'

Carillon scowled at him. 'My uncle gifted me with this sword last year. It was his before that. What do you say?'

When the Cheysuli did not answer immediately Alix looked sharply at him. She was startled to find bleakness in his yellow beast-eyes.

'Long before it was a Mujhar's blade it was a Cheysuli's. Hale made that sword, princeling, and gifted it to his liege lord, the man he had sworn a blood-oath of service to.' He sighed. 'And the prophecy of the Firstborn says it will one day be back in the hands of a *Cheysuli* Mujhar.'

'*You lie!*'

Finn grinned mockingly. '*I* may lie, on occasion, but the prophecy does not. Come, my lord, allow my *lir* to escort you to your horse. Come.'

Carillon, aware of the wolf's silent menace, went. Alix had no choice but to follow.

CHAPTER TWO

Three other Cheysuli, Alix saw apprehensively, waited
silently in the forest. Carillon's warhorse was with them.
She cast a quick glance at the prince, judging his
reaction, and saw his face was pale, jaw set so tightly she
feared it might break. He seemed singularly dedicated to
keeping himself apart from the Cheysuli even though he
was in their midst.

Finn said something in a lyrical tongue she did not
recognize and one of the warriors came forward with a
strange horse for Carillon. He was being refused his
own, and quick colour rising in his face confirmed the
insult.

'We know the reputation of Homanan warhorses,'
Finn said briefly. 'You will not be given a chance to flee us
so easily. Take this one, for now.'

Silently Carillon accepted the reins and with careful
effort was able to mount. Finn stared up at him from the
ground, then moved to the prince and without a word
tore a long strip of wool from Carillon's green cloak. He
tossed it at him.

'Bind your wound, princeling. I will not lose you to
death so easily.'

Carillon took up the strip and did as told. He smiled
grimly down at the yellow-eyed warrior. 'When I am given
the time, shapechanger, I will see the colour of *your* blood.'

19

Finn laughed and turned away. He grinned at Alix. 'Well, *mei jha*, we lack a horse for you. But mine will serve. I will enjoy the feel of you against my back.'

Alix, both furious and frightened, only glared at him. His dark face twisted in an ironic smile and he took the reins of his own horse from another warrior. He gestured toward the odd gear on the animal's back. It did not quite resemble a Homanan saddle, with its large saddletree and cantle designed to hold in a fighting man, but served an identical purpose. Alix hesitated, then placed her bare foot in the leather stirrup and hoisted herself into the saddle. Before she could say anything to prevent him, Finn vaulted onto the horse's rump behind her. She felt his arms come around her waist to take up the reins.

'You see, *mei jha*? You can hardly avoid me.'

She did her best. The ride was long and she was wearied from riding stiffly upright before him when at last Finn halted the horse. She stared in surprise at the encampment before her, for it was well hidden in the thick, shadowed forests.

Woven tents of greens, browns, greys and slates huddled in the twilight, nearly indistinguishable from the trees and underbrush of the forest and the tumbled piles of mountain boulders. Small fires glowed flickeringly across the narrow clearing.

Alix straightened as Finn reined in the horse. She turned quickly to search for Carillon, lost among the black-haired, yellow-eyed Cheysuli warriors, but Finn prevented her. His left arm came around her waist snugly, possessive as he leaned forward, pressing against her rigid back.

'Your princeling will recover, *mei jha*. He is in some pain now, but it will pass.' His voice dropped to a provocative whisper. 'Or I will *make* it.'

She ignored him, sensing a slow, defiant — and somehow frightening — rage building within her. 'Why did you set your wolf on him?'

'He drew Hale's sword, *mei jha*. Doubtless he knows how to use it, even against a Cheysuli.' He laughed softly. 'Perhaps *especially* against a Cheysuli. But we are too few as it is. My death would not serve.'

'You set a *beast* on him!'

'Storr is no beast. He is my *lir*. And he only did it to keep Carillon from getting himself slain, for I would have taken his life to keep my own.'

She glanced at the wolf waiting so silently and patiently by the horse. 'Your — *lir*? What do you say?'

'That wolf is my *lir*. It is a Cheysuli thing, which you could not possibly understand. There is no Homanan word for our bond.' He shrugged against her. 'Storr is a part of me, and I him.'

'Shapechanger . . .' she whispered involuntarily.

'Cheysuli,' he whispered back.

'Is any wolf this — *lir*?'

'No. I am bonded with Storr only, and he was chosen by the old gods to be my *lir*. They are born knowing it. Each warrior has only one, but it can be any creature.' He picked a leaf from Alix's hair, even as she stiffened. 'It is too new for you to understand, *mei jha*. Do not try.'

She felt him slide from behind and a moment later he pulled her from the horse. Alix stifled a blurt of surprise and felt each sinew tighten as his hand crept around her neck.

'You may release me,' she said quickly. 'I can hardly run from a wolf.'

His hand slid from her. She felt her braid lifted from her neck and his lips upon her nape. 'Then you are learning already, *mei jha*.'

Before she could protest he turned her face to his and bent her head back as his mouth came down on hers. Alix struggled against him with no effect except to feel herself held more securely. He was far too strong for her, stronger than she had ever imagined a man could be.

You should not, lir, said a quiet voice in Alix's mind.

21

She stiffened in fear, wondering how Finn spoke without saying anything. Then she was pushed from him unexpectedly as he moved back a single step. She saw he had not spoken, silently or aloud, but whatever had formed the words had greatly upset him. His eyes, watching her warily, were slitted. Slowly he looked at the wolf.

'Storr . . .' he said softly, in amazement.

You should not, said the tone again.

Finn swung back to her, suddenly angry. 'Who are you?'

'What?'

His hand clasped her braid and tugged sharply, jerking at her scalp. 'What manner of woman are you to draw *Storr's* concern?'

The wolf? she wondered blankly.

Finn peered closely at her, fingers painfully closing on her jaw until she had no choice but to look directly into his shadowed face. The gold earring, wolf-shaped, gleamed.

'You are dark enough for one of us, but you have not the eyes,' he muttered. 'Brown, like half of Homana. Yet why else would Storr protest my pleasure? It is not for the *lir* to do.'

'I am none of yours!' she hissed, profoundly shaken. 'I am daughter to Torrin of Homana. Do not *curse* me by naming me Cheysuli, shapechanger!'

His hand tightened and she cried out. Faintly she heard Carillon's worried tone carry across the way. 'Alix!'

Finn released her so curtly she stumbled back. 'Go to your princeling, *mei jha*. Tend his wound like a proper light woman.'

She opened her mouth to protest his unseemly words, then bit them back and whirled, hastening to Carillon. He stood by his Cheysuli mount, unsteady, cradling his bound wrist against his chest. His face, even in the shadows, was drawn with pain.

'Did he harm you?' he asked harshly.

Alix shook her head, recalling the anger in Finn's hand upon her chin. 'No, I am well enough. But what of you?'

He half-shrugged. 'It is my sword arm. Without it I am not much of a prince, nor even a man. Otherwise I would not speak of it.'

She smiled and touched his uninjured arm gently. 'We have nowhere else to go, my lord. Let us move into the firelight where I can see to your wrist.'

Finn came to them silently and gestured toward a green tent not far from where they stood. Mutely Alix followed the Cheysuli leader, keeping one hand on Carillon's arm. That he had said anything at all about his wound worried her, for it indicated the wolf bite was worse then she suspected.

Finn watched them kneel down on a blue woven rug before his tent and then disappeared within, ignoring them. Alix cast a quick glance around the small encampment, seeking a way out, but there were too many warriors. And Carillon's face was already fever-flushed and warm when she set her hand against it.

'We go nowhere, yet,' she said softly.

'We must,' he answered, carefully unwrapping his injured wrist. The flesh was scored with teeth marks. The bleeding had stopped, but the wound was open and seeping.

'We have no choice,' Alix whispered. 'Perhaps in the morning, when you are better.'

Light from the small fire Cairn built before the tent flickered over his jaw. She saw the stubborn set to the prominent bones. 'Alix, I will not remain in a shapechanger camp. They are demons.'

'They are also our captors,' she agreed wryly. 'Do you think to escape them so easily? You could hardly get half a league with this wolf-wound.'

'*You* could. You could reach your father's croft. He could ride to Mujhara for help.'

'Alone . . .' she whispered. 'And so far . . .'

He rubbed his unwounded forearm across his brow. 'I do not wish to send you into the darkness alone, no matter how far the distance is. But I have no choice, Alix. I would go myself, willingly, as I think you know.' He lifted his bloody arm. 'I do recognize my own limitations.' His smile came swiftly, and left as quickly. 'I have faith in you, my girl, more so than in any man who might be with me in this.'

Pain squeezed her heart so that it nearly burst. In the brief weeks she had known him he had become everything to her, a hero she could worship from the depths of her romantic soul and a man she could dream of in the long nights. To have him look at her so warmly and with such trust nearly undid her convictions about not allowing him to see her vulnerability.

'Carillon . . .'

'You must,' he said gently. 'We cannot remain here. My uncle, when he learns of this, will send mounted troops immediately to destroy this nest of demons. Alix, you must *go*.'

'Go where?' demanded Finn from the tent's doorflap.

Alix twitched in surprise at his stealth, but Carillon glared at the Cheysuli. Somehow Finn seemed more substantial, a thing of the darkness, illuminated by the firelight dancing off the gold on his arms and in his ear. Alix forced herself to look away from his yellow eyes and stared instead at the earring half-hidden in thick black hair. It, like the armbands he wore above the elbows, bore a skilful figure of a wolf.

For his lir . . . she realized blankly, and wondered anew at the strangeness of his race.

The Cheysuli smiled mockingly and moved to stand over them. His steps were perfectly silent and hardly left a mark in the dirt.

He is like the shadows themselves . . .

'My prince,' he said vibrantly, 'you must doubtless believe this insubstantial girl could make her way

24

through a hostile forest without aid of any sort. Were she Cheysuli, she could, for we are creatures of the forests instead of cities, but she is not. And I have gone to far too much trouble to lose either of you so quickly.'

'You have no right to keep us, shapechanger,' Carillon said.

'We have every right, princeling! Your uncle has done what he could to slay every Cheysuli in Homana — a land *we* made! He has come closer than even he knows, for it is true our numbers are sadly reduced. From thousands we are hundreds. but it has been fortunate, lately, that Shaine is more concerned with the war Bellam of Solinde wishes to levy against Homana. He needs must steep himself in battle plans again, and forget *us* for a time.'

'So,' Carillon said on a sighing breath, 'you will ransom me back to the Mujhar?'

Finn stroked his smooth jaw, considering, grinning at them both. 'That is not for me to say. It is a Cheysuli Clan Council decision. But I will let you know how we view your disposition.'

Alix straightened. 'And what of me?'

He stared sightlessly at her for a long moment. Then he dropped to one knee and lifted her braid against his lips in a seductive manner. 'You, *mei jha*, will remain with us. The Cheysuli place much value on a woman, for we have need of them to breed more of us.' He ignored her gasp of shock and outrage. 'Unlike the Homanans, who may keep a woman for only a night, we keep her forever.'

Alix recoiled from him, jerking her braid free of his hand. Fear drove into her chest so quickly she could hardly breathe, and she felt a trembling begin in her bones.

He could do this, she realized. *He could. He is a demon* . . .

'Let me go,' she pleaded. 'Do not keep me with you.'

His black brows lifted. 'Do you sicken of my company so soon, *mei jha*? You will injure me with such words.'

25

'Alix is none of yours,' Carillon said coldly. 'If you seek to ransom me, you will do the same for her. And if her father cannot meet your price, the Mujhar will pay it from his own coffers.'

Finn did not bother to look at Carillon. He stared penetratingly at Alix. 'She is a prize of war, princeling. My own personal war against the Mujhar. And I would never take gold from a man who could order his men to slay an entire race.'

'I am no *prize!*' Alix cried. 'I am a woman! Not a broodmare to be judged by her ability to bear young or bring gold. You will not treat me so!'

Finn caught one of her hands and held it, browned fingers encircling her wrist gently. She tried to pull away, but he exerted just enough force to keep her hand imprisoned.

'I treat you how I choose,' he told her. 'But I would have you know *mei jhas* are honoured among the Cheysuli. That a woman has no *cheysul* — husband — and yet takes a man as mate does not make her a whore. Tell me, is that not a better life than the light women of Mujhara receive?'

Her hand jerked in his grasp. 'Let me go!'

'You are not the first woman won in such a fashion,' he said solemnly, 'and doubtless you will not be the last. But for now, you are mine to do with as I will.'

Carillon reached out to grab Finn's arm, cursing him angrily, but the pain of his wrist prevented him. His face went horribly white and he stopped moving instantly, cradling the wounded arm. His breath hissed between his teeth.

Finn released Alix. 'If you will allow it, I will heal the wound.'

'Heal!'

'Aye,' the Cheysuli said quietly. 'It is a gift of the old gods. We have healing arts at our beck.'

Alix rubbed at the place he had held on her arm. 'What do you say, shapechanger?'

26

'Cheysuli,' he corrected. 'I can summon the earth magic.'

'Sorcery!' Carillon exclaimed.

Finn shrugged. 'Aye, but it is a gift, for all that. And used only for good.'

'I will not suffer your touch.'

Finn moved and caught Carillon's wounded arm in a firm grasp. The prince winced away, prepared to make a furious protest, but said nothing as astonishment crept across his face.

'Carillon?' Alix whispered.

'The pain . . .' he said dazedly.

'The earth magic eases pain,' Finn said matter-of-factly, kneeling before the pale prince. 'But it can also do much more.'

Alix stared open-mouthed as the Cheysuli held the lacerated arm. His yellow eyes had gone oddly piercing, yet detached, and she realized her escape lay open before her. He had somehow gone beyond them both.

She moved as if to go, coiling her legs to push herself upright, but the expression on Carillon's face prevented her. She saw amazement, confusion and revulsion, and the beginnings of a protest. But she also saw acknowledgment of the truth in Finn's words, and before she could voice a question, afraid of the sorcery the shapechanger used, Finn released Carillon's wrist.

'It is done, princeling. It will heal cleanly, painlessly, though you will have scars to show for your foolishness.'

'Foolishness!' Carillon exclaimed.

Finn smiled grimly 'It is ever foolishness for a man to threaten a Cheysuli before his *lir*.' Finn nodded his head at the silver wolf who lay silently by the tent. 'Storr will let no man harm me, even at the cost of his own life.' He frowned suddenly, eyes sombre. 'Though that has its price.'

'Then one day I will slay you both,' Carillon said clearly.

Alix felt the sudden flare of tension between the two, though she could not put name to it. And when Finn smiled ironically she felt chilled, recoiling from the twisted mouth.

'You may try, princeling, but I do not think you will accomplish it. We are meant for something other than death at one another's hands, we two.'

'What do you say?' Alix demanded.

He glanced at her. 'You do not know the prophecy of the Firstborn, *mei jha*. When you have learned it, you will have your answers.' He rose in a fluid motion that put her in mind of a supple mountain cat. 'And it will give you more questions.'

'What prophecy?' she asked.

'The one which gives the Cheysuli purpose.' He stretched out his right hand in a palm-up, spread-fingered gesture. 'You will understand what this is another time. For now, I must see my *rujholli*. You may sleep here or within my tent; it is all one to me. Storr will keep himself by you while I am gone.'

He turned and walked away silently, fading into the shadows, lost to sight instantly. Alix shivered as the wolf rose and came to the blue blanket. He lay down near them, watching them with an odd equanimity in his amber eyes.

Alix recalled Finn's odd words earlier; his strange reaction to the gentle tone she had heard in her mind. Carefully, apprehensively, she formed her own.

Wolf? she asked. *Do you speak?*

Nothing echoed in her head. The wolf, called *lir*, did not seem so fierce now as he rested his jaws on his paws, pink tongue lolling idly. But the intelligence in his feral eyes, so unlike a man's, could not be ignored.

Lir? she questioned.

I am called Storr, he said briefly.

Alix jerked and recoiled on the blanket, fighting down nausea. She stared at the animal, horrified, but he had not moved. Something like a smile gleamed in his eyes.

28

Do not be afraid of me. There is no need. Not for you.

'By the gods . . .' she whispered.

Carillon looked at her. 'Alix?'

She could not take her eyes from the wolf to look at Carillon. A shiver of fear ran through her as she considered the madness of her discovery. It was not possible.

'Alix,' he said again.

Finally she looked at him. His face was pale, puzzled; fatigue dulled his blue eyes. But even were he alert and well, she could not tell him she heard the wolf speak. He would never believe her, and she was not certain *she* did.

'I am only confused,' she said softly, mostly to herself. 'Confused.'

He shifted the arm into a more comfortable position, running a tentative finger over the puffy teeth marks left by the wolf. But even she could see it had the look of healing to it.

'You must leave,' he said.

She stared at him. 'You still wish me to go, even after what the shapechanger said?'

Carillon smiled. 'He sought only to frighten you.'

'The wolf . . .'

'The shapechanger will not leave him with us forever. When you have the chance, you must go.'

She watched Carillon ease himself down on the blue blanket, stretching out long legs booted to the thighs and wrapping the green cloak over his arm.

'Carillon . . .'

'Aye, Alix?' he asked on a weary sigh.

She bit at her lip, ashamed of her hesitation. 'I will go. When I have the chance.'

He smiled faintly and fell into an exhausted slumber. Alix looked at him sadly.

What is it about an ill or injured man that turns a woman into an acquiescent fool? she wondered. *Why is it I am suddenly willing to do anything for him?* She sighed and

29

picked at the wrinkles in her gown. *But he would go himself, were he well enough, so I will do as he asks.*

She looked curiously at the wolf, wondering if he could hear her thoughts. But the animal only watched her idly, as if he had nothing better to do.

Perhaps he does not, she decided and drew up her knees to stare sightlessly into the flames.

CHAPTER THREE

The fire had died to glowing coals when she felt an odd
touch in her mind, almost like a probing. It was feather-
light and very gentle, but terrifying. Alix jerked her
head off her knees and stared around wide-eyed, afraid
it was some form of Cheysuli torture.

Nothing was there. The camp was oddly empty, for,
like Finn, each warrior had gone to a single slate-
coloured tent at the far end of the small encampment.

Alix looked at the wolf and found his amber eyes
fastened on her. 'No,' she whispered.

The faint touch faded from her mind. Alix put a
trembling hand to her ear. 'You cannot speak to me. I
cannot hear you.'

You hear, said the warm tone.

'What do you do to me?' she demanded violently,
struggling to keep her voice down so as not to waken
Carillon.

I seek, he answered.

She closed her eyes but was still intensely aware of his
gaze. 'I am gone mad,' she whispered.

No, said the tone. *You are only weary, and frightened, and
very much alone. But there is no need.*

'You said you sought something, wolf.' Alix took a
trembling breath, giving in to her madness for the
moment. 'What do you seek in me?'

31

Storr lifted his head from his paws. *I cannot say.*

His clear gaze made her uneasy. Carillon slept soundly, lines of pain washed from his face, and she wished he could give her the words she needed to banish this strangeness from her mind. She wished also she could lose herself in such soothing sleep, but every fibre in her body was stretched taut with apprehension and a longing to run away.

Wolf? she asked silently.

He said nothing. After a moment he rose and shook himself, rippling his silver coat. He sent her an oddly intent glance, then padded away into the darkness, as deliberate as any dog among his people.

Alix stared after him. A quick glance told her no one was near; she saw no other animals. She looked longingly at Carillon's unmoving form a moment, wanting to smooth the hair from his hot brow, but she kept herself from it. Such intimacy, if it ever occurred, would have to begin with him. She was too far from his rank to initiate anything.

She released a rushing breath, trying to control the raggedness of it, and got to her feet. She shook her skirts free of folds, curling her bare toes away from the cool ground. Her feet were cold, bruised, but she could waste no time regretting her lost slippers.

Silently Alix slipped into the darkness of the encampment. She was no shadow-wraith like the Cheysuli, but she was forest-raised and could move with little noise. Carefully she eased past the last tent and entered the clustered trees.

Needles and twigs snapped beneath her feet, digging painfully into her flesh. Alex bit her lip against the sharp, nagging pain and went on, ignoring the fear in her soul. A shiver coursed down her body as she moved through the silent forest. She longed for the warmth and safety of her father's croft and the hot spiced cider he brewed.

It is for Carillon, she whispered silently. *For him.*

32

Because a prince has asked me. Irrationally she nearly laughed aloud. *But he does not have to be a prince to bid me serve him. I would do it willingly.*

She grasped a tree and felt the rough bark bite into her palms as she dug fingernails into it. Her forehead rested against the tree as she smiled, inwardly laughing at her conflicting emotions. Fear was still the primary element in her soul, but so was her wish to do as Carillon asked. She was fair caught in the trap that bound so many women.

A twig snapped. Alix jerked her head up and stared into the trees, suddenly so badly frightened she lost all track of other emotions. Her fingers clutched spasmodically at the bark and she sucked in a ragged breath.

The wolf stood in the shadows, little more than a faint outline against the darkness beyond. For a moment she felt fear slip away, for somehow Storr did not threaten her; then she realized it was not Storr. This one was larger, ruddy instead of silver. Its yellow eyes held a gleam of invitation.

The fear came back. Alix pressed her body against the tree, seeking its protection. A broken bough jabbed into her thigh but she ignored it, wishing only she could somehow scale the tree into branches far above the ground.

The wolf moved slowly forward into a small clearing. Moonlight set its rich red pelt to glowing, pinpointing yellow eyes into an eerie intelligence. Teeth gleamed, and Alix saw its taunting smile.

The wolf began to change.

Cold, primitive fear crawled through her mind. The form before her eyes altered, subtly blurring outline and colour into a shapeless void. And then Finn stood before her.

'I said you would not win free of us,' he told her calmly. '*Mei jha*, you must stay.'

Alix shivered. Finn was whole again, a man, with yellow eyes glinting in high good humour and heavy

33

gold bands gleaming faintly against folded bare arms.

She gripped the tree. 'You . . .'

He spread his hands slowly, unaggressively. 'Do you question what you have seen, *mei jha*?' His smile was mocking. 'Do not. Your eyes have not deceived you.'

Alix felt nausea roil her stomach and send bile into her throat. She choked it back down. 'You were a *wolf*!'

'Aye,' he agreed, unoffended by her horror. 'The old gods gifted us with the ability to take *lir*-shape, once properly bonded with an animal. We can assume a like shape at will.' He sounded very serious, incongruous in him. 'It is something we honour the gods for.'

'*Shapechanger!*'

Finn's mouth twisted wryly. 'Aye, that is the Homanan name for us, when they do not call us demons. But we are not sorcerers, *mei jha*; we are not servants of the dark gods. We leave that to the Ihlini.' He shrugged. 'We are merely men . . . with a god-gift in the blood.'

Alix could not deal with it; with him. She stared fixedly at him a moment, still stunned by the enormity of what she had seen. Then she scraped herself around the tree and ran.

Underbrush tore at her gown and welted skin already prickling with fright as she raced through the trees. A limb slashed across her face. Alix ignored it all in her panicked flight, seeking only to escape the man, the *demon*, who was everything Carillon had said.

She could hear no pursuit over the noise of her own flight, but it served only to increase her fear. A shapechanger would hardly make noise as he stalked his prey.

Alix stumbled over a log and fell across it, stomach driven against her spine. Breath left her in a whooping rush but she tried to lift herself frantically. Pinpricks of light flashed before her eyes as she struggled to her feet, lungs sucking at air she could not find.

She was driven down again by a hard body from behind.

Alix lay half-stunned, still out of breath. Her face burned from a bleeding welt on her cheek. She lay pressed against the cool gound, sobbing, as she tried to regain her breath, and helpless in his arms.

Her body was lifted from the forest floor and turned over. She lay very still as he set her on her back, unable to close her eyes as he knelt over her. Faint light filtered through the trees. His earring winked coldly.

'Have I not already said escape is impossible?' he asked. 'I am Cheysuli.'

Her chest hurt, but air was beginning to creep into it again. Alix swallowed painfully. 'Please ... let me go.'

'I have said before how much trouble I have gone to get you, and to keep you. At least let me have some repayment for it.'

His fingers touched the cut on her face and she winced. 'You did not need to run from me, *mei jha*.'

She shivered. *This man becomes a wolf at will*. She looked at his hands for signs of the wolf-mark. Finn grinned at her with a man's teeth in a wolfish leer.

'When I wear a man's shape, *mei jha*, I am all man. Shall I prove it to you?'

Alix stiffened as he leaned closer, hands spread across the ground on either side of her shoulders. If she pushed upward it would be to place herself directly in his arms, and he knew it.

'No!' she cried as he leaned closer.

His eyes, oddly feral, looked directly into hers. 'I have watched you for some time, *mei jha*. It was a simple raiding mission we came on days ago, to replenish our Keep. But I found prey of a different sort.'

She closed her eyes.' Please ... '

His knees were on either side of her thighs, holding her prisoner. He bent over her until his lips were nearly touching her face.

'Shaine's soldiers have slain nearly all of us, *mei jha*,

35

and they have not spared our women. What is a proud race to do when it sees its own demise? We must get more of us on the women we have, and take others where we can, even if they be unwilling.'

Her mind flinched from his words, denying them even as she heard the ring of truth in his voice. The Mujhar's purge had begun twenty-five years before. She had grown up knowing the Cheysuli must die, for all she believed the Mujhar's actions unfair in the wake of what her father had said. But now she was faced with a shapechanger who spoke of force, and she was more than willing to forsake her principles to win free of him.

Her fingers on his arm were no more than a feather touch, instinctively seductive. She saw sudden wariness in his eyes and the intensity in his body poised over her.

'Must you make the tales of your savagery and bestial appetites true?' she whispered. 'Must you so readily prove to me you are no better than the demon-spawn others name you?'

Finn scowled at her. 'Soft words will not gainsay me, *mei jha.*'

Her fingers tightened. 'Please ... let me go free.'

He smelled of leather and gold and demand. '*Mei jha,*' he said roughly, 'I cannot ...'

She opened her mouth to cry out as he pressed a knee between her thighs. But before she could make a sound the familiar tone she associated with Storr came quietly into their minds.

Lir, you should not.

It drove Finn from Alix. He shoved her harshly against the ground as she hitched up on one arm, cursing violently beneath his breath, and she winced against the force of his hand against her shoulder. He knelt by her, stiff with tension, and she saw he looked at the wolf.

Storr waited in a thick copse of trees, staring unwaveringly at Finn. Alix could only bless the wolf's timely

36

appearance and intervention, for all she could not comprehend it. Slowly she eased herself onto one elbow.

'Storr!' Finn hissed.

She is not for you.

Finn turned on her, furious. 'Who are you?'

She kept her voice steady with effort. 'I have said.'

He settled one hand around her vulnerable throat. It rested without pressure, promising only, but she felt the violence in his body.

'You have said nothing! Who are you?'

'I am a croft-girl! My father is Torrin and my mother was Leyda. He was arms-master to Shaine the Mujhar before he turned to the land.' She glared at him. 'I am his daughter. Nothing more.'

Finn's eyes narrowed. 'Arms-master to the Mujhar. When?'

Alix took a weary breath. 'I am seventeen. He left the Mujhar's service a year before I was born, and took a valley girl to wife. But I cannot say how long he served Shaine. He does not speak of those days.'

'Does he not?' Finn said musingly, taking his hand from her throat. He sat back on his haunches and frowned thoughtfully, pushing heavy black hair from his face.

Alix, feeling safe for the moment, sat upright and straightened her twisted gown. The welt on her face stung, as did the scratches and bruises on her legs, but she touched none of them. She would not give him the satisfaction.

Finn stared at her impassively. 'Do you know the story of the *qu'mahlin*?'

'There are two of them.' She covered her legs decorously.

He grinned. 'Aye. And I heard you speak of one to the princeling, even when he would dissuade you of it. Which do you believe?'

His change in attitude made her wary, but also

37

relieved. No longer did she fear he would pounce on her like a mountain cat taking a rabbit. With renewed confidence she told him.

'Shaine's daughter broke the betrothal made between the Homana and Solinde. It would have allied the lands after centuries of warfare, but she would have none of Bellam's son, Ellic. She went instead with a Cheysuli.'

'Hale,' Finn agreed. 'Shaine's sworn liege man.'

Alix shrugged. 'I cannot say. I only overheard my father speaking of it once, to my mother, when he thought I could not hear.'

'It is true, *mei jha*,' he said seriously. 'Hale took Lindir with him into the forests of Homana, but only because she asked him to, and only because she wanted no marriage with Ellic of Solinde.'

She scowled at him, strangely confident in the face of his new self. 'What has this to do with me?'

'Nothing,' he told her bluntly. 'It has to do with me, and why you are here. What I said before is true. The *qu'mahlin* has slain most of the warriors and many of the women. As a race we are nearly destroyed, because of Shaine. And now the daughter of the Mujhar's former arms-master — who witnessed the very beginnings of the *qu'mahlin* — is in my hands.' He smiled slowly, gesturing. She saw again the spread fingers and lifting palm. 'It is *tahlmorra*, perhaps.'

'What do you say?'

'Fate. Destiny. It is a Cheysuli word meaning what is meant will happen, and cannot be gainsaid, for it is in the hands of the gods.' Finn smiled ironically at her. 'It has to do with the prophecy.'

'Prophecy,' she muttered in disgust, weary of his attitude and hinted-at knowledge. She looked at the patient wolf. 'What has Storr to do with me?'

Finn scowled. 'I cannot say, but it is something I would learn. Now.' He fixed her with a baleful glare. 'Why does he keep me from you?'

38

She glared back. 'That *I* cannot say, shapechanger, save to compliment his actions.'

He startled her by laughing. Then he got to his feet and reached for her, pulling her up. She stood stiffly, wary of him, ignoring the provocative appraising look in his eyes.

Storr yawned. *I think she is not as frightened of you as she would have you believe, lir.*

Finn smiled at the wolf, then looked back at her. His dark brows rose. 'Are you so brave, *mei jha*? Do you dissemble before me?'

Alix slanted a reproving glance at the wolf. 'He knows me not at all, shapechanger. Do not listen to him.'

'To my own *lir*?' He laughed. 'If I forsake Storr, I forsake my soul. You will learn that, soon enough.'

Storr shook himself and padded into the clearing. *Enough, lir; you do not understand the girl. And she does not understand what is in her blood.*

'My blood?' Alix asked, shaken.

Finn's eyes narrowed as the equanimity left his face. He turned slowly to her, reaching to close a wide hand on her jaw. 'What do you say?'

She swallowed, suddenly frightened again. She fought back a shudder at his touch. 'The wolf. He said something of my blood. What does he say?'

The hand tightened until she winced. 'My wolf?' he hissed. 'You *heard* him?'

She closed her eyes. 'Aye.'

Finn released her. Alix opened her eyes and found him staring at her speculatively. The gold in his ear glinted as he shoved hair back from his face. Slowly he smiled.

'Then the story is true.'

'Story?'

He folded his arms over his chest and grinned at her. 'Your crofter father did not tell your mother all he knew, or else you did not hear it.'

'What do you say?'

Finn flicked a glance at Storr. 'Do I have the right of it, *lir*?'

Can you not see it for yourself?

The warrior laughed to himself and turned back to her. Playfully he caught her braid in one hand and threaded blunt fingers into the loosened plait.

'You hear Storr, *mei jha*, because you are only half Homanan. The other half is Cheysuli.'

'No!'

He frowned. 'But even for all that, it is strange. The women do not take *lir*, nor do they converse with them. Yet it only serves to make me certain who you are.'

Alix felt a renewal of fear. 'I have said who I am. You speak lies to me.'

He tugged on her braid. 'You have much to learn, *mei jha*. You have grown up apart from your clan. You are sadly lacking in the wisdom and customs of the Cheysuli.'

'I am *Homanan*!'

'Then say to me how it is you can hear my *lir* when no other can, save myself.'

She opened her mouth to reply angrily but no sound came out. After a moment she jerked her braid free of him and turned away, hugging herself for warmth and security. She stiffened as his hands came down on her shoulders.

'*Mei jha*,' he said softly, 'it is not so bad a fate. We are children of the Firstborn, who were sired by the old gods. The Homanans are nothing when you understand the heritage *we* claim.'

'I am not a shapechanger!'

Fingers dug into her shoulders. 'You are Cheysuli. *Cheysuli*. Else Storr would not offer you his protection.'

'You accept the word of a wolf?' Abruptly Alix clapped hands over her mouth and spun, staring at him. 'What do I say? What do I hear from my own tongue?' She swallowed heavily. 'He is a wolf. A *beast*! And you are demon-sent to make me believe otherwise!'

'I am not a demon,' Finn said, affronted. 'Nor is Storr. I have said what I am, and what he is, and — by all the old gods! — what *you* are. Now, come with me.'

She wrenched away from his reaching hand. 'Do not touch me!'

Finn glared at her. 'Your blood has saved you from my attentions, *mei jha*, for a time. Do not seek to anger me, or I may renew them.'

Alix stiffened as he took her arm and led her through the trees. He brought her to a slate-coloured tent set in a tumbled circle of stone. The fire cairn still burned next to a blood-red rug, and she dragged her eyes from it in time to come face-to-face with a hawk perching on a staff before the tent. She stumbled back, gasping.

The bird was large, even with wings folded. He was a myriad of rich browns and golds, with dark eyes that watched her, half-lidded. His deadly, curving beak shone in the muted firelight, and she felt a whisper of awe and appreciation in her mind.

A man who has such a lir is powerful indeed . . .

'Cai,' Finn said quietly. 'This is my brother's pavilion. He is clan-leader, and needs to be told who you are.'

Wearily Alix rubbed a grimy hand across her brow. 'And what will you tell him, shapechanger?'

'That Hale's daughter has come back to us.'

She felt the strength pour out of her limbs. 'Hale's . . .'

His eyes were bright and mocking. 'What do you think I told you of Lindir and the Cheysuli she wanted? You are their daughter.'

Alix felt very cold. She hugged herself against his words. 'No.'

'You have only to ask my *lir*.'

'A wolf!'

'The *lir* are kin to the old gods, *mei jha*. They know many things we do not.'

'No.'

He sighed. 'Wait here, *rujholla*. I will speak to Duncan first.'

41

Anger spurred her out of her immobility. 'What do you call me *now*, shapechanger?'

'*Rujholla?*' His smile faded into regret. 'It is Cheysuli — the Old Tongue — for sister.' He sighed. 'Hale was my father, also.'

CHAPTER FOUR

When Finn at last pulled the pavilion doorflap aside and motioned her inside, Alix went numbly, without protest. She had considered, briefly, running again, but his words had dulled her senses. She was incapable of making a decision. She answered his beckoning hand.

First she saw only the torch in the corner, squinting against its acrid smoke. Then Alix's eyes fell on the seated man who held a compact bow in his hands. Transfixed, she stared at his hands; firm and brown, long-fingered and supple. Slowly he smoothed fine oil into the dark wood, rubbing it to a gleaming patina of age and richness. As she stared he put aside the bow and waited.

He was much like Finn, she saw, recognizing characteristic features of the Cheysuli race. But there was something more in the bones of his face. Promised strength, calm intelligence and the same inherent command she saw maturing in Carillon.

He rose smoothly to his feet and she saw he was taller than Finn; long-boned and less heavy. His face was wide-browed with a narrow nose, with the same high cheekbones and smooth planes as Finn's. Like his brother he wore a sleeveless jerkin and leather leggings, but his gold armbands bore the sweeping image of a magnificent hawk, lined with odd runes. At his left ear

43

hung a golden hawk with wings outspread.

Alix straightened under his calm perusal, lifting her chin as she tried to regain some of her vanished composure. He put out a hand and turned her head so the torchlight fell on her cheek.

'What has happened to your face?'

His voice was untroubled, smooth and low. Alix was taken aback by his question. 'A tree limb, shape-changer.'

Something glinted in his eyes as she used a purposely rude tone. For a moment she was very afraid.

This man is more subtle than Finn, she thought apprehensively, *and far less predictable*.

He released her chin. 'How did a tree limb come to desire the taste of your skin?'

She slid a look at Finn, who remained exceedingly silent. But the other man saw the exchange and laughed softly, surprising her. It also drew quick resentment from her.

'Do *you* propose to force me, shapechanger, as your brother intended?'

He studied her solemnly. 'I force no woman. Did Finn?'

Alix gritted her teeth. 'He tried. He wished to. The wolf would not allow it.'

'The *lir* are often much wiser than we,' he said significantly.

Alix was shocked as she saw dark colour move through Finn's face. For a moment her perception of him altered through the eyes of his older brother. Alix saw him as a rash young man instead of a fierce, threatening warrior. The image surprised her.

'Shapechanger . . .' she began.

'My name is Duncan. Calling me by it will not make you accursed, girl.'

She recoiled from his reprimand and answered glumly, 'What is it you want of me, now I am made prisoner?'

Duncan's lips twitched. 'If you are indeed Hale's daughter, you are no prisoner. You are of the clan, girl.'

'No.'

Finn shifted. 'Do you see, *rujho*? She will not listen.'

'Then I will have to convince her.'

Alix blanched and drew away from him. He let her get as far as the doorflap, then smoothly reached out and caught her arm.

'If you will remain with me, I will answer the questions in your mind. This is new for you. Understanding, I promise, will come with time.'

His hand pulled her steadily away from the doorflap. Alix was frightened again. 'I do not believe what he has said. I am Homanan. I am not Cheysuli.'

'If you will be seated, I will tell you a story,' Duncan said quietly. 'I am no *shar tahl* to give you the birthlines and the prophecy, but I can tell you much of what you must know.' His eyes flicked to Finn. 'Leave her with me. You had best tend to Carillon.'

Finn smiled crookedly. 'The princeling sleeps, *rujho*. The earth magic has removed his cares for a time.' He straightened under the silent command. 'But I will see to him, for all that. Tend her well, *rujho*; she was gently reared.'

His departure left Alix alone in the pavilion with Duncan. She waited mutely, unable to force her mind into coherent thought.

Duncan gestured to a spotted grey pelt on the floor and she assented silently, gathering her skirts about her knees as she sat. 'What will you do with me?'

He stood over her, arms folded. The torch painted his dark angular face and danced in his yellow eyes. Like Finn, he wore his black hair cut to his neck, where it fell loosely. Unlike Finn, he did not seem so inherently violent.

Duncan settled himself cross-legged before her, hands resting on his knees. 'I do nothing with you save welcome you to your clan. Do you expect to be slain?'

She stared at her own hands, clasped tightly in her lap. 'You are shapechangers. I have been raised to fear you. What else can you expect?'

'Finn said your *jehan* was arms-master to Shaine when the *qu'mahlin* began. Surely he has not raised you to believe the lies.' His calm voice forced her to look at him. 'Torrin was a faithful man, and honourable. He would not plant the seeds of untruth, even at Shaine's bidding.'

'You speak as if you know my father.'

Duncan shook his head. 'I never met him. I know few Homanans, now, because of Shaine's *qu'mahlin*. But Hale spoke of him when he came to the Keep.'

'I do not understand.'

He sighed. 'It will take much time. But first you must believe *Hale* is your father. Not Torrin.'

Her chin rose stubbornly. 'I cannot accept that.'

Duncan scowled at her, suddenly very like Finn. 'Foolishness has no place here. Will you listen?'

'I will listen.'

But it does not mean I will believe.

He seemed to hear her rebellious, unspoken words. For a moment Alix was nonplussed by the feeling but dismissed it quickly as Duncan began the story.

'Hale took Lindir into the forests. Her *jehana* — Shaine's wife, Ellinda — died soon after. Shaine took another wife, who miscarried three times and then bore him a stillborn son, which made her barren. The Mujhar claims it was Cheysuli sorcery that stole his daughter, slew his first wife and denied his second living children.' Duncan paused. 'And that began the *qu'mahlin*.'

'War,' she said softly.

'The *qu'mahlin* is more than war. It is annihilation for the Cheysuli race. The Mujhar wants every last one of us slain; the race destroyed.' His yellow eyes met hers. 'His decree touches even his granddaughter.'

Alix felt colour drain from her face. 'Shaine's grand-daughter ...'

'Your *jehana* was Lindir of Homana. You are the Mujhar's granddaughter.'

'No. No, you tell me lies.'

Duncan smiled for the first time. 'I do not lie, small one. But if you wish, you may ask my *lir*. Cai has told me you have a gift of the gods, and can converse with all the *lir*.'

'The hawk ...' she whispered.

A golden tone stirred within her mind, softly. *You are Hale's daughter, liren, and bloodkin to us all. Do not deny your heritage, or the gift of the gods.*

Duncan saw the anguish and fear in her face. He touched her trembling hands gently. 'If you wish to rest, I can finish the story another time.'

'No!' she said wildly. 'No, I will listen! What more can you say that will not destroy what comprehension I have left to me?'

He took his hand away. 'Hale was slain in the *qu'mahlin* by Shaine's troops, as he sought from the beginning. Lindir, carrying a child, returned to her *jehan* to beg his understanding. She wanted shelter for her child.' Duncan's face was grim. 'The Mujhar needed an heir. He had no son, and his lady-wife made barren. Lindir's child, were it a boy, would be that heir.'

A chill washed through her, leaving apprehension in its wake. 'But there was no son ...'

'No. Lindir bore a daughter, and died. The Mujhar, still dedicated to his purge, ordered the halfling girl-child taken to the forests and left to die.'

'But it was only a child ...'

'A shapechanger. A demon.' His voice was rough as he said the Homanan words. 'A halfling best left to the beasts.'

Alix looked up into his impassive face. She saw it soften into understanding and sympathy and sternness. He had told her, she realized, and he expected her to believe him.

'How do you know this?' she asked. 'You?'

'It has been told to the *shar tahl*, who has given it to the clan.'

'The *shar tahl*?'

'Our priest-historian, the Homanans would call him. He keeps the rituals and the traditions, and makes certain all know the proper heritage of the Cheysuli. Mostly he tends to the words of the prophecy.'

'What *is* this prophecy you prate of?' she asked, irritable. 'Finn speaks of little else.'

'That is not for me to say. The *shar tahl* will speak with you when it is the proper time.' He shrugged, lifting his spread-fingered palm. '*Tahlmorra*.'

Alix looked at him in the flickering shadows of the slate-coloured pavilion. He was alien to her, part of the vague dreams she had dreamed over the years, growing up knowing the Cheysuli were accursed and outlawed and sentenced to death by the Mujhar. But she knew he did not lie to her, for all she wished to believe it. There was no deceit in his eyes.

'If what you tell me is true, there is one more thing,' she said hollowly. 'You are my brother, like Finn.'

Duncan smiled. 'No. Finn and I share a *jehana*, but Hale was to me what the Homanans call foster-father. My *jehan* died when I was very young.'

She smoothed the weave of her skirts. 'I do not entirely understand. You said Hale took Lindir away and got a child on her. Me.' The word was dry in her mouth. 'But if he was father to Finn and foster-father to you ... I do not understand.'

'Hale was liege man to Shaine. It is a Cheysuli thing; hereditary service to the Mujhars and their blood. Until the purge, the Mujhars of Homana ever had a Cheysuli liege man.' Duncan smiled faintly. 'Hale spent most of his time at Homana-Mujhar, serving his lord, according to custom. Lindir was a golden child who took great joy in teasing her *jehan's* fierce liege man; it was a game to her. Then she was no longer a child, and Hale was no longer indifferent to the promise of her beauty. She had fulfilled that promise.' He saw Alix's shocked face and laughed softly. 'The Homanans hide their *mei jhas* and call them light women. The Cheysuli keep *cheysulas* and *mei jhas* — wives and mistresses — and honour them both.'

'But Hale *left* your mother!'

'He did what he wished. That is understood among us. Men and women have the freedom to take whom they choose, when they choose.' He grimaced. 'Though now we have few warriors, and fewer women.'

Alix swallowed with effort. 'I would rather be Homanan.'

Duncan's eyes narrowed. 'But you are half Cheysuli. In our clan, that is counted as whole.'

But her mind had gone past that, grasping the slippery strands of comprehension. She put the relationships together until she had an understanding of them. Then she looked at Duncan.

'Lindir bore a daughter and Shaine lost the heir he wanted.'

'Aye,' he agreed.

'So he turned to his brother, Fergus, who had a son.'

'Aye.'

Alix took a shaking breath. 'He made that son — his nephew — heir. Prince of Homana.'

Duncan watched her closely. 'Aye.'

She felt her heart begin to hurt. 'Then Carillon is my *cousin!*'

'Aye,' Duncan said softly, understanding.

Alix drew up her knees and clasped her arms around them tightly. She pressed her forehead against them and squeezed her eyes shut in denial and realization.

Before I was only a croft-girl, but one who put him at ease. Now I am Cheysuli — shapechanger! — accursed, and his bastard cousin. Grief surged into her throat. *He will never come to me again!*

She hugged her knees and keened silently in the shape-changer's tent.

CHAPTER FIVE

Alix, at dawn, sat warmly wrapped in a brown blanket, numbly aware she had slept in the shapechanger's presence. She had not meant to. She vaguely recalled her silent tears and his urging of her to sleep, but no more. Now she sat alone in his pavilion, bereft of the heritage she had known all her life.

The doorflap stirred and Alix glanced up, expecting Duncan. Instead she saw Carillon and stood up with a cry, letting the blanket slide to the ground.

Then she froze. His eyes were withdrawn from her, strange, and she saw none of the warm welcome she had come to expect.

They have told him ...

Alix's arms dropped to her sides. Desolation swept in to fill her soul. She would not look into his face and see his rejection of her.

'Alix ...'

'You need say nothing, my lord,' she said remotely. 'I understand how a prince must feel to learn the croft-girl he has kept company with is a shapechanger.'

He moved into the pavilion. 'Are you so certain they have the right of it?'

Her head jerked up. 'Then you do not believe them?'

He smiled. 'Do you think I am so easily manipulated, Alix? I think they lie to you. There is nothing Cheysuli about you. Your hair is brown, not black, and your eyes amber. Not beast-yellow.'

Carillon let her melt against his chest, sobbing quietly. Her fears of suggesting an intimacy she was not due faded away as she sought solace in his strength. His arms slipped around her and held her close, for the first time since they had met.

'You will come with me when I am released,' he said into her tangled hair. 'They cannot keep you.'

She lifted her face. 'Duncan has said I must stay.'

'I will take you back with me.'

'How do you know they will let *you* go?'

He smiled wryly. 'I am worth too much to my uncle for them to keep me long.'

'And I?'

'You, Alix?'

She wet her lips. 'If I am what they say, then I am the Mujhar's granddaughter. Lindir's daughter.'

'So you will admit to shapechanger blood if only to get royal blood as well,' he said, amused.

Alix pulled away from him. 'No! I only seek acknowledgment . . . the truth! Carillon, if I am Shaine's granddaughter — will he not free me from this place?'

'Do you think the Mujhar will acknowledge a half-shapechanger bastard granddaughter?'

She recoiled from the cruel question. 'Carillon—'

'You must accustom yourself. If what the shape-changers say is true, we are cousins. But Shaine will never claim you. He will never offer a single coin for your return.' Carillon shook his head. 'They are harsh words, I know, but I cannot let you expect something you cannot have.'

She set cold hands against her face. 'Then you will leave me here . . .'

He caught her arms, pulling her hands from her face. 'I will not leave you here! I will take you to Homana-Mujhar, but I cannot say what your reception will be.'

'You would not have to tell him who I am.'

'Do I say you are my light woman, then? A valley-girl I have been seeing?' He sighed as he saw her expression. 'Alix, what else would I tell him?'

'The truth.'

'And have him order you slain?'

'He would *not*!'

His hands tightened on her arms. 'The Mujhar has declared the Cheysuli accursed, outlawed, subject to death by anyone's hands. Do you think he will gainsay his own purge for the daughter of the man who stole *his* daughter?'

Alix jerked away from him. 'She was not stolen! She went willingly! Duncan said—' she broke off abruptly, horrified.

Carillon sighed heavily. 'So, you accept their words. With so little a fight, Alix, do you deny your Homanan blood and turn to the shapechangers?'

'No!'

You are Cheysuli, liren, came the hawk's golden tone. *Do not deny yourself the truth. Remain.*

Alix ripped the doorflap aside and stared into the sky. Cai drifted far above, floating on a summer breeze.

'I must go!' she cried.

This is your place, liren.

'No!'

'Alix!' Carillon moved to her and grabbed her arm. 'To whom do you speak?'

Homana-Mujhar is not for you, the bird said softly.

'I cannot stay,' she insisted, amazed at her willingness to speak to a bird. 'I cannot!'

'Alix!' Carillon exclaimed.

She gestured wildly. 'The bird! The hawk! There.'

He dropped her arms instantly, staring at her in alarm. Slowly his eyes went to the graceful hawk.

'Let me go with Carillon,' she pleaded, knowing only that the bird sought to keep her.

I cannot gainsay you, liren. I can only ask.

Alix tore her eyes from the hawk and looked

beseechingly at Carillon. Frantically she reached out to catch her hands in his black leather doublet.

'Take me with you. Tell the Mujhar whatever you choose, but do not make me stay in this place!'

'You understand what the *bird* says?'

'In my head. A voice.' She could sense his shock and sought to convince him. 'Not words. A tone ... I can understand what he thinks.'

'Alix ...'

'You said you would take me,' she whispered.

He put out a hand to point at Cai, ruby signet flashing. 'You converse with *animals!*'

Alix closed her eyes, releasing him. 'Then you *will* leave me.'

'Shapechanger sorcery ...' he said slowly.

She looked at him, judging his face and the feelings reflected there. Then his hands grasped her shoulders so hard it hurt.

'You are no different,' he said. 'You are still Alix. I look at you and see a strong, proud woman whose soul is near to destroyed by these shapechanger words. Alix, I will still have you by me.'

You are meant for another, the hawk said gently. *The prince is not for you. Stay.*

'By all the gods,' she whispered, staring blindly at Carillon, 'will none of you let me be?'

'Alix!'

But she tore herself from him and ran from them both, seeking escape in the forest.

She fled to a lush grassy glade lying in a splash of sunlight. There Alix sank to her knees and sat stunned, trying to regain control of her disordered mind. She shook convulsively.

Shapechanger! Spawn of a shapechanger demon and a king's daughter! She cried within her soul.

Alix scrubbed at her stinging eyes with the heels of her hands, fighting back tears. She had never been one for crying, but the tension and fear of the past hours had taken away her natural reserve. She wanted security and solace like a child seeking comfort at a mother's breast.

Mother! she cried. *Was I birthed by a Homanan valley girl, or a haughty, defiant princess?*

Alix felt the conflict in her soul. She longed for Carillon's confidence in her Homanan origins, yet felt the seductive tug of mystery attending the legendary magic of the Cheysuli. And though Torrin had raised her to be fair to all men in her thoughts, even the Cheysuli, he had also instilled in her the apprehension all felt concerning the race.

She heard a rustle in the leaves and glanced up swiftly, frightened Finn had followed her again. She did not entirely trust his intentions, for all he claimed to be her half-brother. Alix sensed something elemental in him; untamed and demanding.

A hawk rested lightly on a swinging branch, feathers ruffling in the breeze. Though its colouring was the same, she realized it was not Cai. This hawk was smaller, more streamlined; a swift hunting hawk able to plummet after small prey and snatch it up instantly.

Alix shivered involuntarily as she thought of the deadly talons curving around the branch.

Have you decided to stay? it asked.

She stared at it, astonished to discover the great distinction between its tone and Cai's. It regarded her from bright eyes, unmoving on the branch.

Do you stay? it asked again. *Or do you go?*

Resentful and defiant, Alix started to push the tone away. She would not allow the Cheysuli so to manipulate her mind. She would keep herself apart from them and their sorcery, regardless of the seductiveness of their power.

But even as she decided she felt the fear slip away, replaced by wonder. First she had spoken with a wolf who seemed perfectly capable of speaking back; then Cai. And now this smaller hawk.

By the gods, the animals are mine to converse with! She took a trembling breath. *If this is sorcery, it cannot be demon-sent. It is a true gift.*

The hawk regarded her approvingly. *Already you begin to learn. The lir-bond is truly magic, but does harm to no one. And you are special, for no other can converse with all the lir. Through you, perhaps, we can win back some of our blood-pride and esteem.*

'You lost it through Hale's selfish action!' she retorted, then winced at her audacity. Carefully she looked at the hawk to see if it was offended.

It seemed amused. *For the Cheysuli, aye, it would have been better had he never set eyes on Lindir. But then you would not live.*

'And what am I?' she shot back. 'Merely a woman a foolish warrior wanted for his own.'

Finn does, occasionally, allow his emotions to overrule his judgment. But it makes him what he is.

'A beast,' she grumbled, picking a stem from the grass.

He is a man. Beasts have more wisdom, better sense and far better manners. Do not liken him to what he cannot emulate.

Alix, startled by the hawk's wry words, laughed up at him delightedly. 'I am sorry he cannot hear you, bird. Perhaps he would reconsider his rash actions.'

Finn reconsiders very little.

She stared at the bird, eyes narrowing shrewdly. The stem she had picked drooped in her fingers. 'If you are not Cai, who are you? Show yourself.'

Another time, perhaps, the bird said obliquely. *But know I am one who cares.*

It detached itself from the swinging branch and flew into the blue sky.

Alix dropped the stem and stared after the fleet bird dispiritedly. For a moment she had felt an uprush of awe and amazement that she conversed with the *lir*; now she was a frightened and confused girl. Slowly she got to her feet and wandered back to the Cheysuli encampment.

She was startled to find the tents pulled down and rolled into compact bundles. The warriors tied them onto their horses and made certain the fire cairns were broken up and scattered. Alix stood in the centre of the naked clearing and realized her soul and self-image had been as neatly swept clean.

Carillon came to her as she stared blindly at the swift alteration of the camp. He touched her hand, then folded it into his much larger one.

'I will be with you,' he said softly. 'They have said I must go with them.' He grimaced. 'They say I am not yet strong enough for the ride to Mujhara, but they did not lie about the wound. It is near healed, and I feel strong enough to fight any of them.'

She looked at the wrist and saw healing ridges marking the wolf bite. The swelling and seepage was gone, replaced by new skin.

They have healing arts at their beck, she said silently, unconsciously echoing Finn's words.

'Well, my lord, perhaps it is best,' she said aloud. 'I do not seek to lose you so soon.'

'I have said you will come with me to Homana-Mujhar.'

She smiled sadly into his face. 'As your light woman?'

Carillon grinned and lifted her hand to brush his lips across her wrist. 'If it must be done, Alix, I will not prove unwilling.'

She blushed and tried to withdraw her hand, but he held it firmly. He shook his head slightly and smiled. 'I do not seek to discomfit you. I have merely said what is in my mind.'

'I am your cousin.' She did not entirely believe him.

Carillon shrugged. 'Cousins often wed in royal houses, to secure the succession. *This* bond would not be a thing Homanans disapprove of.'

Alix tried to answer. 'My lord . . .'

His brows lifted ironically. 'Surely you can dispense with my title if we discuss our futures in this way.'

56

Alix wanted to laugh at him but could not. She had longed for such thoughts and words from him all through their brief acquaintanceship, though she had never thought them possible. Now she could not comprehend it. The revelation of her ancestry destroyed the roots she had depended on.

'I will wed a princess, one day,' he said lightly, 'to get heirs for the throne. But princes have mistresses often enough.'

She heard the echo of Duncan's voice in her mind, explaining the casual Cheysuli custom of wives and mistresses. An open practice she could not comprehend.

Yet Carillon offers me much the same ... She shivered convulsively. *Who has the right of it — the Cheysuli or the Homanans?*

'Alix?'

She carefully freed her hand from his and met his blue eyes. 'I cannot say, Carillon. We are not even free of this place yet.'

He started to say something, but Finn's approach drove him into silence. Carillon glared at the Cheysuli warrior, who merely laughed mockingly. Then Finn turned to Alix.

'Will you ride with me, *rujholla*?'

She noted the change of address and felt a mixture of gratitude and resentment. She would acknowledge no blood relationship to him; nor would she accept the sort of physical commitment he wanted from her.

She moved closer to Carillon. 'I ride with the prince.'

'And likely have him fall off the horse from in front of you.'

Carillon glared at him. 'I will keep to my horse, shapechanger.'

Finn's earring winked as he laughed. 'You had better change your name for us, princeling, or you insult your cousin as well.'

'*You* seek to do that, not him!' Alix snapped.

He grinned at her, then shot a mocking glance at Carillon. 'Have you forgot? You have gained more than just your light woman as a cousin this day. You also have kin among the rest of us.'

'Kin among you?' Carillon asked disparagingly.

'Aye,' Finn said equably. 'Myself. She is my *rujholla*, princeling, though only by half. But it makes you and I cousins, of a sort.' He laughed. 'I am kin to Homana's prince, who would serve his liege lord by slaying us all. But to do that you would have to slay *her*, would you not?'

Colour surged into Carillon's face. 'If I slay any shapechanger, it will be you. I leave the rest to my uncle the Mujhar.'

'Carillon!' Alix said, horrified.

Finn laughed at them both, spreading his hands. 'Do you see, princeling? What you say of us concerns her. Beware your intentions, do you seek to keep her safe.'

Carillon's hands dropped to the heavy sword belted at his hips; Alix was still amazed the Cheysuli had let him keep it. But he did not draw the blade. Finn smiled at them both and walked away, calling to another warrior in the Old Tongue.

'He only seeks to goad you,' Alix said softly. 'To satisfy his own craving for a place.'

Carillon glanced at her in surprise. Then he smiled. 'Do you prophesy for me, Alix? Can you see into my heart as well as his?'

Inwardly she flinched from the reference to sorcery, and that at her own command. 'No. I only say what I feel in him. As for you ...' She hesitated, then smiled. 'I think you will be Mujhar, one day.'

He laughed at her and pulled her into his arms, lifting her into the air. 'Alix, I thank the gods I rode my warhorse through your garden that day! Else I would not have you sharing such wisdom with me.'

She grinned down at him, delighting in the feelings spilling through her body. His hands on her waist were firm and sure, possessive, betraying no signs of weakness from the wolf-wound. Alix let one hand curve itself around his neck, tangling in his tawny hair.

'And did I not share my wisdom with you when you trampled all my fine young plants?'

He spun her again, then set her down with a rueful grin. 'Aye, that you did. You near made me ashamed of my birth.'

Alix laughed at him. 'Even a prince can manage to go around a garden when his prey avoids it. I cared little for the fine clothes you wore or the gold you threw at me to pay for the damage.' She lifted her head haughtily, mimicking the actions of a high-born court lady. 'I cannot be *bought*, my lord prince, for all you are heir of Homana.'

'But can you be won?' he asked steadily.

Her smile faded. She averted her face. 'If I can be won, it is something left for me to discover. I cannot say.'

'Alix—'

'I cannot say, Carillon.'

Duncan came up before Carillon could speak again. He led a bay horse and carried the oddly compact bow he had polished the evening before. Carillon, looking sharply at it, sucked in his breath.

Duncan frowned at him. 'My lord?'

'Your bow.'

The Cheysuli held it up. 'This? It is not so much. I have better at the Keep. This is for raiding and hunting, and expendable.'

'But it is still a Cheysuli bow,' Carillon said seriously. 'I have heard of them all my life.'

Duncan smiled briefly and held it out. 'Here. But keep in mind it is not the best I have made.'

Carillon disregarded the modest statement and took the bow almost reverently, fingering his enemy's weapon. It was finely crafted, age-polished hardwood. The grip was laced with leather to cushion a man's palm. Odd runic symbols ran from top to bottom, winding around the bow like a serpent.

Carillon looked at Duncan. 'You know what is said of a Cheysuli bow.'

Duncan smiled ironically. 'That an arrow loosed by one cannot miss. But that is all it is, my lord; a legend.' His eyes narrowed in cynicism. 'Though it serves us well. If Shaine's troops fear a Cheysuli bow, it is all the better for us.'

'Do you say a man *can* miss with this bow?'

Duncan laughed. 'Any arrow can miss its mark. It is only rare for a Cheysuli to loose one with poor aim.' His smile faded into implacability. 'It comes from fighting for survival, my lord. When you are hunted down like a be-plagued animal by the Mujhar's guardsmen, you learn to fight back how you can.'

Carillon's face tautened. 'The legend of these bows was known *before* the purge, shapechanger.'

Duncan's mouth twisted. 'Then let us say the skill was *refined* by it, prince.'

Carillon thrust out the bow. Duncan took it without comment and looked at Alix. 'It is time to go. Will you ride with me?'

Her head lifted. 'I told your brother — I ride with the prince.'

Duncan handed the reins of the bay horse to Carillon. 'Your warhorse will be returned when you are better, my lord. For now you may have mine.'

Carillon mounted silently. Before Alix could attempt a scrambling mount Duncan lifted her up behind the Cheysuli saddle. She looked down into his impassive eyes and felt a faint tug of familiarity. But he walked away before she could question it.

Finn, mounted on a dun-coloured horse, rode up beside them. 'Should the princeling falter before you, *rujholla*, I will be more than happy to take you onto my horse.'

Alix looked directly into his angular, mocking face and said nothing at all, ignoring him as pointedly as she could.

Finn merely grinned and fell into place before them. The journey was begun.

60

CHAPTER SIX

The long ride took the heart from Alix as she clung to Carillon. She drooped dispiritedly against his broad back, longing for respite from the steady motion of the horse. Whenever Finn rode by she straightened and arranged her face into an expression of determined spirit, but when he left them she returned to her haze of weariness.

The Cheysuli did not tell either captive where they rode, only that their Keep lay at the end of their journey. When Carillon demanded his instant release and that of Alix, threatening the Mujhar's displeasure and retribution, Duncan refused courteously. Alix, watching him silently during much of the day's ride, wondered at the difference so evident in the brothers. Finn seemed the more aggressive of the two; Duncan kept his own council and gave nothing away to supposition. Though Alix wanted nothing more than to leave the shape-changers' presence with Carillon accompanying her, she far preferred Duncan's company to Finn's.

In the evening she sat before a small fire with Carillon, staring into the flames in exhaustion. The prince had shed his green cloak and draped it over her shoulders. She folded it around herself gratefully. He looked as tired and worn as he stretched his hands out to the fire's warmth; for all it was the beginning of summer, the nights were still cold. Alix knew her own appearance was no better. Her braid was loosened and tangled and her gown showed the results of too long a time spent in it. Her face felt grimy and the welt left by the tree stung.

The Cheysuli, she marked, took little with them on a raiding mission. Their mounts were packed lightly and the warriors carried only a belt-knife and the hunting bows for weaponry. Alix eyed them glumly as they quickly set up a small camp, spreading blankets where they would sleep and building tiny fires to heat their evening ration of journey-stew. The coloured pavilions were kept packed away; Alix realized she would spend the night unprotected by anything save a blanket.

Uneasily she slanted a glance at Carillon, seated next to her on Duncan's blood-red blanket. 'I would near give my soul to be safe in my own bed in my father's croft.'

Carillon, gazing blankly into the fire, looked over to her with an effort. Then he smiled. 'Had I a choice, I would be in my own chambers within Homana-Mujhar. But even your croft would do me well this night.'

'Better than here,' she agreed morosely.

Carillon shifted and sat cross-legged. The flames glinted off the whiteness of his teeth as he smiled maliciously.

'When I have the chance, Alix, these demons will regret what they have done.'

A strange chill slid down her spine as she looked sharply at his determined face. 'You would have them all slain?'

His eyes narrowed at her reproving tone. Then his face relaxed and he touched her ragged braid, moving it to lie across her shoulder. 'A woman, perhaps, does not understand. But a man must serve his liege in all things, even to the slaying of others. My uncle's purge still holds, Alix, I would not serve him by letting this nest of demons live. They have been outlawed. Sentenced to death by the Mujhar himself.'

62

Alix pulled the cloak more tightly around her shoulders. 'Carillon, what if there was no sorcery used against your House? What if the Cheysuli have the right of it? Would you still see to their deaths?'

'The shapechangers cursed my uncle's House when Hale took Lindir away with him. The queen consequently died of a wasting disease, and Shaine's second wife bore no living children. If not sorcery, what else could cause these things?'

Alix sighed and stared at her hands clasping the green wool. She pitched her voice purposely low, almost placating. But what she said had nothing to do with placation.

'Perhaps it was what the Cheysuli call *tahlmorra*. Perhaps it was no more than the will of the gods.'

His hand moved from her braid to her jaw and lifted her face into the light. 'Do you champion the demons again, Alix? Do you listen to them because of what you have learned?'

She looked at him steadily. 'I do not champion them, Carillon. I give them their beliefs. It is only fitting to acknowledge the convictions of others.'

'Even when the Mujhar denounces them as sorcerers of the dark gods?'

Alix touched his wrist gently and felt the ridged scars of the bite from Storr. Once again the image of Finn shifting his shape before her eyes rose into her mind, and it was only with considerable effort she kept the frightened awe from her voice.

'Carillon, will you allow him to denounce *me*?'

He sighed and closed his eyes, withdrawing his hand. He rubbed wearily at his brow and irritably shoved hair from his eyes.

'Shaine is not an easy man to convince. If you go before him claiming you are a shapechanger, and his granddaughter, you touch his pride. My uncle is a vain man indeed.' Carillon smiled at her grimly. 'But I will not allow him to harm you. I will have that much of him.'

Alix drew up her knees, clasping her arms around them. 'Tell me of Homana-Mujhar, Carillon, I have ever been afraid to ask before, but no more. Tell me of the Mujhar's great walled palace.'

He smiled at her wistful tone. 'It is a thing of men's dreams. A fortress within a city of thousands. I know little enough of its history, save it has stood proudly for centuries. No enemy force has ever broken its walls, nor entered its halls and corridors. Homana-Mujhar is more than a palace, Alix; it is the heart of Homana.'

'And you have lived there always?'

'I? No. I have lived at Joyenne, my father's castle. It is but three days from Mujhara. I was born there.' He smiled as if reminiscing. 'My father has ever preferred to keep himself from cities, and I echo his feelings. Mujhara is lovely, a jewelled city, but I care more for the country.' He sighed. 'Until my acclamation as formal heir last year, I lived at Joyenne. I spent time at Homana-Mujhar; I am not indifferent to its magnificence.'

'And I have not even seen Mujhara,' she said sadly.

'That is something I cannot understand. The city belongs to the Mujhar and is well-protected. Women and children go in safety among its streets.'

Alix kept her eyes from his. 'Perhaps it was a promise made to the Mujhar by Torrin; that he would not allow Lindir's shapechanger daughter to enter the city.'

Carillon stiffened. 'If you are that child.'

Alix closed her eyes. 'I begin to think I am.'

'Alix . . .'

She turned her head and rested her unblemished cheek against one knee, looking solemnly into Carillon's face. 'I converse with the animals, my lord. And I understand. If that is not shapechanger sorcery, then I must be a creature of the dark gods.'

His hand fell upon her shoulder. 'Alix, I will not have you say this. You are no demon's get.'

'And if I am Cheysuli?'

Carillon's eyes slid over the shadowed camp, marking

each black-haired, yellow-eyed warrior in supple leathers and barbaric gold. He looked back at Alix and for a moment saw the leaping of flames reflected in her eyes, turning them from amber to yellow.

He swallowed, forcing himself to relax. 'It does not matter. Whatever you are, I accept it.'

Alix smiled sadly and touched his hand. 'Then if you accept me, you must accept the others.'

He opened his mouth to deny it, then refrained. He saw the bleakness in her eyes and the weariness of her movements as she shifted into a more comfortable position. Carillon put a long arm out and drew her against his chest.

'Alix, I have said it does not matter.'

'You are the heir,' she said softly. 'It must matter.'

'Until I am the Mujhar, what I believe does not matter at all.'

And when you are the Mujhar, will you slay my kin? she wondered.

In the morning Duncan led Carillon's chestnut warhorse to them. Alix looked from the horse to the clan-leader and marked his solemn expression. Finn, standing with him, smiled at her suggestively. Alix coloured and ignored him, watching Duncan instead.

'You rode well enough yesterday, my lord,' he said quietly. 'You have our leave to go. Finn will accompany you.'

Carillon glared at him. 'I can find my own way back, shapechanger.'

Duncan's lips twitched. 'I have no doubt of that. But the Cheysuli have spent twenty-five years fleeing the unnatural wrath of the Mujhar, and we would be foolish indeed to lead his heir to our new home. Finn will see you do not follow us to the Keep.'

Carillon reddened with anger but ignored the Chey-suli's dry tone. He took the scarlet leather reins from Duncan and turned to Alix.

'You may ride in the saddle before me.'

Duncan stepped swiftly between the horse and Alix as she moved to mount. His eyes were flat and hard. 'You remain with us.'

'You cannot force me to stay!' she said angrily. 'I have listened to your words, and I respect them, but I will not go with you. My home is with my father.'

'Your home is with your father's people.'

Alix felt herself grow cold. Without thought she had spoken of Torrin, but the clan-leader reminded her, in a single sentence, she was no longer a simple Homanan croft-girl.

She steadied her breath with effort. 'I want to go with Carillon.'

His hawk earring swung as he shook his head. 'No.'

Finn laughed at her. 'You cannot wish to leave us so soon, *rujholla*. You have hardly learned our names. There is much more for you to learn of the clan.'

'I am still half Homanan,' she said steadily. 'And free of any man's bidding save my father's.' She challenged Duncan with a defiant glance. 'I will go with Carillon.'

The prince moved beside her, setting a possessive hand on her shoulder. 'By your own words you have said she is my cousin. I will have her with me in Homana-Mujhar. You cannot deny her that.'

Finn raised his brows curiously. 'Can we not? Your fates were decided in Council last night, while you slept. It was my position we should keep you both, forcing you to see we are not the demons you believe, but I was overruled. My *rujholli* would have you returned safely to your uncle, who will send guardsmen to strike us down.' He shrugged. 'Some even believed you would be won to the belief we are only men, like yourself, did you spend time with us, but I think you would only plan to harm us how you could.' Finn smiled humourlessly. 'What would you have done, princeling, had you stayed with us?'

Carillon's fingers dug into Alix's shoulder. 'I would

have found my escape, shapechanger, and made my way back to Mujhara. You have the right of it. I would aid my kinsman in setting troops after you.'

'At the risk of her life?' Finn asked softly.

Alix shivered. Carillon's hand dropped to his sword hilt. 'You will not harm her, shapechanger.'

'We do not harm our own,' Duncan said coldly. 'But does Shaine bid his men spare the life of a single Cheysuli? They are not discriminating men. If you allow them to follow us and attack, you risk the girl.'

'Then let me go,' Alix said. 'Perhaps the Mujhar would not send his troops.'

'Alix!' Carillon said sharply.

Finn grinned cynically. 'Do you see, *mei jha*, what manner of man your princeling is? Yet he would have you believe *we* are the bloodthirsty demons. I say it was the Homanans who began the *qu'mahlin* and the Homanans who perpetuate it. It was none of Cheysuli doing.'

'No more of this!' Alix cried. 'No more!'

Carillon stepped from her and drew his sword hissing from its sheath. He stood before them with the massive blade gleaming, clenched in both hands. Alix saw the ruby wink redly in the sunlight, then drew in her breath. Down the blade ran runic symbols very similar to those on Duncan's bow.

'You do not take her,' Carillon said softly. 'She comes with me.'

Finn crossed both arms over his chest and waited silently, armbands flashing in the light. Alix, frozen in place, felt an odd slowing of time. Carillon stood next to her with blade bared, feet planted, his size alone warning enough to any man. Yet Duncan stood calmly before the weapon as if it did not concern him in the least.

Her skin contracted with foreboding. *Will I see a man die this day because of me?* She swallowed heavily, wishing she could look away and knowing she could not. *Lindir's*

*actions set the purge into motion; if I am truly her daughter,
does this not add to it?*

Duncan smiled oddly. 'You had best recall the maker
of that blade, my lord.'

Finn's teeth showed in a feral smile. 'A Cheysuli blade
ever knows its first master.'

Alix looked again at the runes on the sword, transfixed
by their alien shapes and the implications of them.

Carillon held his ground. 'You do not even use swords
yourselves, shapechanger!'

Finn shrugged. 'We prefer to give men a close death. A
sword does not serve us. We fight with knives.' He
paused, glancing at Alix. 'Knives . . . and *lir*-shape.'

'Then what of your bows?' Carillon snapped.

'They were for hunting, originally,' Duncan said
lightly. 'Then the Mujhars of Homana began requiring
our services in war, and we learned to use them against
men.' His yellow eyes were implacable. 'When the
qu'mahlin began, we used them against those we once
served.'

Finn moved forward, so close to Carillon the tip of the
broadsword rested against his throat. 'Use it,' he
taunted in a whisper. 'Use it, princeling. Strike home, if
you can.'

Carillon did not move, as if puzzled by the invitation.
Alix, sickened by the tensions, bit at her bottom lip.

Finn smiled and put his hand on the blade. His
browned fingers rested lightly on the finely honed
edges. 'Tell me, my lord, whom Hale's sword will
answer. The heir of the man who began the *qu'mahlin*, or
Hale's only blood-son?'

'Finn,' Duncan said softly. Alix thought he sounded
reproachful.

Her fingers twined themselves into the folds of her
yellow skirts, scraping against the rough woolen fabric.
She knew she would see Finn die; even with his hand on
the blade the warrior could never keep Carillon from
striking him down. She owed no kindness to Finn, who

68

had stolen her so rudely, but neither did she wish to see him struck down before her eyes. The sour taste of fear filled her mouth.

'Carillon ...' she begged. She swallowed back the constriction in her throat. 'Do you begin your uncle's work already?'

'As I can,' he said grimly.

Finn's fingers on the blade shifted slightly. Alix thought he would drop the hand and move into a defensive posture, but he did not. Before she could cry out he twisted the sword aside with only a hand. His own knife flashed as he stepped into Carillon.

'No!' she cried, lunging forward.

Duncan's hand came down on her arm and jerked her back. She tried to pull free and could not, then stood still as she saw the Cheysuli blade against Carillon's throat. The broadsword was in his right hand, but she realized the weapon was too bulky to draw back and strike with in close quarters, particularly with Finn so close.

'Do you see, lordling, what it is for a man to face a Cheysuli in battle?' Finn asked gently. 'I do not doubt you have been trained within the walls of your fine palace, but you have not faced a Cheysuli. Until that is done you have not learned at all.'

Carillon's teeth clenched as they shut with a click. The muscles of his jaw rolled, altering the line of his face, but he said nothing at all. Nor did he flinch before the knife at his throat.

Finn slid a bright glance at Alix. 'Will you beg me for his life, *mei jha*?'

'I will not,' she said clearly. 'But if you slay him here, I myself will see to *your* death.'

His eyebrows shot up in mock astonishment. Then he grinned into Carillon's still face. 'Well, princeling, you have women to argue for you. Perhaps I should respect that.' He shrugged and stepped away, returning the knife to his belt. 'But she *is* Cheysuli, and my *rujholla*, and I will not risk it.'

Duncan bent and picked up the scarlet reins Carillon had dropped. He held them out. Silently the prince slid his sword home in its silver-laced leather sheath and took them.

'Finn will escort you to Mujhara.'

Carillon looked only at Alix. 'I will come back for you.'

'Carillon . . .'

'I will come back for you.'

Alix nodded and hugged herself, hunching her shoulders defensively. She knew he could not win her freedom without sacrificing himself, which would give her no freedom at all. The Cheysuli had disarmed both of them.

Carillon turned away from her and mounted the big chestnut. From the horse's great height he looked down on them all.

'You are foolish,' he said stiffly, 'to free me without requiring gold.'

Finn laughed. 'You seek to instruct us at the risk of your own welfare?'

'It is only that I do not understand.'

Duncan smiled. 'The Cheysuli do not require gold, my lord, save to fashion the *lir*-tokens and the ornaments our women wear. We desire only to end this war the Mujhar wages against us, and the chance to live as we once did. Freely, without fearing our children will be slain because of their yellow eyes.'

'If you had not sought to throw down Homanan rule—'

Duncan interrupted sharply. 'We did not. We have ever served the blood of the Mujhars. Hale, in taking Lindir from her *jehan*, freed her of a marriage she did not desire. In doing that he performed the service to which he bound himself — he served the Mujhar's blood.' He smiled slightly. 'It was not what Shaine expected of his service, perhaps, for Hale was his man. It was only he wanted Lindir more.'

'Your *jehana* was a wilful woman,' Finn said to Alix,

70

deliberately distinct as if to hammer the point home. 'Do you echo her?'

She brought her head up haughtily, defying him. 'Were *I* within Homana-Mujhar, I would not leave it to go into the forests with a Cheysuli warrior. Do not judge me by my mother.'

Finn grinned, triumphant. 'If I have at last got you to admit to your blood, *mei jha*, I will judge you by anything.'

Before she could retort he turned and faded into the trees. Alix glared after him, then scowled as he returned a moment later on his dun-colored horse.

Duncan moved to Carillon's horse, looking up at the prince. 'I would send greetings to Shaine the Mujhar, did I think he would accept them. We do not desire this war.'

Carillon smiled mirthlessly. 'I think the Mujhar has made *his* desires clear, shapechanger.'

Duncan put a hand on the warhorse's burnished shoulder idly. 'If you seek to continue the *qu'mahlin*, my lord, you are not the man I believe you are. The prophecy has said.' He smiled and stepped away, using the spread-fingered gesture. '*Tahlmorra*, Carillon.'

'I renounce your prophecy,' the prince said flatly.

The clan-leader reached out and caught Alix's arm, drawing her close. 'If you do that, my lord, you renounce her.'

Alix shivered once under his hand. 'Let me go with Carillon.'

'No.'

Finn moved his horse alongside the chestnut and smiled sardonically at the prince. 'Waste no more time. I would not wish the Mujhar angrier than he must be. Come, princeling. We ride.'

He brought his hand down on the chestnut's wide rump and sent him lunging forward. Finn crowded his mount behind so that Carillon could not wheel back, and the last Alix saw of the prince was his tawny-dark head ducking a low branch.

She made an involuntary movement to follow and again Duncan's hand held her back. After a moment he released her.

'It is not so bad,' he said quietly. 'You have much to learn, but it will come quickly enough when you have accepted your blood.'

Alix drew a shaky breath and stared hard at him. 'I will not claim you a liar, shapechanger, but neither will I submit to your rule. If I accept this as your — *tahlmorra*, I do it on my own terms.'

A tall warrior smiled at her. 'A Cheysuli could do it no other way.'

Alix scowled at him. Mutinously, she followed him through the trees to his waiting horse.

CHAPTER SEVEN

Alix was so weary by the time evening fell she let Duncan lead her to his fire and push her down onto a thick tawny pelt without saying a word. A crofter's daughter spent little time on horseback; her muscles ached and her legs had raw sores rubbed on them. She huddled on the pelt numbly and pulled her tattered skirts around her bare feet as best she could. When Duncan put a bowl of hot stew into her hands she thanked him shakily and began to spoon it into her mouth.

He sat down on another pelt across from her and picked up the bow Carillon had praised. Silently he began to rub it with an oiled cloth, eyes on his work.

Alix sipped at the cup of honey brew he had given her, nearly choking on its vitriolic taste. She kept her reaction from him by covering her mouth with a hand, trying not to gasp aloud. She did not wish him to see her disability, or her weariness.

He seemed oblivious to her as she scraped up the last of the stew and set the bowl aside, rattling the wooden spoon. She felt better for a full stomach, but it also made her more alert to the dangers she faced. She could no longer take refuge in the haze of exhaustion and helplessness that had dogged her during the long ride. Now she could look across the small campsite and see the dark warriors so intent on taking her away from her people.

Alix was still apprehensive, but most of the over-powering fright had left her. Duncan had treated her with calm kindness all day, and with Finn gone she sensed no threat to her person or her equilibrium. She had the chance to consider her plight from a more sensible angle.

'Will you answer my questions, shapechanger?'

Duncan did not look up. 'I have told you my name. Use it if you would speak with me.'

Alix studied his bowed head, marking how the black hair fell forward into his face as he worked. The gold earring winked through thick strands. Then she glanced at the hawk who sat so silently in the nearest tree.

'How does one get himself a *lir*?'

The bow gleamed in his supple hands. 'When a Cheysuli becomes a man he must go into the forests or mountains and seek his *lir*. It is a matter of time, perhaps even weeks. He lives apart, opening himself to the gods, and there the animal who will become his *lir* seeks him out.'

'Do you say the *animal* does the choosing?'

'It is *tahlmorra*. Every Cheysuli is born to a *lir*, and a *lir* to him. It is only a matter of finding one another.'

'Yet not all animals are *lir*, Finn said.'

'No. Just as all men are not Cheysuli.'

Unwillingly, she smiled at his wry tone, though he did not look at her. 'What happens if the *lir* is not found?'

His hands stopped their work as his eyes came up to meet hers. 'A Cheysuli with no *lir* is only half a man. We are born with it in our souls. If it lacks, we are not whole.'

'Not whole . . .'

'It is a thing you cannot comprehend, but a man who is not whole has no purpose. He cannot serve the prophecy.'

74

Alix frowned at him thoughtfully. 'If you are not whole . . . what happens to you if Cai is slain?'

Duncan's hands tensed on the bow. First he looked at the hawk perching in the tree, then he set the bow aside and gave her his full attention. He leaned forward intently and Alix felt the full power of his strength.

'You do not ask out of mere curiosity. If you seek to escape by slaying my *lir* you will be Cheysuli-cursed. It is not a simple thing to live with.' A flicker passed across his face. 'But you would not live long enough to truly suffer.'

Alix recoiled from the deadly promise in his voice. She shook her head in speechless denial.

'I will tell you, regardless of your intent,' he said quietly, 'so you will know. I put my life in your hands.' He watched her closely: judgmental. 'If a man seeks to slay a Cheysuli, he need only slay his *lir*. Does he imprison that *lir*, he imprisons a Cheysuli. He is powerless, without recourse to the gifts the gods have given us.' He relaxed minutely. 'And now you know the price of the *lir*-bond.'

'How can it be so consuming?' she demanded. 'You are a man; Cai a bird. How is it you keep this bond?'

Duncan shrugged as he smoothed the leather of his snug leggings. 'I cannot say clearly. It is a gift of the old gods. It has been so for centuries, and will doubtless continue.' He grimaced. 'Unless the Mujhar slays us all. Then Homana will lose its ancestors.'

'Ancestors!' she exclaimed. 'You would have me believe *you* made this land what it is, if you speak so.'

Duncan smiled oddly. 'Perhaps.'

Alix scowled at him. 'I do not believe you.'

'Believe what you wish. If you ask, the *lir* will tell you.'

Her eyes went to the hawk. But she refused to hear it from the bird. She preferred to draw Duncan out. 'And if you are slain, what becomes of the *lir*?'

'The *lir* returns to the wild. For the animal the broken link is not so harsh.' He smiled. 'Creatures have ever

75

been stronger than men. Cai would grieve for a while, perhaps, but he would live.'

Do not dismiss my grief so lightly, the bird chided. *Else you ridicule our bond.*

Duncan laughed silently and Alix, surprised by his response, stared at him. The solemnity she had learned to associate with him was not as habitual as she had assumed.

After a moment she put out her arms and stretched them, cracking sinews. 'What truly becomes of you if the *lir* is slain?' she asked lightly.

Duncan grew very still. 'A Cheysuli without a *lir*, as I said, is not whole. He is made empty. He does not choose to live.'

She froze, staring at him. 'Does not choose ...'

'There is a death-ritual.'

Her arms dropped. 'Death!'

Duncan looked again into the trees, eyes on Cai. 'A Cheysuli forsakes his clan and goes into the forests to seek death among the animals. Weaponless and prepared. However it comes, he will not deny that death.' He shrugged, making light of the matter. 'It is welcome enough, to a *lirless* man.'

Alix swallowed back her revulsion. 'It is a barbaric thing. Barbaric!'

Duncan was impassive. 'A shadow has no life.'

'What do you say?' she snapped.

He sighed. 'I cannot give you the proper words. You must accept what I say. A *lirless* man is no man, but a shadow. And a Cheysuli cannot live so.'

'I say it is barbaric.'

'If it pleases you.'

'What *else* must I think?'

He leaned forward and placed more wood on the small fire. It snapped and leaped in response, high-lighting his pale eyes into a bestial glow.

'When you have learned more of your clan, you will think differently.' Duncan relaxed, setting the bow aside as he studied her impassively. Then a faint flicker of curiosity shone in his eyes. 'Would you wed Carillon?'

Alix stared at him. 'Carillon?'

'Aye. I have seen what is between you.'

For a moment she could find no proper answer. The question stunned her, both for its audacity and the implications. In all her dreams of a tall prince, she had never considered marriage with him. Somehow the thought of it, and the regret that it could never be, hurt.

'No,' she said finally. 'Carillon would never take me to wife. He is meant for a foreign princess; some highborn lady from Atvia, perhaps, or Erinn. Perhaps even Solinde one day, if this war between the realms ends.'

'Then you will be his light woman. His *mei jha*.'

She disliked his easy assumption. 'That is difficult to do if I must stay with this clan you prate about.'

Duncan grinned, suddenly so much like Finn it startled her. But the similarity vanished when she looked closer, for there were none of Finn's roguish ways about Duncan.

'You are not a prisoner, though it must seem so to you. As for the prince . . . I think he means what he says. He will come back for you.' He sighed, losing the animation in his face. 'I cannot say when, but he will do it.'

'I will welcome it, shapechanger.'

Duncan regarded her solemnly a moment. 'Why do you fear us so much? I have said we do no harm to our own.'

Alix looked away from him. '*I* have said. I was raised to fear you, and to acknowledge the sorcery in your blood. All I have ever known is that the Cheysuli are demons . . . dangerous.' She looked back at him. 'You raid crofts and steal the livestock. People are injured. If that is no harm, you have a strange way of showing your peaceful intentions.'

77

Duncan smiled. 'Aye, it would seem so. But do not forget ... Shaine has forced us to this. Before we lived quietly within the forests, hunting when we would and having no need to *raid* for our food. The *qu'mahlin* has made us little more than brigands, like those who ply the tracks to steal from honest folk. It was never our nature — we are warriors, not thieves — but Shaine has left us little choice.'

'Had you the choice ... would you return to your former way of life?'

He fingered the gold hilt of the long-knife at his belt absently, eyes gone oddly detached. When he answered Alix heard the echoes of prophecy in his voice.

'We will never regain our former way of life. We are meant for another way. The old gods have said.'

She shivered, shrinking from the implications of his words. She picked up the wooden cup, intending to drink to cover her confusion, saw it was empty and set it down.

'You will be Carillon's light woman?'

The cup fell over as her fingers spasmed. 'I will be no man's light woman.'

Duncan's smile was crooked; disbelieving. 'I have been led to believe most women would slay for a chance to be so honoured.'

'I am not most women,' she retorted. She sighed, picking at the twigs caught in her tangled braid. 'I cannot conceive of it ever happening, now, so there is no need for me to consider it.'

'Then you give him up so easily?'

Alix dropped the braid and stared at him despondently, forgetting that he was her enemy and thinking only of the sympathy in his voice.

'I cannot say what I will do. I cannot even say what I *want*!'

He grunted. 'Those are the restraints put on you by your Homanan upbringing. Among the Cheysuli, a woman takes what man she will.' A fleeting shadow passed across his face as he frowned. A shrug banished the expression. 'A woman of the clan may refuse one man and take another, easily.'

'My father did not bring me up to be a light woman,' she said firmly. 'One day I will wed a crofter, like my father, or a villager.' She shrugged. 'One day.'

'Your father did not bring you up at all,' he said bluntly.

Alix opened her mouth to protest *yes, he most certainly did*, then realized Duncan referred to Hale. Once again she recalled the astonishing story behind her own birth — if she would accept that story as truth. But she could not tell him what she thought, so she settled for the familiar litany she had repeated each evening.

'Carillon will wed a princess. Of course.'

'Of course,' he mocked. 'If he lives at all, he will wed a princess.'

'Lives!'

Duncan stretched one eyelid and rubbed at it. 'The Ihlini will see to it Carillon does not live to wed.'

'The Ihlini!' Alix stared at him, horrified. 'The sorcerers who serve the dark gods? But why? What do they care for Carillon? Is it not Bellam who dictates what Solinde will do?'

Duncan picked up his bow and studied it, then began to oil it once more. His voice, deep and quiet, took on an instructive tone. 'Solinde has ever been a strong land, but her kings are greedy. They are not satisfied with Solinde; they also want Homana in vassalage. Bellam has sought to achieve that all his life, but these constant skirmishes at the borders — and the full battles that slay so many — have won him nothing. He seeks to gain Homana how he can, now.'

'By turning to the *Ihlini*?'

'Already Solinde is much stronger than before. Bellam seeks the unnatural power of Tynstar, who rules the Ihlini — if a sorcerer can be said to rule his own race.'

He bent his head over his work. 'Tynstar is the might behind Solinde, not Bellam.'

'Tynstar . . .' she whispered. For a moment she allowed her mind to recall the tales she had heard as a child, when her mother — despairing of winning Alix's attention to chores — had threatened her with Ihlini retribution.

Until my father said she should not, for to speak of Tynstar and the Ihlini was to invite his power over you. Alix shuddered once, seeking to throw off the spectre, but Duncan did not seem to notice.

'Tynstar, called the Ihlini,' he said, 'perhaps the most powerful of all those who serve the dark gods of the netherworld. He has arts at his command no man should have, and he uses them for Bellam's gain. This time Homana cannot stand against her enemies.'

Alix sat upright, flushed with affrontedness and defiance. 'Homana has never fallen! Not in all the years the kings of Solinde have sought to defeat us.' She thrust her chin up. 'My father said.'

Duncan looked across the fire at her, showing her an expression of such amused tolerance she longed to throw the cup at him. 'And in all these years the Mujhars of Homana had the Cheysuli by their sides. We used our own god-gifts to defeat the Solindish troops. Not even the Ihlini could halt us.' The tolerance faded. 'Twenty-five years ago we helped Shaine hold his borders against Bellam, putting down a massive force that might have destroyed Homana. The peace that resulted from our victory would have been solidified by a marriage between Lindir and Bellam's son, Ellic. When that was broken, so was the peace. Now Shaine slays us, and Homana will fall to the Ihlini.'

'Twenty-five years . . .' she echoed.

'Lindir remained hidden with Hale for eight years of the *qu'mahlin*, fleeing her *jehan's* wrath. When he was slain she returned, and bore you but weeks later.'

'Well . . . if the Ihlini are so powerful, how is it you have withstood them before?'

'That is a thing between the races. I cannot say.' He frowned faintly. 'The Ihlini have no real power before us. Oh, they have recourse to some of their illusions and simple arts, but not the dark magic. But we also suffer, for though the Ihlini cannot overcome us with their arts, neither can we take *lir*-shape before them, or hear our *lir*. We are as other men before them.'

Alix, stunned by his words, said nothing. All her life she had known the Cheysuli had awesome arts at their call, though she could not have named what they did; to hear Duncan speak of the Ihlini as the demons she had ever thought a Cheysuli characteristic upset her preconceived notions of the order of things. Already Finn had destroyed her innocently confident childhood. Duncan had further shaken her foundations by speaking of a prophecy and the future she faced with his clan. Now, to think of the Ihlini as a real threat to the land she loved, Alix felt a desperation building in her soul.

Too much is being shattered . . . she thought abstractedly. *They are taking too much of me, twisting me, promising things I have ever feared . . .*

'Here,' Duncan said gently, 'you have suffered long enough.'

She dragged her eyes from the fire, blinking at the residue of flames that overlay his dark face. He held something in his hand, offering it to her. She saw it was a silver comb, gleaming in the firelight. Slowly she put out a hand and took it, fingering the intricate runic devices that leaped and twisted in the flickering shadows.

'You may have it,' Duncan said. 'I carried it for a girl in the Keep. But you have more need of it.'

Alix hesitated, staring at him. She could not, even as she tried, view him as her enemy. Finn's threat was very real, substantial; Duncan's was not.

Or else he hides it from me . . .

'Use it,' he urged gently.

After a moment she set the comb down and began to

undo her tangled braid. Duncan stirred the fire with a stick, coaxing life back to the rosy coals.

She picked twigs and leaves from the heavy plait, gritting her teeth at the pain of snarls set so deeply she would have to rip most of them out. To cover her grimaces she spoke to Duncan.

'You have a wife?'

'No, I have no *cheysula*.'

She dragged the comb through her hair. 'Then you have a ... *mei jha*?'

He glanced at her briefly, face closed. 'No.'

She scowled at him as she ripped at a tangle. 'Why did you go to such effort to explain the freedom of your race, if you do not subscribe to it yourself?'

Duncan continued to stir the fire, though it did not particularly require it. 'I am clan-leader. It came on me eight months ago, when Tiernan died. With it comes much responsibility, and I chose not to divide myself between a *cheysula* and the leadership this year.' He waved the stick idly. 'Perhaps next year.'

Alix nodded absently as she freed the last tangle from her hair. Her attention was not really focused on Duncan, but she sensed an odd tension in him as he watched her silently. His eyes followed her hands as she pulled the silver comb through the heavy length of her dark hair.

The exercise improved her disposition and her feelings toward the clan-leader. No man, did he want to sacrifice her to some unspeakable god, would allow her the amenities common to courtesy. She was grateful to him.

'My thanks,' she said gravely, then smiled warmly at him across the fire.

Duncan was on his feet in one movement, muttering something in the lyrical Old Tongue. His lips compressed into a thin line and his eyes were suddenly hostile as he stared at her, transfixed.

'What have I done?' she cried, aghast.

'Can you not feel it?' he demanded. 'Can you not hear the *tahlmorra* in you?'

Alix dropped the comb. 'What do you say?'

He swore and turned from her, hands curling into fists. Then he gathered up a bundled blanket and tossed it at her violently.

Alix caught it before it could fall into the fire, recoiling from his cold anger until she felt a tree against her back. As he continued to stare at her with an unwavering, bestial glare, Alix pushed herself to her feet and hugged the blanket as if it would protect her.

'What do you say?' she whispered.

'*Tahlmorra* ... and you know nothing of it,' he snapped.

'No!' she cried, illogically angry when she should be frightened. 'I do not! And do not mutter to me of it when I cannot comprehend what it is. How am I to conduct myself if you tell me nothing?'

Duncan took a trembling breath and visibly controlled himself, as if he knew he had frightened her. 'I had forgot,' he admitted quietly. 'You cannot know it. But I question that you feel nothing.'

'Feel *what*?'

'We serve the prophecy,' he said with effort, 'but we cannot know it perfectly. The *shar tahls* tell us what they can, but even they cannot know everything that the gods intend. The *tahlmorra*, as a whole, is unknown to us. But we feel it. Sense it.' He sighed constrictedly and ran a stiff hand through raven hair. 'I have come to face a part of my *tahlmorra* I did not know. I should welcome it ... but I cannot. I cannot accept it. And that, in itself, is a denial of my heritage.'

Alix felt the measure of his pain, amazed at the depth of his turmoil. His solemnity had vanished; the man she had thought so controlled and implacable was no different from herself. But she did not understand, and said so.

Duncan relaxed minutely. 'No. You cannot. You are

too young . . . and too Homanan.' His eyes, focused on the heavy curtain of her hair, were bleak. 'And Carillon has already won your heart.'

'Carillon!'

He gestured to the blanket still clasped in her arms. 'Sleep. We ride early.'

Alix watched him walk into the shadows, disappearing as easily as if he were a part of the night. She wondered, as she shook out the blanket and lay it by the tree, if he were.

The gods sent her a dreamless sleep.

CHAPTER EIGHT

Alix rode with Duncan the next day, hands clasping the saddle and body held carefully upright so she would not touch his back. With Finn she had kept herself from him because of his undisguised interest in her; Duncan's dignity seemed to demand such behaviour on her part. She could not imagine hanging onto him or otherwise interfering with anything he did. And he had closed himself to her since their conversation of the evening before. For all he was still courteous, he was also cool toward her.

When evening came and the band of Cheysuli stopped to set up camp, Alix found herself delegated to tend Duncan's fire as if she were a servant. She disliked the sensation. It made her feel a true prisoner, even though she was treated mostly like a visitor.

Alix dumped a tree limb onto the fire and scowled at it blackly, angry with herself for remaining so acquiescent to orders and angry with the circumstances in general. When she sensed a presence on the outer fringes of the firelight she straightened, then gasped and stumbled back a step as she saw the baleful gleaming eyes of a ruddy wolf.

It came closer, into the light, and blurred itself before her. Alix released her breath and gritted her teeth as she saw the form shape itself into Finn.

'Do you seek to frighten me to death?'

Finn laughed at her and squatted to pour himself a cup of honey brew from the pot Duncan had set over the fire. After several restorative swallows he fixed her with a bright gaze and scratched idly at his cheek.

'Well, I have returned your princeling to safety.'

Alix knelt down on a thick dark pelt, disgruntled enough to speak rudely even to him. 'You did not slay him?'

'Carillon is meant for a death, like all men, but it will not come at my hands.'

She shot him a dubious glance. 'You would do whatever you could in this personal war you wage against the Mujhar. Even to slaying his heir, were you given the chance.'

'But Duncan would not let me do it.' He laughed at her startled glance. 'No, I would not slay Carillon. He has a part in our own prophecy, if we are to believe he is the one the runes show us. There is no name; only his deeds are written down. The prophecy does not foretell the prince's death so soon, so you may take comfort in that. First he must be Mujhar.' Finn studied her over the cup as he drank from it, still squatting by the fire. 'You do not seem to fret for him, *mei jha*. Have you retrieved your heart from him so soon?'

Alix lifted her chin defiantly. 'I will be with him soon enough, when he returns for me.'

'Your place is with us,' he said seriously. 'We are your people. You do not belong with valley crofters *or* the majesty of the Mujhar and his heir.'

She knelt on the thick fur, leaning forward in supplication. 'You took me from my people. You *stole* me, as the Homanans say Hale did to Lindir. Can you not understand how I feel about the race you say is mine? By the gods, Finn, you even threatened to force me!'

'I did not think you would have me willingly.'

Alix released a breath in frustration. 'Why will you not hear me? Are you ever so witless as you seem?'

86

'Witless!'

'Do you do anything with any thought put to the consequences?'

'The *qu'mahlin* has left us little time for thought. Most of the time we act because we must.'

'You use that as an excuse!' she cried. 'You prate about the *qu'mahlin* as if only you have suffered. Yet you leave me no room to think perhaps your race has the right to curse Shaine, because you behave as if you are free to do what you wish. Duncan would have me see you are men like any other, yet you behave as if the Cheysuli *are* demons with no understanding of what you do to others.'

'You need learning,' he said bluntly. 'When we have reached the Keep and you have spoken to the *shar tahl*, you will understand better what it is to be Cheysuli. You will understand what the *qu'mahlin* has done. Until then you are lost.'

'Take me home,' she said softly. 'Finn, take me home.'

He set the cup down and looked at her levelly. 'I do.'

Alix ground the heels of her hands against her eyes, feeling the grittiness of exhaustion and tension. Her desperation was growing, swelling up inside her until it threatened to burst her chest and force tears from her eyes. She had no wish to cry before Finn of all people, and the sensation of futility and helplessness hurt so bad she could think only to hurt back.

'I will escape,' she said firmly. 'When I have the time, and the opportunity, I will win free of you. Even does it come to putting a knife into you.'

He smiled. 'You could not.'

'I could.'

'You have neither the spirit nor the strength to do it.'

Furious, Alix snatched up the pot of bubbling honey drink and threw it at him. She saw the contents strike his upraised arm and part of his face, then she was on her feet running.

Finn caught her before she reached the edge of the firelight. Alix cried out as he caught one arm and twisted it behind her back. Then he jerked her around until she faced him, and she was suddenly terrified as he bent over her.

'If you would be so bold as to do that, *mei jha*, and yet be caught, you had best be prepared to suffer the consequences.'

Alix cried out again. She could feel his breath on her face; the dampness of the spilled drink as it stained her gown. She felt her lip caught in his teeth, then stumbled back as Finn was jerked away from her.

Alix gasped in pain and shock as Finn came off the ground, hand to his knife. Then he froze, staring angrily at his assailant.

'You will not force a Cheysuli woman,' Duncan said coldly.

Finn took his hand from his knife. 'She may have our blood, Duncan, but she has been reared Homanan. She wants humbling. If you leave her to me, I will see to it she behaves with more decorum.'

'We do not humble our women, either,' Duncan snapped. 'Leave her be.'

'Why?' Finn demanded, all affronted male pride. 'So you can take her?'

'No.'

'If she is what you want as *cheysula*, clan-leader, then you had best follow tradition and ask for her clan-rights in Council.'

Duncan smiled thinly. 'I ask for no clan-rights of any woman this year, *rujho*. But if you are so hot to take her, you should hear your own words. She is no light woman, Finn. Ask for her clan-rights, when she has been proven to have them.'

Finn glared at him. 'I have no need of formal clan-rights where a woman is concerned. There are enough to be had without taking a *cheysula*.'

'Stop!' Alix cried, so loudly they both stared at her in

surprise. Self-consciously she swept back her loose hair and scowled at them. 'I know nothing of these traditions you speak of, or clan-rights, or Council . . . or *anything*! But you had best know I will do *nothing* against my will! You may have forced me to come with you now, but there will be a time when you do not watch me, and I will get free of you all. Do you hear? You cannot keep me!'

'You will stay,' Duncan said calmly. 'No one escapes the Cheysuli.'

Finn smiled. 'The clan-leader has spoken, *mei jha*. We may disagree, my *rujho* and I, but not on this.'

Alix felt the tears welling in her eyes. She widened them instinctively, trying to take back the moisture, but the first tear fell. On a choked sob she spun and ran from them, wondering what animal they would send to fetch her back.

She found a damp mossy area beneath a huge beech tree not far from camp and sat down quickly, loose-limbed and awkward. For a moment she gazed blindly at the shadows and wondered forlornly if she would ever see her home again. Then the enormity of her plight crept upon her. Alix pulled her knees to her chest and hugged them, hiding her face in her torn and stained skirts.

Liren, said a gentle voice, so empathetic it nearly undid her. *Liren*.

Alix turned her head against the rough weave of her gown and saw Storr waiting quietly in the moonlight. For a moment resentment replaced her grief, then it faded. She knew, somehow, Storr had come on his own, not because he was sent to take her back to camp.

I was not sent, he said. *I came because you are in pain, and in need.*

'You speak as a wise old man,' she whispered.

I am a wise old wolf, he said, sounding amused. *But there is not much difference, for all that.*

Alix smiled at him and put out a hand. Storr moved to

her and allowed her to place a hand on his head. For a moment she was stunned at what she did; *touching a wolf*, she thought silently. But Storr was patient and very gentle, and she did not fear him.

'You are Finn's *lir*,' she murmured. 'How can you be so wise and trustworthy and belong to *him*?'

Storr's eyes closed as she ran fingers through his thick pelt. *My lir is not always so hasty and unwise. You have confused him.*

'I!'

He saw you and wanted you. Then he found you were Cheysuli, and his rujholla. He has had no one but Duncan for too long.

'Well, he will not have me.'

You must take someone . . . someday.

'I will not have a beast like him!'

Storr sighed. *Remember, what name you give him fits you also. You are Cheysuli. It may seem strange now, but you will be happier among us than elsewhere.*

'I would sooner go home. *Home* home; not this Keep.'

Even knowing you are not like others?

'Aye. And I am no different.'

But you are. Knowing yourself makes you different. Think of the qu'mahlin. The Mujhar's decree applies also to you.

'I am his granddaughter.'

And Cheysuli. You do not know Shaine. But know this — if your kinship to him were more important than your race, you would be in Homana-Mujhar.

She knew he was right. But she could not say it, even when he nudged her hand and went away.

'I am sorry for my *rujholli*.' Duncan moved softly out of the shadows. 'You must not give credence to his words. All too often Finn speaks without thought.'

Alix looked at him and wished herself as far from Duncan and his brother as could be. But since the wish did not work, she answered him.

'You are nothing alike.'

'We are. You have not seen it yet.'

'You cannot make me believe you are as angry, or as cruel.' She sighed in surrender and picked at the moss. 'Or else you do not show it.'

Duncan squatted before her, hands hanging loosely over his knees. 'Finn was but three when the *qu'mahlin* began. He has little memory of peace in our clan — or in the land — before it. He knows only the darkness and blood and pain of Shaine's war.'

'What of you?'

He stared at the moss she was destroying with rigid, nervous fingers. 'I was five,' he said finally. 'Like him, I awoke in the middle of the night when our pavilion fell under the hooves of Homanan horses. It was set on fire even though the Mujhar's men saw we were only children, and too small to do much harm. They did not care.' He caught her hand suddenly, stilling it as if its movements disturbed him. His eyes were pale in the moonlight. 'You must understand. We were small, but such things remain clear.'

'What do you say?' she whispered, sensing his need to have her comprehension.

'That you should understand why he plagues you. He is bitter toward Shaine, and Homanans in general. Carillon is the Mujhar's heir.' He paused. 'And you want *him* . . . not Finn.'

'But if your story is true, Finn is my brother!'

Duncan sighed. 'You were raised apart. Why should he not desire a woman, even *after* he has learned she is bloodkin to him?'

Alix stared at him, hand still caught in his. The stubborn conflict she felt rise at Finn's name faded beneath a new — and more frightening — comprehension. She saw before her a solemn-faced warrior who seemed to be waiting for something from her.

For a moment she nearly rose and fled, unable to face the conflict. But she restrained the instinct. There was the faintest whisper of knowledge within her soul, the realization of a power she had never thought she might have, and it astonished her.

'Duncan ...' she said softly, 'what is this *tahlmorra* you say I should feel?'

'You will know it.'

'How?'

'You will know it.'

'And do you say ... do you say every Cheysuli has this *tahlmorra*?'

'It is something that binds us all, as tightly as the prophecy. But it has weakened in many of us because so many of us have been lost and forced to take Homanan women to get children.' His mouth twisted into a wry smile. 'I am not proud of that. But it must be done, if we are to survive. But there are some of us who feel *tahlmorra* more clearly than others.' He brought her hand up, smoothing his thumb over the back of her palm. 'Mine has told me what will come. When we reach the Keep I will seek out the *shar tahl* and have him show me the prophecy runes to be certain. But I know it already.'

Alix withdrew her hand, uneasy. 'It has nothing to do with me.'

'It is never wrong. The prophecy was given to us by the Firstborn, who were sired by the old gods. It unveils itself in the fullness of time, and to those who listen and understand. I am one of those who follow its path, Alix. I would give my life to see the prophecy fulfilled.' He smiled suddenly. 'I *will* give my life to see the prophecy fulfilled. That much is clear.'

'You know your own death?' she whispered.

'Only that I will die as I am meant, serving the *tahlmorra* of the prophecy. The Firstborn have said.'

Alix looked away from the steadiness of his gaze. 'You confuse me.'

'When you have spoken with the *shar tahl*, the confusion will leave you. Be sure of that.'

'And does Finn serve this same *tahlmorra*?'

Duncan laughed. 'Finn follows a *sort* of *tahlmorra*. I think he makes his own.'

'I am no part of it,' she told him severely.

His eyes were gentle. 'Of Finn's ... no. The threads of your *tahlmorra* are entwined with those of another man.'

'Carillon?' she asked in a blaze of sudden hope.

He did not answer. She understood him then. Her head came up until she met his gaze squarely. Then she got to her feet and shook out her tattered skirts.

'If I am Cheysuli, I make my own *tahlmorra*. Like Finn.' She looked down on him. 'You cannot force me, Duncan.'

'I would not.' He shook his head and rose, looming over her in the darkness. 'There is no need.'

'You will not force me!'

His hand touched her face gently. 'I would not, small one. Your own *tahlmorra* will.'

Alix stepped away from him, holding his eyes with her own and denying him what she saw in his face. Then her resolution wavered.

She turned and fled into the shadows of the camp.

CHAPTER NINE

The warning came as the warrior band rode through the thick forest, making their own track. Cai broke through the thin veil of tree limbs and foliage to seek out Duncan. Alix, glancing up in surprise, saw the hawk wing down and light upon a branch.

They come, lir, the bird said. *Mounted men in the Mujhar's colours. Half-a-league; no more.*

Duncan pulled his horse to a halt. Alix, seeking to remain upright on the animal, caught at Duncan's waist. She felt the tension in his body as if it were her own.

He half-turned in the saddle, muttering something under his breath. Then, 'I must find a place for you.'

'You will fight them?'

'They will give us no choice, Alix. Why do you think they come, save to slay us all?'

Alix opened her mouth to retort but suddenly could find no words. Her mind was ablaze with sound so intense she knew it was not something she heard with her ears. She thought her head would burst with words, and it was only grabbing at Duncan's waist that kept her on the horse. She mumbled something, closing her eyes against the weight of voices, and vaguely heard the approach of a horse. Duncan took no note of her sudden weakness.

94

'Well, *rujho*,' Finn's voice said, 'the princeling did not lie. He has given us little time.'

Alix forced her eyes open and glared at him, though a part of her attention was still claimed by the multitude of voices.

Do they not hear them? she wondered.

Duncan reached around and caught her arm, easing her down from the horse until she had to scramble to stay upright. 'Take her,' he told Finn.

Alix forcibly detached her mind from the other voices. 'No! Not with him!'

'See to her, *rujho*,' Duncan said calmly. 'I will not have her harmed. These men would do her injury. I leave her to you.'

Finn grinned down at her. 'Do you see, *mei jha*? The clan-leader passes you back to me.'

'I will have none of you,' she said with effort, trying to speak beneath the weight of words in her mind. 'Do you hear?'

Duncan said something to her but Alix heard nothing; she saw only that his mouth moved. She clapped hands over her ears and bowed her head, trying to withstand the patters and tones in her mind.

Finn's hands came down on her shoulders. Dimly she saw Duncan lead his horse away, leaving Finn on foot with her. She peered at him uncertainly.

'You have been given into my keeping,' he announced. 'I do not intend to let you out of it.'

'Is it sorcery?' she gasped. 'Do you seek to take my mind from me?'

Finn scowled at her. 'You do not make sense, *mei jha*. But I have no time to listen to you now ... can you not hear them?'

'I hear their voices!' she cried trembling. Finn's look on her was strange. 'I speak of their horses, *mei jha*. I hear no voices.'

For a moment she pushed away the soundless words and listened to reality. Through the forest came the

95

sounds of men battering their way through delaying brush. Her eyes flew to Finn's.

'They will slay you,' he said gently.

The weight began to fall from her mind. Faintly she heard echoes of the tones and patterns, but she did not feel so bound by them. Her strength was spent. She nodded wearily at Finn and did not protest as he led her deeper into the forest.

'Storr?' she asked softly.

'He is behind, watching. He — like the others — will fight the Mujhar's men.'

Finn pulled her down under cover of a broken tree trunk leaning drunkenly against another. Quickly he set deadfall over them, weaving a rapid shelter. When it was done he pushed her down on her stomach and knelt beside her. Alix, still shaken from the silent voices, watched from a distance as he loosened his belt-knife and effortlessly nocked a yellow-flecked black arrow to his compact, powerful bow.

Alix put her head down on one arm and longed for the security of her father's croft.

'Watch my back, *mei jha*,' Finn said roughly. 'I have no time for women's fears.'

She wrenched her head up and glared at him. His back was to her, presenting an excellent target for a furious fist, but the precariousness of their position was uppermost in her mind. She put away the urge to do him harm and turned instead to watch behind him, as he had bidden.

Alix's head ached. She scrubbed at her forehead as if to drive the pain away, but it did no good. The voices were gone, only a figment of memory, but it was enough to leave a residue. Her entire body ached with the indignities she had been forced to endure: sores remained on her legs from continued riding; bruises dotted her flesh and her bones and muscles felt like rags. Her mind, she knew dimly, was as exhausted. For all they insisted they would do her no harm, the

Cheysuli had accounted for more pain and fatigue than she had ever thought possible.

At first she thought it was a Cheysuli horse crashing through the brush toward their thin shelter. Alix stared silently up at the man a moment before she realized he was a mailed man-at-arms in the scarlet-and-black tunic livery of the Mujhar, sword drawn.

Relief flooded through her. She would escape Finn and the others now, putting herself into the care of a Mujharan guardsman, who would surely rescue her from her plight. Alix sighed in relief and crawled forward as the man's eyes fell on hers. The beginnings of her smile of greeting faded.

The sword lifted in a gloved hand, swinging back over his shoulder. Transfixed, Alix stared at the bright blade. It hung over her, poised to fall, and in a blinding flash of realization she knew Duncan's words were true. They would slay her where she stood and call her shapechanger.

Alix lunged backward into Finn. He turned sharply and hissed something, then saw why she moved. He said nothing more. The arrow's flight was unmarked in passing, but Alix saw the feathered shaft quiver out of the guardsman's throat. He fell back in the saddle, crying out something in a gurgling voice. Then he tumbled from his bolting horse.

She stuffed a fist into her mouth to keep from screaming, aware only that Finn had left her and was fighting hand-to-hand with yet another guardsman. Alix recoiled, staring open-mouthed at the straining men. A bough jabbed her in the small of her back, tearing through the woolen fabric and into her flesh, but she was oblivious to the pain.

Finn bent the man's knife arm away from his throat, a fearful rictus of concentration baring his teeth. Muscles bulged beneath his armbands as he fought to keep the blade from his throat.

Alix mumbled something to herself, unaware she

97

spoke. Finn drove his knife upward into the guardsman's stomach, but not before the man managed to
bring his own weapon down in a slashing motion that
penetrated Finn's rib cage.

Alix cried out again, then heard a strange moaning
sound and saw the Cheysuli blur himself into his wolf-
shape. Before her horrified eyes the wolf leaped on the
man and bore him to the ground, ripping his throat
away.

Sickened, she leaped to her feet and fled the shelter.

'Alix!'

She ran on, ignoring Finn's human cry.

'*Alix!*'

An agonized glance over her shoulder showed him
coming after her, bloodied knife in one hand. She
blurted out a garbled denial and ran on, breaking her
way with outstretched hands.

A horse drove through the brush before her, pawing
hooves flailing at her head as its rider jerked it to a halt.
Alix ducked down and threw up a beseeching hand,
expecting a blow from one of the hooves. She saw an
enraged face hanging over her as the guardsman drew
his broadsword.

'Shapechanger witch!'

'No!' she shrieked. '*No!*'

'You'll not live to bear more of the demons!' he cried,
lowering the blade in a hideous slash.

Alix threw herself flat onto the ground and heard an
eerie whistle as the blade flew past her head. Then she
scrambled up and instinctively dashed directly at the
horse.

The wolf-shape hurtled past her, leaping, and took
the man from the horse in one sweeping lunge. Alix
heard the guardsman cry out. The horse screamed and
reared, striking out.

The guardsman's broadsword fell at her feet as she
stumbled away from the terrified horse. The man, now
on foot, lifted his knife to slash at the wolf leaping

toward his throat. The point slid sideways and tore open one furred shoulder, driving the wolf back.

The soldier bent for his sword, caught it up and advanced on the snarling animal. 'Demon!' he hissed. 'Know what it is to *die* in that shape!'

Alix threw herself forward and grabbed at his arm, thwarting his blow. The mail bit into her hands and face as she hung onto the arm. One jerk knocked her to the ground so hard she lay there, half-stunned.

Gloating, the man turned back to the wolf. But the animal was gone. In its place stood a Cheysuli warrior whose knife found a new sheath in the guardsman's throat. His blood splattered Alix as the body fell next to her.

Finn stood over her, clasping his left shoulder. His jerkin was heavy with blood from the wound in his ribs. Amazed, Alix saw a grin on his battered face.

'So, *mei jha*, you feel enough for me to risk your own life.'

Burgeoning panic and the sickening smell of blood drove her to her feet. Alix stood before him unsteadily, trembling with rage and reaction. She wiped a hand across her face and felt the dampness of the man's blood.

'I wish death on no one, shapechanger. Not even you.'

Another horse crashed through the trees, leaping mailed bodies as they lay scattered on the forest floor. Alix swung around in panic and saw Carillon on his chestnut warhorse. He wore his Cheysuli sword but had not unsheathed it.

'Alix!' He jerked the horse to a halt, staring down at the man Finn had slain. The Cheysuli warrior, weaponless, glared wrathfully at the prince.

'Do you slay me now, lordling?' he demanded, lowering his hand from the wound in his shoulder.

Carillon ignored him and reached out to Alix. 'Quickly. Climb up behind me.'

She moved forward, stunned by the suddenness of her rescue, but Finn's bloody hand on her arm stopped her.

'*Mei jha* . . .'

She wrenched her arm free. 'I go with Carillon,' she said firmly. 'As I told you once before.'

'Alix, waste no time,' Carillon urged.

'*Mei jha*, stay with your clan,' Finn said.

Alix grasped Carillon's hand and pulled herself onto the horse's broad hindquarters. Her arms settled around the prince's hip, resting on his swordbelt. She sent Finn a significant look of triumph.

'I do not stay. I go home . . . with Carillon.'

Finn scowled blackly up at them. Carillon, smiling oddly, tapped his sword hilt. 'Another time, shape-changer.' He spun the chestnut and sent him leaping back the way he had come.

Alix, clinging to him, saw with horror the carnage as they passed. Liveried guardsmen lay scattered through the forest, some displaying the marks of beasts. She shuddered and pressed herself against Carillon's back, sickened by the results of the forest battle.

Carillon's horse broke into a clearing and galloped across a lush meadow. The edge of the forest fell behind them, and with it the grim toll of dead.

'I said I would come,' Carillon said above the sound of pounding hooves.

'So many are slain . . .' she said.

'The Mujhar's vengeance.'

Alix swallowed and put a hand to her tangled, blood-matted hair. 'I saw only slain *guardsmen*, Carillon. There were no Cheysuli.'

She felt him stiffen and expected a curt reply, but the prince said nothing. The golden hilt of his sword pressed against her left arm as she hung on, and she stared at its huge ruby and the golden Homanan lion crest in wonder.

Hale's sword . . . she whispered within her mind. *My father?*

A hawk broke free of the trees and flew to catch them. It circled over them, drifted a moment, then drove closer. The warhorse, shying as the bird neared his head, plunged sideways.

Alix saw the hawk as it streaked by them, circling to return. It was the smaller one she had conversed with in the forest, and she nearly fell from the plunging horse as her grip loosened in shock. Carillon cursing, tried to rein the stallion into control.

The hawk drove close again, wings snapping against the horse's head. Alix felt the smooth hindquarters bunch and slide from beneath her, though she grabbed at Carillon's leather doublet. She cried out and tumbled awkwardly to the ground.

Carillon called her name but the frightened horse would not allow him to approach. The prince wrestled with the reins, muttering dire threats under his breath, but Alix saw no good come of his words. She sat up dazedly and fingered the lump on the back of her head.

Stay with me, the bird said. *Stay*.

'Let me go!' she cried, getting unsteadily to her feet.

Stay.

'No!'

I ask, small one. I am not Finn, who takes. The bird hesitated. *I ask*.

Realization flooded her. 'Duncan!'

Stay with me.

'Duncan . . . let me go with him. It is what I want.'

It does not serve the prophecy.

'It is not *my* prophecy!' she cried, lifting a fist into the air. 'It is not mine!'

And the tahlmorra?

Alix was conscious Carillon had calmed the warhorse somewhat. The prince jumped off the chestnut and dragged him behind, crossing to her with long steps.

'Alix!'

She stared at the hawk drifting idly in the sky. 'It is not

101

my prophecy,' she said more quietly. 'Nor is it my *tahlmorra*.'

But it is mine . . .

Alix turned to Carillon, shoving tangled loose hair out of her face. 'I go with you. If you can keep your horse in check, I will stay aboard.'

She saw questions in his eyes but he did not ask them. Eloquently, silently, he gestured toward the hawk.

Alix stared up at it, aware of a sensation of regret. 'If you would stop me, shapechanger, you must do as your brother. And to do that earns you my enmity.'

The bird paused in mid flight. *That*, it said after a moment, *is not entirely what I seek*.

'Then let me go.'

The hawk said nothing more. It circled a last time, then soared higher into the sky and flew away.

Carillon touched her shoulder. 'Alix?'

Strangely defeated and somehow bereft, she turned to him. She spread her hands. 'You may take me to Homana-Mujhar, my lord, and to my grandsire.'

His hand tightened on her shoulder. 'I have warned you what he may feel when he sees you.'

She smiled grimly through her dirt and blood stains. 'I will take that chance.'

Carillon caught her waist and swung her up on the quieted horse. He put her in the saddle and she clutched at it, surprised. He mounted behind her and took up the reins, setting his arms around her waist.

'I think the Mujhar may find his granddaughter is no simple crofter's child.'

Alix smiled wearily as the stallion moved on. 'He raised a wilful daughter. Let him see how that spirit serves Lindir's child.'

BOOK II
'The Mei jha'

CHAPTER ONE

Carillon took Alix first to the croft so she could see Torrin and show him she was well. As they rode down the hills into the valley Alix had known all her life, she felt a strange sense of homecoming mixed with loneliness. Her relief at seeing the lush valley again was tinged with sadness and regret, for she realized her few days with the Cheysuli had altered her perceptions forever.

'It seems odd,' Carillon said quietly as he guided the chestnut toward the stone crofter's cottage built along the treeline.

'Odd?'

'Torrin lived among the halls of Homana-Mujhar, privy to much of Shaine's confidences. Yet he gave it up to work the land like a tenant-crofter owing yearly rents to his lord.'

Alix, slumped wearily in the saddle, nodded. 'My father—' She broke off, then continued in a subtly altered tone. '*Torrin* has ever been a man of deepness and dark silences. I begin to see why, I think.'

'If the story is true, he has carried a burden on his soul for many years.'

Alix straightened as the whitewashed door of the croft squealed open. Torrin came out and stood staring as Carillon took the horse in to him.

'By the gods . . .' Torrin said hoarsely, 'I thought you taken by beasts, Alix.'

She, seeing him through different eyes, marked the seams of age in his worn face and the thinning of his greying hair cropped close against his head. His hands, once so powerful, had calloused and gnarled with crofter's work over the years, so different from an arms-master's craft. Even his broad shoulders had shrunk, falling in as if the weight of the realm rested on them.

What manner of man was he before he took me from the Mujhar? she wondered. *What has this burden done to him?*

Alix slid free of the horse as Carillon halted him, standing straight and tall before the man she had called her father all her life. Then she put out her hand, palm up, and spread her fingers.

'Know you what this is?' she asked softly.

Torrin stared transfixed at her hand. Colour leached from his weather-burned face until he resembled little more than a dead man with glistening eyes.

'Alix . . .' he said gently. 'Alix, I could not tell you. I feared to lose you to them.'

'But I have come back,' she said. 'I have been with them, and I have come back.'

He aged before her eyes. 'I could not tell you.'

Carillon stepped off his horse and walked slowly forward, skin stretched taut across the bones of his face. 'Then it is true, this shapechanger tale. Lindir went willingly, forsaking the betrothal because of Shaine's liege man.'

Torrin sighed and ran a gnarled hand through his hair. 'It was a long time ago. I have put much of it away. But I see you must know it, now.' He smiled a little. 'My lord prince, when last I saw you, you were but a year old. It is hard to believe that squalling infant has become a man.'

Alix stepped up to Torrin and took one of his hands in hers. She felt the weariness and resignation in his body.

'I will go to my grandsire,' she said softly. 'But first I

will hear the truth of my begetting.'

Torrin led them inside and gestured for Carillon to seat himself at a rectangular slab table of scarred wood. Alix paced the room like a fretful dog, seeking security in the familiarity she had ever known.

Finally, knowing it eluded her, she stopped before the fireplace and faced Torrin. 'Tell me. I would know it all.'

He nodded, pouring a cup of thin wine for Carillon and another for himself. Then he sat down on a stool and stared fixedly at the beaten dirt floor.

'Lindir refused Ellic of Solinde from the very first. She would not be marriage bait, she said, to be given to Ellic like a tame puppy. Shaine was furious and ordered her to do his bidding. When she remained defiant, he said he would place her under guard and send her to Lestra, Bellam's city. Lindir was ever a determined woman, but she also recognized the strength in her father. He would have done it.'

'So she fled,' Alix said softly.

'Aye.' Torrin blew out a heavy breath. 'Hale did not steal her. That was a tale the Mujhar put out, to justify the affront to his pride. Later, when Ellinda died and Lorsilla bore no living children, he decided it was a curse laid against his House by the Cheysuli. What Lindir did made him half-mad, I thought. She had kept her secret well. None knew of her feelings for Hale.'

'He had a woman at the Keep,' Alix said. 'Yet he left her for Lindir.'

Torrin looked at her steadily. 'You will understand such things one day, Alix, when you have met the man you will have. Lindir was the sort all men loved, but she would have no one, until Hale.' He shrugged. 'She was eighteen, and more beautiful than anything I have ever seen. Had she been born a boy — with all her pride and strength — she would have made Shaine the finest heir a king could want.'

'But she *refused* Ellic.'

Torrin snorted. 'I did not say she was acquiescent.

Lindir had a way about her that ensorcelled all men, even her father, until he would wed her to the Solindish heir. Then she showed her own measure of the Mujhar's strength and stubbornness.'

Carillon sipped his wine, then set the cup down. 'My uncle never speaks of it. What I have heard has come from others.'

'Aye,' Torrin agreed. 'The Mujhar was a proud man. Lindir defeated him. Few men of so much pride will speak of such things.'

'What happened?' Alix asked, hugging herself before the fire.

'The night of the betrothal, when all the lords of Solinde and Homana gathered in the Great Hall, Lindir walked out of Homana-Mujhar in the guise of a serving woman. Hale went as a red fox, and no one knew either of them as they left the city. He was not seen again.'

'What of Lindir?' Carillon asked.

Torrin sighed. 'She disappeared. Shaine sent troops after them, of course, swearing Hale had stolen her for himself. But neither was ever found, and within a year the Lady Ellinda was dead of a wasting disease. Shaine's second wife, the Lady Lorsilla, was made barren when she lost the boy who would have been prince. But I have told you that. Shaine began his purge the morning after the boy was born dead, and it has continued since.'

Alix shivered. 'But . . . Lindir came back.'

Torrin's hands clenched against his knees. 'She came back eight years after Shaine began the purge. Hale was dead and she herself was ill. The Mujhar accepted her only because he needed an heir, and when Lindir died after bearing a girl he would not accept it. He said the purge would continue. The Lady Lorsilla and myself pleaded with him not to have the child left to die in the forests. He said I could take the girl, if I left his service and swore never to allow her in Mujhara. I agreed.'

Alix stared at him. 'You did all that for a halfling girl-child . . .'

He swallowed heavily. 'Had Shaine cast you out, I could not have served him again. Taking you was the best thing I have ever done.'

'Then they are not demons?'

Torrin shook his head slowly. 'The Cheysuli have never been demons. They have arts we do not, and most of us fear them for it, but they do not use them for ill.'

'Why did you allow me to believe they were?'

'I never called them demons, Alix. But neither could I tell you differently, or your own innocence in defending them would draw suspicion. Had Shaine ever heard of you, he might have called you to him. He might have rescinded his decision to let me keep you as my own.'

'And Hale?' she asked softly.

Torrin's head bowed. 'Hale served his lord with a loyalty no other man could hope for. It was Lindir who twisted that loyalty. Hale was a good man. You have no need to fear the memory of your father.'

Alix went to him and knelt before him, placing soft hands over his hardened ones. She put her forehead down on his knee.

'*You* will ever be my father!' she said brokenly.

Torrin placed one hand on her bowed head. 'You are my daughter, Alix. If your blood begins to show you another way, I understand. There is magic in a Cheysuli soul.' He sighed and smoothed her hair. 'But you will be my daughter as long as I live.'

'I will never leave you!'

He cradled her head, lifting it so she could see his face. 'Alix, I think you must. I served with the Cheysuli years before your birth; I know their strength and dedication and their magnificent honour. They did not ask for this *qu'mahlin*. But they realize it is a part of their *tahlmorra*.'

'*You* speak of that!'

He smiled sadly. 'I have reared a Cheysuli girl-child in my house, and in my heart. How could I not?'

A chilling sensation rippled through her body. 'Then you knew . . . one day . . .'

'I have ever known.' He leaned forward and kissed her brow softly. 'A Cheysuli can never deny his *tahlmorra*. To do so angers the gods.'

'I did not want this,' she said dully.

Torrin removed his hands and sat back from her as if to illustrate the sacrifice he made. 'Go with the prince, Alix. I would keep you, if I could, but it is not the will of the gods.' He smiled, but the pain remained in his eyes. 'The path to your *tahlmorra* lies another way.'

'I will stay,' she whispered.

Carillon rose quietly and moved to her. 'Come, cousin. It is time you met your grandsire.'

'You have brought me home, Carillon. It is enough.'

He bent and grasped her arms, pulling her upright. Alix jerked around and glared at him. 'You would have me think you no better than Finn — ordering me this way and that!'

He grinned at her. 'Then perhaps he has the right of it. What else can a man do when a woman defies him, save force her?

She took a step away from him. 'I will see the Mujhar another time.'

'If you do not come now, you will never do it.' Carillon glanced at Torrin and saw the confirmation in his eyes. The prince smiled faintly and took her arm once again.

'You will come here another time,' Torrin said.

Alix, testing Carillon's grip tentatively, gave it up. She looked down on the slump-shouldered man who had been a king's arms-master before taking a halfling girl-child to his heart.

'I have loved you well,' she whispered.

Torrin rose, looking at her as if he hurt. Then he cradled her head in his gnarled hands and kissed her forehead.

Carillon led her from the croft.

The prince took her out of the forests and the valleys into

110

Mujhara, and through its cobbled streets. Alix sat behind him silently, clinging to his waist as if his closeness would give her confidence. The gleaming city with its winding, narrow streets took away her powers of speech. Alix was acutely aware of her torn and stained garments and bare feet.

'I do not belong here,' she muttered.

'You belong wherever you wish to be,' Carillon said. He gestured. 'Homana-Mujhar.'

She looked past his arm and saw the stone walls rising before her. The fortress-palace stood on a gentle rise within the city itself, hidden behind time-worn walls of rose-coloured, undressed stone. Before them towered massive bronze-and-timber gates, attended by eight men liveried in the Mujhar's colours. Alix saw red tunics over light chain mail, emblazoned with a rampant black lion. It was the proud coat-of-arms she had seen etched into Carillon's ruby seal ring; and stamped into the heavy gold of the sword hilt.

The guardsmen swung open the huge gates, acknowledging Carillon with brief salutes. As their incurious eyes fell on her she let go of Carillon's waist, blushing in shame.

'Carillon . . . take me back to the croft! I should not be here!'

'Be silent, Alix. This place is your legacy.'

'And Shaine sent me *from* it!'

He did not answer her. She was forced to sit quietly on his warhorse and ride inexorably toward the huge palace. Alix closed her eyes as they entered the bailey and wished herself elsewhere.

Duncan was right . . . Homana-Mujhar is not for me.

Carillon stopped the horse before a flight of marble steps that led up to the palace of Homanan kings. A groom raced over to catch the reins and bowed reverently; Carillon jumped down and lifted Alix from the horse before she could protest. She kept her head lowered as he took her up the smooth, dark-veined steps into the rose-coloured palace, until she saw the first servant stare at her with undisguised contempt. Carillon did not see it, but Alix was instantly aware how her arrival would be regarded. Everyone would think her some lice-ridden woman of the streets if she behaved as one, so she resolutely lifted her head. She summoned her pride and confidence and went with Carillon as if she belonged with him.

She saw magnificent tapestries picked out in rainbow colours; candleracks holding fresh candles glowing with flame; thick rugs and clean rushes; ornaments and heavily embroidered arrases at doorways. Liveried servants bowed respectfully to Carillon and included her in their homage. Inwardly she smiled at the change in attitude a little arrogance brought.

But when Carillon escorted her up a winding stairway of red stone to a doorway of hammered bronze, Alix halted abruptly. 'Where do you take me?'

'These are the chambers of the Lady Lorsilla.'

'Shaine's *wife*?'

'She will see to it you are bathed and dressed as befits a princess, before you meet the Mujhar.' He smiled at her. 'Alix, I promise you will be safe.'

She swallowed and glared at him. 'I do not wish to be safe. I wish to go back to the croft.'

Carillon ignored her and rapped on the bronze door. Alix closed her eyes and consigned herself to the netherworld. The defiance she had held in abundance when first learning of her heritage fled, leaving her cold and lonely within the massive palace.

'Carillon!' cried a woman's voice as the door swung open. 'You are returned so soon?'

Alix opened her eyes. She saw a chambermaid at the door, curtsying to Carillon, and beyond her a tiny blonde woman in a silken blue robe banded with white fur.

'I have brought back what I said I would,' Carillon said gravely.' Regardless what my uncle wishes.'

The woman sighed and smiled wryly. 'You are more like Shaine than you know, at times. Well, let me see her.'

Carillon led Alix forward. She heard the door shut behind them and swallowed against the sudden fear in her throat.

The woman sat on a cushioned bench of dark stone. She settled the rich robe more comfortably around her shoulders. 'Alix, you are well come.'

'No,' Alix said. 'I am not. Shaine cast me out before; I have no doubt he would do so again.'

Lorsilla, queen of Homana, smiled warmly. 'He must see you, first. And I think he will hold his tongue, if only from sheer amazement.'

'Or hatred.'

'He cannot hate what he does not know,' Lorsilla said gently. 'Alix, he is your grandsire. His anger was never at you, but at himself for losing Lindir. Had he treated her more gently when she refused Ellic, she might have remained here.'

Alix gestured helplessly, indicating her tatters and blood-streaked face. 'I am not the sort a king would acknowledge.'

Carillon laughed. 'You will be, when *she* has done with you. As for me, I will leave you to the lady. When I come for you, you will be ready to face even the harshest of men.'

Instinctively she whirled and caught his hand. 'Carillon!'

He detached himself gently. 'I must go, Alix. It is not my place to see you bathed and dressed.' His grin was amused. 'Though I would not mind it so much, myself.'

Lorsilla lifted a delicate brow. 'Carillon, conduct yourself with more decorum.'

He laughed at her and bowed, then took his leave.

Alix stood before the queen of Homana and shivered once, involuntarily. Her feet ached and her face burned with shame.

113

Lorsilla rose and moved forward. She touched a soft hand across the healing welt on Alix's face and brushed away the dried remains of the guardsman's blood. Her voice was very gentle.

'You have no need to fear me, Alix. I am your grand-dame.'

Alix's voice shook. 'But I am a *halfling* . . .'

The tiny woman smiled sadly. 'I will have no children of my own, and no grandchildren. Let me at least have Lindir's daughter, for a time.'

She bowed her head and nodded, hiding the welling of grief in her heart. She heard the woman order a bath drawn and clothing to be prepared. Then Lorsilla laughed softly.

'You have been raised as a croft-girl, Alix. Now you will know what it is to claim the heritage Shaine denied you. I will make you a princess, my girl.'

She swallowed painfully. 'But I am Cheysuli.'

Lorsilla's delicate face grew stern. 'It does not matter. You are Shaine's granddaughter, and that is enough for me.'

But what of him? she wondered apprehensively. *What of the Mujhar himself?*

CHAPTER TWO

Alix went before her grandsire in silks and velvets, girdled with gold and garnets. The rich brown fabrics whispered against her legs and fine slippers hugged her bruised feet. Her head felt heavy with the weight of her hair, laced with pearls and tiny garnets. Her ears ached dully with fresh piercing, but the gems glittering in them assuaged her pain.

The croft-girl was gone as she stood before the Mujhar of Homana, and she wondered if that girl would ever return to her.

Carillon, standing next to her in the huge audience hall, radiated pride and confidence. But Shaine dominated the hall with inborn power and strength of will.

'My lord,' Carillon said quietly, 'this is Alix. Lindir's daughter.'

The Mujhar stood on a low marble dais that spread the entire width of the hall. Behind him, raised on grasping lion's claws, stood a carved throne banded with bronze and silver; cushioned in silks and velvets. Etched deeply within the throne was scroll-work of gold paint, and the wood gleamed with polishing. The scent of beeswax and power hung in the air. Shaine himself wore black and gold, and the harsh pride of an arrogant man.

His grey eyes narrowed at Carillon's announcement.

115

Alix stared at him, concentrating on the fact he was her grandsire and not Homana's king. It did not help.

A wide circlet of emeralds and diamonds set in gold banded his brow, smoothing his silvering dark hair. He was bearded, but it did not hide the determination of his jaw or the tight line of his lips.

There is no forgiveness in this man . . . Alix realized.

Accordingly, she lifted her head proudly and firmed her own mouth. Carillon stepped away from her, renouncing his right to speak for her, but it did not disturb her. She was beyond fear or reticence and let the instincts she had only sensed rule her actions. Her defiance flashed across the Great Hall to strike Shaine like a blow.

'I see nothing of Lindir in you,' the Mujhar said quietly. 'I see only a shapechanger's stamp.'

'What does it tell you, my lord?'

He stared at her, face taut and remote. 'It tells me you have no place here. It speaks of treachery and sorcery, and a Cheysuli curse.'

'But you admit it is true I might be Lindir's child.'

A flicker shadowed the grey eyes a moment. Alix could sense Shaine's consideration of rejecting her outright, but she knew his pride too well for that. He would not quail before acknowledging his wish to rid himself of a halfling child, even at birth.

'Carillon says you are that child,' he said finally. 'Also that Torrin had the raising of you. So you may call yourself Lindir's child if you wish — it does you no good. I will not acknowledge you.'

'I did not come expecting acknowledgment.'

His dark brows rose. 'You did not? I find that difficult to believe.'

Alix kept her hands away from the golden girdle with effort, fighting down her nervousness. 'I came because I wished to see the man who could cast out a child and curse an entire race. I came to see the man who began the *qu'mahlin*.'

'Use no shapechanger words to me, girl. I will not have it in this place.'

'Once you welcomed them.'

His grey eyes burned with inward rage. 'I was deceived. Their sorcery is strong. But I will take retribution for it.'

Alix lifted her head in a reflection of his arrogance. 'Is what Lindir did worth the destruction of an entire race, my lord? Do you seek to be no better than Bellam of Solinde, who wants only to humble this land?'

Carillon drew a quick breath of dismay but she paid it no heed. She held Shaine's eyes with her own and felt the power in the man. She began to wonder, deep within her soul, if she had not her own measure of it.

'You are Cheysuli,' the Mujhar said harshly. 'You are subject to death . . . like all of them.'

'You would have me slain, then?'

'Cheysuli are under penalty of death.'

Carillon moved closer to her. 'What Lindir did was long ago, and best forgotten. You cast Alix away once. Do not do it again.'

'You have no place in this, Carillon!' Shaine lashed. 'Take yourself from this hall.'

'No.'

'Do as I bid.'

'No, my lord.'

Shaine glared at him, hands knotting on his gold belt. 'The Cheysuli took you prisoner and set a wolf on you. This girl is one of them. How can you defy me like this?'

'Alix is my cousin, my lord. Bloodkin. I will not see her treated so, even by you.'

The Mujhar's breath hissed through his teeth as he stepped wrathfully from the dais. He stood before the empty firepit running the length of the hall.

'You do not speak to *me* so! I am your liege lord, Carillon, and I have made you my heir. Am I to believe the shapechangers have used sorcery on you, to win you to their side? Must I disinherit you?'

117

Alix looked sharply at Carillon and saw his face go bloodless, jaw clenched as tightly as Shaine's.

'You may do as you will, my lord, but it seems futile to disinherit the only possible heir to Homana's throne. Did you not live through too many empty years in hopes of getting one before?'

'Carillon!'

'You have made me your heir,' he said steadily. 'But it does not take my humanity from me.'

'Get yourself from this hall!'

Alix stepped forward. 'So you may deal with me alone? So you may have me taken from this place and slain on the altar of your pride?'

Shaine's face blanched white. '*You* do not speak freely in this hall, shapechanger witch! You will do as I bid you!'

Alix opened her mouth to answer but a sudden chiming tone within her mind banished the words. Stunned, she stared blindly at the Mujhar. Cai's gentle tone wove its familiar pattern in her mind.

I am here, liren. Should the man grow too full of himself, we shall show him something; you and I.

Cai! she cried silently.

I am here for you, liren. This petty lord cannot harm you.

Alix began to smile. 'Cai.'

Carillon stiffened. 'Alix, what do you say?'

She ignored him. She looked steadily at the Mujhar and spoke softly, with renewed confidence. A sense of power and resolve was growing within her.

'My lord, you rule here through the sufferance of the Cheysuli. You owe them more than you will admit.'

'I will drive them from this land!' he roared, face congesting. 'They are demons! Sorcerers! Servitors of the dark gods . . . no better than the Ihlini. I will see they are destroyed!'

'And you will destroy the very heart of Homana!' she shouted. 'Foolish man — you do not deserve to be king of an honourable land!'

He raised his hand to her, stepping forward. Alix, unflinching, stood before him, but before the blow could fall she felt a flaring of power within her mind. It reached out, seeking, and the magnificent hawk answered it.

The velvet arras hanging at a narrow casement rippled and billowed aside as the *lir* winged into the hall. His passage set the candles guttering, throwing eerie shadows against the stone walls. Many of the tapers winked out, plunging the hall into flickering relief. Wall sconces flared and smoked as his wingspan flurried them.

Shaine turned as he felt the beat in the wind. His raised hand fell to his side as he stared speechlessly at the hawk. A garbled sound broke from his throat as Cai whipped a slash of air across his face.

The bird of prey circled the lofty hammer-beamed hall gracefully; eloquently powerful. Alix felt a welling of pride so sharp it hurt. As she watched him she began to understand the magic of her blood, and to understand what it was to be Cheysuli.

They have not lied . . . she whispered silently. *They have said the truth — that it is better to be part of an accursed race with a god-gift in the blood, than to be a lirless Homanan.*

Cai circled and flew toward them again, dark eyes brightened by the flames of the sconces and candle-racks. He slowed, stalling with broad wings, and settled himself upon the back of the throne. He mantled once, then perched in perfect silence on the dark lion throne of Homana.

There, liren; have we made the man take notice?

Alix laughed joyously within her mind, welcoming her god-gift, and felt the hawk's approval.

Shaine stumbled away from her, but neither did he go near the throne with its hawk headpiece. The Mujhar's hand raised and pointed at the bird.

'Is this your doing? Do you summon the familiars of demons?'

119

'He is a *lir*, my lord,' she said evenly. 'Surely you recall them. Hale had one, did he not?'

'Go from here!' Shaine cried hoarsely. 'Leave this place! I will not suffer a Cheysuli within Homana-Mujhar!'

'Willingly, my lord grandsire,' she said clearly. 'Nor will I suffer a foolishly vain man longer than I must.'

His face contorted. 'Leave this place before I have my guard take you!'

Alix was so angry she ached with it. She turned her rigid back on the Mujhar and walked to the open doors at the end of the hall. There she swung around once more.

'I see now why Lindir took her leave of you, my lord. I only wonder she did not do it sooner.'

Alix went unaccosted into the darkness of the cobbled bailey courtyard. As she picked up her skirts to hasten toward the tall gates she heard the clash of gold and gems at her girdle and realized she fled with some of the Mujhar's riches. Then she hardened her heart and determined to keep them, if only to have a legacy of her mother. She had no coin; the gems would serve.

Alix glanced over her shoulder apprehensively, expecting to be followed. From all accounts Shaine was too vain to let such an affront to his pride go unremarked; if she did not win free of Homana-Mujhar quickly she might soon taste the hospitality of his dungeons. When she turned back, hitching her skirts higher, she saw a shadow detach itself from the wall and come at her.

She stumbled back in alarm as the looming figure caught her. Before she could cry out a hand fastened firmly over her mouth.

'Be silent!' hissed a whisper.

By the gods, Shaine will have me slain! She struggled against the hard body, fighting the guardsman with all her strength. The hand clenched against her jaw

120

painfully, restraining her teeth as she sought to bite. Her free hand clawed for his face and missed, dragging across a bare arm and stopping against the warmth of embossed metal.

Alix froze.

'*Now* will you be still?' the man asked. He removed his hand from her mouth.

'Duncan. *Duncan!*'

He shook her, hissing at her vehemently. 'Be silent! Will you give us both away?'

'This is *Homana-Mujhar*! Shaine will have you slain!'

'Only if he learns I am here,' Duncan said grimly. 'But that should not be difficult if you persist in shouting.'

'I am not shouting,' she said sullenly, lowering her voice.

He dragged her toward the wall, ignoring her protests. When they reached the shadows he set her against the cold stone and stood before her, blocking out the torchlight from the palace.

'Have you learned what you wanted?' he demanded, not bothering to hide his anger. 'Have you seen what it is to be Cheysuli in Shaine's presence?'

She could not make out his features in the darkness, but his odd violence told her what he felt. 'Duncan, it was a thing I had to do.'

He sighed, still gripping her arms. 'You are no better than Lindir. The Mujhar's get are wilful women.'

'Why are you here?' she whispered, peering at his shadowed face. '*Here?*'

'I will give you answers later. First we must leave this place. I have horses waiting outside the walls.'

Alix planted her feet as he sought to lead her toward a small wooden gate hidden in shrubbery. She felt his startled hesitation and nearly laughed. But she did not let him see her amusement.

'Duncan, I told you to let me be when Carillon came for me. Why have you come?'

He shifted slightly. Faint torchlight illuminated his

face and showed her an odd glint in his yellow eyes. He smiled coldly.

'You said I must do as my brother to stop you. I let you go then. I will not do it again.'

'Let me be!'

'You are Cheysuli,' he said flatly. 'You have a place with your clan.'

'I *refuse* it!'

His hands clamped on her arms, hurting her. He ignored her wince of pain. 'Alix, you will have us found if you persist. What sense is it to have us both slain in the name of Shaine's purge?'

'If you do not explain yourself I will shout for the guardsmen. I am surprised they have not found you already, if they are so skilled.'

He laughed softly. 'The Cheysuli move in silence, small one.' He paused significantly. 'Except, perhaps, for you.'

She glared at him. A strange sense of defiance and exhilaration crept into her heart and nearly consumed her. She smiled at him in vindictive joy and opened her mouth as if to cry out.

Duncan silenced her instantly. This time he did not use his hand. Alix, shocked to the core, felt herself caught in a harsh embrace and kissed as if he would take the soul from her.

She stiffened instantly, pressing palms against his chest to push him away. In that moment she realized the absolute strength of a determined man and was amazed by it. She sought to escape but was trapped within his arms.

Alix shuddered once, recalling Finn's harshness and the instinctive fear he had provoked. Then, oddly, the thought fell away.

A new awareness slid through her as Duncan's mouth moved on hers. It was imperceptible, yet she felt it, and he no longer forced her. The pain he had inflicted at first was gone, altering in some subtle fashion. When a second shiver coursed through her it was of another origin.

Duncan is not his brother, she thought dazedly, *and I do not fear this man . . .*

Alix felt the wall at her back as he lifted his mouth from hers. An odd expression of inner conflict moved through his pale eyes, tautening his face into blankness. Alix, wanting only to see the possessive determination in him again, touched his chin.

'Is this your *tahlmorra*?' she asked breathlessly. 'Is this why?'

The tight line of his mouth relaxed. 'Perhaps it will not be so long a time to wait after all.'

'Duncan . . . I do not understand.'

'I have come to you as Finn, forcing myself on a woman who does not wish it,' he said grimly. 'Have I earned the enmity you promised?'

'I have forgot what I said.'

His lips twitched. 'Forgot? You?'

Alix turned her head away, realizing she still clung to him. Her wantonness made her ashamed, but when she tried to slide away he kept her pressed against the wall.

'Alix, you have only to listen to what is in you. Heed it. I will not force you again.' Duncan moved away from her, releasing her to stand in solitude against the wall. Alix sensed impatience in him and the slow rising of an odd anxiety and urgency in herself.

By the gods, what has this man done to me? Why do I want him by me? She closed her eyes. *It is Carillon I want, not this Cheysuli warrior I have known so brief a time.*

'Alix,' he said gently, 'I am sorry. You are too young to understand.'

Her eyes opened. The torchlight from the palace painted his shoulders and glinted off the gold on his arms. Suddenly she wanted the warmth of him against her again.

'Duncan, I think no woman is too young to understand.'

He blinked in surprise. Then he laughed silently and relaxed visibly. His hand slid around her neck and caught in the braids coiled against her head, cradling her against his chest. He murmured something in the Old Tongue, and Alix wished she spoke it.

Hastening footsteps echoed across the bailey, scraping on the cobbles. 'Alix!' Carillon cried.

Duncan cursed and jerked around. His hand slipped to the knife at his belt.

'No!' Alix cried, grasping at his hand.

'Alix!' Carillon shouted again.

'Here,' she answered, and heard Duncan's swift indrawn breath.

The prince found them in the darkness. For a moment he stiffened as he saw Duncan, but he made no hostile movement. His mouth was a grim line as he looked at Alix.

'You have driven the Mujhar into a rage. He swears he will have the hawk hunted and slain, and you exiled upon the Crystal Isle. Imprisoned.' He sighed. 'Alix, I have spoken with him. It does no good. I will take you to Torrin's croft.'

'She comes with me, Homanan,' Duncan said ominously.

'Does she?' Carillon snapped. 'Do you speak for her, shapechanger?'

'You have no place in this,' Duncan answered. 'She is not for you.'

Alix moved between them. 'Carillon, something happened to me in the hall. Something . . . came to life in me. When the Mujhar called me witch and cursed me for my blood, I felt no shame. I felt no horror; no fear. I felt only anger that a man could hate so powerfully, and do so much harm to a race. It was as if the Cheysuli in me finally came to life.' She touched his arm beseechingly. 'I want no more of this place.'

'I have said I will take you to Torrin. When I can, I will come to you.'

She shook her head slowly. 'I think — I think what is between us must stay unknown, or unnamed.' She pressed his arm. 'Do you know what I say?'

'No,' he said, so harshly she knew he did.

'The Cheysuli are not your enemy,' Alix said softly. 'It is the Solidish, and the Ihlini. Turn your anger on them. Do not let Shaine's madness infect you also. You said once you would accept me whatever I was. Now I ask you to accept the others of my race.'

'Alix, I cannot.'

'Do you sentence yourself to serve the Mujhar's insanity?'

He reached out and clasped her shoulders. 'Alix, I want you where you will be safe.'

She smiled at him, certain of her words. 'Duncan will see I am kept safe.'

His fingers tightened painfully. 'Do you go willingly with him, then? Or has he ensorcelled you with shape-changer arts?'

'No,' she said softly. 'I think it is something within myself. I have no words for it, but it exists.'

Duncan, eloquently silent, stretched out his hand. She saw the familiar gesture of spread fingers and bared palm.

And she understood.

Alix stepped away from Carillon. His empty hands fell limply to his sides. He looked at Duncan, then at her, eyes shadowed with pain and confusion. But she also saw acknowledgment.

'I will get you mounts,' he said quietly.

'I have horses,' Duncan answered.

'How do you propose to get over the walls with her? Alix cannot fly in the guise of a hawk.'

Duncan's face tightened. 'No. But the eight guardsmen are simple enough to put out of my way, if I must.'

Carillon sighed wearily. 'Shapechanger, I begin to understand the arrogance of your race. And its strength, as Torrin said. Do you know Shaine sent fifty

125

men against you in the forests and only eleven survive?'

'I know.'

'How many did you lose?'

'Of twelve men, we lost two. One to death; one to the soulless men.'

Alix shivered at the relentless tone in his voice. She sensed the purpose and determination in the man and realized had she refused to go with him he could easily have forced her.

Carillon nodded. 'I will escort you through the gates. The guard will not stop me, even do I walk with a shapechanger.'

Duncan laughed harshly. 'Once we walked *freely* within this place, prince. But you will have my gratitude, regardless.'

Carillon turned to lead them to the bronze-and-timber gates. Before he could move away Duncan reached out and caught his arm. The prince stiffened.

'Carillon. There is much you do not understand. Perhaps you cannot, yet. But Shaine will not always be Mujhar.'

'What do you say, shapechanger?'

'That we are not your enemy. We cannot alter the *qu'mahlin* while Shaine lives. He has struck well and quickly, reducing us to less than a quarter of what we were. Even now we grow fewer with each year as the *qu'mahlin* continues. Carillon, it is in you to stop this.'

The prince smiled. 'I have been raised on tales of your perfidy. Stories of your demon ways and cruel arts. Tell my why I should halt my uncle's purge.'

Duncan's hand rested on Alix's shoulder. 'For her, my lord. For the woman we both want.'

Alix stood immobile, unable to answer the resolve in Duncan's voice. Something in him had reached out to her, seeking something from her, and she wanted very much to give it to him.

Carillon swallowed. 'It is true, the Mujhar alarms me with his vehemence in dealing with your race. He does

126

not even curse Bellam or the Ihlini as he does the Cheysuli. There is an unnatural anger in him.'

Duncan nodded. 'Hale served him for thirty-five years, my lord, with a loyalty only the Cheysuli can give. They were more than brothers. It is a binding service which our race had honoured for centuries. Hale shattered that bond and hereditary service by his actions. Any man would take it ill and swear revenge, but Shaine also lost a daughter and consequently found his realm plunged into war once again. I understand why he has done this thing, Carillon, even as it destroys my race.'

'Then you are more forgiving than the Mujhar.'

'What of you?' Duncan asked calmly. 'Do you serve the *qu'mahlin* when you are king?'

Carillon smiled crookedly. 'When I am king,' he said gently, 'you will know.'

He turned and walked to the gates. The guards, answering his bidding, opened them instantly. Duncan took Alix's arm and led her silently from Homana-Mujhar.

CHAPTER THREE

Duncan took her through the shadows of tall buildings to the horses. From his saddlepack he pulled a dark hooded cloak and gently draped the folds around her.

'You wear fine clothing and rich jewels, my lady princess,' he said quietly. 'I am only one man, and thieves may think it a simple matter to slay me and steal your wealth. Or even you.'

He pinned the cloak at her left shoulder with a large topaz brooch carved into a hawk shape and set in gold. Silently he pulled the hood over her garneted hair and settled it.

'Duncan,' she said softly, trembling even at his lightest touch.

'Aye, small one?'

'What is this thing? What is this within me?' She swallowed and tried to hide the hesitation in her voice. 'I have lost myself, somehow.'

He smoothed back a strand of dark hair from her cheekbone, fingertips lingering. 'You have lost nothing, save a measure of your innocence. In time, you will understand it all. It is not my place to tell you. You will know.' He removed his hand. 'Now, mount your horse. We have a long way to ride.'

She was muffled by the weight of the unaccustomed gown and the folds of the cloak. Duncan's firm hands held her close as he lifted her into the saddle. Alix settled her wrappings as he turned to his own mount, then dutifully set out to follow him through the city streets. She was well aware of what she did, though days before she would never have admitted she could act so strangely. But something within her told her she would be safe with him.

'Duncan,' she said quietly, 'you spoke of losing someone to the soulless men. What did you truly say?'

Torchlight caught and flashed on his armbands, but he remained shadowed and indistinct as he led her through Mujhara. She thought again how easily the Cheysuli melted into the darkness.

'I have said what it is to be *lirless*,' he said at last, pitching his low voice to carry over the tap of hoof on stone. 'A *lir* was lost, and Borrs seeks the death ritual in the forests.'

'And you let him go?'

'It is our way, Alix. Our custom. We do not turn our backs on what has been within the clan for centuries.'

Wearily she pushed the hood off her face and let it fall to her shoulders. 'Duncan, where do you take me?'

'To the Keep.'

'What will happen to me there?'

'You will see the *shar tahl*, and learn what it is to be Cheysuli.'

'You are so certain your clan will accept me?'

He cast her a sharp glance over a shoulder. 'They must. I have little doubt of your place in the prophecy.'

'Mine!'

'The *shar tahl* will explain it to you. It is not my place.'

Frustration rose within her, sharpening her voice into a demand. 'Duncan! Do not shroud your words in obscurity and expect me to meekly accept them. You have taken me from all I have ever known, and even now you lead me into *more* I cannot comprehend. Tell me what is before me!'

He reined in his horse and allowed her to catch up.

129

Faint illumination showed his face clearly to her, lining rigid determination. His mouth was a taut line.

'Must you know all before its time?' he asked harshly. 'Can you not wait?'

She glared at him. 'No.'

His eyes, bestial in the torchlight, narrowed into pale slits. 'Then I will speak plainly, so plainly even you may understand.'

She nodded.

'What I have seen in my own *tahlmorra* is that the old gods intended you and I for one another. From us will come the next link in the prophecy of the Firstborn. You are Cheysuli. You have no choice.'

He was a stranger suddenly. The gentleness he had used before fled beneath the hardness of his voice and words and Alix nearly quailed from it. Then the full meaning and implications of what he had said flared within her mind.

'You and I . . .'

'If you would feel your own *tahlmorra*, you would see it as clearly as I.'

Alix's breath came harsh in her throat. Her hands tightened compulsively on the reins. 'Ten days ago I was a valley girl tending her father's animals. Now you tell me I must accept the will of this crooked prophecy and serve it accordingly.' Her voice wavered, then grew firm again. 'Well, I will not. I choose my own way.'

'You cannot.'

She glared at him through angry tears. 'I have been cast from my grandsire's palace; threatened with imprisonment and death. Even *Torrin* says I must follow this *tahlmorra*, as you do. But I will do as I choose! I am not an empty vessel to be filled with other men's desires and plottings! I am more!'

Duncan sighed. 'Have you not yet learned all men are no more than empty vessels for the gods? *Cheysula*, do not rail so at your fate. It is not so bad.'

'What do you call me?'

He stiffened, rigidly upright in the saddle. 'I have some honour, girl. I will accede to the dictates of my own *tahlmorra*, but I will also honour yours. I know how it is with Homanans and their propriety, so I will renounce my vow of solitude. You I will take according to Cheysuli custom, and make you a wife.'

'You will *not!*'

'Alix—'

'No! When I become a wife it will be because I wish it, and to a man I can be at ease with. You frighten me with your shadowed soul and mutterings of prophecy I cannot even understand. Leave me to *myself!*'

He pressed his horse closer and caught her arm. Alix struggled against him as he pulled her effortlessly out of her saddle and sat her upright against his chest. In one terrifying instant she saw the echo of his brother in him, and all of Finn's fierce determination.

'Duncan — *no!*'

'You have asked for it!' he snapped, settling her across his lap.

Cai, drifting down from the rooftops, circled over them. *You should not, lir.*

Alix, trapped within the hard circle of Duncan's arm and fearful of his intentions, saw the conflict in his face. His hand was on her jaw, imprisoning it, but he made no further move against her. She waited stiffly, not breathing; afraid even to move.

Abruptly he kneed his horse to hers again and deposited her roughly into her own saddle. Alix grabbed at the reins and pommel, fighting to stay upright. When she cast an anxious glance over her cloaked shoulder she saw him visibly constrain the force of his emotion. Then his face was a mask to her.

'It seems,' he began stiffly, 'you have all the *lir* at your bidding. First Storr gainsays my *rujholli* from forcing you; now Cai does so with *me*. There is more within you than I thought.'

'Perhaps you should heed it!'

Duncan's face twisted. 'I think the gods laughed when they determined we should serve the prophecy together. It will be no simple task.'

She glared at him. 'It will be no task at all, shape-changer. *I* have determined that.'

He swore something in the Old Tongue, forsaking the control he had so recently won back. Alix, startled by the savagery in his voice, reined her horse back two steps.

Lir! Cai cried in warning.

Duncan turned swiftly in the saddle, hand to his knife, but the men were on him. Three of them, clothed in dark garments, dragged him from his mount.

Alix gasped as she saw him stand braced against his horse, knife drawn to face the men. Suddenly her anger and frustration evaporated, replaced by stark fear for his life.

A swift feathered weight plummeted from the night sky, wingtips brushing her hair. Cai shrieked into the darkness and fell, talons outstretched. Alix's horse, terrified by the bird, reared.

She cried out and scrabbled for a solid handhold, tangling reins and mane in her rigid fingers She had little knowledge of horses; always before she had ridden with someone. Now she struggled to keep the horse from striking Duncan with its pawing hooves.

A hoarse outcry followed Cai's attack. Alix tried to see if Duncan was safe, but her horse denied it to her. It reared again and danced backward, then spun and bolted.

Shod hooves slid on cobbles, striking sparks. The horse cared little for obstacles in its path, leaping anything in its way. Alix clung to the animal with all her strength, unable to control its flight, and sought the mercies of the gods.

The horse leaped a bushel and slipped badly on landing, sliding spread-legged, nearly throwing Alix from the saddle. The cloak, whipping back, dragged at her. She felt the woven strands of garnets break free of her hair, spilling loosened braids over her shoulders in disarray. She took two trembling wraps in the reins, snugging them around her hands, and pulled the horse's head sideways in an instinctive bid to slow it.

Dimly she heard the animal's wheezing breath and felt the lash of bloodied saliva against her face. The horse slid and thrashed all four legs in an effort to maintain momentum, but Alix kept her painful grip on the reins. She felt the cloak torn from her, whipped back into the darkness.

The horse folded beneath her suddenly, without warning, and tumbled her painfully into the street.

Stunned, knocked dizzy with the force of her sprawled landing, Alix felt the tug at her left arm. The twisted reins still wrapped themselves about her wrist, threatening to drag her as the animal fought to regain its feet. Dazedly she picked at the taut leather with her other hand, freeing her wrist at last.

She heard a rattle of pebbles and dimly realized the jewelled lacings in her hair had broken, scattering garnets and pearls across the cobbles. A searching hand at her hips told her the girdle was also gone, and her skirts torn and stained. But she dismissed that and got painfully to her hands and knees.

The horse, defeated in its attempt to rise, lay wheezing on its side near her. Alix stared at it blankly, wanting to go to it; afraid of what she might find if she did.

Hair tumbled over her shoulders into her bruised face, dragging on the cobbles. Wearily she pushed it behind her ears and discovered the garnets in her ears remained. Alix got to her feet and waited for the pain to begin. When she found she could stand it, she picked up her heavy skirts and moved slowly back the way she had come.

Duncan was missing when she found the place. Alix

moved into the pool of faint torchlight and stared vaguely at the cobbles, seeing two bodies. One man lay on his back with a deep knife wound in his abdomen. The other, clawing hands clasped to his face in death, had had his forehead rent by talons. He bled freely from a wound in his throat.

The third man was nowhere. Alix wobbled unsteadily and put both hands over her mouth to force back the sour bile rushing into her throat.

A lantern flared in a door across from her as it opened. Alix squinted against it, trapped in the spilling illumination. An old man peered out, one hand grasping the collar of a growling dog. He lifted the lantern to shed more light into the street and Alix instinctively shrank from it, pressing herself against the wall.

But he saw her. His dark eyes widened, then narrowed as he stared at the slain men. His voice came harsh as he looked back at her.

'Witch! *Shapechanger* witch!'

Alix put a trembling hand to her face, realizing how deeply she bore her father's stamp. In the darkness, illuminated by the lantern light, she was branded by the Mujhar's hatred.

'No,' she said clearly.

His hand loosened on the dog's collar. Alix, fearing he would set the animal on her, gathered up her skirts and fled.

She ran until her lungs screamed their protest and her legs faltered. Breathlessly she fell against a stone well set in the intersection of cobbled streets. She clutched at the cross-beams of the well and held herself upright, gasping from knifing pain in her chest and sides.

When some of the breath-demand had gone she cranked up the bucket. The cool water was sweet on her raw throat, trickling down to soothe her heaving stomach. It splashed over the rim and stained the velvet of her fine garments, but she did not care.

'Could you spare some water for a thirsty horse, my lady?' asked a quiet voice.

Alix jerked upright, dropping the bucket down the well. Her hands clenched spasmodically in her skirts as she stared at the man.

He moved softly, silently, forsaking the shadows like a wraith. She saw a dark cloak falling to his booted feet. An oddly twisted silver brooch pinned it to his left shoulder, but he had pulled the folds back from a silver sword hilt at his hips. Somehow, though he moved in darkness, he brought the light with him.

His face was smooth, serene. Strength of a sort she had never seen shone from the fine features, and his smile was gently beguiling. His hair and beard were inky dark, carefully trimmed, and flecked with silver. His eyes, black as the horse who followed him, were soothing and sweet.

'Do not fear me, my lady. I seek only water for my horse.' He smiled gently. 'Not some light woman for the evening.'

Alix, even bruised and weary, felt the insult keenly. She drew herself up and glared at him, disdaining to answer. But as her eyes met his the defiance slid away, leaving her powerless before him.

She gestured weakly. 'The well is yours, my lord.'

He cranked up the bucket and held it steady in gloved hands, letting the horse take its fill. He watched her in a manner almost paternal.

'You have seen trouble this night, lady,' he said quietly. 'Are you harmed?'

'No. I am well enough.'

'Do not seek to hide the truth from me. I have only to look at your eyes.'

She swallowed, aware of her loose hair and stained clothing. 'We were set upon by thieves, my lord.'

'You are alone now.'

'The man I rode with stayed to fight the thieves. My horse was frightened and ran. In order to stop him I was forced to put him down on the stones.' She shrugged slightly, dismissing the remembered fright. 'So now I walk.'

'What of your escort?'

Alix looked away from him. 'I cannot say, my lord. Perhaps he is slain.' The vision rose before her eyes, showing her Duncan twisted on the cobbles, slain. She shuddered and felt the horrible anguish in her soul.

'With such words you place yourself in my hands,' he said gently.

A chill of apprehension slid through her, but she was aching and weary, too dazed to care. 'If it be so, my lord, what will you do with me?'

He sent the bucket back to the depths of the well and caressed the horse's silky jaw. 'Help you, lady. I will give you my aid.' His beguiling smile soothed her. 'Come into the light and look upon me. If I truly seem treacherous, you have only to leave me. I will not gainsay you. But if you find me honest in my intentions, you are welcome to come with me.'

Slowly Alix answered his summons, moving into the torchlight. His appearance was calm, gentle-seeming, and his affection for the horse indicated goodwill. She met his eyes for a long moment, searching for an answer there.

At last she sighed. 'I am so wearied from this day and night I care little what your intentions may be. Where do you go, my lord?'

'Where you wish, lady. I serve you.'

Alix looked into his smooth face, seeking an indication of his true intent, but she saw only serenity. He was richly clad, though not ostentatious, and his manner was that of some high lord.

'Do you serve the Mujhar?' she asked, suddenly apprehensive.

He smiled, white teeth gleaming. 'No, lady, I do not. I serve the gods.'

It relieved her past measure. Silently Alix took the

gems from her ears and held them out.

But he would not take them. 'I have no need of your jewels, lady. What I do for you requires no payment.' He gestured smoothly. 'Where do you go, lady? I will take you there.'

'A croft,' she said quietly. 'In the valley. It is perhaps ten leagues from here.'

His eyes glinted in gentle humour. 'You do not have the appearance of a croft-girl, lady. I see more in you than that.'

Her hand gripped the garnet earrings. 'Do you seek to humble me, my lord? There is no need. I know my place.'

He moved closer. The light seemed to follow him. His eyes were soft, sweet, like his voice, and deep as the well from which they drank.

'Do you?' he asked softly. 'Do you truly know your place?'

Alix frowned at him, baffled by his manner, and lost herself in the dominance of his black eyes.

He lifted his right hand. For a moment she thought he would make the Cheysuli gesture of *tahlmorra*, but he did not. Instead a hissing line of purple light streaked out of the darkness and pooled in his hand, throwing a violet glare over her face and his.

'So you have learned your legacy,' he said quietly. 'After all this time. I had thought Lindir's child lost, and of no more account.'

Alix gasped.

The flame leaped in his hand. 'You hold more of the prophecy within you than any I have yet seen. And I have watched for years ... waiting.'

Her voice hurt. 'What do you say?'

Black eyes narrowed and held dominion over her. 'Can it be you do not fully understand? Have the Cheysuli not yet bound you to their *tahlmorra*?'

'*Who are you?*'

He smiled. 'I have many names. Most are used by

137

petty men who fear me. Others are revered, as they should be.'

Alix shivered. 'What manner of man are you?'

'One who serves the gods.'

She wanted to leave him but the power in his fathomless black eyes held her. Purple light glowed in his palm.

'What do you want of me?'

'Nothing,' he said calmly, 'if you remain unknowing. It is only if you recognize the *tahlmorra* within yourself that I will be forced to gainsay you. In any way I can.'

Her palm burned where the earrings bit into her flesh. 'You are not Cheysuli.'

'No.'

'Yet you speak of their *tahlmorra*, and the prophecy. What is it to you?'

'My bane,' he said softly. 'The end of me, should it be fulfilled. And the Cheysuli know it.'

Cold knowledge crept within her mind. Consciously she forced her body to relax, then lifted her head. 'I *know* you. I *know* you.' She took another breath. '*Ihlini*.'

'Aye,' he said softly.

'Tynstar ...'

His eyes smiled. 'Aye.'

'What do you do here?' she whispered.

'That is for me to know. But I will tell you this — already Bellam breaks Shaine's borders and invades. Homana will fall, lady ... soon. It will be mine.' He smiled. 'As it was ever meant.'

'Shaine will never allow it.'

'Shaine is a fool. He was a fool when he sent the Cheysuli from their homeland and sentenced them to death. Without them, he cannot win. When he does not, the prophecy will fail. And I will be lord of this land.'

'By your unnatural arts!' Alix cried.

The sorcerer laughed softly. 'You are party to your own unnatural arts, lady ... you have only to learn them. But until you do, you remain insignificant, and of no account to me.' He shrugged. 'So I will let you live.'

'Let me live ...' she echoed.

'For now,' Tynstar agreed lightly

A winged shadow passed over them, blotting the violet glow a moment. Tynstar glanced up and watched the shadow, then looked at Alix.

'You summon the *lir*, lady, even though you do not know it. Perhaps you are not the naïve child you would have me believe.'

Cai! she cried silently, staring up at the hawk.

Tynstar's hand was on his horse. The other still held hissing purple flame. He smiled at her across its glow and sketched a twisted rune in the air. Its path glowed against the darkness a moment, then flared into a column of cold fire. When it had gone, so had he.

'Alix.'

She spun and stared at Duncan. He stood silently with his horse at his back, left arm streaked with blood. A bruise darkened his cheekbone and he bore a shallow slice across his forehead, but he seemed whole.

Alix looked at him. The defiance she had struck him with earlier had faded. Her words then, angry and frightened, had no more meaning. Something whispered in her soul, tapping at her mind, and she began to understand it.

'The horse ran away,' she said unsteadily.

His eyes were fixed on her. 'I found him. He is lamed, but will recover.'

'I am glad he was not badly hurt.' She knew the words they said held no meaning. Their communication lay on another level.

'Will you suffer to ride with me?' he asked. 'I cannot waste more time seeking another horse. The clan has need of me.'

Alix walked slowly toward him, eyes dwelling on every visible wound and bruise. A strange trembling weakness crept into her limbs as his yellow gaze remained on her in a calm, deliberate perusal. The hawk-earring glittered in the strands of his black hair.

She halted before him. 'It was Tynstar.'

'I saw him.'

She put out a hesitant hand and gently touched the drying blood on his arm. 'Duncan, I did not mean to hurt you.'

He flinched at her soft touch but she realized it was not from pain. Something told her this man was hers to hold, to keep, and the enormity of it stunned her.

'Duncan ... ' She swallowed heavily and met his blazing eyes. 'Duncan, please hold me so I know I am real.'

He whispered something in the Old Tongue and took her into his arms.

Alix, hair spilling down her back, melted against his firm warrior's body until she was boneless. The strange weakness was new to her, but she welcomed it.

Duncan sank a hand deep in her hair and jerked her head back. 'Do you deny it? Do you deny the *tahlmorra* in our blood?'

She did not answer. She caught her hands in the thick hair curling at his neck and dragged his mouth down on hers.

CHAPTER FOUR

Duncan found them a cave in the hills beyond Mujhara and spread furred pelts over the stone floor. Alix sat on one, pulling his red blanket around her shoulders, and watched him build a small fire. When it was done he took the small grouse he had caught, spitted it, and set it over the fire.

'Does your arm hurt?' she asked.

He flexed the scabbing forearm. 'No. The men were not skilled with their weapons.'

'Finn has said you can heal. Will you not do it?'

'Not for myself, or for so trivial a wound. The healing arts are used only in great need, and usually only on others.'

'Finn healed Carillon's wrist.'

'Because Carillon required convincing we were not the demons he believed.'

She shifted, easing a sore hip. Her entire body ached with the fall from the horse. 'What did you mean when you spoke to Carillon as we left? It sounded as if you spoke from certain knowledge.'

He tended the sizzling grouse and sipped at a cup of honey brew. 'I spoke from the knowledge of the prophecy. Carillon is not named in it — no man is — but I think he is the one.'

'Speak plainly with me.'

141

Duncan smiled crookedly at her. 'I cannot. You have no knowledge of the prophecy. That will be given to you by the *shar tahl*, and then you will know.'

'Why must you shroud your words in so much darkness? You would have me think it is some sorcery you seek to do.'

'It is no sorcery to serve the gods.'

'As does Tynstar?'

He stiffened. 'Tynstar serves the dark gods of the netherworld. He is evil. He seeks only to end the prophecy before its time is come.'

'So he said.' Alix sighed and rubbed at her brow. 'Where did you go when my horse ran?'

'First I slew two of the thieves. The third ran. I went to find you.'

'Why did you not simply send Cai? Or seek *lir*-shape?'

'I could not take *lir*-shape. I sensed the presence of an Ihlini, though I did not know who. As for Cai ... him I sent to Homana-Mujhar.'

'Homana-Mujhar!'

'I thought you had returned to Carillon.'

She stared at him, astonished, then felt a strange bubble of laughter welling within. 'You will have me think you are jealous of him.'

He scowled. 'I am not jealous.'

Alix smiled in wonder, then laughed outright. 'So, I am to think the Cheysuli are not capable of such a Homanan emotion? Yet your brother — who is also mine — seems well able to display it.'

'Finn is young.'

'And you not much older.'

Color came into his face. 'I left my youth behind the day my first Keep was invaded by the Mujhar's men. It was only the will of the gods I was not slain, as so many others were.'

'Duncan—'

'You will see when we have reached the Keep.'

'Are so few left?'

'Perhaps fifty women, half of which cannot bear children. The rest are old men; girls, and boys. Of warriors . . . there are perhaps sixty.'

The horror of the *qu'mahlin* swept into her for the first time. 'Duncan . . .'

He looked old suddenly. 'Once this land was ours. More than fifty clans ranged Homana, from Hondarth on the Idrian Ocean into the mountains of the north, across the Bluetooth River. Now they are all slain, leaving only my own clan. And we are not so strong as we were.'

'Shaine's doing . . .'

He reached out and caught one of her arms, eyes beseeching her. 'Do you see it now? Do you understand why we steal women and force them to bear our children? Alix, it is the survival of a race. It is not *you* the Council will see, but your race and your youth. You must serve your race, *cheysula*.'

She sat straight upon the pelt. 'And will they hear you have called me that?'

He released her arm. 'I will ask for you. It is my *tahlmorra*.' Duncan gestured slowly, spreading his fingers. 'You are Hale's daughter. I think they will not deny me.'

She felt chilled. 'But — they *could*? They could refuse you?'

His hand dropped. 'Aye. First you must be acknowledged within the clan, given the knowledge in the old fashion, made aware of your birthlines. The *shar tahl* will say if you are truly Cheysuli.'

'But — *you* have said!'

Duncan smiled sadly. 'There is no doubt, small one; it is only custom. But you have been raised Homanan. In the eyes of the Council, you are tainted. Until the *shar tahl* has declared you free of it.'

Desolate, she closed her eyes. Her growing security in him was destroyed with but a few words. Then her eyes snapped open.

143

'They would not give me to *Finn*!'

Duncan's face was a mixture of suprise and amusement, then consideration. He frowned.

Alix was suddenly frightened. 'Duncan, they would not!'

He turned the spitted bird slowly. 'I am clan-leader, but not the sole power in the clan. It is Council that says what will be.'

She leaped to her feet and stumbled to the rock wall facing her. She stared at it blindly, hugging the blanket around her aching body. The new knowledge of what Duncan meant to her twisted in her entrails like a serpent, setting jagged teeth into her spirit.

To lose him when I have only just found him . . .

Duncan's hands settled on her shoulders. 'I will not let you go so easily.'

Trembling, she turned to him. 'Could you gainsay it, if they wished to give me to another man?'

Muscles rolled beneath the smooth flesh of his jaw. 'No.'

'Then what of this *tahlmorra* you prate about?'

'It is mine, Alix,' he said sombrely. 'It does not mean it is the clan's.'

She whispered his name. Then she lifted her face and touched his arm. 'If I went before this Council already carrying your child . . . ?'

His eyes flickered in surprise. Then he smiled faintly. 'If you made such a sacrifice, small one, there would be little they could say about the match.'

Alix let the blanket drop. The gown beneath, ungirdled, hung loosely. Slowly she undid the fastenings at the neck. Duncan watched her mutely, held by the strength in her eyes. His breath came harsh.

When the gown was undone she let it fall to her feet. Her hair unbound, streamed over her shoulders like a mantle.

'I am new to this . . .' she whispered, trembling with something other than fear. 'Duncan . . . it cannot be so very difficult to conceive . . .'

144

'No,' he breathed, reaching for her. 'It is not so very difficult.'

He took her from Homana into Ellas, the realm bordering Homana's eastern side. Alix, clasping his lean waist with a new and wonderful possessiveness, felt regret and anger stir within her that her grandsire could so malignantly drive her race from their homeland into a strange realm.

When at last Duncan halted Alix saw before her a large half-circle wall of piled stone. The wall ran a distance before circling back, and at the wide opening she saw three warriors with their *lir*. They waited silently, and she realized they were guards.

'The Keep,' Duncan said, and rode past the warriors.

Huge oiled pavilions billowed in a faint breeze. All were dyed warm colors, dwarfing the small tents she had seen at the raiding camp. Each had its own firepit before flapped entrances, but smoke drifted from the poled peaks and she realized smaller fires were tended within. Each pavilion, regardless of its color, bore a painted animal on its sides. By the shapes she could know what *lir* lived there.

The curving wall of undressed, unmortared stone hugged the shoulder of a craggy mountain. The half-circle blended into thick, sheltering trees. Alix realized such anonymity was the safety of the Cheysuli.

Duncan halted the horse before a green pavilion. She looked for the hawk painting on its side but saw only a wolf.

She stiffened. 'Why do we stop here?'

'I would see my *rujho*,' he said quietly, slipping from the horse. He turned to lift her down.

'Why? I want nothing to do with Finn.'

Duncan eyed her thoughtfully. 'When last I saw him, he was feverish from the wounds gotten in the forest battle.' His mouth was firm. 'Wounds won protecting you.'

Chastened, Alix slipped silently into his arms and allowed him to lead her into the pavilion.

Finn was stretched out on a pallet of thick furs, wrapped in a soft woven blanket. As he saw them he hoisted himself up on one elbow and grinned at her.

'So, my *rujho* managed to win you away from the wealth of Homana-Mujhar . . . and Carillon.'

She had been prepared to wish him well, feeling guilty over his injuries gotten in her behalf. But now, facing his mocking eyes and words, her good intentions evaporated.

'I came willingly enough, when my grandsire called me shapechanger witch and threatened to have me slain.'

'I *said* your place was with us, *mei jha*; not among the walls of Shaine's palace . . . or within the princeling's arms.'

She glared at him. 'You do not look feverish to me.'

He laughed. 'I am fully recovered, *mei jha*. Or nearly. I will be plaguing you soon enough, when I am on my feet.'

'You do not require feet to do that!' She scowled at him. 'You need only be in my presence.'

Finn grinned and ran a hand through his hair. She saw his eyes were alert and unclouded by illness, though his color was not as deep as usual. Inwardly she was grateful he had not been badly injured, but she would not say it to him.

'Will you two never admit peace between you?' Duncan growled. 'Must I ever seek to placate you, one at a time?'

'She is a woman, *rujho*,' Finn said airily. 'And they are ever the cause of much agitation.'

Before Alix could answer Duncan put a firm hand on her shoulder, pressing gently. She said nothing, but saw Finn's eyes narrow suspiciously. Alix could not keep her face from turning bright red.

He smiled slowly, watching her, eyes very bright. He

was not stupid, she knew. He looked at Duncan with a blank mask on his face.

'Malina has conceived.'

Duncan's hand bit into Alix's shoulder. She stared at him in surprise, seeing him go pale beneath his Cheysuli coloring. She was new to a woman's intuition for her mate, but understood instantly that something had deeply shaken him.

'Is it certain?' Duncan asked in a peculiar voice.

Finn nodded. 'She is four months gone.' His face twisted mockingly. 'Was it not four months ago when she turned from you to Borrs, and took him as her *cheysul*?'

'I count, Finn!' Duncan said angrily.

The younger man looked at Alix's uncomprehending face. He smiled more broadly. 'And now Borrs is among the soulless men, seeking his death-ritual. Malina is free again.'

Instinctively Alix reached for Duncan's clenched fist. But he withdrew his hand from her seeking fingers and stepped away, putting distance between them.

'Has she declared the unborn child before Council yet?' he asked harshly.

Finn, solemn again, shook his head. 'She has been in formal mourning for the last three days, since she learned of the news. But it will have to be a brief mourning, if she is to take another *cheysul*.'

'Did Borrs know of the child?'

Finn hunched a shoulder. 'He said nothing of it to me. But then he knew you and I are close, *rujho*, and he would hardly speak of such a thing to the *rujholli* of the man who first had his *cheysula*. Would he?'

'Then she has not named the *jehan*.'

A mocking glint crept back into Finn's eyes. 'Perhaps even Malina does not know the *jehan* of her unborn child, *rujho*. Do you?'

Alix stepped toward him. 'What do you say? What has this to do with Duncan?'

'It would be better, perhaps, he told you himself.'

'*Tell* me!'

Finn slid a glance at his silent brother, then nodded slightly. His smile was wolfish and triumphant. 'Duncan would have asked for formal clan-rights of Malina next year, taking her as his *cheysula*. She had been his since I can say . . . in the clans children are close and often wed when they are of age.' He scratched at an eyebrow. 'But Borrs also wanted her, and when Duncan wished to wait because of becoming clan-leader, Malina did not. I cannot account for a woman's whim to punish one man by taking another, but it is what she did.' He looked intently at Duncan. 'Yet now Borrs is among the soulless men, clanless, and she is free to choose again.' he paused significantly. 'Or *be* chosen.'

Alix, aware of Finn's natural perversity, sought the truth in Duncan's eyes. He turned from her and went out the flapped entrance, saying no word.

Finn's low laugh stung her. Alix turned on him, furious, fist upraised in his direction. But he laughed again, amused by her action, and she dropped the hand back to her side.

'Why?' she asked. 'Why do you punish me this way?'

He sat up, crossing his legs beneath his blanket. He wore no jerkin and she saw the bronze of his broad chest was ridged with scars. The wound in his shoulder was unbound but healing, and she recalled again his savagery as he slew the guardsmen who would have slain her.

'So,' he said in a low, taunting voice, 'you recognize the *tahlmorra* in yourself at last. I see you have chosen my *rujholli* after all, forsaking even Carillon. Only now Duncan returns to his first woman.' He clucked his tongue. 'Poor little *mei jha*.'

'I require no pity from you!'

'Duncan differs from me in many ways, *mei jha*; particularly in his women. He has long been satisfied with Malina, requiring no others.' He shrugged. 'I take

148

a woman where I will; freely. Save for you, they have never denied me.'

'What do you say!'

'That Duncan makes a life-bond when he takes a *cheysula*. If Malina is offering clan-rights with proven fertility, he would be a fool to deny her.' He stretched idly, cracking tough sinews. 'My *rujho* is many things, but he is not a fool.' Finn grinned at her. 'Do not worry, *mei jha* . . . I will still have you. You will not be lonely.'

She longed to scream at him but did not. Somehow she summoned a regal elegance, even in a torn and stained gown.

'I am Hale's daughter . . . I believe it now. Therefore I am Cheysuli. Therefore I have free choice of any man, *rujholli*, and I tell you now — you would be the last warrior I would ever consider. The *last*.'

Alix left him feeling a strange satisfaction that she had so easily bested him. The look on his face had assured her victory. But the satisfaction faded as she recalled the cause of it. Outside Finn's green pavilion, Alix hugged herself and longed for Duncan.

Cai drifted down from the skies. *Come with me, liren.*

Where? she asked dully.

To my lir.

Your lir seeks the company of another woman.

Cai's tone was exceedingly gentle. *You are weary and filled with sorrow and confusion. Come with me.*

Silently Alix followed the bird across the Keep to a slate-coloured pavilion embellished with a painted gold hawk. As Cai settled on his polished wooden perch she pulled the doorflap aside and went in.

Duncan had filled his pavilion with thick soft pelts and a richly embroidered tapestry. Alix stared at it blankly, unable to decipher the runes and odd symbols stitched in the blue pattern. Then she knelt before the ash-filled fire cairn.

She felt very small. An ague seemed to have settled in her bones, rattling them even as she sought to calm

149

herself. Her breath seemed to have gone completely; repeated gasps only worsened her need for air. Finally she bowed her head and clutched at her head, pressing against her temples.

'By the gods . . .' she whispered, 'what have I done?' She drew in a deep breath. 'I have left my croft . . . I have been sent from Homana-Mujhar . . . I have ridden into a strange realm with a man I cannot understand, and he has forsaken me as easily as Shaine.' Alix clenched her fists as if to drive demons from her skull. 'I have *given* myself to him . . . and now he seeks another!' She lifted her head and stared blindly at the tapestry. 'What have I done?'

The tapestry did not answer her; nor did Cai. Alix longed for his warm tone and reassurance, but the hawk remained silent. She became aware of other whispers in her mind. They formed patterns and tones like the ones she had heard before the forest battle, but did not oppress her as much.

'I am gone mad,' she whispered.

The whispers and tones continued, rising and falling as any ordinary conversation. She began to separate the sounds, frowning in concentration as she tried to understand the implications. Alix dragged fingers through her hair as if to untangle the threads of the patterns and realized how tangled her hair was. She took the silver comb Duncan had given her from her bodice and began to drag it through the snarls, hoping the pain would rid her of what she could not understand.

When her hair was smooth again she braided it into a single plait, tying the end with a strip of velvet torn from her gown. Its splendour was ruined; the silken overtunic was in shreds and the hem ragged and stained. But she cared not at all for the vanished elegance of her clothing; she wanted only to win back Duncan's regard.

When he came it was silently, without the warmth she

was accustomed to. His face was drawn as he settled the doorflap behind.

'You must come with me.'

'Where?'

'To Raissa.'

'Who is Raissa?' she asked, knowing it was not truly the answer she sought.

'She is the woman who will keep you until you go before the *shar tahl*, and Council.'

'Can I not stay with you?' she asked softly, hands folded in her lap.

Duncan knelt and shifted the wood resting in the small pavilion fire cairn. He took up a flint and fired the kindling.

'No,' he said at last. 'You would do better to stay elsewhere.'

Alix bit at her lip to fight back tears. 'Then what Finn said is true ... there is another woman you would have.'

His hand snapped a stout branch. After a moment he tossed the pieces on the fire, settling on his knees to face her through the rising smoke.

'When I came for you in Homana-Mujhar, Malina was *cheysula* to another man. I had put her from my mind. I thought only of you.'

She swallowed painfully. 'But now you can no longer put her from your mind.'

He moved to her, still kneeling, and took her face in his browned hands. 'I will not give you up.'

Alix stared at him, holding back the trembling in her bones. 'Then what do you say, Duncan?'

'Our *tahlmorra* is one, Alix. I feel it, even if you do not. I will not give you up.' He sighed, brow creased. 'Malina will be my *cheysula*, as I promised her when we were children, but you hold a place in my soul. *Mei jhas* have honors and rights within the clan ... there is no disgrace among the Cheysuli. I will keep you by me.'

Alix reached up and grasped his wrists firmly. Then

151

she jerked his hands away. 'What did you promise *me!* What did you say to me in the cave, when I offered to conceive your child so we would never be separated, even by your Council?'

'Alix—'

'I will be no man's light woman, Duncan . . . not even yours. It is a thing I cannot consider. . . . perhaps it is my *tainted* Homanan upbringing!' She glared at him. 'Do you think what I did is so easy for an untried girl?'

'Alix—'

'No.'

His hand reached for her but she avoided it, sitting back on her heels. After a moment he let his hand drop back to his thigh.

'What would you do, were you free to do it?' he asked.

She scowled at him, understanding what the delicate question asked. He was perfectly capable of denying her the right to leave the clan; she expected it. But she would try it nonetheless.

'I will go back to Carillon.'

Duncan stared at her. His face was a mask but he could not quite hide the cold anger in his yellow beast-eyes.

'To be light woman to a prince.'

'No. For his help.' Alix picked at a tear in her skirt, avoiding his eyes. 'He would help me in whatever I asked.'

'You cannot leave, small one,' he said gently. 'I understand your feelings, but I cannot allow you to go.'

Her hand clenched in the soft velvet. 'And your reason, clan-leader?'

Duncan's face softened. 'You might have conceived.'

Realization flooded her. Angrily she pressed a fist against her stomach. 'If I have conceived by you, I will name the child fatherless and raise it myself!'

Duncan went white, bolting to his feet like a wounded man. He caught her arm cruelly and dragged her to her feet, ignoring her cry of pain.

'If you have conceived by me, it is *mine!*'

She gritted her teeth and hissed at him. 'And do you not already have an unborn child, shapechanger? In the belly of the woman you will take as *cheysula!*'

'If it is mine I will keep it by me, just as I will if *you* bear me a child.'

She paled beneath the pain of his hand on her arm. 'You cannot take a child from its mother!'

'Here you live among the Cheysuli,' he said grimly. 'You will abide by our customs. If you will not have me then you will not, but if you have conceived the child is mine ... and a link in the prophecy.'

Alix spoke through the pain. 'And will you force me to do what my mother did ... run away? And bear my child in solitude?'

He drew her near. Alix stiffened rigidly as his arms went around her. It was no gentle lover's kiss. He was forcing her, as Finn had once, and she hated it. Warring emotions filled her soul and she struck out in bitterness, but her fist was trapped between his chest and her own. Slowly, against her will, it crept up to grasp his hair and pull him closer. Whatever power he had to inflict pain on her also inflicted something deeper, and instinctively she recognized her need of him.

'*Cheysula,*' he whispered against her lips.

Alix jerked free of him. 'I am *not!* You said you will choose another ... and I *will not* be your light woman!'

His mouth was compressed into a thin line. 'Then you will be *cheysula* to no man.'

She lifted her head. 'I will not.'

'Nor *mei jha.*'

'Nor *mei jha.*'

His eyes glittered strangely. 'Do you hold with your Cheysuli blood, Alix? Do you follow our customs?'

'I have little choice!'

'Do you accept them?'

'*Aye!*' she cried bitterly.

153

A muscle twitched in his jaw. 'Then you must accept *all* customs as your own.'

She glared back at him defiantly. 'I do.'

His hand darted to his belt and came up with his knife. Alix, terrified, spun to flee.

Duncan caught her by the heavy braid and in one slash severed it at her neck.

Alix, stumbling, gasped in shock as the hair fell away. Her hands clasped the ragged edges left to her. Duncan stood silently, dark braid hanging from his hand.

'What have you done?'

'A Cheysuli custom,' he said, deliberately casual. 'When a woman refuses her place within the clan as *cheysula* or *mei jha*, her hair is shorn so all men know her intent. This way she cannot change her mind.'

'I see a stranger before me . . .' she whispered.

He dropped the braid to the fire. It caught and smouldered, filling the pavilion with the stench of burning hair.

Duncan returned the knife to his belt and gestured toward the doorflap. 'Now, *rujholla*, I will escort you to Raissa.'

CHAPTER FIVE

Duncan took her to a brown pavilion that bore a gold-colored fox on its sides. He pulled the doorflap aside and gestured her to go in; Alix did so without meeting his eyes. She felt horribly shamed without the braid, for though she still felt more Homanan than Cheysuli Duncan's disparagement of her brought the implications of her braidless state home with real impact.

A woman stepped from behind a curtain dividing the pavilion into two sections. Her black hair was generously threaded with grey, but she had woven silver laces into multiple braids cunningly, fastening them to her head with an intricate silver comb. Her dress was fine-spun black wool threaded with scarlet ribbons at collar and cuffs, and a delicate chain of silver bells clasped her waist. She was no longer young, but she was a handsome woman. Her face reflected her Cheysuli blood with its high cheekbones, narrow nose and wide, smooth brow. Her yellow eyes were warm as she looked at Alix.

'Raissa, this is the girl,' Duncan said. 'Alix.'

The woman smiled at Alix and then looked steadily at Duncan. 'Who has shorn her hair?'

His jaw tightened. 'I have.'

Her brows lifted. 'But it is for Council to decide if she remains solitary.'

Alix heard the unspoken reproach and stole a glance at Duncan, surprised to see him bow his head in acceptance. Then it lifted again.

'She had made the decision for herself ... I merely acquiesced.'

'He did not tell me he would cut off my hair,' Alix said bitterly.

Raissa moved forward. The tiny bells chimed and winked in the folds of her black gown. Her slender hand touched the ragged curling tendrils at Alix's neck and jaw.

'I am sorry he acted so hastily. He should have explained the custom to you.' Her lips twitched with a half-hidden smile. 'I have never known Duncan to act without reason, so he must have been driven to it.'

'He did it out of jealousy.'

Raissa withdrew her hand. 'Duncan? Why do you say so?'

Alix slewed her eyes sideways to look at him. 'He told me he would ask for me in Council ... as his *cheysula*. Then — finding his former consort had conceived and was free again — he refused me honourable marriage and offered only to have me as his light woman.' She looked back at Raissa. 'Of course I refused.'

The woman was solemn. 'Among us a *mei jha* has honor, Alix. Here she is not treated like filth, as are the whores of Mujhara. We are too few, now, to place so much value on a woman's married or unmarried status. *Mei jha* is not a dishonourable position.'

Alix's stubborn chin came up. 'I have much left to learn of Cheysuli customs, but this will take the most trouble, I think.' She swallowed and set her jaw. 'I will not accept a lesser position with any man.'

The older woman smiled. 'Ah ... it is everything or nothing, with you. Well, perhaps you are not so wrong. Once I said the same to my *cheysul*.' She glanced at Duncan. 'All of this will be settled in Council. Until her birthlines are studied and she is formally accepted, I will

156

keep her by me and teach her what she must know. My thanks, Duncan, for bringing a lost one back to us.'

He said nothing, merely inclined his head and left the pavilion without looking at Alix. She stood there, bereft, hating Finn all the more for beginning it all with his abduction of her.

Raissa guided Alix to a grey pelt and gestured for her to sit. Alix did so, staring at her hands as they twisted themselves into the fabric of her gown. Raissa arranged her own skirts and sat down before her.

'Duncan would not offer unfairly,' she said quietly. 'I know the man . . . he is not one to trouble a girl that way.'

'He did not know about Malina until we arrived,' Alix admitted. 'But Finn wasted no time in making certain his brother learned of it quickly enough.'

'Finn has ever been jealous of Duncan,' Raissa said.

'Why?'

She spread her hands eloquently. 'An elder son is ever favored by a *jehan*. It grates particularly hard when your own blood father favors a foster son. Hale treated them equally, but Duncan matured quickly. He felt the weight of the *qu'mahlin* more. And it has cost him, though Finn does not fully understand that.' Raissa's eyes were expressive. 'And now, Alix, you have given Finn reason for jealousy again.'

'*I* have?'

Raissa looked at her solemnly. 'Would you have Finn as your *cheysul*!'

'No. Never.'

'You see? You will have Duncan, or none. It cannot be easy for Finn to know once again his *rujholli* takes precedence.' She smiled. 'Wanting Duncan, you could not want Finn. I know that. They are too dissimilar. But Finn is not so bad as he seems, Alix . . . he might make a fine *cheysul*.'

'Finn stole me. He would have forced me, had Storr not kept him from it. How can you say he would be a good husband?'

Raissa smiled. 'There is much of men you do not understand. But you must learn that for yourself; it is not my place to teach you such things.'

Alix recalled the determination in Finn's face when he said he would have her. And now she was no longer promised to Duncan.

'Raissa!' she said, suddenly frightened. 'They would not force me to take Finn, would they?'

Raissa glanced down at her skirts, settling the tiny bells into perfect symmetry. 'This will be hard for you, I know. Particularly since you were raised Homanan and feel no loyalty for your true race.' The yellow eyes came up. 'We are too few, now. The clans have been destroyed, save for us, and even now Shaine works to slay what remains of us. We need children . . . we need women who will bear them.' Light flashed off the silver in her hair. 'You are Cheysuli, Alix. You must take your place in the future of the clan . . . in its *tahlmorra*. You must bear children for us. If you will not have Duncan, or even Finn, then it will have to be another warrior.'

'You would *force* me!'

Raissa reached out and grabbed her hands, holding them even as Alix sought to withdraw. 'No woman wishes to be used as breeding stock, Alix! Children are a gift of the gods . . . not coin with which to barter! But we have too few . . . we are dying. You will not be forced to lay with a man you cannot abide, but the censure of the clan is no light burden to bear.'

'Then I will go back,' Alix said flatly. 'I will go back to the croft.'

Raissa squeezed her hands. 'No. You must stay. By the gods, Alix, you are Hale's daughter! We need his blood.'

'Through Finn?' Alix disengaged her hands. 'He is my half-brother.'

'Aye, but you were raised apart. Hale's blood must come back into the clan.'

'Then tell *Finn* to get himself children!' she said angrily.

'He would do so willingly enough ... were you his *cheysula*. Or *mei jha*,' Raissa said steadily.

'What if I have already conceived?' Alix asked in desperation.

Raissa's eyes sharpened. 'Already conceived ... you have lain with Duncan?'

Alix nodded silently, suddenly apprehensive. 'Was it wrong?' she whispered. 'Is it wrong to lay with a clan-leader while he rules?'

The older woman smiled. 'A clan-leader does not rule ... we have no kings, Alix. And no, it was not wrong. Do you think Duncan keeps himself chaste? It would be a burden no man should carry.'

Alix looked away, embarrassed. 'Then what will happen?'

Raissa sighed. 'Well, it would change things. The Council might be willing to let you remain solitary ... they would respect your shorn hair, regardless of the reasons for it. You would have the freedom you desire if you refuse to take a *cheysul*, and have already conceived. But that is still a Council decision.'

'I should never have come,' Alix said. 'I should never have allowed Duncan to take me out of Mujhara.'

'This is your home.'

'I should have let Carillon take me back to the croft.'

'It will not be so harsh — I promise — when you are accustomed. Alix, we are your people.'

Alix looked at the woman and saw the innate strength and pride reflected in her Cheysuli face. She put a hand to her own, tracing the identical high cheekbones. Her skin was not so bronze; her hair not so dark; and her eyes amber, not beast-yellow ... but she knew herself Cheysuli.

She sighed. 'Where is Malina's tent?'

Raissa's eyes flickered but she said nothing of her surprise. 'Near the gates. The blue one with Borrs's *lir*-symbol, a mountain cat. There is only one.'

Alix took the silver comb out of her bodice and stared

159

at it. Then she met the woman's eyes and smiled. 'I have something to return. My thanks for your kindness.'

Raissa nodded and Alix left the brown pavilion.

Alix found the blue tent and jerked the entrance flap aside, somehow not surprised to find Duncan there. But Malina did surprise her.

The girl did not look Cheysuli. Her hair was dark blonde and her eyes blue. She lacked the feral, feline grace of the true Cheysuli woman, but she was beautiful nonetheless.

Duncan rose to his feet. Alix moved swiftly to the woman and held out the comb. 'This is yours.'

'Mine?' Malina asked in surprise.

Alix saw she did not show her pregnancy yet; no swelling belly evident beneath the soft green gown banded with amber beadwork and bronze platelets.

'He let me use it because I had none ... when I still had hair enough to need it.' She glanced at Duncan a moment, then looked back at Malina. 'But it is yours. He said so, once.' Alix put the comb into the girl's hand and silently left the pavilion.

Duncan caught her before she had gone more than five steps. He swung her gently to face him, one hand going tenderly to her shorn hair.

'*Cheysula*, forgive me. I had no right.'

His gentle voice nearly finished her. 'I have no claim to that title, Duncan. You have given it to another.'

His hands cupped her jaw and lifted her face so he could see her welling tears. His own face was stark and tight. 'You have only to say it, Alix. It is yours to decide. We would not be happy apart.'

'I would not be happy sharing you.' She swallowed heavily. 'I doubt Malina would care for it, for all that.'

'Malina knows I have asked for you as *mei jha*.'

'She *knows*?'

His hand smoothed back a ragged tendril of hair. 'It is often done among us, Alix.'

160

'I cannot.' A tear spilled over and slipped down her cheek.

'And if you have conceived?'

She closed her eyes and put her forehead against his chest. 'Why must you take her back? What I have done is no light thing for me, and now it is all for naught. Duncan . . . I did not know I would have to fight a woman and an unborn child. I thought I had only to think of the Council.'

'I am sorry, small one. I did not intend this.'

Alix sucked in a trembling breath. 'They will try to make me take Finn as a husband.'

His hands stiffened. 'What do you say?'

'Raissa told me. It is doubtful I can keep my wish to remain apart.' Alix shivered. 'Unless I have conceived. Raissa said it would change matters.'

'Aye, you could live apart with the child . . . or become *mei jha* to me. Which would you choose?'

She lifted her head. 'I have said I will be *mei jha* to no man, Duncan. Even you.'

'And Finn?'

'I want no one but you.'

'I have said how you may have me.'

'And *I* have said no.' She stepped back from him and smiled sadly. 'Perhaps Finn will have the forcing of me yet.'

'Alix . . .'

'Duncan, I know there is much of the Cheysuli I cannot comprehend. But there are things in me *you* cannot comprehend. Do not ask me again to be your *mei jha*, for I will not.'

She waited for his answer. When he said nothing at all, remote and unattainable before her, Alix turned and walked away.

Alix felt the weight of her decision as she walked slowly back to Raissa's pavilion. She knew, instinctively, Duncan wanted her as much as she him, but the pride inherent in his race would not allow him to come after her.

161

Nor will mine allow me to accept his offer.

She considered it carefully again, as she had since Duncan first suggested she be his *mei jha*. The shiver of distaste that ran briefly through her body once more told her she could not be so free with the man she loved. It was not a Homanan custom.

If I cannot have him to myself, I will not have him at all.

But the decision, once made, gave her no contentment.

She slowly became aware of the voices as she walked. They were different from those she had heard spoken by Cheysuli in the Keep; these were not sounds her ears heard but what her mind sensed. Alix fingered her brow as if touch might tell her what it is, but no answer came. Whispers floated through her awareness, drifting in wisps of tonal patterns similar to what she heard as words from Cai and Storr.

Alix stopped abruptly, staring around to search for those who tormented her, but no one seemed to pay her mind except passing curiosity. The Cheysuli, she had learned, did not exhibit the open emotions of the Homanans.

She pressed hands against her head as the oppression increased. No one said anything to her, yet she was so sensitized to the gentle waves of sound in her mind that she thought she had gone mad. Alix stopped walking and waited for the madness to take her completely.

Liren, do not fight so, said Storr's gentle voice.

Alix opened her eyes and saw the wolf before her. She gasped and knelt, putting grasping hands to his neck ruff.

Storr, is this a punishment? She wailed silently. *A curse?*

It is a gift, liren, from the gods. It is only new to you.

Alix glanced up as a shadow passed over her. Cai circled in the air, dipping and playing among the currents.

Liren, he said, *you must learn to control your gifts.*

Control them! she cried, startled.

Come with us, Storr said gently. *Come with us, liren, and we will teach you.*

They took her out of the Keep, to a huge oak scored with an old lightning-wound. The charred hole left behind was enough to hide her, and Alix crawled into it as if seeking security in a mother's womb. Storr lay down at her feet and Cai perched on an overhead limb.

'What must I learn?' she asked aloud.

To accept, Cai said. *Not to rail against your tahlmorra.*

'You are Duncan's *lir*,' she accused. 'You will support whatever he says.'

I am his lir but I am also myself. I am not a dog, liren, who answers its master's voice with unthinking loyalty. I am of the lir, and we are chosen by the gods.

Storr's tone agreed. *We are not echoes of those we bond with, or I would have all of my lir's faults*

Alix laughted softly and stretched out a hand to caress Storr's silver pelt. 'You have none of Finn's faults.'

Then will you listen?

Her hand fell away. 'Aye.'

Cai mantled once and settled more comfortably. *You bear the Old Blood, liren. It has gone out of the clan. You will bring it back.*

'By bearing children.'

Aye, Cai agreed. *How else does a female give more to the world?*

Alix scowled at her bare feet.

Storr's eyes glinted. *It is not that you do not want children, liren*, he said. *It is that you wish to choose who will father them.*

'Aye!' she shouted. 'Aye, you have the right of *that*!'

We cannot tell you who to take, Cai said calmly, ignoring her outburst. *That is for you to decide. But we can aid you accept your tahlmorra, and the gifts the gods have given you.*

'What have they given me?'

The ability to hear us.

Alix frowned. 'I have ever heard you. From the beginning.'

But you hear us all, liren, Storr said. *Each lir in the Keep.*

You are not mad, Cai said reassuringly. *It is only you hear what no one else hears.*

'I hear . . .' she whispered distantly.

The weight in your mind, Storr told her. *It is the voices you hear, when the lir converse. You must set it aside until it is needed.*

'And if I cannot?'

Then it could drive you mad, Cai said at last.

Alix closed her eyes. 'It *is* a curse.'

No, said Storr. *No more than the ability to take lir-shape.*

Her eyes snapped open. 'I could *shapechange?*'

You have the Old Blood, Cai said quietly. *And with it comes all the old gifts.*

Alix set a hand against the tree as if to steady herself. Her thoughts ranged far ahead of what she had just heard, conjuring visions of herself in the shape of any animal she wished. Then she frowned.

'I have no *lir.*'

You need none, Storr told her. *That is what the Old Blood means . . . freedom to speak with all lir and assume any shape.*

'By the gods!' she whispered. 'How is it possible?'

Others have also asked that, Storr said, sounding suspiciously like Finn. *But they have not been the get of the gods.*

She slanted him a sharp glance. 'No one else in the clan can do this?'

No. It is a thing long lost to us, for the Cheysuli have taken Homanan women to increase their numbers. It has weakened the gifts. Storr paused. *It is for you to bring the Old Blood back.*

'We begin again,' she said suspiciously. 'You have said this before.'

That does not make it less true, Cai commented.

She craned her head to stare up at the hawk. 'Then teach me,' she said. 'Show me what it is to shapechange.'

First you must decide which of us to bond with.

164

She considered it. 'Flight must be difficult. Perhaps it would be better if I remained earthbound, this first time.

You are wise, liren. My lir near broke his arm his first time in the air.

Alix, struck by a vision of Duncan having difficulties, laughed aloud and nodded. 'Then I will be a wolf.'

Storr approved. *Then listen, liren. He paused. Your sight, while good, has become secondary to your ability to smell. Allow yourself to judge the world by scent, liren. The earth, trees, insects, worms, birds, leaves, pollen, breezes. And more. Do not depend solely on mere sight, for it can fail. Think with your nose.*

She concentrated, closing her eyes and trying to separate individual scents.

Now you must feel the damp earth beneath your paws; mud clinging to your claws. Be wary of sharp stones that can trap themselves between your pads, and thorns that pierce the tender webbing between toes.

Alix put her hands to the mouldy, leafy ground and felt the dampness.

Winter is coming. Your coat must be thick and warm. A heavy layer of fat forms beneath your skin, thickening your undercoat. It itches, but you know it will mean added warmth in the coldest season. You tail grows bushier, more luxuriant, and you are lovely, liren.

She was.

You have the endurance to travel many leagues in a single day, without food and little water. Your sinews and nerves are strongly knit and your heart is large. You are young and strong and joyous in life.

Alix felt warm blood pulsing through her veins; felt the vibrancy and exhilaration of youth. She opened her eyes and met Storr's on a level, realizing she knelt in the leaves like any four-footed creature.

The world spun. It picked her up like a leaf on a whirl-wind and turned her upside down.

Alix put a hand out toward Storr, silently asking his help, but she saw only a padded, furred paw with black nails.

She cried out, and heard her voice echoing in the woods like the howl of a lonely wolf.

Disorientation took her. Dizzily she clasped her head in her hands, conscious they were human once more.

'Storr . . .' she said weakly.

It was too fast, liren. You must not fear the shapechange. You cannot harm yourself in lir-shape, but it is not wise to shift too quickly. The mind cannot adjust.

Slowly her stomach settled itself. Her eyes saw clearly again and the ache in her head died to nothingness. She smiled wearily, triumphantly, and looked into the wolf's wise eyes.

'I have done it.'

It will be better, after this.

Perhaps, Cai said gently, *you will amaze even my lir.*

CHAPTER SIX

Alix sat hunched on the broken stump of a felled tree, toes digging through the velvet of her court slippers into the soft ground. The slippers were torn and stained, nearly useless, for they had been made for Shaine's palace and not the wildness of a Cheysuli Keep. Her ruined gown had been changed for a woolen dress of palest orange; her ragged hair trimmed so that it did not straggle so much, but she had retained the slippers to recall her brief moment of glory.

The glory had gone. Only in her dreams did she recall the richness of Homana-Mujhar and the fine glittering city surrounding its rose-coloured walls. Her days left her no time to think, for the hours were filled with Raissa's words as she taught Alix the customs she must know. Her hands were never still; she needs must learn how to weave a tapestry, how to tend two fires at once, how to cook Cheysuli dishes ... and how to prepare herself to take a *cheysul*. The *shar tahl* had yet to see her personally but Raissa said there was no need; the man spent his time researching the birthlines to trace her history and ancestors so that no one could question her birth.

They bind me ... she thought. *They seek to bind me tightly within the coils of their prophecy, so I have no choice but to do as they wish.*

Alix smoothed the soft wool over her knees, fingering the nap. She had been shocked to find the skill so evident in Cheysuli craftsmanship. She had grown up believing them little better than barbarians without the niceties of Homanan culture and crafts, but five days with the clan had already altered her perceptions. Their fabrics were close-woven and fine, dyed muted shades of every color and often beaded with semi-precious stones or brightened with gleaming metals.

And the jewelery ... Alix realized even the finest of Mujhara's goldsmiths could not match the skill of Cheysuli craftsmanship. The warriors wore thick *lir*-bands on their arms and a single earring, but their talents stretched farther than that. Already Alix had seen small casks filled with delicate ornaments fit to bedeck any king or queen.

A strange thing ... she thought, *that a race so dedicated to war can also make such delicate, beautiful things.*

The hands came over her shoulders and rested there, one thumb caressing her neck. The intimacy of the touch brought home all the longing she felt for Duncan, for he had not seen her except in passing. Alix lowered her head and stared blindly at the leaf-carpeted ground, wishing Duncan would not play with her emotions so.

'I have missed you,' he said.

Alix stiffened and spun out from under the hands, leaping up and stumbling away. Finn's hands slowly dropped back to his sides.

Her breath came harshly, whistling through her constricted throat. One hand spread across her neck, guarding it; the other tangled itself in her skirts.

'What is it you want of me?' she asked.

Finn's lips twitched. 'That, I think, you know already.'

Alix lowered her hand and stood stiffly before him. 'Why have you come?'

'To speak with you.' He sat down on her deserted stump and stretched out his legs. Thigh muscles bunched and rolled beneath the snug fit of his leather leggings. His face still bore the thread of pinkish scar tissue over one black eyebrow.

'What would you and I have to speak about?'

'You and I,' he said quietly.

Alix frowned at him. 'I do not understand.'

Finn sighed and gesture. 'I will not leap on you, *mei jha*, I promise. But I cannot speak to you if you persist in being so frightened of me. Your eyes are like those of a doe when facing a hunter.' He smiled. 'Sit, if you will.'

Alix hesitated, still defiant before him, but she was caught by the lightness in his tone. He had shed the ironic mocking she hated so much. Carefully she settled down in the leaves and spread her skirts around her folded legs.

'Council has been called for this night.'

She felt blood leave her face. 'Council . . .'

'At sunset.'

'What is the subject of it?'

'All manner of things; many of which concern you.'

Alix bit at her lip. 'I thought it might be that.'

'I have come to save you some trouble.'

Her chin lifted. 'You do not save me trouble, Finn; you make it.'

He had the grace to color. 'For you . . . perhaps I did. I admit it.' He smiled crookedly. 'But admitting is not an apology, and I will never apologize for following my judgment.'

Alix stared at him, growing more baffled by the moment. 'Finn, you had best be plain with me.'

He pulled his legs in and sat upright on the stump. 'You did not conceive.'

Heat coursed through her face as she went rigid. 'What do *you* know of it?'

His eyes were amused, though he did not laugh at her. 'Among the Cheysuli such things are not kept locked behind doors. We are too few to look upon it as a woman's mystery. It is a reason to rejoice, Alix, when a

169

Cheysuli woman has conceived.' He paused as she stared hard at the ground. 'Raissa told me when I asked this morning. There is no child.'

'Raissa had no right to tell you anything, nor you the right to ask.'

'I had every right. I intend to ask for your clan-rights in Council this night.'

Alix's head jerked up. 'No!'

'Duncan will not have you,' he said ruthlessly. 'That has been made plain to all of us. He will take Malina, as he has ever intended. There is no hope left to you.'

'There is ever hope,' she said fiercely, though she knew he was right.

He moved off the stump and knelt in the leaves before her, catching her hands before she could escape his closeness.

'You have said you will be no man's *mei jha*. That is your Homanan blood speaking, but I will respect it. I am not entirely blind to your needs, Alix.' He smiled at her ironically. 'I will sacrifice a part of my freedom.'

She tried to break free of his clasping hands but could not. Once again she felt helpless, trapped, and the familiar fright rose up. She knelt before him, trembling, hands icy cold in the warmth of his.

'Finn . . . I cannot. There can never be peace between us. You made that impossible from the very first day. I would hardly be a docile, accommodating *cheysula*.'

His grin flashed. 'If I wanted that sort of *cheysula*, I would never ask for you.'

She managed to glare at him. 'Then why *do* you ask for me?'

'I have wanted you from the beginning,' he said deliberately. 'I will take you however I can get you.'

Alix recoiled from him, finally breaking free. 'I would never take you . . . *never*! By all the gods, Finn . . . you are my half-brother! You *stole* me! You took my life and destroyed it, and now you seek to make a new one I want no part of. It is Duncan I want . . . *not you*!'

170

His face remained set and closed, but the color drained slowly until he resembled a dead man. But the intensity in his eyes showed his blood still ran beneath his flesh.

'Duncan wants Malina,' he said coldly. 'Not you. Else he would renounce the old oath he made to her so long ago, and take you as his *cheysula*.' He shrugged dismissively. 'You will grow out of wanting Duncan, my Homanan *rujholla*, if only because such desires die if not fed.'

'There is ever hope,' she said blankly.

'There is none,' he told her. 'You turned from Carillon to Duncan. In time, you will turn from my *rujholli* to me.'

'You cannot *make* me!' she cried.

'I will not have to.' Finn glanced down at his hand as he idly separated the leaves by colors. 'I spoke to the *shar tahl*. You will be acknowledged at Council, and formally accepted into the clan. With that acceptance comes clan-rights, which any warrior may ask for.' He looked at her. 'Others may ask for you, Alix, because you are young and healthy and new to the clan. But I think you will take me, because — for all that has happened between us — you *know* me.'

'I will take Duncan,' she said firmly, knowing it as a weapon against Finn. 'Duncan.'

Finn's mouth twisted. 'I also spoke with Duncan about your clan-rights, *rujholla*. He is clan-leader. It is his place to know what clan-rights will be asked, and who will do the asking.'

She stared at him. 'I do not understand.'

'A clan-leader can ever deny a warrior the woman he wishes. Taking a *cheysula* is a formal thing. The clan-leader must give his permission.'

Alix felt cold and hollow, and very much alone. 'And Duncan . . .?'

'He gave me permission, Alix. He will not interfere.'

Duncan! she cried within her soul.

'If it is not me, it will be another,' Finn said gently.

Alix looked at him. For the first time he spoke softly to her, without the mocking mannerisms she had come to expect. She summoned up the image of him shape-changing before her, but it no longer frightened her. She had her own ability, though no one knew of it yet. Part of him, she knew, must be like Duncan. If he was harsh and taunting and impulsive, it was because Duncan was not, and Finn must make his own way.

She moved forward on her knees, sitting before him with leaves spread all around them. Alix slowly touched his hand, then pulled it into her own. She saw the startled flicker in his eyes.

'Finn,' she said softly. '*Rujho* . . .' She swallowed and smiled. 'Take me home.'

His hand stiffened and jerked away. 'Home . . .'

'To the croft,' she said. 'To Torrin. To the life I know.'

His face masked itself. 'This is your home. I will take you nowhere.'

'Finn . . . she said softly, 'I give you a chance to pay back what you took from me. Take me home.'

Finn got to his feet and looked down on her as she knelt in the leaves. 'I could not let you go,' he said clearly. 'Not now, when you are nearly mine. You forget, *rujholla* . . . I stole you because I wanted you, I will not give up so easily.'

'But if Duncan said no —'

'Duncan said aye,' he reminded her. 'Duncan has said I may have you.'

She stared up at him. 'And if I refuse you? If I stand up in Council and say I will not have you?'

The mocking smile was back. 'Do not forget our third gift, *mei jha*. What you will not do willingly, you may be forced to do.'

'Please,' she said.

Finn looked down on her pleading face. 'No,' he said, and left her.

Alix stood outside the slate-colored pavilion and closed her eyes, summoning her courage. Finally she scratched at the doorflap and waited. Duncan called for her to enter.

She hesitated, then pulled the doorflap aside. It dropped behind her as she stood there, letting her eyes adjust to the dim light. Duncan was hunched over a low worktable, a slender metal stylus held in one hand as he scraped carefully at gleaming gold.

'Aye?' he asked, without looking up.

Alix wet her lips. 'Duncan.'

The line of his shoulders and arms stiffened. For a moment he continued working on the gold ornament, then he set it aside and dropped his tool down. It rattled against the gold and wood, rolling across the table. Alix watched it move, unable to meet his eyes.

'I have come because you are clan-leader,' she said carefully.

'Sit down, Alix.'

She knelt on the other side of his worktable, still not looking at him. Her heels dug into her thighs as she folded her legs under her. Finally she brought her head up.

'Finn came to me. He said he has spoken to you; that he will ask for my clan-rights at Council.'

He wore his solemn clan-leader face. 'Aye.'

Her breath was unsteady as she drew it in. 'Duncan . . . I do not wish for Finn. You know that.'

'It has been settled,' he said remotely. 'And if you bring this up again, I cannot be only a clan-leader to you.'

Alix smiled at the unspoken warning. At least he was not totally indifferent to her. 'I have not come to ask you to reconsider what you offer to me,' she told him. 'You have made it plain what you will do, and I am done begging for more.'

His eyes flickered. 'Then what do you seek, Alix?'

'I want you to withdraw your permission to Finn. I

173

want nothing to do with him. We could never make a marriage between us ... and I think it might be the death of one of us if we were forced. I think it would be *his* death ... not mine.'

Duncan smiled briefly, though he banished it quickly enough. 'It would not be a tedious match.'

'It will not be a match at all,' she said darkly. 'Duncan, withdraw your permission.'

'On what grounds?'

She scowled at him. 'I do not want him!'

He shrugged. 'Those are not grounds. That is merely contrariness speaking, and women are prone to that.'

Alix stared at him. 'You cannot *want* me to take him!'

His face twisted. 'No,' he said at last. 'I do not want you to take him. But to refuse him because of that speaks of prejudice, and a clan-leader cannot be so petty. Alix, the match will be good for the clan.'

'Is that all you can say?' she demanded. 'Can you only see the clan, and not me? By the gods, Duncan, I thought we had more between us. What has become of this precious *tahlmorra*?'

Color surged into his face, then slowly fell away. 'Will you accept another warrior?'

'You know there is only one warrior I will accept.'

'Then the choice is yours,' he said softly. 'Be *mei jha* to me ... or *cheysula* to another man.'

'*Why?*'

'I promised Malina when we were eight years old,' he said quietly. 'A Cheysuli oath is binding.'

'*She* broke it.'

'She did not think I meant what I said.' Duncan touched the golden ornament on his table. 'She went to Borrs because she thought I would change my mind. When I did not ... she was fairly caught. The clan-leader had given his permission for Borrs to ask for her clan-rights, and once done that is not rescinded. It is binding.' He looked at her bleakly. 'I did what you have done. I asked the clan-leader to withdraw his

174

permission to Borrs, so that I could ask for Malina. He would not do it ... and they were formally acknowledged before Council.'

Alix frowned. 'But I thought you were clan-leader, and that was why you would not take a *cheysula*.'

He looked weary. 'Tiernan died of a sickness. It took months. All knew I would be his successor, so I made my decision to remain solitary before he died. But he was still clan-leader. And when he died, Malina was already *cheysula* to Borrs.'

'But the child ...'

'It could be mine. It could be Borrs's.' He sighed faintly. 'We are not a race that places much honor on fidelity.'

She recoiled. 'She was *wed* to him!'

Duncan smiled. 'I did not think you would understand.'

'Do you mean you are willing to take Malina and myself, and yet may also seek other women?'

He frowned thoughtfully. 'I cannot say what I will do. What man could?'

This new side of him shocked her. She peered into his face uncertainly. 'Duncan ... do you mean this?'

He shrugged. 'I have never been a man for all women. One suffices. I doubt I would trouble you that way.'

'Duncan!'

'Alix, she carries a child that may be mine.'

'And I do not,' she said dully.

'Alix—'

'If she had not conceived, would you be so ready to make her your *cheysula*?'

He looked away. 'If Borrs had lived, and the child still mine ...' Duncan sighed deeply. 'I think I would have said nothing.'

She stared at him. 'Then it is the *child*...'

'I have ever cared for Malina,' he said steadily.

'And if the child is not yours?'

His jaw tightened. 'I cannot take that chance.'

'Yet she is willing to share you with me?'

'I made it a condition,' he said softly. 'I said I would take her for the sake of the child ... and if she would accept you as my *mei jha*.'

'Duncan!'

'Small one, had she said no I would have made you my *cheysula*. But there is much between Malina and myself, and I could not forsake her so easily.'

'But you forsake me ... you give me to *Finn*!'

'Because he has asked, and there is no reason to deny him. It is not for me to do.'

'I will not have him. I have told him that, and now I tell you.' She fisted her hands in her skirt. 'I am Cheysuli, clan-leader, and you cannot compel me.'

'We will do whatever we must, Alix,' he said gently. 'Even to one of our own.'

She rose slowly, shaking her skirts into order. Somehow she summoned a smile. 'You cannot force *me*, Duncan. That you will see.'

She turned on her heel and left him.

BOOK III
'The Cheysula'

CHAPTER ONE

Alix stood before Raissa's pavilion and called Cai and
Storr to her. The *lir* came and accompanied her to the
lightning-scored tree, saying nothing, though she was
sure they knew what she planned to do. She needed
practice in assuming *lir*-shape; if she wanted to impress
upon the Council the magnitude of her abilities, she had
better do it competently.

Cai perched above her on a stout limb, preening his
feathers into perfection. Storr sat down and watched
her from wise amber eyes.

'Help me,' she said.

You need only think yourself a wolf, he said, *and you will be
one.*

She recalled the words he had used before, the
sensations coursing through her body as she made the
transition. A part of it still frightened her, but she also
recognized it for the gift it was. And it might keep her
from Finn, if she showed Council what she could do.

Alix opened her eyes and crawled out of the deep
hollow, shaking her shaggy red-grey coat. Sounds came
more sharply to her twitching ears, and her nose told
her more than she dreamed possible. She smiled, baring
gleaming teeth.

Storr and the young wolf-bitch shouldered through
the underbrush. Alix delighted in the feel and sensation

of things she normally paid no mind to. She found she did not lose awareness of herself as a person, rather that knowledge and awareness were enhanced and extended until she could comprehend both life processes. Her intelligence was neither diminished nor improved; she merely understood things as both human and wolf.

She had lost her human speech but needed no words with the *lir*. Thoughts from Cai and Storr still formed themselves in patterns easily comprehended. With an uprush of pride and ecstasy she knew in full measure what it was to be Cheysuli.

And in that same instant she understood why Shaine the Mujhar hated her race.

He thinks the Cheysuli will use their arts in retribution for the qu'mahlin. He will never rescind it!

Now you fully understand, liren, Cai chimed. *Shaine cannot forgive himself his own pride, or his own fear.*

Alix, new to her wolf senses and lost in contemplation, did not hear the snapping of twigs in the underbrush. Cai winged higher and Storr slipped into the shadows, but she — glowing ruddy-grey in vibrant health — provided an inviting target to the mounted hunter.

A bough cracked beneath the horse's hooves. Alix spun around. Alarm spread through her sinews and charged her thudding heart with shock.

She twisted, leaping into the air, yelping in fear and pain as the arrow sliced into the ruff at her neck.

The hunter, dismounting to locate the downed wolf-bitch, parted the underbrush and found himself looking into the dilated eyes of a woman.

He stumbled back a step as she clasped the flesh at the top of her left shoulder, blood welling between her fingers. She gripped the arrow in her free hand and threw it at him, trembling with shock and pain.

Alix's words tumbled over themselves as she cursed him, hardly able to speak through the violence of clenched teeth. He turned and crashed back through the underbrush to his horse.

She moaned softly and rocked on her knees, one arm clasping her bleeding shoulder, the other stretched across her roiling stomach.

You must return to the Keep! Storr said in alarm as he melted out of the trees.

'I c-cannot . . .' she gasped.

Cai came down to a nearby branch, agitated and mantling. *Liren, you must get to the Keep.*

Alix could only force out a weakened denial and slipped bonelessly to the leafy ground, blood spilling rapidly from her shoulder.

She was aware of pain when the arms took her from the ground and cradled her against a broad chest. Alix fought to open her eyes, achieved it, and stared dimly at Duncan's face. It was drawn and pale, and in his eyes she saw fear.

'Duncan . . .'

'Be silent, small one. I will take you to the Keep.'

'How did you know?' she asked weakly.

'The *lir* came. Cai told me.'

'What of Council?'

His arms tightened. 'Be silent, Alix! I will not have you weaken yourself with such worries.'

He took her to Raissa's pavilion and settled her on her thick furred pallet, shifting her limbs carefully. Though her mind was sluggish and strangely dull she was conscious of his gentleness and concern. But when she tried to ask him another question he placed a hand over her mouth.

'If you will allow it, small one, I will let you feel the healing arts of the Cheysuli. But it must be soon.'

Her ears rang and her bones felt heavy as stone. Her eyes saw only fuzziness. 'I would not consign myself to death,' she whispered as he removed his hand. 'Do what you will.'

He settled himself next to her pallet, crossing his legs. He did not touch her, but his eyes were fixed on her with

181

absolute possessiveness and determination.

Suddenly she found herself trembling, unable to feel the soft furs beneath her or the warmth of the blood still spilling from her shoulder. Only air was beneath her, and when she tensed against its feather touch she felt the earth under her hands. Her fingers curled against it, clawing into its softness. It enveloped her in rich gentleness, entering the pores of her skin.

She opened her mouth to scream but could find no voice. A blurring came into her mind, fogging her eyes, stopping her ears. She sought to lift a trembling hand and found her body would not answer her.

Duncan's hand smoothed hair from her damp forehead. 'It is done, small one. Rest yourself. I promise you will be better.'

Her eyes cleared slowly. She saw him by her, himself again, though he looked weary. 'Duncan . . .'

'Hush,' he said softly, running a gentle hand over the wounded shoulder. 'It is healed, but it will take time for you to recover your strength. The earth magic does not give back everything.'

'What did you do?'

'I summoned the healing touch of the earth. It is magic that resides in all the lands, but only the Cheysuli may summon it.'

'I will miss Council,' she said.

'Aye. It will take time for your strength to return.'

Her eyes closed. 'It is better so. I have no wish to see you ask for Malina.'

'Or have Finn ask for you?'

Her eyes flew open. 'Duncan . . . do not tease me. Not about this.'

'I do not tease,' he said gently. 'And I should not long prolong this for either of us.' He took her right hand and laced his fingers into hers. 'Finn will not be asking for your clan-rights this night. Or ever.'

'You have refused him?'

'There is another warrior who takes precedence over Finn.'

'Another!' Her fingers stiffened. 'Duncan—'

His free hand covered her mouth again. 'Listen to me, small one; do not be so ready to fight me when there is no need.' He smiled at her. 'I went to see Malina after you had left. I had every intention of asking for her clan-rights this night. But she let fall the truth of the child . . . that it was Borrs's, and she knew it. She said nothing because she did not wish to lose me to you.' His expression was wry. 'I had not thought myself the sort of man two women would want so badly, but I will not task myself over it. I will simply accept the wisdom of the gods.'

Alix grinned at him, amused by his masculine assurance. Her fingers tightened in his. 'If you will not have Malina—'

'—I will have you.' He bent and kissed her tenderly. 'If you will take me.'

'There is no question,' she whispered, fighting against drowsiness. 'None.'

He put something in her hand, curling her fingers around the coolness of metal. Alix opened her eyes and stared at the thing. It was a curving neck torque of purest gold, beaten into hundreds of gleaming facets. At the lowest point stretched the fluted wings of a soaring hawk, and in its talons was clasped a glowing lump of dark amber.

'It is a Cheysuli custom,' he said. 'The warrior offers the woman a torque, to signify the bond, and if she accepts it they are considered wed.'

'What of these clan-rights you speak of?'

Duncan smiled. 'I will ask for them formally in Council, but it would not hurt anything if we preceded the formality a little. If you are willing.'

She ran a trembling finger over the gleaming hawk, down to the amber. 'I must ask it, Duncan.'

'Then ask.'

183

'You said your race does not place so much honor on fidelity.'

He smiled. 'I thought it might be that. Small one, you need fear nothing. While it is true the Cheysuli do not often keep themselves to one woman, it does not mean we *cannot*. I respect your Homanan ideals, *cheysula*. I do not intend to give you reason to cast me out of your heart.'

She closed her eyes to hide her tears. 'Duncan ... if this is the *tahlmorra* you spoke of ... I think I can follow it faithfully.'

He bent and kissed her brow. 'Hush. I must leave you now, for Council, but I will return. Rest, *cheysula*.'

She wanted to keep him by her but let him go. When he had left her Raissa came and knelt, covering her with a soft blanket.

'Now you see the strength in him, Alix. For all Shaine's *qu'mahlin* changed his life, it has made him a warrior.'

She felt herself drifting. 'You speak as if you have known him longer than any.'

Raissa smiled. 'I have. I bore him.'

Alix's eyes snapped open. 'You are Duncan's mother?'

'And Finn's.'

She stared at the woman blankly. 'You did not say ...' She thought it over. 'Nor did they.'

'There was no need. But have I not proven a good ear for you to rant of Finn's arrogance while you silently longed for Duncan?'

Alix closed her eyes. 'You shame me, lady. I have said things no mother should hear.'

Raissa laughed. 'I know all of Finn's faults, small one. And you fool yourself if you think Duncan has none.'

'I have not seen any,' Alix said distinctly.

The woman laughed again and smoothed back her shortened hair. 'Only because you will not let yourself. Have you not lost most of your hair because of his jealousy?'

Alix smiled through her exhaustion. 'Perhaps that is one fault I can accept.'

'Rest now, small one,' Raissa said gently. 'He will come back to you.'

Alix struggled for awareness a moment longer. 'I am Hale's daughter, lady. How can you show kindness to the daughter of the man who left you for another?'

'It does not matter, Alix. That is all in the past.'

'I know how Finn hates,' Alix said quietly. 'I would not have you hate me like that.'

'Hale was a Cheysuli warrior. He conducted himself according to his lights. It is the custom among us, Alix, you are welcome in my pavilion. If I can have Hale back through you, I am glad of it.'

'Raissa—'

'Hush. If you wish, we will speak of this another time. Perhaps there are things you would like to know about your *jehan*.'

Alix slid farther into a dreamless sleep, lost within the realization she would be Duncan's woman after all.

But she also wondered at the magic in Lindir's soul to so ensorcel a man.

And she wondered if she had not her own measure of it.

Two days later she was installed in Duncan's pavilion, propped up on her pallet by mounds of rolled furs. It seemed strange to be in his place, knowing it was now hers as well, but as he stood over her solicitously she knew only she was the happiest she had ever been.

'I am well, Duncan,' she said softly.

He looked down at her sternly. 'Then tell me how you came by an *arrow* wound.'

Alix laughed at him. 'It was a young hunter. Ellasian, I must believe.'

He frowned at her. 'Tell me why a hunter would *shoot* you, rather than seek other things with you.'

She looked down at her blanketed legs, wiggling her

toes beneath the wool. Finally she glanced up. 'Because,' she said gently, 'he thought I was a wolf.'

Duncan's brows lifted. 'I hardly see how he could mistake you for a *wolf*, Alix. Perhaps he saw Storr, and simply missed.'

The time had come for an admission. She had missed Council, when she would have shown her skill to them, and had not said anything to Duncan regarding the accident. She had cradled her knowledge to her like a child, keeping it secret and anticipating the joy in telling him. Now it proved more difficult than she had imagined.

'He did not miss,' she said finally, fingering the healing wound in her shoulder. 'He mistook me for a wolf because I *was* one.'

Duncan made a sceptical sound and sat down at his low worktable, picking up his tools and a gold brooch she had watched him work on for two days. The *lir*-torque rested against her throat, warmed by her skin.

'You do not believe me?' she asked.

'You weave me a tale, *cheysula*,'

'I am telling you the truth. Duncan ... I can do more than speak with the *lir*. I take *lir*-shape, too.'

For a moment he continued to work on the brooch. Then, when she said nothing more, he looked at her from beneath lowered brows.

'Alix, would you truly have me believe—'

'You had better!' she flung at him. 'I would hardly lie about something so close to a Cheysuli warrior. I will even prove it to you.'

She moved as if to get up. Duncan, rising rapidly from his cross-legged position as he dropped his tools, reached her bed and stood over her. 'You go nowhere, *cheysula*, until you are better.'

'I *am* better.'

'Better than you are now.' He grinned. 'It will not be long, I think.'

She settled back against the furs. 'I am not lying. Ask

186

Cai. He and Storr taught me how to do it.'

Duncan dropped to his knees beside her. 'Is this true? Alix, you are unique enough that you converse with the *lir*. Can you truly assume *lir*-shape as well?'

'Aye,' she said softly.

He sank back on his heels. 'But this has not been done for *centuries*. Our history says once all Cheysuli could assume any *lir*-shape, but since before my grandsire's time this was only done by men. And then only when bonded by a single *lir*. It was the Firstborn who had the old abilities.'

'Those who made the prophecy.'

'Aye,' he said absently, eyes clouded with thought. 'The Firstborn took any *lir*-shape at will, and conversed with them all. But their blood has been gone from us for a long time.' He looked at her sharply. 'Unless, somehow, you have a measure of it.' Duncan got to his feet rapidly, startling her. 'I will be back.'

Alix stared after him, baffled by his sudden withdrawal, but she assumed he knew what he was doing. She pulled the blanket higher around her shoulders and snuggled down against the pallet, drowsily content. But part of her was still amazed at the new course her life had taken.

Duncan returned with a Cheysuli Alix did not know; a much older man whose hair was pure white and held back by a slender bronze fillet. Alix, struggling to sit upright again, saw he did not wear the leather of the warriors; instead he clothed himself in a fine white wool robe, clasped with a leather belt mounted with bronze platelets. Like Raissa, he wore silver bells at his belt that sent a shiver of sound through the pavilion whenever he moved.

Alix sent a puzzled glance at Duncan, who gestured with all deference for the man to seat himself on a brown bear pelt placed before the small fire cairn. The man did so with great dignity, carefully settling brittle bones into a comfortable position. He put a rolled deerskin on the pelt before him and waited.

187

Duncan sat down at Alix's side. 'This is the *shar tahl*. He keeps the rituals and traditions for the clan, and passes the history down to each generation. Each child born learns his ancestors and what has gone before from this man. You have come late to your clan, but you are here now, and he will tell you what you must know.' He smiled faintly. 'He may also have the answer to my question'

The *shar tahl* nodded to her, then untied the rolled deerskin. It was soft and supple, bleached white as snow, and as it unrolled before him Alix saw the runic symbols and lines twisting on the floor of the pavilion like a snake. He tapped the deerskin with a gnarled finger.

'Your birthline,' he said. 'You are here as surely as your *jehan*, and his *jehan* before him.' The finger moved. 'All the way back to the Firstborn.'

'But what does it mean?' she asked softly.

His finger moved off the main line of runes and traced a second line, like the branch of a tree. Alix followed the movement until it stopped. The finger tapped again.

'There.'

'Where?' she asked.

He looked at her sternly from rheumy yellow eyes. 'There. The answer lies there.'

She looked helplessly at Duncan. He maintained his solemn clan-leader demeanour, though she had come to know he had flashes of Finn-like irreverence. He simply kept it quieter.

'If you know so little of your clan, you had best come to me for instruction,' the *shar tahl* intoned.

Alix nodded meekly. 'I will learn.'

The *shar tahl* touched a red symbol gone dark with age. 'It is here in the birthline. Five generations ago the Mujhar took a Cheysuli *mei jha*, whose clan was so pure it could name members of the Firstborn as direct ancestors. All could assume *lir*-shape, even the women.' His thin shoulders stiffened. 'That clan has

188

since been destroyed by the *qu'mahlin*.'

Alix ignored his controlled bitterness, counting back in her head. Then she shot the *shar tahl* a startled glance. 'Shaine's great-great grandsire?'

'The woman who was *mei jha* to a Mujhar bore him a daughter. She was raised at Homana-Mujhar and wed to a foreign princeling, from Erinn. Shaine the Mujhar first took an Erinnish princess to wife, and so the blood came back.'

'Then I am Cheysuli on both sides.' Alix sat upright. 'There is Cheysuli blood in Shaine!'

'It has been thinned,' the *shar tahl* said firmly. 'Marriage with foreigners has overcome any Cheysuli traits left.' He pushed a wisp of white hair from his brow. 'It is the women who have done this. It is in their blood. Ellinda bore Lindir, who has gifted you with the Old Blood long lost to us all.'

Duncan touched her shoulder and pressed her down upon the furs. 'Perhaps Lindir, unknowing, had her own *tahlmorra*. Perhaps Hale did not forsake his face for a *Homanan* princess, but followed what the gods have set for us.' He smiled. 'If Lindir has passed this gift to you, you can bring it back into our clan.'

She sank back. 'I do not understand.'

The *shar tahl*, surprising her, smiled. 'It is time you learned the prophecy. If you will be silent, I will tell it to you.'

She felt Duncan's silent amusement and shot him a grimace of resentment. But she settled herself upon the pallet and nodded at the old man.

'I am more than ready.'

He sat upright before her, aged yellow eyes taking on the brightness of youth and wisdom. 'Once, centuries ago, Homana was a Cheysuli place. This land was gifted to us by the Firstborn, who were sired by the old gods. Do you hear me?'

'I hear,' she said softly.

'The Cheysuli ruled Homana. It was they who built

189

Mujhara and the palace of Homana-Mujhar. It was the Cheysuli who held sovereignty over all men.'

'But the Mujhars are Homanan!'

He fixed her with a stern glare. 'If you will hear me, you must listen.'

She subsided, chastened.

'Mujhar itself is a Cheysuli word. So is Homana. This was our place long before it came into the hands of the Homanans.'

Alix nodded reluctantly as he looked at her. A faint smile curved his creased lips.

'The Ihlini rose up in Solinde and began to move against us. The Cheysuli were forced to use their own arts to defend the land. The Homanans, ever doubtful of such sorcery, began to fear.

'Within a hundred years the fear turned to hatred; the hatred to violence. The Cheysuli could not convince the Homanans of their foolishness. We gave up the throne to them so they might know peace and security, and took up the bond of service to the Homanan Mujhars. Nearly four centuries ago.'

Alix groped with the knowledge, unable to absorb it all. Finally she nodded to him, silently bidding him continue.

'Until Hale took Lindir away, the Mujhar had ever kept Cheysuli advisors and councillors, and warriors who protected this land in battle. A Cheysuli liege man dedicated his life to the Mujhar. Such was Hale's service.'

'And Shaine ended it,' she whispered.

'He began the *qu'mahlin*.' The *shar tahl*'s face tightened. 'Even that was spoken of in the prophecy, but we chose to ignore it. We could not believe the Homanans would ever turn on us. We were foolish, and we have paid the price.'

'What is the prophecy?'

The bitterness vanished, replaced with pride and great dignity. 'One day a man of all blood will unite four warring realms and two races bearing the gifts of the old gods.'

Alix stared at him. '*Who?*'

'The prophecy does not name a name. It only shows us the way, so we may follow it and prepare Homana for the proper man. But it seems we grow closer to the path.'

'How do we follow it?' she asked softly.

'We have the Old Blood in our clan again, because of you. The Prophecy speaks of a Cheysuli Mujhar ascending the throne of Homana again after four centuries. It is nearly time.'

'But Carillon will be Mujhar,' Alix said.

'Aye. It is his *tahlmorra* to prepare the way for the prophecy's proper path.'

'*Carillon?*' she asked incredulously. 'But he distrusts all Cheysuli!'

The *shar tahl* shrugged. 'It has been foretold.'

Duncan sighed. 'This is what I meant when I spoke to him in Homana-Mujhar, *cheysula*. He must be turned from this hatred Shaine has put in him, and be made to see Homana's need of us. It is time we served the prophecy of the Firstborn . . . as it was meant.'

She looked at him blankly. 'But what have I to do with it?'

'It is up to you to give us back our pride and ancient magic.'

'How?'

He smiled gently. 'By bearing more of us.'

CHAPTER TWO

Alix, tongue clenched firmly between her teeth, wrestled with the knee-high furred boots. Duncan had brought her the black pelt of a mountain cat, cut it to shape with his knife, then handed the remains to her with instructions to begin a pair of winter boots. Aghast, Alix had stared at him and hoped he was teasing. He was not, she found, and now she cursed within her mind as she tried to work the thick hide and fur into something resembling boots.

She worked until her fingers were awl-pricked and sore, troubled by her inability to fashion the boots. She was slowly learning her place within the clan and her responsibilities as a clan-leader's *cheysula*, but her experience was sorely lacking. The warm grey wolfskin boots she wore had been made by Duncan for her when the weather turned cold, and she wished he would consent to making them all.

But he has things of more import to concern himself with! she thought sourly, throwing her half-done black boot aside to stare at the pavilion across the way. *He spends his time hunting or conversing with the Council, speaking ever of the war with Solinde!*

Instantly she was ashamed, for she knew as well as anyone how seriously concerned the Cheysuli were about the war. Increasingly alarming messages arrived from *lir*-couriers sent from Cheysuli secreted with Mujhara, seeking to learn of Shaine's actions. The Solindish, buttressed by Tynstar's Ihlini and troops guided by Keough, Lord of Atvia, had made inroads upon the Mujhar's defence of Homana.

And I said Bellam could never take this land, she thought hollowly. *I, like all the others, have been too impressed with past victories*

She sucked idly at a bleeding finger and recalled Duncan's summing up of the threat to their homeland.

'Homana will fall if Shaine does not commit himself to this war,' he had said one evening, staring gloomily into the flames of the pavilion fire cairn. 'He recalls the victory against Bellam twenty-six years ago, and trusts to the might of his armies. But then he had the Cheysuli, and now he does not.'

Alix had shifted closer to him, resting one hand upon his thigh. 'Surely the Mujhara understands this Solindish threat. He has ruled for many years, and won many battles.'

'He concerns himself more with the *qu'mahlin* than the Solindish war. I begin to think his fanaticism has made him mad.' Duncan's hand idly caressed her arm. 'He sends his brother, Fergus, into the field as commanding general, keeping himself safe within the walls of Homana-Mujhar.'

'He has fought before,' she said softly. 'Perhaps he realizes Fergus is a better soldier now.'

Duncan leaned forward and placed more wood upon the fire. 'Perhaps. But perhaps it is also he prefers to avoid the sacrifices a man makes in war. Shaine is not one who wishes to sacrifice anything.'

Alix stared at the brown pelt beneath them and pushed rigid fingers through the bear fur. 'To send your heir into battle is a sacrifice,' she said quietly, trying to hide from Duncan the fear it brought. 'He has sent Carillon to fight.'

Duncan was not fooled. 'If Carillon is to be Mujhar, he

must learn what it is to lead men. Shaine has trusted to his own council too long; he has neglected Carillon's education.' He grimaced. 'I think the prince could make a good Mujhar, but he has been given little chance to learn the responsibilities.' Duncan slid Alix a carefully blank glance. 'It is no wonder he took to speaking soft words to innocent croft-girls in the valley, to while away his time.'

Alix flushed deeply and withdrew her hand. But when she saw the glint in his eye she realized he only teased, and laughed at him.

'But I am no longer so innocent, Duncan. *You* have seen to that.'

He shrugged, purposefully solemn. 'Better a clan-leader, I think, than a mere warrior.'

'Warrior . . . *what* warrior?'

'Finn.'

'You beast!' she cried, striking him a glancing blow on the shoulder. 'Why must you remind me of him? Even now he calls me *mei jha* and torments me by suggesting I be his light woman.'

Duncan arched his brows. 'He seeks only to irritate you, *cheysula*. Even Finn knows better than to seek a clan-leader's woman, when she is unwilling.' His brows lowered. 'I think.'

'Finn would dare anything,' Alix said darkly.

He smiled. 'But if he did not, small one, he would be a tedious *rujholli* indeed.'

'I would prefer him tedious.'

'You, I think, would prefer him slain.'

She looked at him sharply, startled. 'No, Duncan! Never. I wish death on no man, not even one like Shaine who would have all Cheysuli slain.' She recalled the guardsmen killed in her behalf. 'No.'

His hand was gentle on her head, caressing her shorn hair. It had grown, but still barely touched her shoulders. 'I know, *cheysula*; I only tease.' He sighed heavily as his hand fell away. 'But if we join this war, there may be many deaths.'

194

'But the Mujhar will not have you with his armies. You have said.'

'In time, perhaps, he may *have* to.'

Alix, hearing the weariness of reluctant acceptance in his tone, leaned her head against his bare shoulder and tried to think of other things.

Now, as she took up the black boot again, she wondered how Carillon fared.

She had not lost her affection for the prince, even though she had spent nearly three months with the clan in Ellas. Carillon had been the first man she had fastened her fancy on; though it had been an impossible dream, she dreamed it with great joy. Duncan had replaced Carillon in her dreams, dominating her thoughts and desires, but she did not forget the first one she had loved. That love had been childish, immature and unfulfilled, but it had been true.

Alix fingered the thick black fur absently, lost within her thoughts. Duncan had showed her what it was to be a woman, what it was to be Cheysuli; what it was to have a *tahlmorra*. Already her roots had twined themselves around his own so deeply she knew she could never be herself again without him. She wondered if that was what it was to have a *lir*.

The adjustment had not been easy. Alix missed Torrin and the croft; missed the green valleys she had ever known. At times she awoke in the night sensing an odd disorientation, frightened by the strange man at her side, but it always faded when full awareness came back. Then she would press herself against Duncan's warmth, seeking comfort and safety, and always he gave it; and more.

She thought again of Carillon. She had heard only that the prince was in the field with his father, fighting the Solindish and Atvian troops. Duncan — sensing her loyalty — was unusually reticent with her when speaking of Carillon. Finn was not. He taunted his brother with the fact the prince had shared a place in

195

Alix's heart first, and relished giving her news of Carillon if only to tease Duncan. His attitude irritated Alix, but it was a way of getting news.

As if hearing her thoughts, Finn walked up to her and sat down on the grey pelt spread before the large fire cairn. Alix glared at him, expecting his normal mocking manner, but she saw something else in his face.

'It has come, Alix,' he said quietly.

'What do you say?' she asked in dread.

'It is time the Cheysuli defied the *qu'mahlin* and went again into Mujhara.'

'Mujhara!' She stared at him, shaken by his somber tone. 'But the Mujhar . . .'

Finn smoothed the nap of the pelt absently, staring at his hand. 'Shaine will be too occupied with real sorcerers to waste much time on us.' His eyes lifted to hers. 'The Ihlini have broken into the city.'

'No . . . oh, Finn! Not Mujhara!'

He stood. 'Duncan sent me for you. Council is calling all into the clan pavilion.' He put out a hand to help her up. 'We go to war, *mei jha*.'

Silently she took his hand and rose, shaking out her green skirts. She looked at Finn for more information, apprehensive, but he said nothing else. He merely led her to the Council pavilion, a huge black tent painted with every *lir*-symbol imaginable.

Duncan sat before the fire cairn on a spotted pelt, watching his clan file into the black interior in pensive silence. At his right lay an ochre-coloured rug, and it was to this Finn took Alix. The heaviness of the silence fell on her like a cloak. She sat down on the rug, watching Duncan's face closely. Finn sat beside her.

Duncan waited until the pavilion was filled, ringed with dark faces and yellow eyes. Then he looked to the *shar tahl*, seated across from him, and nodded to himself. Slowly he got to his feet.

'Vychan, in Mujhara, has sent his *lir* to us. The message is one we have expected these past months.

Tynstar has led his Ihlini sorcerers into Mujhara, and they have taken the city.'

Alix, sickened with fear, swallowed against the foreboding in her soul. The others, she saw, waited mutely for Duncan's words.

'The western borders fell three months ago. Keough of Atvia fights for Bellam, marching toward Mujhara where the Ihlini await them. Only Homana-Mujhar has not fallen.'

Alix closed her eyes and conjured the Great Hall with all its candleracks and rich tapestries.

And Shaine . . .

'If Homana-Mujhar falls, Homana herself falls. We, as the descendants of the Cheysuli who built both palace and city, cannot allow it to happen.'

Finn shifted. 'So you will send us into the Mujhar's city, *rujho*, and have us fight two enemies.'

Duncan shot him a sharp glance. 'Two?'

'Aye,' he said briefly. 'Do you forget Shaine? He will set his guardsmen against us, when he would do better to use them against the Ihlini.'

Duncan's mouth was a thin line. 'I do not forget Shaine, *rujho*. But I will set aside our personal conflicts to save Homana.'

'Shaine will not.'

'Then we will give him no choice.' Duncan looked slowly and deliberately around the pavilion, marking each attentive face. 'All of us cannot go. We must leave warriors to defend the Keep. But I have need of strong men willing to go into the city and fight the Ihlini with any method at hand. We are not many. Any force we send will have to be selectively efficient. Open warfare will result in too high a death toll. We must answer the Ihlini with stealth of our own.' His eyes returned to Finn. 'I send the best and the strongest. And some will be lost.'

Finn smiled crookedly. 'Well, *rujho*, you say nothing I do not already know. It is ever so, I think.' He shrugged. 'I go, of course.'

Other warriors echoed Finn's words, committing themselves to a war the Mujhar would not welcome them to. Alix, listening blankly to them, realized why Duncan had wanted to remain solitary. He had known all along the Cheysuli would risk their few numbers to save their ancestral home.

It is tahlmorra, she whispered within her mind. *Ever tahlmorra.*

Alix walked back to the pavilion alone, lost within fears and worries. In her time with Duncan she had learned of his strength of will, determination and selfless dedication to serving the prophecy. Nothing would deter him from leading his warriors into Mujhara. She knew better than to ask him to remain in safety with her, and though she wished he did not have to involve himself so deeply, she also knew he would lessen himself in her eyes if he did choose to stay. Duncan was, perhaps, less aggressive than Finn in his desire to fight, but his pride ran just as deep.

The fire cairn had burned itself to ash, so Alix spent her time rekindling it for warmth and illumination. The pavilion was her security now, as much as Torrin's croft had been. Even the tapestry meant much to her, for Duncan had carefully explained each runic device and the designs stitched within the patterning of rich blue yarns. The tapestry contained much of Cheysuli lore, highlighting the strengths and traditions of the race. She wondered, as she knelt by the fire, if more history would be added with the warriors' return to the city.

Duncan came in softly, easing aside the doorflap. Alix, seeing the quietude in his eyes, met him with a measure of her own solemnity.

'Duncan,' she began softly, 'how soon do you leave for Mujhara?'

He went to his weapons chest and took out his war bow, a compact instrument of death similar to his plain hunting bow. But this was dyed black, polished, inlaid with gold and tiger-eye. The string also was black, humming tautly as he strung the bow and tested it.

He dug his black arrows out of the chest and sat down cross-legged, beginning the laborious examination of each one.

The arrows were fletched with silver feathers, and the obsidian heads gleamed.

Alix waited silently, patiently, and finally he answered her. 'In the morning.'

'So soon . . .'

'War does not wait for men, *cheysula*.'

Carefully she smoothed her green skirts over her thighs as she knelt upon the spotted pelt. 'Duncan,' she said at last, 'I wish to go.'

He meticulously inspected the fletching of each arrow. 'Go?'

'To Mujhara.'

'No.'

'I will be safe.'

'It is no place for you, small one.'

'Please,' she said clearly, not begging. 'I could not bear to remain here, waiting out each day without knowing.'

'I have said no.'

'I would not hinder you. I too can assume *lir*-shape. I would be no trouble.'

He studied her impassively a moment, half his attention on his arrows. Then he smiled. 'You are *ever* trouble, Alix.'

'Duncan!'

'I will not risk you.'

'You risk *yourself*!'

He set down one arrow and picked up another. 'The Cheysuli,' he said slowly, 'have ever risked themselves. For Homana, it is worth it.'

'But for Shaine?'

'The Mujhar *is* Homana. Shaine has held these lands safely for more than forty years, Alix. Our race has not benefited from him, perhaps, but all else have. If he requires help to hold the land now, we must give it to him.' His eyes dropped. 'And we must think of the one who will succeed him.'

Alix took a trembling breath. 'Let me give my aid as well. Shaine is my grandsire . . . and Carillon my cousin.'

He set the arrow aside and clasped his hands loosely in his lap. Alix found herself avoiding his eyes, focusing instead on the heavy gold banding his bared, bronzed arms. She saw the embossed, incised hawk-shape of his *lir* and the runic designs worked into the gleaming metal on either side of the hawk. When she could look at his face again, she saw pride and warmth in his eyes.

'*Cheysula*,' he said gently, 'I know your determination. I am thankful for it. But I will not have you risking yourself, especially for the man who cast you out at birth and then again so many years later.'

'Yet you risk yourself,' she repeated hollowly, sensing defeat.

He sighed minutely. 'It is a warrior's place, *cheysula*, and a clan-leader's *tahlmorra*. Do not deny me it.'

'No,' she said. She reached for the bow and picked it up, caressing the smooth patina and gleaming ornamentation. She slid careful fingers down the taut bowstring, testing its tension and vibrancy. 'Will you be careful?' she asked in a low voice.

'I am usually little else, as Finn often tells me.'

'*Very* careful?'

He smiled wryly. 'I will be very careful.'

Alix gently set the bow in front of him. 'Well, I would not want your first son born without a father.'

He was silent. Alix, eyes downcast in a submissive position unfamiliar to her, waited for his astonishment and joy.

But Duncan reached out and grabbed her shoulders, jerking her upright onto her knees. He glared at her wrathfully.

'And you would *risk that* by coming to an embattled city?'

'Duncan —'

'You are a fool, Alix!' He released her abruptly.

She stared at him open-mouthed as he rose stiffly and stalked from her, halting at the open doorflap to stare out.

'I thought you would be pleased,' she told his rigid back.

He turned on her. 'Pleased? You beg to go to war and then tell me you have conceived? Do you wish to *lose* this child?'

'*No!*'

He glared at her. 'Then remain here as I have said, and conduct yourself as a clan-leader's *cheysula*.'

Alix, driven into speechlessness by the intensity of his anger, said nothing at all as he turned away from her and left the pavilion.

She shivered once, convulsively, then folded both arms across her still-flat belly and bent forward, hugging herself tightly.

She let the tears come unchecked and rocked back and forth in silent grief.

CHAPTER THREE

When the doorflap was pulled aside Alix sat up hastily and wiped the tears away. She was prepared to meet Duncan with dignity, but when she saw Finn staring in at her she lost her composure.

'Duncan is not here,' she said shortly.

Finn studied her a moment. 'No, I know he is not. He passed me but a moment ago, black of face and very black of mood.' He paused. 'Have you had your first battle, *mei jha*?'

She scowled at him, fighting back the impulse to cry again. 'It is none of your concern.'

'He is my *rujholli*; you my *rujholla*. It is ever my concern.'

'Go away!' she cried, and burst into tears.

Finn did not go away. He watched her in ironic amazement a moment, then stepped inside the pavilion. Alix turned her back on him and cried into her hands.

'Is it truly so bad?' he asked quietly.

'You are the last person I would tell,' she managed between sobs.

'Why? I have ears that hear as well as anyone's.'

'But you never *listen*.'

Finn sighed and sat down next to her, carefully avoiding any contact. 'He is my *rujho*, Alix, but it does not make him perfect. If you wish to tell me how abominable he is being to you, I will listen readily enough.'

She shot him a repressive glance. 'Duncan is never abominable.'

His brows lifted. 'Oh ... he can be. Do you forget I grew up with him?'

Something in the lightness of his tone broke her down farther, destroying her last reservation. Most of the tears had gone, but she was still upset.

'He has never been *angry* with me before,' she whispered.

Finn's mouth twitched. 'Did you think Duncan beyond it? Most of the time he loses himself in the burdens of being clan-leader to a dwindling race, but he is like any other. He has ever been more solemn than I, but he has just as much anger and bitterness. It is only he hides it better.'

She thought of the cause of Duncan's anger, but could not tell Finn. It was too new; too private.

'It is too hard,' she said, pushing away the last of the tears.

'Being his *cheysula*?' he asked in surprise. 'Well, there was a way out of that ... once.' He grinned sardonically. 'You had only to be *mei jha* to me.'

'I did not mean that,' she said sharply. 'I spoke of learning new customs, and conducting myself the way a Cheysuli woman does.'

Finn thought about it. 'Perhaps that is true. I had never thought of it.' He shrugged. 'This is the only life I know.'

'I know two,' she told him heavily. 'The one you stole me from, and this. There are times I wish you had never seen me.'

'So you could dally with the princeling and grow up to be his light woman?'

Alix glared at him. 'Perhaps. But *you* ended any chance of that.'

'You had best not say that where Duncan can hear it,' Finn said tonelessly.

Alix was startled. 'Duncan knows how I felt about Carillon. How could he not?'

Finn dragged at his boot, as if delaying his answer. Then his mouth twisted. 'He still fears you may go back to the princeling.'

'*Why?*'

'Carillon offers more than we can.' His eyes were expressionless. 'The magnificence of Homana-Mujhar, wealth, the honour in being a prince's light woman. It is more than any Cheysuli can give.'

'I do not take a man for what he gives me,' she said firmly. 'I take him out of love. Duncan can say it was *tahlmorra* that brought us together — perhaps it was — but it is not that which keeps us together.'

Finn seemed suddenly uncomfortable. 'Then you will remain with the clan?'

'Duncan would not let me go; nor, I think, would you.' Alix held his eyes. 'I have no real wish to go back ... My place is with Duncan.'

'Even though it be hard to learn our ways?'

Alix sighed resignedly. 'I will learn ... eventually.'

Finn lifted her hand, encircling her wrist with his fingers as he had done so long before. 'Does what you feel for him pall, Alix, or he dies in this war we face ... you may come to me.' He silenced her before she could protest. 'No. I do not mean it out of my own desire for you, though that is unchanged.' He shrugged, dismissing it. 'I mean for you to come to me in safety, should you ever need it.'

'Finn—'

He released her wrist. 'I am not always so harsh, *rujholla*. But you never gave me the chance to show you otherwise.'

He left before she could say anything more. Alix, staring after him, wondered if perhaps she had done him an injustice in her thoughts.

Duncan said little to her in the morning as they parted. Though he had come back to the pavilion much less angry and sorry he had frightened her, he was still determined she would do nothing to endanger the child or herself. Aloud she agreed with him, admitting her foolishness; inwardly she calmly considered when would be the best time to assume *lir*-shape and go by herself.

But when Duncan bid her farewell she clung to him in helpless anguish, silent, and made no reference to her secret plans.

Alix found, to her anguish, Cheysuli women did not say good-bye in the privacy of the pavilion. Instead a *cheysula* or *mei jha* stood outside, before the tent, bidding her warrior safe journey in the open. The custom, Duncan said, came from a wish to make parting easier on the warriors. It was difficult to leave a sobbing woman with any degree of confidence.

She stared fiercely after them as they rode out of the stone Keep. The winged *lir* flew ahead, scouting; the four-footed beasts paced beside the horses. Alix saw Cai swoop above the treetops; Storr lope easily beside Finn; and the others go silently with their *lir*.

And I will be them all, she thought in grim satisfaction.

She was calm in her decision, acknowledging the difficulties. She had been a wolf only twice, and then with disastrous results, but that was hardly her fault. She would do better. Yet she was concerned with the knowledge she would have to go as a bird, an unknown shape, for a wolf would move too slowly for her to catch up to the party of warriors.

I wish Cai were here to teach me to fly, she thought uneasily. *It must be frightening to seek the air for the first time, trusting your life to fragile wings.*

But she knew she would go.

Alix prepared rapidly, wanting to leave no later than afternoon. She drew a pair of Duncan's worn leggings and soft jerkin from a chest, cutting both garments to

205

her smaller size. The jerkin she put on over the top half of the gown she had worn at Homana-Mujhar, using it as a rough shirt to cover her arms and hide her figure. A leather strap served as a belt, and she pulled on her wolfskin boots, cross-gartered to the knees. Grimly she looked down at herself.

I look no more a warrior than some Cheysuli boy playing at it. Well, it will have to do. I cannot go to war wearing skirts.

She sat down on the spotted pelt by the fire cairn and stared sightlessly into the coals.

How to make oneself a bird . . .?

Carefully Alix detached her mind from her surroundings, dismissing the familiarity of soft pelts and colored tapestries and the mundane tools of daily life. The coals blurred before her eyes into a collage of rose and grey, transfixing her mind.

She thought of treetops and fields and clouds. She thought of a falcon, swift and light; of feathers and talons and hooked beak; bright eyes and hollow bones and the marvellous freedom of flight.

When she broke out of the pavilion and air rushed gloriously through her outstretched wings she knew she had succeeded, and rejoiced.

At first she wheeled in exultation, dipping and circling, playing among the currents. Below her lay the Keep, spreading to shelter the last of Homana's ancient race. The pavilion was a speck of slate against the neutral tones of the Keep and surrounding forest.

Then Alix put away the joy of such freedom and flew on to seek a *lir*.

But she wearied quickly. Unaccustomed to prolonged flight, Alix at last admitted defeat and perched herself upon a tree. She was weary and hungry, tense with the effort to keep *lir*-shape, and realized she had nearly reached her limit.

She flew again to the ground and blurred herself from her falcon-shape into human form. Again she marvelled at the gods-given ability of the *lir*-bond, for her clothing changed with her when she assumed *lir*-shape, and returned when she shifted back.

That is fortunate, she thought wryly. *I would not care to be caught in the middle of a forest unclothed.*

Alix climbed up a gentle spill of dirt packed against the mountainside and halted as she found a brush-covered hollow half-hidden in the shadows of dusk. Carefully she moved closer, peering through the boughs. The limbs and leafy branches had been woven together roughly, as if to form a cover, and as she inspected it closely she knew it could only be human-made. She pulled the covering aside and crept into the shallow cave.

She discovered a coarse, poorly woven brown blanket spread on the uneven floor of the rocky cave. Next to it lay a leather bag fastened with a wooden pin, and a small fire snapped at freshly piled kindling. She hesitated, wondering suddenly if she would not be welcome. Perhaps she trusted too easily.

The sound of breaking twigs sent her whirling on her hands and knees, eyes widened in fear.

The man ducked his head as he crawled into the cave through the narrow opening, eyes on the stone floor. Over his shoulder he wore a crude bow, but the long-knife at his belt looked more efficient. Under one arm he held the drooping body of a slain rabbit.

Alix withdrew farther, stone wall biting at her back as she pressed against it. The sound penetrated the silence like an enemy's shout. The man dropped the rabbit and drew his long-knife in a single motion, bracing himself on one knee as he came up from the floor to strike.

Then she saw shock and amazement flare in his brown eyes as he realized she was a woman.

He swore softly in wonder and shoved the knife back into its sheath. Carefully he eased into a squatting position, as if he feared to frighten her.

'Lady, I will not harm you. If you seek shelter here, you must be a refugee from Bellam's troops also.'

'Refugee!'

He nodded. 'Aye. From the war.' He frowned. 'Surely you have heard of the war, lady.'

'I have heard.' She stared blankly at his crusted, age-cracked leather-and-mail, and the soiled scarlet tunic bearing the Mujhar's rampant black lion. His mail was rusted, as if washed with blood, and she shivered against the sudden foreboding in her bones.

'My name is Oran,' he said, rubbing a dirty hand through matted, lank brown hair. 'I am a soldier of Homana.'

She frowned at him. 'Then why are you here? Should you not be with your lord?'

'My lord is slain. Keough of Atvia, Bellam's foul accomplice, overran the army twenty days ago like a pack of savage dogs.' His eyes narrowed angrily. 'It was night, moonless and dark. We slept, wearied from a three-day battle. The Atvian host crept upon us in all stealth, and routed us before the dawn.'

Alix wet her dry lips. 'Where, Oran? Mujhara?'

He laughed. 'Not Mujhara. I am not one of the Mujhar's fine guard. I am a common soldier who once was a tenant crofter for Prince Fergus, the Mujhar's own brother.'

'Fergus.' She eased herself away from the rocky wall, kneeling before him. 'Then it was Fergus you served in the field?'

'Aye, seven days' ride out of Mujhara.' He hawked and spat, turning his head from her. He wiped the spittle from his lips and looked at her bleakly. 'Prince Fergus was slain.'

'Why did you not stay?' she demanded. 'Why did you forsake your lord?'

His grimy, stubbled face was ugly. 'I sickened of it. I was not meant to slay men like beasts on the order of a man who keeps himself safe behind the ensorcelled walls of Homana-Mujhar.' Oran spat again. 'Shaine has set wards, lady; instruments of sorcery to keep the Ihlini

208

out. He keeps himself safe, while thousands die in his name.'

Alix drew a trembling breath, clenching fists against her knees. 'What of Carillon? What of the prince?'

Oran's mouth twisted. 'Carillon is prisoner to Keough himself.'

'Prisoner!'

'Aye. I saw him slay two who sought to take him, fighting like a demon, but it was Keough's own son who broke his guard and disarmed him. Thorne. The Atvian prince took Carillon's sword, then Carillon himself, and marched him to his father.' Oran stared at her narrowly. 'They will slay him, lady, or take him to Bellam in Mujhara.'

'No . . .'

He shrugged. 'It is his lot. He is the Mujhar's heir, and valuable. Keough will keep him close until he is in Bellam's hands. Or Tynstar's.'

Alix closed her eyes and summoned up his face, recalling his warm blue eyes and stubborn jaw. And his smile, whenever he looked on her.

Oran shifted and she opened her eyes. He grinned, displaying broken, yellowed teeth, and took up the leather pouch. He undid the pin and spilled the contents across the blanket.

It was a stream of gems glowing richly in the shadowed cave. Brooches, rings of delicate gold and silver, and a wristband of copper. Oran prodded the cache with a finger.

'Solindish, lady. And fine, as you can see.'

She frowned at them. 'Where did you get them?'

He laughed crudely. 'From men who no longer had need of such things.'

She recoiled. 'You stole them from dead men?'

'How else does a poor soldier make his way? I am not one of your rich lordlings, like Carillon; nor am I a Mujhara noble born to silks and jewels. How else am I to get such things?'

Avarice glinted in his eyes. She saw them travel her body expectantly. She wore the golden *lir*-torque Duncan had given her and delicate topaz drops hung at her ears.

'So,' she said on a long breath, 'you will slay me for my wealth as well.'

He grinned. 'There need be no slaying, lady. You have only to give them to me.' He stroked his bottom lip. 'I have never seen your like before. Are you some lord's light woman?'

The insult did not touch her. Oran, in his commonness, did not recognize it as such. And the Cheysuli had begun to change her perceptions of such things.

Alix slowly tensed. 'No.'

'Then how came you by such things?'

Enlightenment flared within her mind. Carefully she damned the sudden realization of her power and looked at him calmly.

'My *cheysul* gave them to me.'

He scowled at her. 'Speak Homanan, lady. What do you say?'

'My husband, Oran. He made me these things.'

He grinned. 'Then he can make more. Here, lady; give them to me.'

'No.' She looked at him levelly. 'It is not wise for a Homanan to seek that fashioned by a Cheysuli.'

'Cheysuli!' His brows slid up. 'You live among the shapechangers?'

'I *am* one.'

For a moment fear flashed in his eyes. Then it faded, replaced with determination and greed. 'The shapechangers are under the Mujhar's death decree. I should slay you, and then all you have would be mine.'

It angered her past caution. 'I doubt you could accomplish it.'

His hand flashed to his knife. 'Can I not, shapechanger witch? You do not frighten me with your sorcery. Only your warriors shift their shape, so you offer little threat.'

210

He grinned and lifted the knife. 'What do you say now, witch?'

Alix said nothing. He effectively blocked the cave entrance with his mailed bulk, and as he moved slowly toward her she saw she had no chance to avoid him. The wall curved snugly against her back.

'Do not,' she said softly.

Oran laughed silently and put his hand on the torque at her throat.

Alix summoned the magic and blurred herself into a wolf.

He gaped at her, then fell back with a cry of terror. The knife fell from limp fingers as he scrabbled on the floor. The wolf-bitch snarled and leaped over him, avoiding his body, but forcing him flat on his back as she moved. She heard his scream of horror as she drove past his trembling body and into the darkened forest.

She paused a moment, free of the place, and sent an exultant howl soaring to the dark heavens.

Then she went on in *lir*-shape.

The wolf-bitch, silvered by moonlight, sifted out of the trees into the Cheysuli camp. She saw the huddled forms of blanketed, sleeping warriors and the shadowed lumps of *lir* scattered throughout the camp. She sent soothing patterns to the animals so they would not give the alarm and moved smoothly toward the fire. She heard Cai, perched in a tree, send a single word to his *lir*.

Duncan rolled over instantly and sat up. His movement awoke Finn, next to him, and they got to their feet in silent unison. They parted smoothly, unsheathing knives, watching the wolf-bitch carefully.

Alix, realizing they thought her some wild creature, laughed within her mind.

And Duncan named me helpless . . .

She sensed his attentiveness. Finn, moving silently, stepped closer to her. She considered leaping at him in mock attack, but gave it up as she realized he would very likely slay her.

Instead, she blurred herself into human form.

Duncan blinked, then frowned.

Finn laughed. 'Well, *rujho*, I have not given you proper credit. You are powerful indeed if she cannot even part with you for two days.'

Alix, suddenly chilled and wearied by the exertion and tension of the past hours, ignored him and walked to the glowing bed of coals. There she dropped to her knees and stretched her hands over the embers.

Duncan slid his knife home in its sheath. He said nothing.

Finn laughed again and gathered up his blanket, dropping it over her shoulders as he moved softly to her. 'There, *rujholla*,' he said mockingly. 'If he will let you freeze, at least I will not.'

She slid him a resentful glance and gathered the folds about her. Finn shrugged eloquently and returned to his sleeping place, settling himself cross-legged on the flattened earth.

Duncan stepped behind her, so close she could feel his knees against her back. 'I suppose you will tell me why ... eventually.'

'It was *not* what Finn said!'

'Well,' Duncan said, sighing, 'it was too much to expect you to obey me. I should have put a spell on you.'

She jerked around so hard the blanket slid off a shoulder. 'You can do that?'

He laughed and moved next to her, squatting down. He took a stick and stirred the coals. 'You do not know all of our gifts yet, *cheysula*. There are three. The Cheysuli can assume *lir*-shape, borrow the earth magic to heal, and also force submission on any save an Ihlini.' He smiled. 'But that we save for extremity.'

'Duncan!'

He grinned at the coals. 'I would not truly do it, *cheysula*. But you tempt me, with your forward ways.'

212

She scowled at him. 'You know I have come mostly because of you, Duncan.' She took a breath. 'But also because of Carillon.'

His hand stopped stirring the coals. 'Why?'

'He requires our help.'

'How would you know that? Or can you also read the minds of men in addition to the *lir*?'

She disliked the mocking glint in his eyes. 'You know I cannot. But I met a man who says he saw Fergus slain and Carillon taken by Thorne, Keough of Atvia's son. It was a bloody battle, from the appearance of his garments.'

'War is often bloody, Alix. Why else would I seek to keep you from it?'

'We must find Carillon.'

'The prince is no half-grown boy, Alix. And he is valuable. His captivity may well be unpleasant, but it will not be the death of him. Bellam — perhaps even Tynstar — will want him alive, for a time.'

She stared at him. 'I begin to think you will allow this jealousy to prevent his rescue.'

'I am jealous of no one!' he snapped, and reddened as he heard Finn's spurt of laughter.

'Duncan, we must go to him.'

'We go to Mujhara, to fight the Ihlini. They are a bigger threat than Keough.'

'Then you sentence Carillon to death!'

Duncan sighed heavily. 'If his death is meant, it will happen. Carillon may not be Cheysuli, but he has his own sort of *tahlmorra*.'

'Duncan!' she cried incredulously, aware the others watched in silent interest. 'You cannot mean to forsake him like this!'

He looked at her harshly. 'The Ihlini have taken Mujhara. If the palace falls, Homana is in the hands of Tynstar. Do you not see? Carillon will be kept alive while Bellam wants him, but if Homana-Mujhar falls he will slay all threats to his control. First Shaine, then

213

Carillon.' He released a weary breath. 'I know you care for him, *cheysula*, but we cannot seek out a single man when an entire city may be destroyed.'

'He is your prince,' she whispered.

'And I am your *cheysul*.'

She scowled at him. 'Do you send me back, then?'

'Would you go if I did?'

'No.'

He grunted. 'Then I will save my breath.' He raised her, removed Finn's blanket and led her over to his pallet. He pressed her down with a hand on her shoulder. 'Sleep, *cheysula*; we ride early.'

'Sleep?' she inquired impishly as he lowered himself next to her and encircled her with his hard arms.

He laughed softly. 'Sleep. Would you give my *rujholli* more to make sport of?'

'It is ever Finn,' she said grumpily, pulling a blanket over them both.

Duncan settled her head upon his shoulder. After a moment he sighed. 'If it pleases you, small one, I will send Cai to the prince. He can bring word of Carillon's welfare.'

'Well,' she said after a silence, 'it is something.'

His hand tightened threateningly on her throat. 'Can you never be satisfied, Alix?'

'If I told you aye, you would cease trying to please me.' She spread her fingers against the hollow of his throat, feeling it pulse. 'Duncan,' she whispered after a moment, 'why have you never said you loved me?'

He was very still. 'Because the Cheysuli do not speak of love.'

Alix sat bolt upright, dragging the blanket from him. 'What do you say?'

His hand reached out and caught hers, pulling her back down against his chest. 'I said we do not *speak* of love. It weakens a warrior, who should think of other matters.' He smiled into the darkness. 'For all that, words do not always serve.'

'Then am I supposed to *guess*?'

He laughed softly and settled the blanket over them again. 'There is no need for you to guess. I have given you answer enough, before.' His hand slid down to rest across her stomach as he whispered. 'You bear my son, Alix. Is that not enough?'

She stared into the darkness. 'For now . . .'

CHAPTER FOUR

Alix spent her days behind Duncan on horseback,
clasping his lean waist and anticipating what they
would do when they reached Mujhara. She had decided
not to bother Duncan with entreaties to go instead to
Carillon, for he had sent Cai as promised four days
before, and his arguments made sense. For all she still
held great esteem and affection for Carillon, she knew
even the prince would be more concerned with the
welfare of Homana-Mujhar than himself.

Duncan was unusually solicitous of her, so much so
that Finn, riding next to them, finally demanded an
explanation. Alix, looking at him in surprise, realized
Duncan had said nothing of the child.

'Well *mei jha*?' he asked. 'Have you sickened, or does
my *rujho* simply worry himself over women's things,
now he has a *cheysula*?'

She felt color rise in her face. 'I have not sickened.'

Duncan shot Finn a dark glance. 'Do not plague her,
rujho. You have done enough of that in the past.'

Finn kneed his horse closer. 'Do you seek to tell me
something without speaking?'

'No,' Alix said quickly.

Duncan laughed softly. 'Perhaps it is time, *cheysula*.
You will not be able to be silent about it much longer.'

'Duncan . . .' she protested.

Finn scowled at them. 'What do you say?'

'Alix has conceived. She bears me a son in six months.'

She waited for Finn's mocking words and twisted mouth, dreading what he might say. But he said nothing. He glanced at her quickly, then away, head bent as if he studied the ground beneath his horse's hooves. His face was masklike, as if he feared to set free an emotion he could not control.

Duncan frowned. 'Finn?'

Finn glanced up and smiled at his brother. His eyes slid to Alix, then away. 'I wish you well of it, Duncan. It is a good thing to know the Cheysuli increase, even if only by one.'

'One is enough for now,' Alix said firmly.

His grin crept back. 'Aye, *mei jha*, perhaps it is. I will be glad enough to be uncle to one.'

She watched him, puzzled by his manner. He was a different man. She saw his yellow eyes settle broodingly on Duncan, then a strange regretful smile twisted his mouth. He glanced up and saw her watching him, then gestured expressively with a hand.

Tahlmorra.

Alix opened her mouth to ask a question, sensing something she could not quite understand. But she said nothing as Duncan stiffened before her. She felt the sudden tensing of his muscles as he shuddered once, violently.

'Duncan!'

He did not answer her. Instead he jerked the horse to a stop so unruly it slid Alix along smooth hindquarters until she clutched helplessly at Duncan, trying to stay horseback. It was futile. She landed awkwardly on her feet, hanging onto the stirrup to steady herself.

'Duncan!'

The horse side-stepped nervously. The reins were slack in Duncan's hands as he bent over the pommel and shuddered again.

Alix stumbled back as the horse moved against her,

nearly stepping on her. She grabbed Duncan's leggings and tugged, trying to gain his attention.

Finn, on the other side, wrenched his mount to a halt and reached out. '*Rujho?*'

Duncan pushed himself upright and slid awkwardly off the horse. He hung onto the stirrup helplessly, unaware of Alix's presence. He set his forehead against the saddle and sucked in air like a drowning man.

'Duncan . . .' she whispered, putting a hesitant hand on his rigid arm. '*Duncan!*'

Finn dismounted rapidly and moved around the riderless horse to Duncan's side. He gently pushed Alix out of the way, ignoring her protests, and took Duncan's arm.

'What is it?' he asked.

Duncan turned his head, gazing blankly at Finn. His eyes were dilated and oddly confused. 'Cai . . .' He gasped hoarsely, shuddering again.

Finn steered him away from the fretting horse to a tree stump, pushing him down on it as Duncan swayed on his feet. There he knelt in the leaves and looked into his brother's face.

'Slain?' he whispered.

Alix, still standing by the horse, understood the implications of the question instantly. She fell to her knees next to Finn.

'Duncan . . . *no!*'

His face was strained and pale. His head dropped until he stared sightlessly at the ground, hands hanging limply against his thighs.

Alix touched his cold hand softly. 'Duncan, say you are well.'

Finn set his hand on her shoulder, silencing her without a word. Then he grasped Duncan's tensing forearm.

'*Rujho*, is he slain?'

Duncan raised his head and stared at them. His eyes were strange, dangerously feral in a hollowed face.

Tautness moved through his body like a serpent, knotting sinews into rigidity. But color began to flow slowly back into his face.

'No,' he said at last. He swallowed against another shudder. 'He is — injured. And far from this place.' He shoved a shaking hand through his black hair. 'His *lir*-pattern is so weak I can barely touch him.'

Alix sent out her own call, trying to discover the hawk, but nothing answered. She had spent time working on screening out the other *lir* so she could think in peace; perhaps it worked against her now.

Finn glanced over his shoulder at the gathered warriors. 'We camp here until morning.' He turned back and looked at Alix out of a face suddenly old and weary. His smile held little reassurance, though he sought to soothe her. 'Cai is not slain. Duncan will be well.'

She swallowed and felt some of the horrible fear slide out of her bones. But much of it remained, and when Finn pulled Duncan to his feet she nearly cried to see his spirit so diminished.

This is what it is to have a lir, she thought miserably. *This is the price of the old gods' magic* . . .

Duncan was made to lie down, wrapped in blankets before a hastily laid fire. But he came out of his shock long enough to stare frowningly at his brother.

'We should go on, *rujho*. We do not reach Mujhara like this.'

Finn smiled and shook his head. 'I know what you feel. When Storr nearly died of an arrow wound, I was close to death myself with the shock of it. You have never had to deal with it, so keep silent until you are better. I am second-leader, after you.'

Duncan pulled the blankets more closely around his shoulders, worn to the bone. 'You have never led men, Finn,' he said crossly. 'How can I know you will not get us into trouble?'

Alix smiled faintly, relieved to hear the brotherly

banter. Finn, standing over his elder like an avenging demon with a newly won soul, grinned and crossed his arms over his chest.

'You will simply have to find out, *rujho*. It may be *I* am better suited, even, than you.'

Duncan scowled blackly at him a moment, then closed his eyes and sank against the ground. Alix watched him fade into sleep as she knelt beside him. She gripped his war bow in her hands.

'He will be well?' she asked softly.

'He is full of Cai's pain,' Finn told her. 'When a *lir* is injured, the Cheysuli feels all of it in the first moments. It will pass.' He sighed. 'He only needs rest.'

'And Cai,' she said softly.

Finn's face tightened. 'Aye. And Cai.'

Duncan recovered rapidly, though his attention seemed elsewhere most of the time, seeking Cai. Alix remonstrated with him to rest longer than a single night, but Duncan declared himself fit enough and ready to go on to Mujhara. Finn, after grumbling about his brother's foolishness, gave in and agreed. So Alix climbed aboard the horse once again and hung onto Duncan more firmly than usual, making certain he was well.

They were two days out of the city when Cai appeared in the sky, winging slowly toward them. She felt Duncan's instant tension and smoothed a hand across his back, as if to quiet a fretful child. Duncan halted the horse and waited.

Lir, the bird sent, sounding pleased, *I was not certain how far you rode from me*.

Alix smiled in relief at the hawk's healthy tone. But Duncan sat stiffly on his horse. He reached out his left arm and let the hawk alight. Talons closed, gripping tightly, and Alix saw a trickle of blood thread its way across the vulnerable flesh. Duncan seemed not to notice.

The bird settled himself. *I am sorry, lir, that I troubled you. I am better now.*

Finn guided his horse to Duncan's and waited mutely, watching Duncan's face. Alix realized once more how special her gift was. The others must wait for Duncan to pass on Cai's speech, but she could hear the hawk's warm tone easily.

Duncan draped the reins over the pommel and put his free hand to Cai's head, stroking the shining feathers gently.

'I would not lose you,' he murmured.

Nor I, you. The bird's eyes sharpened. *I bring news, lir. The war goes badly for Homana. The Mujhar's armies are near destroyed, scattered by the Solindish troops. What men did not flee were taken by Keough of Atvia, who rules the field. It was Atvian archers who loosed arrows at me for sport, and nearly brought me down. But the wing was hardly touched, and I am strong again.* Cai lifted from Duncan's arm and circled the forest clearing. Then he perched himself on a low branch. *You see?*

Relief loosened the constraints of Duncan's muscles. Alix felt him relax for the first time since Cai had been injured. But she also felt his concern for the army's welfare as Cai continued.

It is bad, lir. Of the thousands Shaine sent, only hundreds remain alive. Most are captives of the Atvian lord, like Carillon.

Alix stiffened so quickly her fingers dug into Duncan's back. 'What of Carillon?'

Cai hesitated. *He is well enough, for a man kept chained night and day and plagued by Atvian and Solindish soldiers who wish to ridicule him.*

'He is not hurt?' she asked breathlessly.

Liren, I did not see him well. But he was in a tumbril, heavily chained so he could not move. No man, even uninjured, can bear such close bonds for long without suffering.

She set her forehead against Duncan's back in anguish, vividly picturing the prince a prisoner to the enemy. She hardly heard Duncan telling the others what Cai said.

Finn smiled grimly. 'So, the princeling learns what it is to be a man.'

Alix jerked her head up and glared at him. 'How can you say that? Carillon is a warrior, a *prince!* He was a man before ever you took me captive!'

Finn lifted a placating hand, grinning at her vehemence. '*Mei jha*, I speak no ill of him. I mean only he has not fought for his realm before, and it is a hard thing to learn when one is taken prisoner.'

'Fergus is slain,' she said in a deadly tone. 'Mujhara is in the hands of the Ihlini. And now Carillon is prisoner to this Atvian lord. It seems more than enough for any *man*.'

'Aye,' Finn said gently.

She glared at him, expecting more. But he said nothing.

Duncan glanced at the waiting warriors. 'We must go to the city.'

'No!' Alix cried.

Cai agreed with Duncan. *Even now the Atvian lord moves his men toward Mujhara. If you go there, you will be able to defend the ancient city.*

'No,' Alix said firmly. 'We must go to Carillon.'

Duncan sighed. 'Nothing has changed, *cheysula*. Mujhara is taken. Shaine waits within the palace. It is there we must go.'

'But he is a *prisoner!*'

'You knew that days ago,' he said shortly. 'And you agreed I had the right of it.'

'I did not know he was chained! He deserves our help.'

Finn snorted. 'He wanted nothing to do with us before, *mei jha*. Why should I believe differently now?'

'By the gods!' Alix swore. 'You would have me believe you *desire* his death!'

'No,' Finn said, unsmiling. 'It would not serve the prophecy.'

That silenced her. Finn never spoke of the *tahlmorra*

contained with the prophecy of the Firstborn, and to hear his serious tone made her realize he was not always the disruptive warrior. Alix scowled at him, disliking the unfamiliarity of his new attitude.

Duncan kneed his horse forward. 'We go on to Mujhara.'

'Duncan!'

'Be silent, Alix. You are here because I have allowed it.'

She gritted her teeth and spoke through them. 'If it were *you*, Duncan, and Carillon could come to *your* aid, would you be content to let him go elsewhere?'

Duncan laughed. 'The prince does not even know we move to aid the Homanans. He can hardly miss us.

'It is not fair,' she muttered.

'War rarely is,' Duncan agreed, and led the warriors on.

Alix did not sleep. She lay stiffly under Duncan's sleep-loosened arm, thinking deeply. The Cheysuli camp was silent save for the settling of the coals and the shifting of a *lir*. She had longed to question Cai more closely about Carillon, but could not for fear Duncan would hear. So she pretended sleep when he would speak softly to her, and smiled grimly when he fell asleep himself. Then she began to plan.

If I go to Carillon, they also will have to go. Duncan would not allow me to remain alone in an enemy camp for long. She smiled wryly, half-pleased with the thought. *Not bearing this child who may give the Old Blood and its gifts back to the clan.*

She snuggled more deeply under the blanket. *I will go, and then Carillon will have the help he needs.* She scratched at a bug bite on her neck. *And if the others desire it another way, perhaps I will be enough to win Carillon free of Keough and his Atvian demons.*

Storr, lying at Finn's side, stirred and lifted his head. *You should not, liren. There is danger.*

223

She peered though the darkness but could not see the wolf's silver form. *Storr, I must do this. Carillon would do it for me.*

Your cheysul will not approve.

Then he may beat me, if he wishes, when he comes to find me.

He would never beat you. Storr was silent a moment. *Liren, you are stubborn.*

Alix smiled into the darkness. *I am Cheysuli.*

Cai settled his wings more comfortably. *Perhaps it will be enough.*

It will be, she said firmly, and waited for the dawn.

CHAPTER FIVE

Just before sunrise, when the stillness of the night lay heaviest on her soul, Alix slipped carefully from beneath the blanket. Duncan made no movement as she folded the blanket so the chill would not give away her absence. Cai, perched in the nearest tree, startled her with his resigned tone.

Still you go, liren??

She straightened the twisted jerkin and tightened her belt. *I go. Carillon is deserving of it.*

You carry a child.

Her mouth twisted. *I do. And I will keep it safe.*

The hawk's tone saddened. *I cannot gainsay you, liren.*

She looked at him sharply, peering at his huddled form. *Do you tell your lir of this?*

He will have to know.

But not yet, she pleaded. *First, let me go. Then you may tell him.*

It is not my place to keep things from my lir.

Cai, I will go. Even if Duncan wakes and seeks to gainsay me, I will go. Do you see?

The great bird seemed to sigh. *I see, liren. Then go, if you must.*

Alix smiled fondly in his direction, then blurred herself and went unto the skies as a falcon.

The journey took time, and Alix tired as she soared

over the forests. But she ignored the tension in her wings and kept on, determined to reach Carillon. When at last she broke free of the trees into bare plains, she was near exhaustion. Already it was twilight, and she feared she would not reach the armies until after dark.

Suddenly the Atvian host was below her. Alix circled and drifted over the army, seeking knowledge of the true state of affairs. She saw strange bearded men in red-painted leather-and-mail, wearing keyholed helms that hid their faces. There were archers, she saw, and soldiers bearing heavy broadswords. Among the red-mailed men were Solindish troops in chain mail and breastplates.

She kept one keen eye on the archers, fearing they would shoot at her as they had Cai. But most of the troops seemed more concerned with food, for they squatted around fires with bowls and mugs in their hands. No one paid a lone falcon any mind.

Alix dared closer, drifting in an idle pattern toward a blue field pavilion. Carefully she settled on the ridge-pole, seeking the proper place for a prince held captive.

Her body trembled. She mantled once, settled her feathers and tried to recoup her lost strength. Alix was afraid the exhaustion in her hollow bird-bones might sap her ability to hold *lir*-shape, and she could not risk discovery.

If I am caught, I will be named witch, she thought uneasily. *Shapechanger witch.*

She waited until some of her strength returned. Then she lifted from the ridgepole and drifted over the sprawling encampment.

Alix saw no sign of Carillon. She found the Homanan prisoners, harshly tied and guarded by Atvian men, but Carillon was not among them. She closed her mind to the cries and moans of the wounded, for if she listened their pain would become hers, and she would fail.

She dipped closer when she saw the post set before a scarlet pavilion. For a moment she feared the figure lashed to it was Carillon, but she saw it was a boy. His body was slumped against the post, arms and legs tied securely on the other side. His forehead was pressed against the rough wood and his eyes were closed. The soiled tunic he wore was in shreds, hanging from his back. She saw, with a quickening of revulsion, he had been flogged.

His eyes were shut tight in a pale, grimy face, and his black hair hung limply to his shoulders. She could not tell if he was alive or dead.

Alix flew on, passing over a two-wheeled tumbril near the picket-line of horses. A glance down showed her the figure slumped in it, and the familiar tawny-dark hair.

She sucked in her breath and turned back, driving toward the tumbril. Carillon sat against the front of the cart, legs stretched to hang from the opening. The setting sun glinted off the iron banding his legs and hands.

Like the boy, his eyes were closed. And, like him, he showed no signs of life. Alix flew closer.

He moved. She heard the clash of iron as he shifted his arms, settling the chain links against his chest. His eyes opened, half-lidded, staring out at the tumbril blankly. His face was badly bruised and smeared with blood. But he lived.

Alix felt the fear abate and anger rise in its place. She nearly shrieked her rage aloud but refrained as she realized it would be better not to draw attention to herself. Instead she dropped to the tumbril and settled on its rim.

Carillon stared at her. Now she could see the gauntness in his face; the blackened eyes and poor color. But there was also life in his eyes, and burning resentment.

She could not speak to him in *lir*-shape, and she dared not change back yet. She could only sit by him, and wait.

The prince shifted in the tumbril. The chains clashed and rattled against the wooden flooring, driving empathetic pain into her own heart. The heavy shackles bound his wrists mercilessly, and she saw the ridged, seeping sores beneath.

Keough is a demon! she raged within her falcon-soul. *A demon!*

Carillon raised his shackled hands and rubbed wearily at his eyes. Blood ran up the right side of his face like a flag, but she could not tell if it was his or another man's. His lips were pale and compressed.

'Well, bird,' he rasped, 'do you come to witness my death? Do you seek my flesh like the carrion crows?'

No! she cried silently.

Carillon sighed and rested his head against the tumbril. 'You may not have long, then. Keough has slain hundreds of Homanan soldiers. It is only time before he puts me up to take my head as well.' He grimaced. 'Unless he means me for Bellam, in Mujhara.'

Alix stared at him in anguish, unable to speak to him, knowing he saw only a bright-eyed falcon.

Carillon's smile was that of a man who sees his own death. 'Keep your vigil, then. I can use the company, no matter what sort it may be. The nights are long.'

Alix held her position on the tumbril rim, waiting for the long night to come.

When it did she slipped off the tumbril and blurred herself into human-form. The guard stood far away, as if a chained prince was of little account. She was unable to hold *lir*-shape any longer and slipped back into her human shape with a sigh of relief. Carillon, eyes closed, did not see it.

She moved carefully to him and put a gentle hand on his booted leg. 'Carillon.' He did not stir. 'Carillon,' she whispered again.

He opened his eyes and stared at her. For a long moment he remained expressionless, as if he saw nothing at all, and she feared he was too dazed to acknowledge her presence. Then she saw sense come into his eyes, and the incredulity.

'Alix . . .' he hissed. He sat bolt upright, wincing as the shackles bit into his raw wrists. '*Alix!*'

She raised a hand. 'Be silent, Carillon, or at least quieter. Would you have me made prisoner also?'

He gaped at her. Slowly his mouth closed and he wet his lips. 'Alix . . . have I discovered madness? Is it truly you?'

'Aye,' she whispered. 'I have come to give you what aid I can.'

He shook his head slowly. 'This cannot be. No man could walk into Keough's camp undiscovered. How is it *you* have done this?'

She smiled, suddenly calm and exultant at the same time. 'You have cursed my race, Carillon, but see how it serves you. I came to you in *lir*-shape.'

'You!'

She glanced around anxiously, hushing him with a quick gesture. 'Carillon, there is something in me that allows me to assume any animal form I wish. The *shar tahl* says it is the Old Blood in me, gotten from Lindir.' She saw the scowl begin on his face and slid into the tumbril, covering his mouth with her hand. 'Lindir, Carillon. She had Cheysuli blood in her, from her mother, though it was little enough. Yet it gave me the magic of the Firstborn.'

'I do not believe it.'

'Shaine's great-great grandsire took a Cheysuli *mei jha*, who bore him a daughter. Perhaps you also have a drop or two of Cheysuli blood in your veins.'

'I *cannot* believe it.'

Alix smiled at him. 'Were you not attended by a falcon earlier, my lord?'

He scowled at her. 'That was a bird.'

'*I* am a bird, when I wish it.' She sighed and gently touched a bruised cheek. 'I have come to get you free of this place. Do you wish to discuss my abilities all this night, rather than escaping?'

He grabbed her before she could move, pulling her

229

down until his mouth came down on hers. Alix, shocked into immobility, smelled his sweat and blood and fear, and wondered at her own lack of response.

Is this not what I wanted for so long?

She pulled away from him, one hand to her mouth. Carillon's face, though shadowed, was not at all repentant. His eyes, looking so deeply into hers, saw the answer she could not speak, and he accepted it.

He lifted his arms, chains clashing. 'I go nowhere in these.'

Alix looked away from his face; at the iron locked around his boots and the chain so short it denied him slack enough to walk.

'I will get the iron from you,' she promised. 'I will give you your freedom again.'

'I would not ask you to risk yourself, Alix. I have given you my thanks for what you have done — if you wish an explanation — but I could not ask such a dangerous thing of you.'

'I *offer*. You do not ask.' She smiled. 'If I unlock your chains, could you take a horse from here?'

He stared hard at the tumbril floor and at the muscles that quivered in his thighs. His voice, when it came, sounded old and worn thin. 'I have been chained as you see me for weeks. I doubt I could stand without aid, let alone ride.' His eyes shifted to her face. 'Alix, I would be willing to try, but I will not let you do this. I will not risk your life.'

'You sound like Duncan!' she accused. 'He will not credit my willingness to do this either.'

His brows lowered. 'What has the shapechanger to do with this?'

Alix sat on her folded legs, forcing her frustration down. 'He is my husband, Carillon, after Cheysuli fashion. He has much to do with this.'

He shifted uncomfortably. 'You should not have gone with him from Homana-Mujhar. You could have stayed with me, once I had soothed the Mujhar.'

230

'I chose to go with Duncan.' She sighed and forced herself to relax. 'Carillon, we can speak of this another time. For now, I have come to help you escape. Tell me where the key to this iron is kept.'

'No.'

'Carillon!' she hissed.

'I will not,' he said firmly. 'I would rather remain a prisoner than risk you.'

She glared at him, teeth and fists clenched. 'They will take you to Mujhara! Tynstar is therĕ, with Bellam. Carillon, you will be *slain*!'

He remained silent.

Alix ground her teeth and flung a furious glance around the area. Finally she hunched over, propping her chin on one hand.

'I have come all this way for you, and you will not let me help you. I defied my husband, who said Homana-Mujhar is more important than Homana's prince, and I have risked the life of my child for you, and *still* you will not let me do this.'

'Child,' he said sharply, straightening. 'You have conceived?'

She scowled at him. 'Aye. I have assumed the form of wolf and falcon. I have no knowledge what such magic will do to an unborn child, but I did it for you. For *you*, Carillon.'

He closed his eyes. 'Alix,' he said in despair, 'you have been a foolish woman.'

She picked at the leather of her borrowed leggings. 'Aye, perhaps I have. But I cannot go back now.' She brightened. 'Would it change your mind if I said the Cheysuli will come here?'

He stared at her suspiciously. 'Cheysuli?'

She straightened, growing excited. 'We were on our way to Mujhara, to aid Shaine. But Duncan will doubtless seek me here, when Cai tells him what I have done.' She smiled slowly, proudly. 'He will not let me do this alone. He will come after me.'

231

Carillon sighed wearily and fingered the bruise on his cheek. 'Alix, if you are anything like your mother, I am not surprised she said no to royal betrothal and fled with a shapechanger. I think you are more stubborn than any woman I have known.'

'They will come,' she said softly. 'The Cheysuli. And you will be freed.'

He raised a single eyebrow. 'Duncan has no knowledge you are here?'

She averted her face. 'No. He would have forbidden it.'

'As would I,' he retorted. 'Perhaps he and I are more like than I thought.'

She watched emotion moving in his face, and his struggle to maintain a calm demeanor. She leaned forward and placed a gentle hand on his manacled forearm.

'Carillon, the Cheysuli are not so different from the Homanans. They have only retained the gifts of the old gods.' She paused. 'Do not curse us for it.'

'Alix, you are more eloquent than my uncle's courtiers.'

'Will you not admit it?' she asked earnestly. 'Will you not see we are not demons and beasts . . . not what men brand us?'

'I cannot say. I have been taught to fear and mistrust them all my life. Alix . . . I have seen what they can do to men in battle . . . what they leave when they kill.'

'That is battle,' she said quietly. 'You should know, now, what price it exacts.' Her fingers tightened on his arm. 'You know them, now. You know *me*.'

Carillon drew up his legs, chains clashing, and stared over his knees at her. 'If they come — *if* they come — there is little I can say against them. They will have proven their service to the Mujhar's heir.' He smiled bleakly. 'But they will not come.'

'*I* came.'

For a long moment he said nothing, studying her face.

232

She sensed the conflict within him, realizing she had suffered her own measure of it when Duncan first insisted she go to the Keep.

It is not easily done, she reflected. *And he is no kind of man at all if he accedes so swiftly to words he has been taught not to hear.*

'Alix,' he said finally, 'perhaps, in time, I will believe you. But not yet.'

She removed her hand and stood. 'If I cannot free you, perhaps there is something else. Can I steal food for you? Water?'

'I do not hunger. Inactivity and chains take the appetite from a man.' His eyes were grim, hidden in shadow. 'There is only one thing I would ask, and I cannot ask it of you.'

'Tell me.'

He pushed grimy fingers through tangled tawny hair, baring his face to the moonlight. Alix saw the glitter in his eyes.

'There is a boy. Rowan. A Homanan boy no more than twelve, who came to serve his lord however he could.' His eyes closed a moment. 'He told me he acted as a runner between the captains, carrying messages. But he, like me, was caught and made helpless. Keough's son took Rowan from the prisoners — as he did me — and made him serve the Atvian lords.' Carillon's face tightened into bitterness as he remembered. 'I was forced to watch him, in Keough's field pavilion. His eyes followed me everywhere ... and I could see the confusion in his face. I was his prince — why could I not win his release?'

'Carillon,' she said softly.

Chains rattled and glinted in the moonlight. 'Rowan did well enough at first. But he was tired, aching from the cuffs they had given him all night. They even made him serve me, though it was done as if I were no better than the poorest cur.' Breath hissed between his teeth. 'Rowan tripped and fell across the table, and spilled wine all over Keough himself. When they picked him up he was crying in fear and exhaustion, but his face — when he looked at me — accepted what they would do to him. He knew.' He swore beneath his breath. 'I tried to gainsay it. I tried to assuage Keough's anger by offering to take the boy's punishment myself — by the gods, I begged for it! I got on my knees to Keough ... when I would not do it before, when they asked for it! But the boy was worth it.'

'They would not accept it,' Alix said.

'No. Thorne — Keough's son — took Rowan out and had him flogged until the skin fell off his back ... and then left him tied to the post.'

'I have seen him.'

Carillon gave up his breath as if he would breathe no more. 'Only a boy, who wished to serve his lord. And do you see what that service has won him?'

She felt for the knife in her right boot and found it. Then she smiled at Carillon. 'I will free him for you, my lord. You will see.'

'Alix!' he cried, jerking upright, but she had already blurred into the darkness.

CHAPTER SIX

Alix flew to the post and perched upon it. The boy was still slumped at its base, but now she could see the movement of his back that told her he breathed. The flesh had nearly been stripped from his rib cage. She winced to herself, then looked closely at the field pavilions surrounding the area.

The scarlet one was largest, and the finest. Men had set tall torches in the ground before it, illuminating its front. Two other smaller pavilions stood on either side of it, but the torchlight did not extend to them. Alix assured herself there were no guards near the post, then drifted down and blurred into human form.

She drew the knife from her boot and knelt at the boy's side. She put a hand on his shoulder, carefully avoiding his lacerated flesh. He made no movement and she feared his unconsciousness would hinder her ability to get him away safely.

I will take him to the forest's edge, she decided. *Somehow I will get him there, and have him wait. When Duncan comes, I can take him to this boy, Rowan.*

He winced and moaned, stirring under her fingers. His eyes opened wide, dilated, pale in the moonlight. Fear changed his bruised face into a mask of terror.

Alix moved around so he could see her clearly. 'No, Rowan,' she said softly. 'I am not your enemy. I am sent from Prince Carillon, who would have you free of this place.'

His face was hidden behind his tied arm, but she could see the gleam of his light eyes. He swallowed visibly. 'Prince Carillon?'

Alix set her knife to the robe binding his legs and cut them. 'He knows you have served his House,' she said soothingly. 'He knows what loyalty you have given him. He would not have you so poorly treated for honorable service.'

'I have not served honorably,' the boy said miserably. 'I ran. I *ran*.' His head dropped. 'And I was captured.'

'Carillon was also captured,' she told him. 'He fought, but was beaten.' Inwardly she flinched at so undermining Carillon's prowess. But it was the truth. 'You were here, Rowan. You came to serve. He has seen the honor in you, and he has done what he could to get you free. I have come in his name, because he asked it.' She bent closer to him. 'He called you by name and told me to come straight here, to release you.'

'I am not worthy.'

She freed his hands and moved back to his side, sliding the knife into her boot. Carefully she helped him sit up.

'You are more than worthy. Why else would the prince himself insist you be freed?'

The light fell clearly on his face for the first time. It was bruised and grimy, but his eyes, staring at her, were as yellow as Duncan's.

Alix sucked in a breath. 'Cheysuli!'

Rowan recoiled from her, then winced. 'No!' he cried. 'I am not a demon!'

She put a trembling hand toward his face. 'No . . . oh no . . . you are not a demon. It is not a curse. Rowan—'

'What do you do?' asked an accented voice from behind.

Alix leaped to her feet and whirled, staring wide-eyed

236

at the man. He stood before her like a demon in shadow, backlighted by the torches. He was dark-haired, bearded, and the color of his eyes was indeterminate. Before she could move he reached out and caught her arm.

'Who are you, boy?'

She was thankful for her warrior's garb. 'I am a servant of the prince, my lord. Prince Carillon.'

He glanced down at Rowan, shivering against the post. The man smiled grimly and jerked Alix toward the scarlet pavilion, into the torchlight.

She saw he was near Duncan's age, but there the resemblance ended. He was tall and slender; strongly built. She saw cruelty and determination in the lines of his face; glinting in his brown eyes. He was richly dressed in black save for a blue tunic that bore the crest of a scarlet hand clasping a white lightning bolt. His mail, glinting in the light, was little more than ceremonial.

His hand was tight on her arm. 'You are no boy,' he said, surprised. He turned her face into the light. 'No boy at all.' And he smiled.

She tugged ineffectually against his grip. When she saw she could not break free she gave it up and waited silently.

'Who are you? Why do you free that worthless child?'

'He is not worthless!' she cried. 'He only sought to serve his prince, as befits a loyal man. Yet you punish him for that!'

'I punish him because he threw wine over my father,' the man said firmly. 'He is fortunate I did not order him slain.'

Alix froze. *Thorne . . . Thorne! This man is Keough's heir!*

His dark eyes narrowed. 'What do you do here, girl?'

'You saw me. I cut the boy free.'

'Why?'

She lifted her chin defiantly. 'Because Carillon desired it.'

237

'Carillon is a prisoner.' His accent twisted the name. 'His desires are nothing to me.'

'Let me go,' she said, knowing the request was futile.

Thorne arched a dark brow. 'I think not. But tell me why you desire to leave a prince's presence so quickly.'

'There is another prince whose company I prefer.'

He stared at her malignantly. Alix began to regret antagonizing him, for fear of the reprisals that might affect Carillon.

'My father will wish to see you,' Thorne said abruptly, and dragged her into the scarlet pavilion.

Keough, Lord of Atvia, sat at a heavy slab table in the shadows of the pavilion. Braziers had been set out to ward off the chill and torches flamed in each corner. Alix stared at him and began to be very afraid for the first time.

He was huge. His massive body dwarfed the chair he sat in, which had been bound with iron to lend it strength. His bared forearms rested on the table. She saw freckles and red hairs bleached golden by the sun. A white ridge of scar tissue snaked across the flesh and up his left arm. His hair also was red, threaded with white, and his beard was bushy. His deep-set eyes watched her in calm deliberation.

'What have you brought me, Thorne?'

'A woman dressed as a boy. You will have to ask her the reason for it.'

Keough's eyes narrowed. His Atvian mouth formed the Homanan syllables harshly, without the liquid grace she was accustomed to.

'She does not look like a camp follower. They, at least, wear skirts.' His fingers combed his beard. 'Are you a woman who prefers those of her own sex?'

'No!' Alix hissed, against her will. She saw Keough's small smile, and it rankled. 'I am a Homanan, my lord. That is all you need know.'

'Then you are my enemy.'

'Aye.' It was heartfelt.

The beard and mustache parted as he grinned, displaying discolored teeth as big as the rest of him. 'Have you come hoping to fight? If so, you are too late. The battle is already won. Prince Fergus and the generals are slain; executed. Most of the captains are dead, though I save a few for later exhibition. Even Carillon is in my hands.' Keough paused. 'There is little left for you to champion.'

Alix was done with this. She reached for the magic in her bones that would give her *lir*-shape before their eyes. But Thorne, seeming to sense something, twisted the arm he held until the sinews cracked. The sudden pain drove away the concentration the shapechange required.

'What do I do with her?' Thorne asked. 'Will you use her, or do I take her for myself?'

Keough looked at her as she hung on her tiptoes. 'Leave her with me. See if Carillon is still among us.'

Thorne released her and left the tent. Alix cradled her aching arm against her chest, glaring at Keough. For the moment she was helpless, and knew it.

The Atvian lord smiled and sat back in his massive chair. 'You are not a light woman. You are not a soldier. What are you?'

'Someone who will seek your downfall, Atvian, when I am given the chance.'

'I could have you slain, girl. Or do it myself.' He raised his huge hands. 'Your slender throat would not live long in these fingers.'

'And your heart will not live long with a Cheysuli arrow piercing it,' Duncan said quietly.

Alix swung around, shocked as she saw him standing inside the pavilion. His eyes rested on her briefly, expressionlessly, then returned to Keough. In his hands was the black war bow, its string invisible in the shadows. Eerily, it seemed the bow required no string to send its arrow winging into men's flesh.

Keough made a sound. Alix turned back and saw him

stare at Duncan as if demons pursued his soul. His small eyes slid from Duncan to Alix, and she heard the malevolence in his tone.

'So, you are a shapechanger witch sent to distract me while others work against us.'

'No,' she said clearly. 'I am Cheysuli, aye, but I came only for Carillon. You bind him harshly, my lord. There is no honor in your heart.'

Keough laughed at her. 'I *have* no heart, witch. None at all.'

Duncan moved forward until he stood next to Alix. 'My *cheysula* has the right of it. Carillon deserves better.'

Keough pressed his hands against the table and rose. He was unarmed save for a sheathed knife at his belt, but he did not reach for it.

'I warn you, shapechanger. I am not an easy man to slay.'

Duncan smiled grimly. 'You will not be slain this night, my lord. It is not your *tahlmorra*. It would not serve the prophecy.'

Keough's red brows lanced down. 'What mean you?'

'Nothing, save I desire Carillon's release.'

'Your price for leaving me alive?' Keough laughed. 'What if I refuse?'

Duncan shrugged. 'I have said you will not die this night. I have never lied. Even to my enemies.'

The huge Atvian lord smiled. 'I give you nothing, shapechanger. What you will have, you must take.'

Alix sensed the billowing of the doorflap behind and turned quickly, expecting an Atvian guard. But instead she saw a familiar silver wolf, and Finn beside him.

He grinned at her. 'So, *mei jha*, you will do for yourself what you cannot convince *us* to do.'

'I asked,' she said tightly. 'You would not come.'

'Enough,' Duncan said softly.

Thorne burst through the draped pavilion entrance, sword drawn and raised to slash its way into flesh and bone. Finn spun noiselessly and drew his knife,

240

knocking the blade away. Thorne fell sprawling to the ground, a Cheysuli knife pressed against his throat as Finn knelt by him.

Duncan looked solemnly at Keough. 'Your son's life, my lord, in exchange for Carillon's release.'

Keough spat out an Atvian oath between his teeth and grabbed up the keys from an open chest. He flung them at Duncan.

Alix followed Duncan's silent order and left the pavilion. Duncan followed her out, leaving Finn and Storr to keep the Atvian rulers contained.

'Where is he?' Duncan asked.

'By the horses. Duncan—'

'We will speak of it another time.'

Alix winced. 'What else could I do?'

'We will speak of it another time.'

She stopped to protest, then became aware of the odd stillness shrouding the encampment. She realized not a single Atvian or Solindish soldier moved against the Cheysuli invaders.

Alix turned puzzled eyes on Duncan. 'What have you done?'

He smiled grimly. 'We have used the third gift of the gods, Alix. We could not force all into submission, but we found the captains and took their minds from them for a time. They, in turn, do as we ordered, and keep the common soldiers from fighting. The Homanan captives have been freed.'

She drew back a step. 'By the gods ... you are so powerful?'

'It is a thing we rarely do. It takes the spirit from a man, and that is a thing no Cheysuli would do if there were another way.' His eyes were reproving. 'You have brought this about, *cheysula*.'

Her hands clenched into fists. 'I would do the same for you!' she burst out. 'For you I would give my life. How can you deny me this for Carillon?'

He sighed and jangled the keys against his leg. 'Alix,

241

we will speak of this later. You have forced me to free the prince, so let me be about it. Do you come?'

She started to walk on, then stopped stiffly and turned back. 'The boy!'

'What boy?'

'Rowan.' She gestured at the post and saw the boy was gone. 'He was there. Tied. I freed him.' She frowned. 'I thought he had not the strength to leave this place.' Alix's face cleared. 'But if he *is* Cheysuli—

Duncan took her arm. 'Come, *cheysula*. If the boy is free, it is fortunate for him.'

She went with him to Carillon.

The prince still sat in the tumbril, legs drawn up. Moonlight spilled across the iron on his legs and hands, illuminating the drawn hollows aróund his eyes. When he saw Alix he shifted forward, ignoring the clank of chain.

'You are safe!'

She smiled and slid a quick sideways glance at Duncan. 'Aye, I am.'

Carillon blinked in surprise as he saw the Cheysuli warrior. Then a wariness came into his face. 'What have you come for, shapechanger?'

Duncan regarded Carillon solemnly. 'I lost something, my lord. I came to recover it.' He spread his hands. 'But while I am here, I may as well see to your welfare. My foolish *cheysula* has forced me to do her bidding.'

Carillon nearly smiled. Alix saw the struggle in his face as he tried to keep his emotional distance from the Cheysuli. But his relief and good nature won out.

'She *is* a foolish woman. I told her so when first she appeared, but she would have none of it.' He shrugged. 'Women are wilful creatures.'

Duncan lost his solemnity and grinned. 'Aye, especially this one. I think it is the royalty in her.'

Carillon laughed. Alix, disgruntled by the amusement in them both at her expense, glared at Duncan.

'Have you brought the keys for nothing, Duncan? See to your prince!'

Duncan banished his smile but not the glint in his eyes. He bent and unlocked the leg shackles. Then he unlocked the heavy bands around his wrists.

The iron fell away. Alix hissed as she saw the raw wounds ringing Carillon's wrists, as if he still wore the shackles. Carefully he stretched out his hands and tried to work them.

Duncan stopped him. 'Do not. If you will suffer it, I can take away the pain when we are free of this place.' His eyes were very watchful. '*Will* you suffer it?'

Carillon sighed. 'It seems I must. Alix has chastised me for my unremitting distrust of your race. Perhaps it is time I listened to her.'

A glow came into Duncan's eyes. 'If she has caused you to reconsider the feelings most Homanans hold for us, then her foolishness has some merit.'

'Duncan!' she cried in frustration.

His brows lifted as he turned to her. 'Well, it *was* foolishness. First you left the Keep, where I ordered you to remain; then you joined us when I would have you go back; and now you have come into an enemy camp. What else am I to think of your behavior?'

Alix took a deep breath and glared at him, hands on hips. 'My behavior is mine to do. It has nothing to do with you. Because I have wed you according to your barbaric shapechanger custom and carry your halfling child does *not* mean you have the ordering of me.'

'Alix!' Carillon cried. He looked first at Duncan, then at her. After a moment he looked back at Duncan. 'Does she always speak this way?'

'When it suits her. I have not found her a diplomatic *cheysula*.'

Alix scowled at him.

Carillon shook his head slowly. 'No, I think not. I had not known of her sharp tongue.' He grinned suddenly.

'Well, that is not entirely true. I recall her words when I destroyed her garden.'

Alix shoved her hair back from her face. 'I begin to wish I had not come.'

Carillon frowned at her. 'Who cut off your hair?'

'Duncan.'

Carillon, astonished, looked at the warrior. 'Why?'

Duncan's mouth twisted. 'She required a lesson.' He dropped the keys and stretched out his hand. 'Come, my lord; it is time we took you from this place.'

Carillon heaved himself from the tumbril with Duncan's help. His face went white and he gasped in pain as his muscles screamed their agony. He remained on his feet only because Duncan held him there.

'Give me a sword,' Carillon said between clenched teeth. 'I must have a sword. I owe a death to someone.'

'I have none.' Duncan's eyes were opaque and blank. 'The last sword the Cheysuli held was Hale's. You, my lord, have lost it for us.'

Carillon blanched beneath the quiet reproach. 'I had little to do with it! Thorne disarmed me, and took it.' His pale face twisted. 'I will slay that man. I have been chained like a beast and treated as common filth. They have made me watch as they ordered my men slain, and Thorne has laughed at it all.' He took a slow breath. 'But the worst has nothing to do with me. It was the boy. Because of him, and the rest, Thorne will die by my hand.'

Alix moved closer. 'The boy, Carillon. I saw him closely. Is he Cheysuli?'

Carillon sighed. 'I thought so. He had the colour for it. But he said no, when I asked him. He was afraid. I think, if anything, he is a bastard got on some Cheysuli woman. He said he was raised Homanan by a man and a woman not his parents.' He looked back at Duncan. 'If I cannot have a sword, shapechanger, then lend me a knife.'

Duncan's eyes narrowed. 'I have a name, princeling.

You would do well to use it. I have committed my clan to your survival, and that of Homana. You and I have, I think, gone beyond being opponents of any sort. There is more than that between us, now. My lord.' Duncan studied him dispassionately. 'If you would earn the respect of the Cheysuli — which you must have to keep Homana intact — you would do well to save your hatred for the Ihlini.'

Alix feared they might come to blows. Carillon glared angrily at Duncan, as if he would slay him, and Duncan exhibited no intention of retracting his sharp words.

Finally she put a hand on each of their arms. 'Come, my warriors. We should leave this place.' When Duncan made no signs of moving she deliberately pressed her nails into his bare arm. 'Cheysul, so you forget I carry your son? Get me free of this place.'

That drove both of them into motion. Carillon wavered on his feet, recovered, and made as if to walk. Duncan caught his arm and led him away from the tumbril. But his other hand was on Alix's wrist, and she felt herself dragged after him.

Satisfied she had achieved her goal, she smiled to herself and went along amicably.

CHAPTER SEVEN

Duncan stole an Atvian horse and helped Carillon mount. The prince's face was stretched taut with pain and the struggle to keep it unspoken, but Alix sensed every screaming fibre of Carillon's mistreated body. Silently she watched him compose himself in the saddle, gathering reins with swollen, discolored hands.

Duncan turned to her. 'Ride behind him, *cheysula*.'

Carillon glared at him. 'I have no need of a woman to keep me in the saddle, shapechanger.'

'This *woman* has accounted for your rescue, princeling,' Duncan returned. 'And as for your ability to keep yourself in the saddle, that is for you to do. It is Alix I am concerned about, and the health of our child.'

Carillon, about to say something more, snapped his mouth shut.

Alix shook her head. 'I go with you, Duncan.'

'The others leave this place in *lir*-shape,' he said calmly. 'I will walk, leading this horse. Whether you realize it yet, you are doubtless weary. Ride, Alix.'

Duncan's words awoke all the trembling in her limbs and the comprehension of what she had accomplished. Alix felt her bones turn to water. Though she longed to protest she withheld it as she saw the understanding in Duncan's eyes. Silently she let him lift her onto the horse, and carefully clasped her fingers into the leather of Carillon's belt.

'Where do we go?' he asked.

'Not far. Perhaps two leagues from here.' Duncan took the horse's bridle and led it out. 'Come, we will see to your welfare when we are free of this place.'

Duncan took them from the open plains into the depths of the shadowed forests, moving so silently Alix heard only the horse's steps muffled against the bedding of the forest floor. Occasionally she saw flitting shapes of animals slipping by and realized the *lir* and their warriors gave the clan-leader and his charges protection. She felt very safe.

At last Duncan turned the horse into a tiny clearing invisible to the untrained eye. Alix pushed free of the horse and dropped to the ground, ignoring Duncan's disapproving comment. She stepped out of the way and watched as he helped Carillon dismount.

'I will be well enough,' Carillon said curtly.

Duncan did not remove his steadying arm. 'It is no disgrace to require help after so much time spent in close confinement.' He met Carillon's eyes. 'Or is it only *Cheysuli* aid you spurn?'

Alix sighed wearily and pushed hair from her face. 'Must you ever go at one another with no basis other than pride and arrogance?' she asked. 'Can neither of you forget your race and simply conduct yourselves as *men*?'

Carillon stared at her. After a moment something softened his expression and twisted his mouth briefly. He looked back at Duncan.

'You have proven your loyalty to *me*, at least, this night. It is not my place to reprove you for it.'

Duncan smiled and indicated a fallen log. 'Come, my lord. We will see if you are worth saving.'

Alix followed as Duncan led Carillon to the log. The prince lowered himself carefully to the ground and leaned against the fallen tree, sighing as his limbs fell

247

once more into the positions they had grown accustomed to in captivity.

'Build a fire, *cheysula*,' Duncan said quietly as he knelt by Carillon's side.

She felt a spasm of fear in her chest. 'So close to the Atvians?'

'We must, Alix. Carillon can go no further this night.'

Unhappily she did his bidding, locating stones and building them into a small fire cairn. She lay small sticks and broken kindling upon it, and kept herself from twitching in surprise as a Cheysuli warrior appeared to light it. When she glanced up she saw the clearing was filled with returned warriors.

Flames licked at the kindling and caught, illuminating the clearing into eerie, flickering shadows. Alix saw the dark face of each man and the glowing yellow eyes, acknowledging again her own kinship to the magic of the gods. The *lir*, four-footed and winged, waited silently with their warriors.

Cai? she asked silently.

He rustled in the nearest tree. *Here, liren.*

I accomplished what I said I would.

Aye, liren. He sounded amused. *You are truly Cheysuli.*

Alix grinned. *Those words from you are honor indeed, Cai.*

Yet once you would not admit it, liren.

Alix sighed and knelt by the fire, watching her husband at Carillon's side. *But then I was foolish, Cai, and unwilling to learn.*

You have learned much, the bird agreed. *But there is still much left to you.*

She peered into the tree, trying to distinguish the hawk's form from distorting branches. *What do you say?*

In time, you will know.

A stifled exclamation from Carillon took her attention from the bird and she moved closer to the prince. Duncan, she saw in alarm, manipulated Carillon's hands with little regard for his pain.

248

'Can you not let them be?' Carillon asked between gritted teeth. 'They will heal.'

'It is worth the pain to let me see to them, my lord. Iron can damage more than flesh. It can take away the little life within the muscles themselves. But you, I think, will hold a sword again.'

'And when I hold that sword, I will plunge it into Thorne's black heart.'

Alix's eyes widened as she saw Finn step out of the darkness into the ring of firelight. Storr flanked him on one side.

'What sword will you use, princeling?' Finn demanded. 'You have lost the one my *jehan* gifted to the Mujhar.'

Color flooded Carillon's face. 'I admit it.'

Finn raised one eyebrow. 'Well, I had expected denials and excuses from you. You surprise me.'

'This can wait,' Duncan said reprovingly.

Finn moved closer and drew a tooled leather sheath from behind his back. The gold hilt of a broadsword gleamed in the firelight, and the brilliant ruby in it glistened like blood.

The warrior lifted it into the light, focusing all eyes on it. 'Hale's sword was meant for one man, Carillon. I cannot say if that man is you, but if it is — you had best take care. This is twice you have lost my *jehan's* sword. Next time I may not see it back in your hands.'

Carillon said nothing as Finn held the sheathed weapon down. For a long moment his hands lay still in his lap, where Duncan had released them. Then, when Finn made no move to withdraw it, Carillon closed one hand around the scabbard.

'If you are so dedicated to overcoming my succession,' he began, 'why, then, do you persist in restoring this blade to me? In your hands it might prove far more powerful.'

Finn shrugged, folding bronzed arms across his chest. 'A Cheysuli warrior does not bear a sword. And I am that before anything else.'

249

Carillon set the sword across his lap and stared at the Homanan lion crest stamped into its hilt. Then he let the pain and fatigue take his mind, and he fell asleep with Hale's sword against his chest.

Alix looked on his bruised, gaunt face and suddenly longed for the first days of their meetings in the forest near the croft. His fine clothes were gone, replaced by soiled and scarred leathers and blood-rusted chain mail. His sword-belt was missing and his hair had grown shaggy and tangled in weeks of captivity. The only thing princely about him was the ruby seal ring on his right forefinger, and the determination inherent in his face even in exhausted sleep.

She sighed and felt a hollowness enter her spirit, knowing Carillon's personal *tahlmorra* would take him farther from her yet.

Duncan rose and turned to her, looking down on her expressionlessly. Something in his eyes made her realize her face gave away her feelings, and for an odd moment she saw before her a stern shapechanger warrior who had forced her into his clan against her wishes.

Then the oddness slid away and she saw him clearly. *He is Duncan*, she recalled. *Duncan* . . .

Somehow, it was enough.

He moved to her and slowly raised her. She felt the strength in his hand on her arm and marvelled again that this man had taken an unschooled croft-girl into his pavilion, when he might have had another.

'Come with me,' he said softly, guiding her out of the clearing to the forest beyond.

When he found a shattered tree stump he set her down upon it and stood resolutely before her, dark face unreadable in the shadows.

'Duncan?'

'I cannot fault you for what you have done. You determined what it was that needed doing, and you did it.' He shrugged crookedly. 'As any warrior does.'

Alix stared at the ground, dreading his wrath. Duncan's was ever worse than anyone's.

'I understand what it is to care deeply for someone, so deeply you must do what you can, regardless of outcome,' he said quietly. 'You know I would sacrifice myself for you, or Finn, or any other warrior of my clan.'

After a moment she dared to look up at him. Nervously she wet her lips. 'If you mean to be angry, Duncan, do it. I cannot wait for it all night.'

His face, still in shadow, showed her nothing. But his voice was surprised. 'I am not angry with you. What you did was not *wrong* — only inconsiderate.'

She stiffened. 'Inconsiderate!'

Duncan sighed and stepped forward, into a shaft of moonlight threading its way through the trees. She saw his smile and warm eyes as his hands settled possessively on her shoulders.

'Do you forget the child? Do you forget the magic in your soul?'

'Duncan—'

'I will not risk losing you because of bearing the child too soon. Such things can take a woman's life. But neither will I risk the child, who deserves to live as a warrior. Alix, you have taken *lir*-shape while carrying an unborn child. Had you not thought what that might mean?'

Instinctively a hand slipped to her stomach. Suddenly she was very frightened.

'Duncan — it will not harm the child? It will not take him from me?'

He traced the worried creases from her brow. 'I think it will not harm the child, *cheysula*, but it cannot do it much good. Would you have a poor unformed soul shifting shape before it even knows its own?'

Her fingers tightened spasmodically against her stomach. 'Duncan!'

He sighed and pulled her to her feet, wrapping hard arms around her shoulders. She turned her face against him.

'I have not said this to worry you, Alix. Only to make you think.'

She clung to him. 'I *have* thought, Duncan ... and I am afraid!'

'The child is Cheysuli, small one, and bears the Old Blood. I think it will be well enough.'

She drew back. 'But what if I have harmed it? What if it is not whole?'

Duncan muttered something under his breath and pulled her against his chest roughly. 'I am sorry I said anything. I should not have put this in your mind.'

'You are right to,' she said clearly, trying to see his face in the shadows. 'I have been foolish ... as you said.'

'Would you say that to Carillon, whom you have freed from captivity?'

'*You* freed him.'

'But had you not defied me to begin with, I would not have gone to the Atvian encampment at all. It was Mujhara I was bound for.'

Alix sighed, trying to deal with two fears. 'Do you send me back, then? Do you forbid me to go with you to the city, and make me wait at the Keep?'

He laughed softly. 'Why can you not be as other women? Why must you put on men's garb — my own, I have seen — and act the part of a warrior?'

She scowled. 'How can I say? I am myself.'

He nodded. 'I have seen that. It is not entirely unpleasing, in its place. As for Mujhara, you will have to come with us. I will not have you take *lir*-shape again, and I will not have you return to the Keep alone. I can spare no men to take you.' He shrugged, sighing. 'So you will come.'

Alix said nothing for a long moment. Then she clenched her hands against his ribs. 'I cannot say if I am pleased or not. I would not be happy at the Keep, waiting in fear, but neither will I be happy to see you risk yourself for Shaine's city.'

He smoothed back her hair. 'It is not Shaine's city,

small one. Once it was Cheysuli. We have only to win back what was ours.'

She turned her face up to his. 'Duncan — had the Cheysuli not given up the throne to Homanans — could you have been Mujhar?'

He smiled. 'I am clan-leader, *cheysula*. It is enough.'

Something turned in her heart. 'But you have lost so much . . .'

His eyes were very clear in the moonlight as he looked into her face. 'I have lost something, perhaps, but I have found even more.'

'Duncan—'

'Hush, *cheysula*. It is time you let our child rest.'

She sighed and felt her left hand clasped firmly as he led her back to the tiny camp.

I am not the proper sort of woman for this man . . . she thought in aching regret.

Cai, hidden in the darkness, sent her his warm reassurance. *Liren* . . . *you are the* only *woman for this man*.

Alix drew closer to Duncan and hoped the hawk was right.

BOOK IV
'The Warrior'

CHAPTER ONE

'I will not subject myself to Cheysuli sorcery,' Carillon said firmly in the morning.

He sat upright against his log, hands folded over the scabbarded sword Finn had returned to him. The Cheysuli warriors faced him silently, yet disapproving even in their silence.

Alix saw the defiant determination in the prince's battered face. 'Carillon,' she reproved softly.

His eyes flickered as he looked at her, standing at Duncan's side. 'Alix, such sorcery is evil. I cannot deny your own measure of it, but I know you. You would never seek to bring down Homana's heir.'

'Nor would we,' Duncan said flatly. He sighed. 'You would not believe it, perhaps, but the Cheysuli never meant to give up their proper place next to the Homanan Mujhars. Until Hale left, Cheysuli warriors ever served Homanan kings. We seek no quarrel with you.'

Finn stood apart from the others, smiling crookedly in his familiar mocking manner. '*You* seek the quarrel, I think.'

Carillon's mouth tightened. 'I seek only to get to Mujhara and free my city from the Ihlini demons. And Bellam of Solinde.' His fingers were bone-white as he clenched them on the sword.

'You will not get there without our aid,' Finn said curtly. 'Yet last night you were willing enough to let us use our gifts on the enemy.'

'Using your magic to release your liege lord is one thing,' Carillon retorted. 'Subverting my will with it entirely another.'

Finn laughed scornfully. 'See how quickly he calls himself our lord! Only months ago you lay in our hands, princeling, and did our bidding. Could we not have forced sorcery on you *then* if we wished it? Or is it that you lift yourself higher, now, because Fergus of Homana is slain?'

'*Rujho*,' Duncan said quietly.

Carillon's eyes were hard as stone as he shook his head. 'Let him speak. I have learned much of men because of this war, and I find there are times a man must consider himself first. Long have I allowed the Mujhar to manipulate me, but no longer. My father is slain by Atvian hands and it is my place to do what he would.' Carillon smiled slowly, without humor. 'You may not like it, shapechanger, but I will be lord of Homana one day. You had better accustom yourself to it.'

Color surged into Finn's face as he stiffened. The yellow blaze in his eyes gave away the depths of the rage he felt, and Alix grinned delightedly. She caught his eyes on her and did not hide her reaction, which only angered him further. Finn turned and walked away from the clustered warriors.

Duncan, legs spread and arms folded, smiled ironically down on Carillon. 'My lord prince, you may well be our liege lord. But it remains: you cannot ride into Mujhara in this fashion. You would not last the journey.'

Carillon placed one hand flat against the ground and pushed himself upright, tensing his body with the effort it took. Alix stifled the movement she longed to make to help him, knowing to do so would diminish the impact of his rising. He stood taller than most of them, though the Cheysuli were a tall race, and his broad shoulders stretched against the leather-and-mail he wore. Only his eyes gave away the immensity of effort it took for him to remain standing erectly before them.

'If I cannot ride into my own city, I have no business attempting to free her from the Ihlini terror.'

'Carillon,' she said softly, 'it will not hurt. It will only strengthen you.'

His eyes burned into hers as he stretched out his left hand. The stiff sleeve of his fighting leathers and mail drew back on his arm, baring the ridged purple weals still weeping fluid from the shackle-wounds.

'I care little if it hurts, Alix. Have I not learned to deal with pain?'

Duncan's hand pressed against her shoulder as if bidding her into silence. Alix longed to answer Carillon's bitterness but refrained. As she listened to Duncan she realized nothing she said could change Carillon's mind. But Duncan's words might.

'Homana lies in her death struggle,' he said clearly. 'I believe you realize that. It is a harsh thing to comprehend, when you are prince of a land and must someday ascend the throne, but it is something you must deal with. The Cheysuli denied the truth of the prophecy once, Carillon, and suffered because of it. If you deny it, you also will suffer.'

'I am not Cheysuli,' Carillon said sharply. 'A shape-changer prophecy cannot foretell what will become of a Homanan. I have no place in it.'

'You cannot know,' Duncan said softly. 'Nor can any man. You must allow things their own path if you are to survive. This prophecy *has* foretold what will become of you, my lord, even though you be Homanan. I believe you are the Mujhar it speaks of — the one who will end the *qu'mahlin* and restore our race to peace and our homeland.' Duncan sighed as Carillon's face expressed patent disbelief. 'We cannot turn the flow of the prophecy. But we *can* withstand the dark arts of Ihlini interference.'

'You cannot tell me what has happened was *meant*!' the prince snapped. 'My father's death?'

'A man must die before his son is fully a man,' Duncan said gently. 'And the throne of Homana must once again fall into Cheysuli hands.'

Alix saw bitterness and resentment wash colour from Carillon's face. 'Cheysuli hands?' he asked ominously. 'You say Homana's throne will be in *shapechanger* hands?'

She stepped from Duncan and stood between them, fearing little would be settled over such an emotional score. Gently she touched Carillon's hand as it clung to the sword.

'I have learned once this land was Cheysuli,' she said softly, 'before ever the Homanans came. It was the Cheysuli who gave the throne to your ancestors. Duncan does not mean he will deny your right to it. It is only that you must *have* it before it goes again to a Cheysuli Mujhar.' Alix took a careful breath. 'Carillon, can we not be one race instead of two?'

'You will rule in Mujhara, my lord,' Duncan said calmly, 'but only if we get you there.'

Carillon said nothing. It was Alix who smiled into his face and insisted gently. 'I will not let them harm you. I promise.'

His free hand slid up to her face and cupped it gently. 'Then I leave my fate in your hands.'

'No,' she said softly. 'Your fate is your own. *Tahlmorra*.'

The Cheysuli went into Mujhara under cover of darkness. Carillon, submitting to the summoning of earth magic that renewed his strength and sent vigour sweeping through his bones, rode the Atvian mount stolen for him. Alix sat behind Duncan once more and stared in dismay at the city.

It lay in shambles. The glittering magnificence had

260

shattered beneath the continued onslaught of Ihlini sorcery. Walls lay tumbled, oddly charred as if unholy fire had leached life from stone blocks once raised by Cheysuli hands so many centuries before. Many of the dwellings had been destroyed completely; others showed no signs of life within. Crumbling casements stared blindly at the streets as if the eyes had been plucked from them by unseen hands.

Alix shivered and held more tightly to Duncan. Here and there someone moved out of the shadows to avoid them, as if they feared Ihlini retribution, and Alix longed to tell them differently. But she could not find her voice.

Mujhara ... she mourned within her heart.

She looked at Carillon and saw him sitting erect in the saddle, Cheysuli sword fastened to his leather belt. His face, as he looked on the city, was perfectly blank. His eyes were not.

Duncan halted his horse and waited until the warriors gathered around him in a narrow alley. Their silence was eloquent.

'We are too late to keep the city from the Ihlini,' he said. 'It is Homana-Mujhar we must look to. If the palace falls, so falls the realm.'

Carillon shifted in his saddle. 'The palace has stood against strong foes for centuries, shapechanger. It will not fall to dark sorcery.'

Duncan slowly lifted his head and indicated the charred, still-smoking ruins of a tall dwelling near them. 'There is the smell of death in the air, my lord. Does it matter so much if it is achieved at the hands of sorcerers, or mere men?'

Carillon scowled. 'What do you say?'

'That if you continue to believe in the infallibility of Shaine and the palace in which he hides himself, you are foolish indeed.' He smiled bitterly. 'Carillon, once my own race was arrogant enough to believe we would ever hold the regard of the Homanans. See how that

261

faith has turned to folly? Tynstar is powerful indeed. If Homana-Mujhar can be taken — and any castle can be — the Ihlini will do it.'

The prince's blue eyes were bleak. 'I do not deny the demon his arts, nor his strength. I have only to see what he has done already. But it is a hard thing to realize the strength of a land resides in a single Mujhar.' His mouth thinned. 'I am not so much like my uncle, I think. But I will do what I can to keep this land free of Bellam's grasp.'

Finn's dun-colored horse stomped against the ash-covered cobbles, raising fine grey dust. The warrior astride the animal set his hand to the hilt of his knife.

'We accomplish little here, *rujho*. Let us go on to Homana-Mujhar.'

Alix felt Duncan's subtle sigh. Then he straightened and nodded. 'What we do now may well settle the future of the Cheysuli.' He stared levelly at Carillon. 'Can you truly cling to the belief that we mean the Mujhar's blood only ill, my lord?'

Carillon slid the sword free of its sheath. The moonlight and dying flames from the burning buildings glinted off the blade and set the ruby to glowing like a crimson eye.

'I have said you will know what I believe when I am Mujhar, shapechanger. Shaine still lives.' His grim face softened slightly. 'But your aid is welcome this night.'

Finn laughed curtly. 'That is something, I suppose, from you. Well, princeling, shall you show us how a fine Homanan lord fights to save his land?'

'I will fight how I can, shapechanger. As you will see.'

Duncan gathered the reins of his mount. 'We go separately,' he said quietly. 'Cheysuli-fashion, when the odds are so high. When we have reached Homana-Mujhar, we will see to the Mujhar's welfare.'

Alix watched as the warriors melted into the darkness.

After a moment only she and Duncan remained with Carillon.

Finn kneed his horse out of the shadows. 'Duncan, I hope this is what you have wanted so long,' he said obscurely.

Alix frowned at him. 'What do you say?'

Finn stared at his brother. 'He has ever warned the clan against unrestrained retribution for the *qu'mahlin*. It has ever been Duncan, swaying the Council, who kept us in the forests of Ellas, when we would strike against Shaine's patrols and any other serving the Mujhar.' Something glinted wickedly in his eyes. 'You do not know, *mei jha*, what it is to fight a Cheysuli in all extremity. We might have slain many more who sought to slay us, had Duncan allowed it.'

'The prophecy does not speak of utter annihilation, Finn,' Duncan retorted. 'It speaks of a final peace between warring lands and races. Should it not begin within our own realm?'

'Shaine would sooner see us dead.'

'Shaine will see us, *rujho*, but we will not be dead.' Duncan kneed his horse forward. 'Do you come with us?'

'No.' Finn gathered his reins. 'I fight alone, Duncan, as ever.' His eyes flickered over Alix. 'You are a foolish woman, *mei jha*. You should be at the Keep, with the others who wait.'

'I could not bear it,' she said quietly.

Finn stared harshly at her a moment longer, then wheeled his horse and rode into the shadows. A silver wolf loped silently at his side.

Alix wrapped her arms around Duncan and pressed herself against his back as they rode through the streets. 'Duncan, I am afraid.'

'There is no dishonor in fear. It is only when you fail to do what you must that the dishonor comes.'

She sighed and put her forehead against his shoulder. 'Do not speak to me as a clan-leader, Duncan. I am in no mood to listen.'

263

Carillon, riding abreast, grinned at her. 'Have you ever been in the mood to listen? No. Else you would not be here, and afraid.'

She shot him a dark glance and refrained from saying anything for fear it would not be seemly.

They rode through streets unfamiliar to her, and even Duncan at last gave way to Carillon, who knew the city better than any. The people who passed them went cloaked and hooded, saying nothing. Carillon rode silently but Alix saw the tension in his body and realized what the knowledge of what had happened did to him.

Duncan pulled his horse to a halt at a large recessed stable opening of a deserted dwelling. Alix waited, uncomprehending, as he slipped from the saddle and turned to help her down. When she stood on the cobbles she stared into his face and opened her mouth to speak.

Duncan put gentle fingers across her lips. 'I would have you remain here, *cheysula*; out of harm's way. That you have come so far with me is risk enough. I will not have you come farther into the enemy's trap.'

She pried his fingers away. 'Do you leave me here?'

'Aye. The street is empty, the buildings deserted. I think you will be safe here, if you do as I say.'

Alix glanced briefly past him and saw Carillon's silhouette against the shine of moonlight. He had halted his horse near the end of the street, giving them privacy.

'Then I will be waiting again; unknowing,' she protested. 'It will be no different than at the Keep.'

His hands clasped her belted waist possessively. 'Alix, I understand what you fear. In your place, I could not do it. But I cannot have you by my side as I go into war. It would divide my concentration, and that is deadly to any warrior.'

'By myself?' she whispered.

'I will leave Cai. I would not have you go unattended.' He smoothed back her tousled hair. '*Cheysula*, say you will do as I ask.'

'Duncan, how am I to deal with this? You leave me in the middle of a fallen city and say I must not worry. That is the cruellest torture I could know.'

He glanced over his shoulder and saw Carillon returning. He sighed and left his horse in the street, taking Alix into the building half-destroyed by Ihlini sorcery. Before she could protest, Duncan lifted her and set her on a tumbled wall.

'You will stay here, with Cai.'

'Without your *lir* you cannot shapechange.'

'There are Ihlini here. I cannot seek *lir*-shape anyway.'

'Duncan—'

'Do as I ask. Keep yourself safe here, away from fighting.'

He sighed and one broad, long-fingered hand slid to cover her stomach. 'I must name the child, *cheysula*.'

'Name it . . . now?'

'Aye. It is a warrior's custom to name an unborn as he goes into battle.' He shrugged. 'So that it is gods-blessed, regardless of the *jehan's* fate.'

Cold slid through her bones as she grabbed at his hands. 'Duncan, I would sooner have you stay with me!'

'I cannot,' he said gently. 'It is not my *tahlmorra* to turn my back on Homana's need.'

'You will come back for me!'

'Of course, *cheysula*. Do you think so poorly of my warrior skills?'

'But I am not a warrior. I cannot judge.'

'You are warrior enough for me.' He silenced any protest with a kiss of such longing and poignancy she could say nothing when he at last released her. She stared into his face beseechingly, and saw the pride and strength she had ever loved.

'He shall be Donal,' he said softly. 'Donal.'

Perversely, she scowled at him. 'And if I bear a girl?'

Duncan grinned. 'I think it will be a boy.'

'Duncan—'

'l will come for you, when it is done.'

Anguish filled her. '*Cheysul*—'

'It is *tahlmorra*, small one,' he said firmly, and left her in the darkness.

CHAPTER TWO

Alix paced through the rubble like a madwoman. For a long time she saw nothing of the place in which Duncan had left her, feeling only the turmoil and anger of her spirit, until at last she stopped in the middle of the tumbled building and stared into its shadowed depths. The emptiness of the place oppressed her until she wanted to run screaming from it. Then she realized it was not the tumbled wreckage that beat at her so much, but the acknowledgement of her own futility.

She wrapped both arms tightly around herself as if they would lend her warmth and security. She attuned her senses to her surroundings and heard the skittering of rats in dark corners, and the creaking of weakened timbers. Slowly she lifted her eyes to the broken roof and stared into the black night sky with its scattered stars.

I am here, liren, Cai said softly. *I am here.*

Her mouth twisted. *I respect you, Cai, but you are not Duncan. You are not the father of this child I carry.*

The bird shifted somewhere above. *He has left me to make certain you fare well. Not to take his place.*

She smiled into the blank open doorway. *Cai ... sometimes I forget you are a hawk and think of you almost as a man.*

A tiny pebble fell from the timber over her head. *I am*

267

not so different, liren. Because I have wings and talons does not make me insensitive to a woman's fears. His tone warmed. *He is a brave warrior, liren.*

'But they die,' she said aloud. 'Even the bravest die.'

The hawk seemed almost to sigh. *I cannot say if he lives or dies this night, liren. Only that he fights for his beliefs. Should he die, I will be lirless and you without a cheysul. But he would be content he had done what he could for the prophecy.*

'Prophecy!' she cried aloud, clutching at the abdomen that carried Duncan's child. 'I think it is more like a curse!'

Cai shifted overhead and scattered another handful of pebbles to the floor. Alix stared blindly at the invisible fall.

The propehcy is your tahlmorra, the hawk said at last, gently. *As it is mine, and my lir's. Even, I think, your child's.*

Alix jerked her head up and stared at his shadow-shrouded form. 'What do you say? Do you tell me you know what will come to all of us? Do you say we are only game pieces the gods move as suits their will?'

Liren, he said softly, *we were the first. The gods made lir before they made man. We know many things.*

She wrenched her hands from her abdomen. 'Then will you not tell me? Will you not say what road lies before me?'

I cannot, liren. The prophecy unveils itself in the fullness of time. The lir cannot precipitate it.

'Cai!'

No, he said calmly.

'It is not fair!' she cried. 'If he should die, you will tell me it is his *tahlmorra* and I should not grieve. Yet if he lives, and returns to me to see his child when it is born, you will say *that* is meant also! Cai, you speak to me in tangled words and snarled threads. I cannot say I like this tapestry you weave!'

The hawk was silent a long moment. *It is not my*

268

tapestry, he said at last, *but that of the gods. They have said what will come. It is up to the shar tahls to show you what has gone before, and what may follow.*

'It is not fair,' she repeated.

No, he agreed, *nor ever shall be.*

Alix stared blindly into the darkness and cursed her soul for its unquiet depths. After a moment she went to the wall Duncan had perched her on and climbed up to seat herself on it gingerly.

Repeating the action did no good. Duncan was not there, and she felt only the emptiness of her heart.

'Cai,' she said at last, hearing the whisper of an echo in the shattered dwelling, 'I am not meant to wait so patiently, or silently.'

You are never silent, liren.

She did not smile. 'I will not remain here.'

He wished it.

'*I* wish to be with him.'

Silence crept into the ruin. Then Cai shifted on the beam and sent a brief shower of debris raining down on her.

Liren, he has said what he wants from you.

'I will work myself into a frenzy,' she said calmly, 'and that will do the child no good at all.'

Yet if you go, you risk both of you.

She closed her eyes. 'Duncan does what he must, and expects me not to question it. But I do, Cai. I must. There is something — different — in myself. I cannot sit calmly by and wait for him to return to me . . . if he can.'

Liren . . .

Alix opened her eyes, decision made. 'I must do what I must, bird. Perhaps it is my own *tahlmorra*.'

The great hawk lifted and flew from the timber to the broken wall before her. She saw his dark eyes glinting in the moonlight.

Liren, it is not for me to gainsay you. I have said what I can.

Alix smiled. 'Cai, you are truly a blessing of the old gods.'

269

The hawk fixed her with a bright eye. *So is the child you carry.*

She slid off the shattered wall and straightened her creased leathers. 'Cai, I will carry this child to full term. It is a part of my own *tahlmorra*.'

He sounded oddly amused. *You have only just come to us, liren, yet you speak as a learned one who has the magic of the shar tahls.*

Alix walked from the dwelling into the cobbled street and stared down the empty alley. 'Perhaps I have a measure of that magic, Cai. Now, do you come?'

The great hawk mantled and took to the air. *I come, liren.*

Alix moved softly, mimicking Duncan's stealth. She was very aware of the knife in her boot, wishing she had better but knowing she would be incapable of using it against another anyway. She was no warrior.

Cai winged overhead silently, saying nothing to her as she walked carefully through the empty streets and alleyways. The night sky was clear save for stars, but she felt a heaviness in her bones as if the buildings of the Mujhar's city leaned in on her. And she smelled the stench of death, unable to escape its cloying touch.

Occasionally she passed a tumbled wall still smouldering, still caressed by odd purple fire. She swallowed heavily as she recalled Tynstar and his odd method of departing her presence. A shiver of foreboding coursed through her body as she stepped carefully through the broken fragments of a dwelling, and her right hand dropped instinctively to shield her unborn child.

Alix froze suddenly as a shadow streaked across the street before her, hissing malevolently. Instinctively she pressed herself against the nearest wall, hoping the bricks might provide protection. Then she saw it was only a cat, fur raised and ears flattened as it fled the night terrors. For a moment she held herself against the wall, eyes closed tightly as she tried to still her lurching heart. Cai drifting over her, sent her a burst of his own confidence.

Alix pushed away and moved on, releasing a breath that rasped through her dry throat. After a moment she paused, bending, and took the knife from her boot. The feel of it in her hand gave her a measure of renewed confidence, and she walked on softly.

You can go back, Cai said. *You can wait for my lir, as he wished.*

No, she said silently.

Liren . . .

No.

Alix felt better for her determination, recalling the urge that had originally driven her into the streets. For all she was frightened of what might befall her, she was more frightened of what might happen to Duncan. She would far prefer being with him, in danger, than without him in comparative safety.

A stone rattled on the cobbles before her. Alix slipped into a recessed doorway, knife drawn up to her chest in readiness. Another stone skittered across the uneven street and came to rest near her foot. She followed its path with her eyes until she saw the figure move silently through the street.

It was a man, she thought, for the cloaked form was tall and moved with the subtle grace of a warrior. She had seen its like in warriors of the clan, marvelling at the body's ability to take on the aspect of animal suppleness while maintaining human form. For a moment she thought the man Cheysuli, then recalled none had gone cloaked on this mission into Mujhara. Alix drew in a breath and waited.

He moved past her, half-hidden in the shadowy folds of his cloak. For a moment he paused, very near her, and she feared discovery. A hand rose and pushed the hood free of his face, sliding the draped material to his shoulders. Alix, certain he somehow knew her presence, waited for him to speak.

But the man said nothing. He glanced into the sky, marked the hawk's idle flight, and smiled to himself. Then he moved on.

Alix waited until he was gone. Then she slipped out of the doorway and hastened from the street, fearing belated discovery. When she reached for Cai's soothing pattern she felt an odd current pushing against her, almost as if it sought to prevent communication with the hawk. She strengthened her call and relaxed as the bird's tone came to her.

Ihlini, liren.

Alix paused, frowning against the effort it took to hear him. *Ihlini?*

Aye, the cloaked man.

She stared into the darkness. *Then why do I hear you at all?*

Perhaps it is the blood in you, liren. Perhaps whatever power it is that prevents other Cheysuli from seeking their lir does not block you from it. His shadow drifted over her. *Liren, you are fortunate indeed.*

But she felt the strain within the pattern and sensed a draining of her resources. It frightened her, for she dared not risk the child. She broke off the link to Cai and decided to keep it broken, for fear it might harm the unborn. Cai seemed to approve, and she went on in greater solitude than before.

Alix knew herself lost. Her visit to Mujhara with Carillon had not accustomed her to the twistings and turnings of the narrow streets, and she realized she might be moving farther from Homana-Mujhar instead of going to it. Frustrated and fearful, she turned yet again and kept her steady pace. She longed to question Cai, knowing he could tell her, but fought down the instinct. She would not involve the hawk unless forced to.

She heard a child crying in the distance. As she drew closer the piteous wail drove into her spirit like a shaft, beckoning her. Alix broke into a trot, then a run as the crying seemed to weaken. She was breathless as she rounded a corner and tripped over a body in the street.

It was a woman, clothed in a soiled and torn gown.

Alix got to her knees and replaced her knife as she put a trembling hand toward the woman's face. Then she saw the staring eyes were blank, bulging in death, and something elemental curled deeply within her soul. She hesitated, then put gentle fingers to the eyelids and closed them. The cold stillness of the flesh shot a convulsive shudder down her spine.

The crying renewed itself. Alix jerked her head around and stared wide-eyed into the darkness. After a moment she located the focus of the sound and rose, moving quietly to the broken wall of a charred building. Behind the scattered stone, placed carefully beneath a sheltering piece of broken door, lay a naked baby.

Soundlessly Alix cried out. Then her hands were on the infant, lifting it free of its protection. It was a boy-child, cold to the touch, and his chest rose feebly in an attempt to breathe. Alix knelt and cradled him to her breast, feeling a mixture of longing and pain in her soul as she sensed the ambiance of her own unborn child.

She crooned to him softly, smoothing his silken head. He was no more than a few weeks, she knew, and helpless as a blind, newborn rabbit. His slender limbs trembled from explosure and unknown fear, and after a moment Alix lay him down in the street and stripped out of her supple jerkin and belt. The leather was not much, but she realized some wrapping was better than none. Carefully she lifted the child and folded the jerkin around his body, snugging the belt over it to swaddle him as warmly as possible. Chill nipped through the loose weave of her improvised shirt, but she ignored it as she lifted the baby and walked on.

At last Alix turned a corner and saw before her the red stones of Homana-Mujhar. The walls rose mutely in the moonlight, throwing dark shadows into surrounding streets. And she saw the Solindish and Atvian guards surrounding the place, posted at every gate. She wondered if Tynstar had yet broken through Shaine's wards, taking the palace for Bellam.

Alix drew back in the sheltering shadows, suddenly at a loss for what to do. She had anticipated finding Duncan no matter how impossible the task seemed, even in the cul-de-sacs and strange turnings. Now she stared worriedly at the bronze-and-timber gates and feared she had acted wrongly.

Where are they? she asked fearfully. *Where are the Cheysuli?*

The child whimpered in her arms. Alix shifted him closer to her chest and placed gentle lips against his forehead, silently promising him safety. But she also feared for her own.

She glanced back the way she had come and stiffened. Through the narrow street walked a cloaked figure, moving with familiar grace. The hood was drawn up again to hide the man's features, but she knew him by his movements. Alix pressed back against the wall.

Then a second figure slid out from the shadows, just behind the cloaked Ihlini. Alix watched in painful silence as the second man moved into the moonlighted street, then caught her breath in a gasp as muted light glinted off gold *lir*-bands.

'*Ihlini!*' the Cheysuli whispered.

The cloaked figure spun and froze. Alix saw him push his hands out sideways, away from his body, as if to indicate his innocent intent. The Cheysuli moved closer and a shaft of moonlight slanted clearly across his face.

'*Duncan!*' she whispered in horror, clutching the child.

The Ihlini's voice, quiet but pitched to carry, came clearly to her. 'We should not fight, you and I. The Cheysuli and Ihlini are much alike. You have your gifts, I mine. We could use them in concert.'

She heard Duncan's soft laugh. 'There is no likeness between us, sorcerer, save equal determination to serve our own gods.'

The Ihlini lowered his hands, then pulled his cloak off and dropped it to the cobbles. 'Then I will serve my

274

gods, shapechanger, by ridding this land of one more Cheysuli.'

The fight was sudden and vicious. Alix gasped as Duncan closed with the Ihlini, movements half-hidden. She saw only the glint of knives and heard their grunts of effort as each sought to slay the other.

'By the gods,' she whispered to herself, horrified, 'it is much worse than I thought. *Much* worse!'

The child whimpered again and she hugged him closer, seeking her own strength in his need for security. But her mind was with Duncan.

She saw the Ihlini stumble back. A metallic glint flashed from his left shoulder and she saw the hilt of a Cheysuli knife stand out from his dark leathers. Duncan, crouched in readiness, straightened. Alix felt overwhelming relief flood her body, then realized how much she had longed for the sorcerer's death. The emotion shocked and sickened her.

The Ihlini did not fall. His back turned to her and she saw his right arm move to pull the knife away from his shoulder. Duncan, hands empty, waited warily.

Die, Ihlini ... she whispered silently, hating herself for desiring another's death. *Die!*

The sorcerer went to one knee. She saw Duncan clearly in the moonlight, feet spread to brace himself against the enemy. Darkness slid down one arm, dulling his *lir*-band, and she realized the Ihlini's knife had found at least part of its target. She bit her lip and fought back the instinct to run to him.

A rattle behind Duncan spun him around. He was unarmed, vulnerable to a second attack, but something in his stance told her he was prepared. Then she saw the Solindish soldier move into the moonlight, sword bared.

Cai! Alix cried. *Cai — do something!*

The pattern was faint. At last Cai answered her. *Liren, I cannot. It is an Ihlini he faces ... the lir do not interfere. It is part of the gods' law.*

The Solindish soldier made no move against Duncan.
He stood braced, ready to fight, yet did not step in
against his shapechanger enemy. Alix saw the Ihlini
come out of his crouch and realized the Solindish man
acted only as a decoy.

Her cry of warning was lost in the Solindish soldier's
shout. Alix spun and set the baby down in the darkness
near a wall, dragging the knife from her boot. Then she
pushed herself free of the wall and ran toward the Ihlini.

She saw Duncan stiffen spasmodically as the sorcerer
snaked a gleaming wire around his throat. Both hands
flew to the wire and clawed at it, seeking to rip it away.
But the Ihlini stood unmoving, slowly tautening the
thin garrote until blood broke from Duncan's throat.

'No!' Alix shrieked.

The Solindish soldier stared past the Ihlini and his
prisoner in alarm. His sword shifted, rising, and she
realized he would move to stop her.

But she could not hesitate. Her fear had been replaced
by the overwhelming need to strike down the Ihlini who
threatened Duncan. Her veneer of civilization and
gentle ways was stripped from her easily, leaving her
naked before all men, and she knew herself as capable of
slaying a man as any warrior.

Duncan's knees were buckled. The Ihlini stood firm,
bending slightly as he tautened the garrote even further. Alix was oddly aware of the flash of the Solindish
sword as she stumbled to a halt behind the sorcerer. But
it did not matter. She lifted the knife, clutching it in both
hands, and brought it down with all her strength.

The shock ran through her arms as she drove the knife
through leathers and into the flesh of the Ihlini. She felt
him stiffen spasmodically, crying out. One gloved hand
clawed briefly at his back, fingers stretching and
scraping, then it dropped slackly at his side. The sorcerer sagged over Duncan and fell into the street.

Alix heard the soldier swear a violent oath, unable to
decipher his words. She saw the malevolent gleam in

his eyes as he lifted the sword over one shoulder, preparing to unleash the killing stroke. Somehow, she was unafraid.

'By the gods!' cried a clear voice, 'you will *not*!'

Dimly she heard the clatter of hoof on stone and saw the horse rearing behind the soldier. Before the Solindish man could turn, a flashing sword swung through the air in a swift arc and severed head from shoulders.

Alix staggered back, gagging, as blood sprayed from the falling trunk. It splattered over her face and clothing, staining her hands as she raised them to cover her eyes. Then she peered through her fingers into the blazing blue eyes of the prince of Homana.

Instantly she forgot Carillon. She stumbled forward, reaching frenziedly toward the sprawled bodies. Blood ran through the cobbles, muddying the ash and dust, but she ignored it all as she clawed at the Ihlini's still form.

Alix tugged ineffectually at the heavy body until Carillon flung himself from his horse and helped her, dragging the slain sorcerer free of Duncan.

'No!' she cried, falling to her knees. '*No!*'

The wire, she saw, had fallen partially free of Duncan's throat. It had bitten deeply but had not yet sliced into the vulnerable windpipe. Carefully she pulled the wire away and threw it into the street, moaning as she saw the vivid discoloring as blood stained his neck.

'He is alive, Alix,' Carillon said, kneeling over the warrior. 'Alive.'

She put gentle fingers to his bloodied throat, feeling the erratic pulse-beat. Carefully she cradled his head in her lap, fighting back the rush of bile into her throat as she realized how close he had come to death.

Duncan's hand twitched and moved instinctively to the empty sheath at his belt. Carillon reached out and stopped the searching hand.

'No,' he said clearly. 'We are not your enemy.'

277

'Duncan!' she cried. '*Duncan . . .*'

His eyes opened and blinked. For a moment he said nothing, lying limply against her lap, then bolted upright into a sitting position. Carillon moved back, squatting, and Alix hastily wiped tears off her cheeks. Duncan, in all his Cheysuli pride, would not want to see her cry.

Duncan looked silently at the body of the Solindish soldier. Then his eyes travelled to the felled Ihlini, lying so close. After a moment he put bloodstained fingers to his throat.

He looked directly at Carillon. 'Tell me I did not hear her,' he rasped. 'Tell me I somehow imagined she was here.'

Carillon began to smile. His eyes slid past Duncan to Alix, and his smile became a grin. Then he shook his head.

'I will not lie to you, shapechanger. You have only to look.'

Duncan winced and turned his head. Alix swallowed welling tears away as she saw the sliced welt rising on his throat, still weeping blood. But Duncan ignored it as he looked at her in dismay.

'*Alix . . .*'

She bit her lip in response to the ragged sound of his voice. Then she shrugged her shoulders uncomfortably.

'I am sorry, Duncan, that you are burdened with such a disobedient woman. I am not at all the proper sort for a clan-leader's *cheysula*.'

She saw his eyes travel over her blood-smeared face to the dark stains on her ragged shirt. One hand reached out and touched her arm, tracing the sticky flesh. Then he drew up his legs into a cross-legged position and sat there. Silent.

'Duncan—' she began tentatively, then broke off as she recalled the infant. She jumped to her feet and ran, ignoring Carillon's startled question.

Alix knelt by the jerkin-wrapped child and smiled, gathering it up carefully. 'There is someone you should meet, small one,' she whispered. 'Someone very special.'

She half-rose, cradling the child against her chest. Then something stopped her, cutting through her happiness like a scythe.

The child was cold, too cold. He made no sound as her hand gently touched his face. Carefully Alix knelt back on the cobbles and fought down the sudden painful fear as she slid a hand beneath the jerkin and felt his body.

Horror came slowly. Then the pain. 'No!' she cried. 'Not the *child!*'

He lay unmoving, unbreathing. Alix shuddered over him, rubbing hands against his cold flesh as if her warmth would bring him back to life. She heard footsteps behind her and the clank of a sword sliding home in its sheath.

'Alix,' said Duncan's hoarse voice.

She shook her head violently in denial, still rubbing the child's cold flesh.

Duncan's hand was on her shoulder, pulling her away gently. 'There is nothing to be done, *cheysula.*'

She jerked away and knelt over the child. 'He is mine. *Mine!* I will not let him die.'

Duncan pulled her away. Dimly she saw Carillon kneel by the infant and touch a hand to its chest. Then he glanced up at Duncan and shook his head.

'He is mine,' she repeated.

'No,' Duncan said hoarsely. He put his hand against her stomach. '*Here* is our child.'

She stared into his face. 'I only put him down for a moment. You needed my help. The Ihlini would have slain you. So I put him down to go to you.' Her eyes closed. 'Why did the gods make me choose between you?'

Duncan sighed. 'Do not torture yourself like this, Alix. It does no good.'

'It was only a *child!*'

'I know, small one. But he was more fortunate than most. He did not know what he faced, before it claimed him.' Something crept through his eyes and she saw the vestiges of remembered horror. 'He did not know what it was to look into the eyes of death so close.'

Alix shivered and pressed herself against him. 'Duncan, I could not bear to lose you. I could not bear it.'

'Well, you have made certain I will live a little longer.' He smiled crookedly at her and traced the bloodstains on her nose. 'I have taken myself a warrior instead of a woman.'

Carillon's boots scraped against the cobbles. Alix looked at him and saw the weariness and determination in his face.

He gestured toward the red walls rising in the near distance. 'Homana-Mujhar, my friends. It waits for us.'

Duncan nodded. Alix slipped from his arms, cast one more longing glance at the jerkin-wrapped bundle in the corner, then turned from it resolutely.

But the pain remained.

CHAPTER THREE

They found shelter in the shadows of the high walls, avoiding the Solindish soldiers who gathered in the torchlight spilling from sconces set into the red brick. Cai perched himself in a nearby tree, for the proximity of Ihlini kept him from conversing with Duncan, and even Alix felt the weakness in her mind. She did not wish to expend energy she might need later, so she kept herself from conversing with the hawk.

Duncan leaned one shoulder against the cool walls and looked at Carillon. 'We need a way in, my lord. As normal men. I have no recourse to *lir*-shape here.'

Carillon's hand idly caressed the hilt of his massive sword. 'There is a way. I played here as a child, and I know all the secrets of this place. I am only glad the Solindish do not.'

'Alone?' Alix whispered.

Duncan shook his head and felt gently at his bruised throat. 'If you can, Alix, summon the *lir*. They will bring the warriors.'

Apprehension flared in her. 'But you said I should not use what power I have. Because of the child—'

'We have no choice. If we are to succeed, we must get to Shaine.' His hand engulfed and pressed her shoulder. '*Cheysula*, I would not ask it otherwise.'

She nodded and leaned back against the wall,

detaching herself from immediate awareness. She no longer felt Duncan's hand on her, or heard Carillon's startled question. She was aware only of the heaviness in the air and the great effort it took to reach the *lir*.

At last she felt Storr's familiar pattern questioning her. Alix smiled weakly and told him to bring his *lir*, and the others. His acquiescence came just as her strength failed her.

Alix sagged limply against the wall and felt Duncan catch her. He swore something in the Old Tongue that broke halfway through his exclamation and set her upright, pressing her against the wall. She heard Carillon's sharp question, but Duncan made no answer. At last she dragged her eyes open and looked into their faces, seeing their mutual fear.

Alix managed a faint smile. 'They come. The *lir*, and their warriors.'

'I am sorry . . .' Duncan rasped uneasily.

She shook her head. 'It — it was only that they are so far. I will be well enough in a moment.'

Carillon flicked a dark glance at Duncan. '*I* would not use her so, shapechanger.'

Duncan's face hardened. 'It is for *your* sake I asked it, princeling.'

Alix put a hand up and pushed herself away from the wall, straightening her tired shoulders. 'Enough of this. If you wish Homana reconciled with her Cheysuli forebears, you will have to begin with yourselves.' She glared at them. '*Yourselves!*

Carillon looked guilty. Duncan, mouth twisting in Finn's ironic manner, nodded to himself.

Alix sighed and rubbed wearily at an eye. 'I think they come. Here is Storr.'

The silver wolf came out of the shadows silently, feral eyes gleaming in the darkness. With him came Finn, who had a wide smear of blood across his jerkin and a victorious glint in his eye.

'You wanted me, *mei jha*?'

'*Duncan* wanted you. And the others.'

Finn glanced at his brother, then frowned. He stepped close and examined the bloody slice in Duncan's throat. After a moment he stepped back and raised his brows.

'Did you tangle, somehow, with an Atvian bowstring instead of an arrow?'

Duncan smiled. 'An Ihlini garrote, *rujho*.'

Finn grunted. 'They are ever troublesome. We should teach the Ihlini something, someday.' His eyes belied the irony in his tone. '*Rujho* . . . you are not badly hurt?'

Duncan shrugged. 'I am well enough. Growing voiceless, perhaps, but you may prefer me that way.'

Finn's teeth flashed. 'Aye, *rujho*, I believe I may.'

The others had gathered. Alix saw not a single warrior was missing. She wondered, in remembered horror, how many men lay dead at shapechanger hands.

'We will go in,' Duncan said in his broken voice. 'We will go in and give what aid we can to Shaine the Mujhar.'

'How?' demanded Finn. 'We cannot seek *lir*-shape so close to the Ihlini. And we can hardly scale the walls without being seen.'

Duncan gestured to Carillon. 'The prince has said he can get us in.'

Finn's face expressed doubt. No one else moved, but Alix sensed their unspoken disbelief. Then Carillon shifted against the wall and stood upright.

'You have little enough reason to trust me. It would be a simple matter for me to let you in and lead you into a trap of the Mujhar's making.' He smiled grimly. 'While I have not precisely been your enemy, neither have I been your ally.'

'I think we are in agreement for the first time, princeling,' Finn said in careful condescension.

Carillon, to Alix's surprise, appeared unoffended. He smiled calmly at Finn. 'You need my aid, shapechanger. *Mine*.'

Finn grunted. 'I need nothing of yours.'

Carillon turned to Duncan. 'I will get in, and then I will open one of the smaller gates. I leave it to you to rid your-selves of the Solindish guards.' He gestured toward the darkness. 'It is but a short distance that way. I will meet you.'

He faded into the shadows. Finn spat out a curse between hs teeth and looked as if he had swallowed something sour.

Duncan observed him impassively. 'I trust him, Finn. He will do as he says.'

'He is Homanan.'

'They are not our enemy.'

Finn's eyes narrowed. 'Then what of the *qu'mahlin*?'

'It was begun by a single man, not by a nation. It can also be ended by a single man.' Duncan sighed and felt at his tender throat. 'Shaine began it. Carillon, I think, is the man who will end it.'

'Do not speak so much,' Alix admonished him, then shot Finn a scathing glance. 'Carillon expects us, *rujholli*. Should we not go where he said?'

He grinned at her and gestured with a flourish in the direction Carillon had indicated. When she did not move he shook his head reprovingly and went into the darkness. The others followed.

Alix turned away as the Cheysuli slew the Solindish guards. Her flesh crawled as she remembered the sensations in her when she had plunged her knife into the Ihlini's back. She would have run from the renewed violence had Duncan not kept her by him.

As the last man died, the narrow gate swung open. Carillon stepped through. His leather-and-mail dripped with water, pooling at his feet. His hair was plastered darkly against his head, but his smile was subtly triumphant as he gestured.

'There is a culvert few know about. Now, through here, if you please. And you are well come to Homana-Mujhar.'

He led them into a small bailey, avoiding the larger one which opened onto the front of the massive palace. He paused as Duncan whispered to him, and waited as the clan-leader turned to his warriors.

'It would be better to go in separately, should the Mujhar send men against us. Slay only if you must, for these men are not truly our enemies. When you can, make your way to the Great Hall.' He smiled at Carillon's involuntary start of surprise. 'Have you forgot, my lord, that Hale was my foster-father? I was here as a small child. I know this place.' He looked up at the dark bulk of stone. 'A long time ago, I walked the halls and corridors with impunity. Shaine once called me by name and bade me serve him as well as Hale did.' His mouth tightened. 'A very long time ago.'

Finn stepped between them. 'But I was never here, princeling. I was left at the Keep. You may serve as my guide.'

Carillon turned away and moved toward the palace. The others melted away. Alix walked at Duncan's side as they followed Carillon and Finn into the castle.

They went unaccosted, though the servants and guardsmen within the halls grew red-faced or frightened as they saw the Cheysuli. Only Carillon's presence kept the guardsmen from moving against them, and Alix saw that Finn marked it. She wondered if it made a difference to him.

At last they reached the hammered silver doors of the audience chamber she remembered so clearly. She felt a shiver of remembered apprehension run down her spine. Shaine had frightened her that day, before he made her angry. Then she smiled as she called to mind the Mujhar's terror as Cai swept into the hall.

'Borrowed glory,' Finn muttered. 'Borrowed.'

Alix glanced at him. 'What do you say? This place is magnificent!'

'This place is Cheysuli,' he retorted. After a moment his voice softened as he glanced around. 'Cheysuli.'

Carillon thrust open the unattended doors. Alix would have gone through immediately but Duncan held her back. She looked at him in puzzlement, then saw his gesture toward Carillon. Understanding, she stepped back.

The prince entered the long hall slowly. He left a trail of water behind. For a moment Alix saw a vision of the tall prince forcing his way through the narrow culvert, and smiled. Then she went in with Duncan.

Shaine sat upon the throne, hands clasping the curving lion paws. His eyes stared broodingly into the massive firepit. It had died to coals and the hall was chilly. The Mujhar seemed to notice no one as they approached the dais.

Duncan paused at the firepit, allowing Carillon to continue on alone. Alix waited also, as did Finn. They watched as Carillon paced the length of the firepit and halted before the dais.

'You, my lord Mujhar, have been a fool,' he said coldly.

Shaine looked at Carillon. Slowly he rose to his feet, taller than his heir only by virtue of the dais, staring at him in amazement.

'*Carillon* ...' he whispered.

'A fool,' Carillon repeated.

But Shaine was not undone by Carillon's unexpected presence. He was a king before all else, and could still command a powerful presence when he chose.

'You will not speak to me until you find the proper words of respect to your liege lord.'

The prince laughed openly. '*Respect*. You have earned none of mine, uncle.'

Shaine's grey eyes glared. His voice dropped to the ominous tone Alix recalled so clearly.

'I will excuse your poor manners this once. Doubtless you grieve for your father, and you appear to have been poorly treated at Keough's hands. But I will not hear such words from you again.'

Carillon smiled grimly. 'My father is fortunate in his death, uncle. He does not face the knowledge that the Mujhar has failed Homana. *I* have to deal with that . . . and so must you.'

'You call me a fool!' Shaine roared. 'What do *you* know of the things I have had to order these past months? What do you know of the harsh decisions I have had to make?'

'Safe within your walls!' Carillon shouted back. '*I* have been in the field with thousands of Homanan soldiers — some of them *boys!* What do you know of *that*, my lord Mujhar? You make the commands — we carry them out. And *we* are the ones who die beneath Bellam and Keough's hordes, uncle — *not you!*'

Shaine's face congested. 'You would have me die, then, my lord heir? So you may do better in my place? Is that what you seek?'

Carillon was rigid. 'I want Homana safe again, my lord Mujhar. And you alive to see it.'

Before Shaine could reply a quiet voice echoed down the hall. 'And *I* want you alive as well, Shaine the Mujhar. Else I cannot have the pleasure of taking your life.'

Alix stiffened as Finn threw the words down the hall, moving to approach the Mujhar. Storr padded at his side silently. She sensed the wolf's loyalty to Finn more strongly than ever before. She nearly went after them both, suddenly frightened, but Duncan kept her back.

'It is for him to do,' he said softly. 'It is his *tahlmorra*.'

'He will *slay* him!'

'Perhaps. Be silent, Alix. This is for Finn to do.'

She clenched her teeth and turned back, hating the calm acceptance in Duncan's broken voice. Like him, she could only watch.

Finn stopped before the dais. He waited.

Shaine stared at him. Color drained from his face until only a death mask remained. His lips were bluish; hands shaking. An inarticulate sound burst from his throat. Then he swallowed visibly and forced a single word between his lips.

'*Hale.*'

Finn laughed. 'No. His son.'

'Hale is . . . slain . . .'

'By your order.'

'He had to die . . . *had* to . . .' Shaine stiffened before Finn and brushed a trembling hand across his staring eyes. 'He had to die.'

'*Why?*'

Shaine blinked. 'He took her away. Lindir. My daughter.' He swallowed. 'Took her from me.'

'She *chose* to go. You drove her away, my lord Mujhar. You. Lindir left Homana-Mujhar of her own will, because she desired it. Because she desired a Cheysuli!'

'No!'

'*Aye, my lord!*'

Carillon stepped toward the Cheysuli. 'Finn—'

'Silence yourself, princeling!' Finn snapped. 'This is a thing between men.'

'Finn!'

'Go, princeling. You have served your purpose. You have delivered the Mujhar to me, as I have long desired.' Finn glared at him. '*Go.*'

Alix started forward but Duncan's hand inexorably drew her back.

Carillon turned again to his uncle. 'This is *your* doing! Once the Cheysuli served Homanan kings more faithfully than any — now they seek only to destroy the man who ordered the *qu'mahlin*. Is this what you wanted?'

Shaine's face was deathly white. His breath came hoarse and loud. 'Hale . . . it is *Hale* . . .'

'No!' Carillon shouted.

The Mujhar's face cleared and sense crept back into his blank eyes. He looked upon Finn a long moment, then reached out to point at the Cheysuli.

'I will not suffer a shapechanger in my presence. In my realm. I have ordered your race destroyed and I will have it done. *I will have it done!'*

The roar swept through the hall. Finn met it with a smile. 'He was your sworn man, Shaine the Mujhar. A Cheysuli blood-oath. He fought for you, slew for you, loved you as his liege lord. And you had him slain like some crazed beast.'

'Finn,' Duncan said at last.

Shaine's eyes sharpened as he looked past Finn and Carillon. His chest heaved.

'No.' He choked. 'Not the Cheysuli . . .'

Carillon glanced at him. 'My lord?'

The Mujhar's breath was uneven. 'I—will—not—have —Cheysuli—*here* . . .'

'It seems you have little choice, uncle.'

'I will not have it!' Shaine moved to the throne and drew a scarlet silk bag from its cushioned seat. He turned back to them with an expression of gloating triumph in his eyes. Slowly he poured glowing blue cubes into the palm of one hand.

Carillon stared. 'The wards—?'

'Hale's, given to me forty years ago . . . should I ever face harsh odds. There are no more in all of Homana.' Shaine swallowed as heavy color rushed into his face. 'They have kept the Ihlini from Homana-Mujhar. It is the only thing. And I will willingly destroy them if only to destroy Cheysuli!'

Surprising them all with his swiftness, the Mujhar moved agilely to the coals of the firepit. Carillon said something incoherently and leaped for him, grabbing for the outstretched hand clutching the blue cubes. Finn drew his knife and advanced.

But the Mujhar was too quick.

Blue flames roared up as the wards burned. Eerie illumination crept across Shaine's tortured features. He stood stiffly before his nephew and Finn.

'I declared *qu'mahlin* on the Cheysuli twenty-five years ago,' he rasped. 'It has not ended!'

Alix gasped. She saw Shaine look past Finn, and as his eyes fell on her face she saw loathing enter them.

'Shapechanger ...' he hissed. *'Shapechanger!'* He drew a gasping breath and pointed at her. 'My daughter gave her life in exchange for a *halfling witch!'*

Alix stared at him in shock and mute pain, stunned by the virulence of his hatred. Then Finn said something in the Old Tongue and lifted his knife to strike.

Carillon leaped, grabbing the raised arm. Finn spun to dislodge him but a garbled sound broke from the Mujhar's throat and stopped them both.

Shaine fell slowly forward to his knees. His eyes remained locked on Alix, but his face was no longer that of a sane man. It twitched, discolored, and he pitched loosely onto the stones.

Alix was frozen in horror. She saw Finn standing over the Mujhar, still clasping his knife.

Silence reigned. No one moved, as if made immobile by the sudden collapse of Shaine. Then Finn turned a strangely impassive face to Carillon.

'Is he slain, princeling? Is the Mujhar dead at last?'

Carillon knelt by Shaine's side. Carefully he turned the body over and they all saw the twisted travesty of a face. Alix gulped back a sour taste in her throat.

After a moment Carillon lowered the body and rose, facing Finn bitterly. 'You have accomplished your goal, shapechanger,' he said flatly. 'The Mujhar is slain.'

Alix began to tremble. She saw an expression in Finn's face that frightened her. It was a mixture of conflicting emotions: pleasure, relief, satisfaction and something very strange. It turned her cold.

For a long moment Finn looked down upon the body stretched by the firepit. Then he turned and stared at the throne a very long time. Finally he looked back at Carillon and stretched out a restraining hand as the prince moved away.

'No,' he said.

Carillon frowned at him. 'I go only to tell the guardsmen their lord is slain.'

'The *old* lord is slain,' Finn said clearly.

'Because of you!' the prince snapped.

Finn looked down at the knife in his hand as if surprised to see it. For a moment he seemed bewildered. Then he glanced back at Duncan.

Alix felt the intensity of their locked gazes and looked from one to the other, shaken. But she did not interfere.

Finn smiled. Something in his face had surrendered. When he looked again at Carillon he seemed resigned. Swiftly he flipped the knife in his hand and slid the point beneath the underflesh of his forearm. Alix winced as blood welled quickly around the blade, staining it.

'Is this expiation for a dead Mujhar?' Carillon asked harshly.

Finn did not answer. He dropped to one knee, head bowed. 'It is a Cheysuli custom, my lord, that the Mujhar is ever attended by a liege man.' A deep breath lifted his shoulders briefly. 'Fifty years ago Hale of the Cheysuli swore a blood-oath to take Shaine the Mujhar as his liege lord until death.' His eyes moved to Carillon's face as he held out the knife, hilt first. 'If you will have it ... if you will accept it, my lord Carillon ... I offer you the same service.'

Carillon, staring at the kneeling warrior in absolute astonishment, slowly opened his mouth.

'I?'

'You are the Mujhar. The Mujhar must have a Cheysuli liege man.' Finn smiled without his customary irony. 'It is tradition, my lord.'

'Cheysuli tradition.'

Finn remained unmoving. 'Will you accept my service?

'By the gods, Finn, we have never met without railing at one another like jackdaws!'

Finn's mouth twisted. 'It is unsettling for a Cheysuli to recognize his own *tahlmorra* when he wants no part of it. What else would you expect me to do?' He waited, then sighed. 'Do you accept me, or do you refuse me the sort of honor my *jehan* ever respected?'

Carillon stared down at him. 'Well ... I cannot have

291

you bleeding all over the floor. Although once I said I would see the color of your blood.'

Finn nodded. 'If you see much more, I will have nothing left to spare in your service.'

Carillon smiled and held out his hand. The hilt was placed in it, and he accepted the knife without comment. Then he drew his own, slid Finn's blade home in his sheath, and gave the Cheysuli his own untarnished knife.

'A blood-oath is binding,' he said quietly. 'Even I know that.'

Finn rose, shrugging. 'It is only binding until it is broken, my lord. But that has only been done once before.' He smiled crookedly. 'And you have seen the result.'

Carillon nodded silently. Then he moved past Finn as one dazed and walked to the huge silver doors. There he paused and looked briefly at Alix, then to Duncan.

'Have you known he would do this? *Him?*'

Alix, who wanted to ask that question for herself, waited expectantly.

Duncan grinned. 'Finn does as he chooses. I cannot explain the madness that comes on him at times.'

Carillon shook his head and glanced back at the Cheysuli warrior who stood silently with his wolf.

Alix, also staring at Finn, felt a strange bubble of laughter burst in her soul. She grinned at Carillon.

'I think you have your revenge, my lord. How better to overcome a Cheysuli than to appeal to his eternal *tahlmorra?*'

Carillon grinned back. Then he lost it as he heard the first shouts from without the Great Hall. His voice turned harsh.

'The Ihlini,' he said. 'My uncle has destroyed the wards.'

'Then it is time we left this place, my lord Mujhar,' Duncan said quietly.

Carillon glanced back at Shaine's body. Then he turned on his heel and departed the Great Hall.

CHAPTER FOUR

Almost instantly they were surrounded by Solindish and Atvian troops who shouted triumphantly as they made their way past slain Homanan servitors and guardsmen to begin their destruction of the fallen palace.

Alix bit her bottom lip as Duncan thrust her against a wall that blocked an Atvian soldier's cursing attack. She slid back against the wall in horror, seeing only the blood-lust in his eyes and the sudden savagery in Duncan's.

Carillon's sword clanged against another as a Solindish man sought to bring him down. The prince fought well, though badly outweighed and outreached. He fell to one knee, gasping as he tried to bring up his broadsword, but Finn was there before him. Alix saw the royal knife that now belonged to a Cheysuli sink home in a Solindish throat, and bit back an outcry as the man fell at Carillon's feet.

The prince pushed himself upright and turned, staring fixedly at Finn. 'Is this what it is to have a liege man?'

Finn, retrieving his new knife, grinned. 'I am newly-come to the service, my lord, but I know it is my task to keep you alive.' He paused significantly. 'When you foolishly engage someone stronger than you.'

Carillon scowled at him, but Alix saw the gratitude

and realization in his blue eyes. She nearly smiled to herself, pleased beyond measure that they could be in accordance after so much discord, but Duncan grabbed her arm and dragged her down the corridor.

'Shaine has done his work well,' he said roughly. 'We have little time to win free of this place.'

'Win *free!*' Carillon called breathlessly from behind. 'This place is Homanan! I will not have it fall into enemy hands.'

Duncan turned to say something more, saw the approaching enemy soldiers and shouted something to Finn. The younger Cheysuli turned back, shoulder-to-shoulder with the prince, and beat back four soldiers. Duncan grabbed Alix's shoulder and shoved her through a tapestried doorway.

She stumbled into a small ceremonial chamber, protesting inarticulately at Duncan's roughness. He remained at the doorway, holding the tapestry aside as he peered out to search for the enemy. Alix turned from him and surveyed the chamber.

It was deserted but oddly comforting, like the eye of a bad storm. Braziers warmed the room against the chill of mortared stone, and fine rugs and arrases bedecked the floors and walls.

She fingered the back of an ornate wooden chair and wondered at its fineness. Then she heard Duncan expel a sudden breath and whipped around, crying out as the Atvian plunged through the door tapestry with an iron spear.

The flanged head slid easily into the back of the chair and shattered it, spraying her with splinters. She stared speechlessly at the bearded Atvian who clawed at his belt-knife.

Duncan lunged for the man. 'Alix! Find a place to hide yourself — I cannot spare the time to watch out for you!'

She retreated instantly, staring as Duncan engaged the man. Finally she wrenched her eyes away and sought a place.

An indigo curtain shrouding a huge casement billowed and she ran for the wide bench of stone sill. Alix climbed up and pressed her back against the cold stone, dragging the velvet around her body. But she left gap enough to watch.

Duncan slew the Atvian soldier and stood over the body, gasping as he tried to recover breath through his torn throat.

'And who prophesied *your* death, shapechanger?' asked Keough from the door.

Duncan straightened instantly, meeting the Atvian's satisfied, expectant eyes. The Cheysuli stood straddle-legged over the dead soldier as Keough advanced into the room through the only door. Behind him stood his son, blocking the exit.

'Where is your vaunted bow, shapechanger?' Keough challenged. 'Where is your animal?'

Duncan said nothing as he stepped around the body and settle into a readied position.

Keough laughed. 'Before you had your bow. Now you bear only a knife, and I a sword.'

Duncan watched the gleaming blade dance before his eyes. The lord of Atvia was huge and unbelievably swift for a man of his bulk. Thorne, smirking in the door, folded his arms and watched his father drive the Cheysuli across the hall until his back pressed against a colourful tapestry.

Keough smiled in his red beard, sword tip drifting to touch Duncan's neck gently. 'It seems someone has already tried to take your head shapechanger. Shall I finish it for him?'

The sword flashed to the side lightly and Duncan brought up his knife, flipping it to throw.

Keough slapped it from his hand with a frighteningly smooth motion. The sword tip moved again to the bruising on Duncan's throat. A trickle of flesh blood welled in the ugly wire cut.

'Here, shapechanger? Do I strike *here*?'

Thorne cried out as the ruddy wolf flashed from the casement, ripping through the velvet arras. Duncan's yellowed eyes widened in unfeigned surprise and Keough, warned by it, whipped the sword around.

He met the snarling jaws of a wolf-bitch, compact body hurling itself against the Atvian's huge chest. Off-balance, Keough went down at Duncan's feet. A terrified cry broke from his wailing throat.

Thorne rushed the length of the hall, sword drawn and raised to strike the wolf from his father's body. Duncan bent swiftly and grasped his knife, thrusting himself forward to block Thorne's furious charge.

Keough's son went down with a cry of pain, clutching at the knife buried in his chest. Duncan straightened and turned, moving unsteadily to the wolf-bitch.

The animal stood across the unmoving lord of Atvia, feral eyes blazing with silent rage. Slowly knowledge crept into them as she saw Duncan staring wordlessly down at her, face drawn.

'He is slain,' he said hoarsely.

Keough, face congested, bore no wound. But the man lay dead within Homana-Mujhar.

'Cheysula,' Duncan whispered.

The wolf-bitch blurred before his eyes and Alix moved to him, arms crossed slackly across her stomach as if to protect the child.

'He would have slain you.'

'Aye, Alix.'

She blinked empty eyes. 'I know you said I should not shapechange, cheysul, but you would have died. I think I would be like a lirless man if you died, and lose my very soul.'

'It was done out of fear and a wolf's fierce protectiveness for its mate. I could not have asked for or expected different, child or no.'

'Then you are not angry with me?'

He put out his arms and took her to him, cradling her head against his shoulder. 'I am not angry, small one.'

296

'Duncan . . . we are losing Homana-Mujhar.'

'Aye. Carillon will have to wait a while longer before he can assume the Mujhar's throne. We must gather ourselves and go before Bellam finishes the *qu'mahlin* Shaine began.'

Thorne, at Alix's feet, groaned. She shuddered and whipped her head around to look, hand to her mouth. Duncan took her away from the young Atvian, heading toward the door.

'Duncan — he is still alive!'

'He will have to remain that way. We can spare no more time, Alix. Come.'

Getting out of Homana-Mujhar safely proved more difficult than getting in. Twice Duncan had to fend off Solindish soldiers and Alix shrieked once as a wounded Atvian rose from the floor. A thrown knife bearing Carillon's royal crest quivered in the man's back and she looked up to meet Finn's eyes across the corridor.

'So, *mei jha*, you still trail after my *rujho*.'

Alix, faced with Finn's obvious exhaustion and blood-smeared features, laughed at him. 'Aye, I still do. And ever will.'

Finn smiled at her and retrieved the knife that was now his, shooting his brother a searching look. Duncan gestured for him to follow and they moved down the corridor silently.

'The prince?' Duncan asked hoarsely.

'I left him in Shaine's own chambers, effectively dispatching two Atvians. Our princeling has learned how to kill. He did not need my help.'

'Are you ready to go from this place?'

Finn laughed shortly. 'Though I hate leaving such work unfinished, I am more than ready. All we do here is die.' He sighed. 'We will take Homana-Mujhar another time.'

'Carillon might not wish to go.'

'He will when I have told him. He may be my liege lord, but I have more sense.'

'*Do* you?' Alix demanded, grasping Duncan's belt as they moved.

'Aye, *mei jha*, I do.'

'Well, *rujho*,' Duncan said, 'perhaps you have gained some in the past months. You never had any before.'

Finn, affronted, followed them as Storr moved closely at his heels.

They found Carillon where Finn had said and convinced him to join their flight from the palace. He was not particularly happy with the idea, but gave in when Duncan explained their chances. Carillon sighed and pushed a forearm across his damp forehead. His hair had dried into unruly curls.

'This way,' he said and led them through winding corridors.

Twisting and turning in the bowels of the immense palace, they followed the prince out of Homana-Mujhar, glad of a respite. They found no Atvian or Solindish troops and it gave them all a chance to breathe again.

Alix followed Carillon out of a recessed doorway into the small bailey at the back of the palace. Behind her were Duncan and Finn, murmuring to one another in the Old Tongue she had not yet quite learned. Then she came to an abrupt stop as Carillon halted before her, and stepped around him to question their pause.

She came face-to-face with a cloaked figure very like the man she had slain in the streets of Mujhara, and suddenly she was very afraid.

A gloved hand slid the hood back, baring exquisitely fine features and a sweetly beguiling smile. 'Alix,' he said softly. 'And my lord prince of Homana. I could not have hoped for better fortune.'

'Tynstar . . .' she whispered.

Duncan stepped beside her, keeping her between himself and the prince. Finn stood at Carillon's right hand, making certain the prince had room to use his sword. Storr, hackled and growling, waited at Finn's right side.

Tynstar smiled. 'A tableau. I have before me the three men most responsible for attempting to ruin Bellam's bid to take Homana.' His black eyes flickered. 'And the woman.' He moved closer soundlessly, staring into her face. 'Alix, I said you should remain insignificant. You have not heeded me.'

She swallowed heavily and fought down the fear that threatened to turn her knees to water. The man who had been so kind and unassuming when first they had met displayed his true colors to her at last, and she understood the magnitude of his dedication to his dark gods.

Tynstar smiled more broadly. 'Shaine is dead. And Keough. Even Prince Thorne lies dying of a Cheysuli knife. You have accounted for a large toll, this night.' His voice dropped to a whisper. 'But it is for naught.'

'Naught!' Carillon echoed.

'Aye. Bellam holds Homana-Mujhar. Homana is his.'

'Yours,' Alix said softly. 'Homana is *yours*.'

The Ihlini smiled sweetly.

Carillon's hand settled on his sword hilt. Tynstar's eyes moved from Alix to him.

'Were I you, my young Mujhar, I would leave Homana-Mujhar instantly.'

Carillon's hand twitched. 'You tell me to *go* . . .'

Tynstar affected a casual shrug. 'You are nothing to me. Bellam wants you for parading before his men, and to show the Homanans your defeat, but *I* see no use in that. It only makes a man determined to have retribution.' A hand gestured smoothly. 'You have seen what such desires have done to the Cheysuli.'

'The *qu'mahlin* is ended,' Carillon snapped. 'Ended. The Cheysuli may come and go as they please, as before.'

Alix felt the surge of joy in her chest, but did not move. Before Tynstar, she could not.

The Ihlini gestured toward the small gate in the high walls. 'Go, my lord, else I change my mind.'

Carillon drew his sword. Before he could complete the action of lifting it against Tynstar he was rudely halted. He uttered a single choked-off cry and the Cheysuli blade clanged to the stones from nerveless fingers. Carillon, collapsing like a drunken man, fell forward to his hands and knees in front of the sorcerer. His head bowed as if in submission.

Alix gasped and moved forward. Duncan caught her arm and pulled her back.

'Wait . . .' he breathed.

Tynstar's eyes were expressionless as he looked on Carillon's taut shoulders.

'I hold your life, Shaine's heir. I could crush your heart in my very hand, yet never touch you. I could steal the very breath from your lungs in an instant. I could make you blind, deaf and dumb with no more wits than a mewling infant.' His teeth gleamed in a terrifying smile. '*But I will not.*'

Alix, angered by his words and that neither Duncan nor Finn moved against the sorcerer, jerked free of Duncan and walked toward Tynstar. She stopped at Carillon's side.

'If you take his life, you must also take mine. Do you think I will stand by while you use your dark arts against my kinsman? I am of this House also, Ihlini!'

Tynstar lifted a gloved hand as if in benediction. Another shudder wracked Carillon's body and Alix sucked in a frightened breath.

'I can harm none of *you* with my arts,' Tynstar said calmly, 'and my strength is lessened within your presence. But there is enough left to me. Carillon is solely within my care. Speak again, Lindir's daughter, and see the result.'

'You cannot touch me, Ihlini,' she whispered. 'My own magic is stronger than any other Cheysuli's. I have only to show you my wolf's fangs, and you will die as Keough did, of fear alone.'

Tynstar's eyes narrowed. 'It is true, then, that Lindir

gifted you with the Old Blood of this land.' He smiled and shrugged. 'Well, I can wait. Time is nothing to a man who is already three centuries old.'

He glanced regretfully at Carillon. Slowly the prince gathered his strength and got shakily to his feet, lifting the sword loosely as he rose. He stared in cold fury at Tynstar a moment, then looked at Alix. His hand touched her arm.

'I heard, cousin. And I give you my thanks.'

Tynstar stepped back from them smoothly. His beguiling smile blanketed them all.

'Bellam will hold Homana-Mujhar, Carillon, and you will have to fight him for it. But not this night.'

He raised a hand, called purple flame hissing from the darkness, and disappeared.

EPILOGUE

The darkness, illuminated only by eerie Ihlini flames as purple demon fire consumed the magnificence of Homana-Mujhar, was oppressive. Yet somehow they gathered the surviving Cheysuli warriors and left the palace, forsaking the Homana city Bellam of Solinde had won.

Carillon said very little on the long ride back to the Keep, so many leagues into Ellas, but Alix knew he had not given himself up to depression. Carillon, the boy-prince who had grown into a king, planned.

When at last they reached the Keep and the warriors scattered to their pavilions and women, Carillon solemnly accepted Duncan's invitation to stay in the slate-colored clan-leader's pavilion.

And it was there, six days later, he told them his decision.

Alix shook her head repeatedly. 'You should stay here. *Here*.'

He sat before the fire cairn in his scarred leathers and crusted mail. His wrists, though nearly healed, displayed the deep wounds left by Atvian iron.

Carillon's blue eyes were steady. 'Bellam sends troops to find me. He is not a man who gives up easily. The Cheysuli have suffered enough at Shaine's hands; I will not have them dying because the Mujhar's heir shelters in their Keep.'

'*You* are the Mujhar,' Finn said quietly.

Alix glanced at him and saw the odd calmness she had come to acknowledge in him. For all the confrontation within Homana-Mujhar had changed Carillon, it had also worked its power on Finn.

Carillon gestured dismissively. 'It is a title, Finn; no more. And empty. Bellam — on the throne of Homana — claims it his.'

'Homana knows it false,' said Duncan in his husky voice. Alix still winced when she heard it, fearing his normal tone would never return; knowing Duncan, like Carillon, would carry his scars for life.

'Homana is a defeated land,' Carillon said quietly. 'It is folly to deny it. To survive, Homana must do Bellam's bidding . . . for a time.'

'And Tynstar's,' Alix said softly, shivering.

Finn shrugged casually. 'We need only wait, Carillon. You will take back Homana-Mujhar.'

The last surviving male member of the House of Homana sighed heavily. 'Not, I think, for a long while. Thorne heals in Atvia, swearing he will avenge his father's strange death.' His eyes flicked to Alix, who stared fixedly at the fire cairn. 'Tynstar and his Ihlini buttress Bellam's hold on the thrones of Homana and Solinde. This land's strength is diminished, and must renew itself before the battle begins once more.' He smiled faintly. 'I cannot ask my battered realm to go so quickly into war again.'

Alix met his eyes at last. 'Where will you go?'

'We are safe here, across the Ellasian border. Your Keep has been left unbothered by High King Rhodri's soldiers for years. I think no one will mind a lone prince wandering through. I will fade into the land for a time.' Carillon's faint smile, older now, came quickly. 'But I will not risk another Cheysuli life until it benefits us all.'

'It matters little that we risk ourselves,' Duncan said

quietly. 'The prophecy says that one day you will ascend the throne of Homana. One day . . . you will.'

'The Cheysuli throne, Duncan?' Carillon mocked, and grinned. 'I have not forgotten.'

'Nor have we.'

Carillon abruptly got to his feet. He stared down at Alix.

'Cousin, once you told a naïve, arrogant princeling the truth of Shaine's *qu'mahlin*, and he denied it. He even denied you. I am sorry for it. You are wiser than any I have known.' He reached down and took her hand, pulling her to her feet. 'You have been truer to your blood than I could ever hope.'

'Carillon . . .'

He shook his head and released her hand. 'I have a horse. And, I believe, a shapechanger sworn to be the Mujhar's liege man. Like his father.'

Finn rose and grinned into Alix's stricken face. 'There, *mei jha*, you rid yourself of me at last.'

She said nothing, unable to speak past the pain closing her throat.

Finn looked at Duncan. '*Rujho*, care for your *cheysula*. She is not one to be treated lightly.'

Duncan smiled and rose, sliding a hand around Alix's waist. With the other he held out the black war bow, ornamentation gleaming.

'Here, my lord Mujhar. Finn will show you how to use it.'

Carillon hesitated. 'But only a Cheysuli may shoot a Cheysuli bow.'

'Traditions change,' Duncan said softly.

Carillon took it silently. Then he walked from the pavilion like a man turning his back on a past, intent on making a future.

'Storr!' Alix cried.

The wolf's eyes were warm. *Tahlmorra, liren.*

Alix watched in mute pain as Finn followed Carillon, silver wolf flanking him. She was hardly aware of

Duncan's hands settling at her hips, pulling her close against him. She was conscious only of the deep anguish and regret swelling in her breast.

'They will be well, *cheysula*.'

'Why must they *both* go?'

He laughed softly. 'Have you not longed for Finn's absence from your life?'

She swallowed. 'I have . . . grown accustomed to him. That is all.'

'The Mujhar is ever served by a Cheysuli, as Finn said in Homana-Mujhar. As Hale served Shaine. And even before.'

Alix stared out the open doorflap and wiped quickly at the tears on her face. 'I cannot see Finn and Carillon accomplishing much more than *argument*!'

His hands tightened. 'Argument, as *you* should know, has its place. I am certain Shaine and Hale argued, on occasion.'

'Look at the result.'

Duncan moved behind her and gently rested his chin on her head. 'Carillon is not his uncle.'

'No, he is not.' Alix sighed heavily. 'He is only Carillon.'

'He will come back.'

Alix stiffened, but refused to turn on him for fear she would see something she could not bear.

'Duncan . . . do you speak of *tahlmorra*?'

'Perhaps.' He turned her until she stared into his face. 'Do you think Finn and Storr will allow their princeling to stay long from their home?'

Something fluttered briefly within her. In amazement Alix put a hand to her stomach, then smiled and placed Duncan's hand there as well so he could feel the child move.

'When Carillon returns, *cheysul*, he will have a new kinsman to see.'

'And a realm to win back from Bellam,' Duncan said gravely.

She stared into his solemn yellow eyes. 'Can he accomplish it? Does the prophecy say he will accomplish it?'

He smoothed back her hair with his free hand. 'I cannot say, small one. It is Carillon's *tahlmorra*.'

Carillon's tahlmorra ... she echoed sadly within her mind, and instinctively sought an answer in the power the gods had given her.

There she found it, and smiled.

THE END